That Stripy Cat

That Stripy Cat

BY NORENE SMILEY

PICTURES BY TARA ANDERSON

Fitzhenry & Whiteside

For Sue R., supernova, and for Pickle Bob,
as spunky as they come
                                                    —Norene

To Dylan and Matthew Racco and their parents
Lucy and Frank, with love always. Never forgotten.
                                                    —Tara

On Saturday morning, Mrs. Cosy made her cinnamon porridge alone in her kitchen to the tick-tock of the big wall clock.

Then she rode lickety-split to the Hummingbird Animal Shelter. When she arrived, Mrs. Cosy met a stripy little cat that had been rescued the night before.

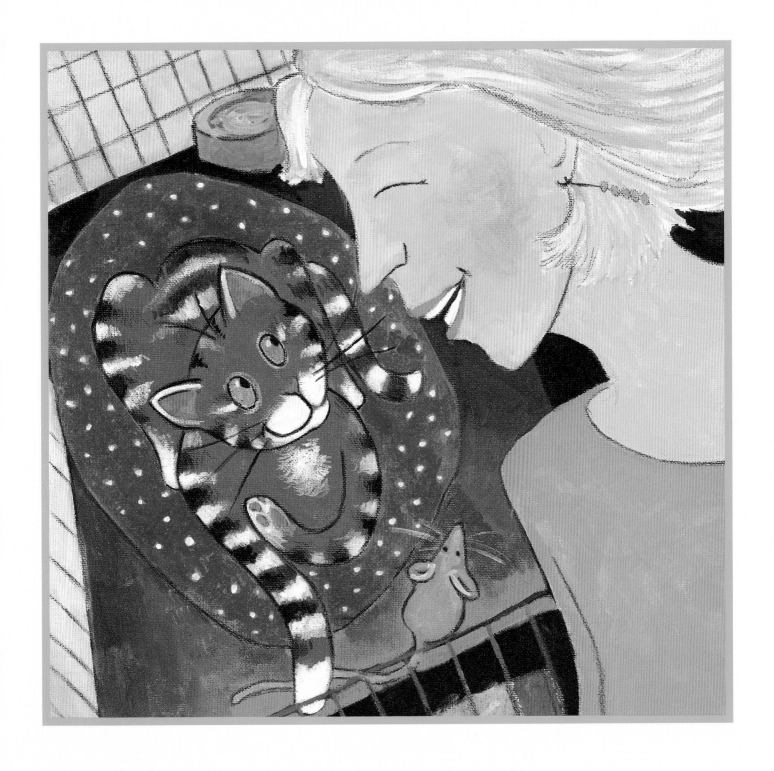

"Good as gold," said Mrs. Cosy. And she went about her work.

But by midmorning the trouble started. The stripy cat would not come out from under the couch. "Your name should be Cantankerous!" said Judy.

Mrs. Cosy just smiled and called the cat Steadfast.

"Persnickety!" cried George, when the stripy cat ran up one curtain and down another.

Mrs. Cosy just laughed and called the cat Spunky.

By lunchtime everyone was in a dither. Mrs. Cosy just peeled the stripy cat off the screen door and called him Full of Beans.

In the afternoon, Alexander Puddle dropped in to adopt a cuddly pet for his sister. But the stripy cat splashed and splooshed in the water dish.

"Too wild!" hooted Alexander. He chose a poodle named Lucy, with fur as soft as cotton balls and eyes like melted chocolate.

The stripy little cat was left behind.

At teatime, the McCurdy sisters hurried in to adopt a cat to catch all the mice in their bookshop. But the stripy little cat wedged himself in a drawer and would not budge.

"Too timid!" said the McCurdys. They chose two frisky kittens named Tootie and Tiger.

The stripy little cat was left behind.

When Millie Greenapple came looking for a cheery pet, the stripy cat shrieked like a fire engine and would not stop.

"Too loud!" cried Millie. She chose a budgie named Hank that crooned "Love Me Tender" at the drop of a hat.

The stripy little cat was left behind.

By closing time, all the animals had been adopted except one—
the stripy little cat with no name of his own.

"My uncle has room for that stripy cat in his barn," said Judy.
But the stripy cat tangled himself around Mrs. Cosy's legs and clung
on tight. Judy went home in a huff.

The stripy little cat was left behind.

"They need a ratter at the dump," said George. "Maybe they could take that no-good cat."

But the stripy cat stuck like a burr to Mrs. Cosy. George went home in a grumble.

The stripy little cat was left behind.

"What a muddle," said Mrs. Cosy. She looked down at the stripy cat. The stripy cat looked back.

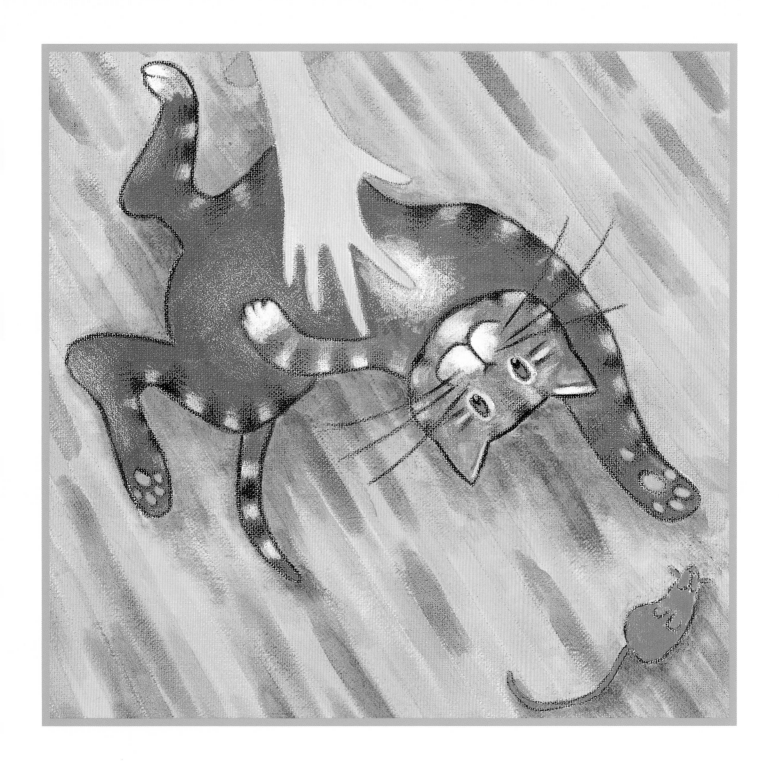

"That's it, then," said Mrs. Cosy.

And she took the stripy little cat home. At sunset, they played hide-and-seek in all the nooks and crannies.

"As hard to shake as gluey paper," said Mrs. Cosy.

Later, in the comfy kitchen, Mrs. Cosy shared her supper of salmon pot pie. The stripy little cat cleaned his whiskers and settled down beside her.

"A comfort sure and true," said Mrs. Cosy.

On the way upstairs, Mrs. Cosy sang "You are My Sunshine." The stripy cat followed close behind.

While Mrs. Cosy soaked, the stripy cat perched nearby and watched the bubbles break, one by one.

"Constant as the sea," said Mrs. Cosy.

By bedtime, the stripy cat was still stuck tight to her side.
"You are plucky," said Mrs. Cosy. "As trusty as the fastenings on my
sneakers." And she nàmed the stripy cat Velcro, then and there.

Then they snuggled together under the crazy quilt as the moon rose in the night sky. Mrs. Cosy read *Puss in Boots*, and Velcro purred in all the right places.

Published in Canada by Fitzhenry & Whiteside, 195 Allstate Parkway, Markham, Ontario L3R 4T8

Published in the United States by Fitzhenry & Whiteside, 311 Washington Street, Brighton, Massachusetts 02135

www.fitzhenry.ca   godwit@fitzhenry.ca

10 9 8 7 6 5 4 3 2 1

Library and Archives Canada Cataloguing in Publication

Smiley, Norene
The stripy cat / Norene Smiley ; illustrated by Tara Anderson.

ISBN-13: 978-1-55005-164-3   ISBN-10: 1-55005-164-4

1. Cats—Juvenile fiction. I. Anderson, Tara II. Title.

PS8637.M54S87 2007   jC813'.6   C2006-906868-2

**U.S. Publisher Cataloging-in-Publication Data
(Library of Congress Standards)**

Smiley, Norene.
That stripy cat / Norene Smiley ; illustrated by Tara Anderson.
[32] p. : col. ill. ; cm.
Summary: Despite Mrs. Cosy's efforts to find a home for the stripy little cat left at
the animal shelter, nobody wants to adopt the little troublemaker. But the stripy cat
has already chosen the one he wants to adopt and he's going to stick to her like glue.
ISBN-10: 1-55005-164-4   ISBN-13: 9781550051643
1. Cats – Fiction – Juvenile literature. I. Anderson, Tara. II. Title.
[E] dc22 PZ7.S655 2007

 Canada Council
for the Arts   Conseil des Arts
du Canada   ONTARIO ARTS COUNCIL
CONSEIL DES ARTS DE L'ONTARIO

Fitzhenry & Whiteside acknowledges with thanks the Canada Council for the Arts, and the Ontario Arts Council
for their support of our publishing program. We acknowledge the financial support of the Government of Canada
through the Book Publishing Industry Development Program (BPIDP) for our publishing activities.

Design by Wycliffe Smith Design Inc.

Printed in Hong Kong, China

EUROPEAN REGULATION OF ADVERTISING

Supranational Regulation of Advertising in the European Economic Community

BY

REIN RIJKENS
Former President, European Association of Advertising Agencies

GORDON E. MIRACLE
Professor of Advertising, Michigan State University

1986

NORTH- HOLLAND
AMSTERDAM . NEW YORK . OXFORD . TOKYO

ISBN: 0444 87972 2

PUBLISHERS:
ELSEVIER SCIENCE PUBLISHERS B.V.
P.O. BOX 1991
1000 BZ AMSTERDAM
THE NETHERLANDS

SOLE DISTRIBUTORS FOR THE U.S.A. AND CANADA:
ELSEVIER SCIENCE PUBLISHING COMPANY, INC.
52 VANDERBILT AVENUE
NEW YORK, n.y. 10017
U.S.A.

Library of Congress Cataloging on Publication Data
Rijkens, Rein.
    European regulation of advertising.

    Bibliography: p.
    Includes index.
    1. Advertising laws – European Economic Community
countries.   2. Consumer protection – Law and legislation –
European Economic Community countries.   I. Miracle,
Gordon E.   II. Title.
KJE6580.R55   1986   343.4′0786591   86-16236
ISBN 0-444-87972-2 (U.S.)   344.03786591

PRINTED IN THE NETHERLANDS

To the memory of Anthony, my grandson

Rein Rijkens

Table of contents

Foreword

The publication of an authoritative treatise on the regulation of the advertising function in the European Economic Community could not have been more timely. The influence of advertising on our attitudes and our way of life has progressed by leaps and bounds in the post-war decades and now affects the way in which we live more continuously and powerfully than is generally realised. There is equally no doubt that some moral standard should be applied to such a critical activity and its expansion and development cannot be left entirely to the economic laws of supply and demand. It is, therefore, essential that appropriate standards should be established which have both the short and long-term interests of the Community at heart.

At the same time the establishment of elaborate and perhaps expensive machinery must be studied with great concern, especially at a time when the cost of government in European countries generally is dramatically higher than that which exists in our major competitive communities, namely the USA and Japan. For these and other reasons, there is a growing pressure for deregulation which could run counter to plans that the advertising function should be monitored especially if such plans appeared to be costly. The watchword of deregulation is on everyone's lips and could create opposition to worthwhile proposals to apply reasonable standards to the advertising function. Proposals for self-regulation mentioned in this publication are particularly appropriate and contemporary as a solution.

The publication also coincides with a growing recognition that the European Economic Community must speak out with one voice and break down the geographic and cultural barriers which accentuate weakness and disunity. It will make a valuable contribution which should speed up the debate and help considerably the attainment of practical and successful conclusions in this important area.

LORD PENNOCK

President of the
Union of Industries of the
European Community (UNICE)

Preface

This book is about advertising regulation at the international level and the efforts of the business community to avoid regulation which limits consumers' freedom of choice and which impairs legitimate private enterprise.

The book has been written for: (1) experienced business executives in the world's most important trade centers, who would like to inform themselves more fully about advertising regulation on an international scale, and what their colleagues in Europe have done in response to it in the past, (2) young advertising executives who wish to receive guidance from those who have gone before on action to be taken today, (3) educators and their students who are interested in the regulatory aspects of international advertising in Europe, (4) legislators and government officials in Europe who are in a position to influence legislation or enforcement of laws relevant to consumer affairs and advertising and (5) consumer representatives and their associations who are interested in an ongoing dialogue with the advertising business on protecting the buying public.

The reader can discern the general content and organization of the book by perusing the *Table of Contents*. Most topics are covered more or less in chronological sequence, although for ease of interpretation we sometimes group matters by subject, regardless of the sequence in which events occurred. We present an *Executive Summary* for the reader who wishes to know our conclusions and recommendations, without accompanying background and reasoning. For the reader who wishes to pursue some or all of the issues in greater depth, we include in our *References* not only those to which we refer directly, but also a number of selected additional references which cover many aspects of international advertising and its regulation. A list of *Abbreviations* is also included. To facilitate reading, in both the Executive Summary and in the chapters, names of organizations and other bodies appear only the first time in full. Subsequently, abbreviations are used.

We have drawn upon a broad spectrum of evidence, opinion and viewpoints. The main sources of information include; (1) the professional experience and files of one of the authors, who participated in many of the events which are dealt with, (2) numerous articles, books, official documents and other published materials, (3) private correspondence and personal interviews with officials of consumer organizations, current and former officials and staff of governments and of the

EEC and with business leaders, representatives of industry associations, international advertising executives, and many others.

In view of the somewhat unusual combination of specialized academic and advertising backgrounds of the two authors – one a European marketing and advertising executive, one an American university professor – it is felt that it would be useful to the reader to know a bit more about each of us. We therefore present the following brief biographical sketches:

(1) From 1966 to 1978 *Rein Rijkens* was a director on the Board of SSC&B:LINTAS International, a worldwide advertising agency based in London. In addition to his responsibilities as a member of this Board, he was President of the European Association of Advertising Agencies between 1975 and 1978, when he became closely involved with the EEC and its consumer policy, then in an important stage. He started his career in marketing and advertising with Unilever in the Netherlands in 1945. In 1954 he became head of Unilever's Toilet Preparations Company in Germany and in 1962 he was appointed head of the SSC&B:LINTAS advertising agency in Germany. In 1964 he became the marketing member of Unilever's Toilet Preparations Coordination in Rotterdam. Upon leaving SSC&B:LINTAS International in 1978, he started his own Consumer Affairs Consultancy in The Hague, where he now resides. He has written a regular column in *Advertising Age* on the subject of EEC developments in the field of consumer protection and has for many years also been a Vice President of the International Advertising Association, of which he now is an Honorary Life Member. Recently he carried special responsibilities for developing and introducing worldwide the advertising educational program of this association. In November, 1982 the Communication Advertising and Marketing Education Foundation Ltd. in the UK awarded him an Honorary Diploma.

(2) *Gordon Miracle* has been Professor of Advertising at Michigan State University since 1966, with prior service as a faculty member at the University of Michigan (1960 – 1966) and the University of Wisconsin (1958 – 1960). His Ph.D. in Commerce and his MBA in Marketing were earned at the University of Wisconsin. Over the years he has been a regular consultant to industry and government; he served as Chairman of MSU's Department of Advertising for six and one-half years; he was visiting professor at the North European Management Institute in Oslo for the academic year 1972 – 1973. He chaired the Ph.D. Program in Mass Media at MSU for one year and served many years on its executive committee. He has authored, co-authored or edited six books and monographs and more than fifty other publications, many of which deal with international advertising, business and marketing. He was employed in Germany for several years early in his professional career and has travelled widely in many countries to work with research colleagues and to lecture at universities and advertising conferences. His current research programs and publications focus on "Comparative Regulation of Advertising," especially in European nations and Japan.

Gathering information for a book such as this required the assistance of many people. We are deeply indebted to those who gave generously of their time and knowledge when meeting with us, or in answering our many queries. They all, without exception, showed interest in what we were doing and gave us their highly appreciated encouragement. Unfortunately, it is impossible to acknowledge adequately each and every contribution, but we would like to extend our warmest thanks to those many people, whose names and affiliates are listed in a separate section at the end of this book and to whom we owe so much. They have generously shared their knowledge and experience with us, for which we are most grateful.

It was sometimes difficult to interpret or reconcile differing points of view and it was necessary to make judgments as to what to include and to exclude. Our sources could do no more than to give us their views. We have done our best to present a balanced and fair account of one of the most important periods in the history of advertising in Europe and we accept full responsibility for the book as it stands.

Finally, we are indebted to the Marsteller Foundation for its generous financial support in the form of a grant to one of the authors. We also want to thank Marlene Corner, who showed so much patience and endurance in typing and re-typing the many drafts of this manuscript.

The Hague   REIN RIJKENS
East Lansing   GORDON E. MIRACLE
February, 1986

Executive summary and recommendations

The following conclusions are a distillation of the main points from our analysis and the recommendations that flow from them. They are presented sequentially so that the interested reader can locate additional information easily in the corresponding chapters. Readers who require details beyond those in the chapters are referred to the *Appendices* and *References* at the end of the book.

Chapter I: Setting the stage

(1) Advertising does not owe its reputation to its importance as a business. Compared with other industries, the amount of money spent on producing and placing advertising, as well as the number of people employed in the advertising business, are relatively insignificant. Advertising owes the widespread attention it receives to its visibility in the marketplace and its sometimes provocative nature; every citizen is exposed to it and some have strong opinions about it.

(2) In the years after World War II European countries experienced a transition from a sellers' to a buyers' market, which advertising helped to create. In the 1950s and 1960s, sellers found it increasingly necessary to compete intensely. This led gradually to mounting criticism of certain marketing and advertising practices, which were not thought to be in the interest of the buying public.

(3) Advertising, as an important element of the private enterprise system, came under attack from consumer groups and politicians.

(4) Gradually consumer organizations grew nationally and internationally, criticizing, among other things, advertising in a variety of ways and demanding not only that advertising should include more and better information, but also that consumers should be protected against forms of advertising which were perceived to be misleading or which appeared to manipulate consumers unfairly. The introduction of television made people more conscious of advertising than they had ever been before. Consumer organizations exerted pressure on governments to introduce or to sharpen existing legislation to control advertising in all its forms, particularly as it appeared on television.

(5) But consumer interest in advertising and dissatisfaction with it have been small compared to the dissatisfaction of active consumerists. Most consumers did not

choose to be represented by consumerists; many were complacent about advertising; and some disagreed directly with consumerists who were felt to be politically inspired and in many cases too extreme.

(6) Advertising has long been accepted by large parts of our society as an integral part of a market economy. It is in many cases an indispensable tool to inform the public about availability and qualities of products and services. It has nevertheless been subjected to controls in a variety of ways in many European countries, particularly to protect competitors from unfair practices, to preserve competition, and, more recently to protect consumers from perceived advertising abuses.

(7) Consumerism has a long history, taking various forms and rising and falling in intensity over the decades. An important period of consumerism for our purposes was the peak reached in the late 1960s and early 1970s. Consumer "leaders" (rather than consumers themselves) were the main source of dissatisfaction with advertising.

(8) In each country there is a relatively small group of people who exercise an important influence in the marketplace as opinion leaders and informed critics. These "information seekers" and opinion disseminators are relatively affluent and well educated; they have an impact on advertising, not only as consumers, but especially as articulate and active opinion leaders. Some of them also become consumer activists when they perceive that the system is not performing up to their personal expectations.

(9) The advertising business and consumer representatives both realize the needs for: (1) *information* to make buying decisions, (2) *education* to know how the economy operates and how buyers and sellers interact and deal with the institutions they encounter, and (3) *protection* against deceptive or unfair acts or practices.

(10) The controversy on the alleged consumer information gap is likely to remain pending continued consumer and marketing research. Research is at best inconclusive regarding the effectiveness of advertising, as well as the need of consumers for more information or protection. The evidence on balance indicates that most consumers feel they are reasonably intelligent judges and that they need little protection beyond the basic requirement to assure the free flow of accurate and truthful information.

(11) Several hundred laws affecting advertising were enacted or adopted in the 1950s and 1960s by Member States of the European Economic Community (EEC). Likewise, during these two decades various systems of advertising self-regulation were introduced or reinforced in many European countries, for the most part based upon the Code of Advertising Practice of the International Chamber of Commerce (ICC), of which the first version dates back to 1937, with periodic updates.

(12) National voluntary codes or other forms of self-regulation have been useful in varying degrees as a means to protect consumers against abuse in the marketplace. When systems of self control are applied effectively, they work quickly and

economically and can be more effective than government regulation by itself. The business world has therefore long favored self-regulation. Consumer activists on the other hand have felt that self-regulation is relatively ineffective and have therefore favored government regulation.

(13) Despite increased governmental self-regulatory controls on advertising, criticisms of advertising continued. Often such criticisms seemed politically motivated, and sometimes exhibited distrust of the market economy and a preference for more controls on the market system.

(14) While in recent years the image of advertising in the eyes of the public has shown positive developments, some criticism of advertising is likely to continue. This suggests the need for continued improvement in advertising practices, as well as the need for vigilance to protect against unwarranted intervention.

(15) Legislation and government enforcement of laws to control advertising seem to be relatively less important now than in the two previous decades, but will continue to be important, particularly as a minimum base on which self-regulatory activities can build.

(16) Many of the criticisms of advertising probably tend to persist because critics do not realize, understand or accept the fact that advertisers and their advertising agencies carefully monitor changing consumer attitudes, tastes and preferences. They do so first and foremost to ensure continued success of their brands in the marketplace. In response to increasingly sophisticated and informed consumers, advertisers adjust products and services in accordance with the ever changing profile of consumers. Content and presentation of advertising form an important and integrated part of this process of adaptation which is intended to give long-term consumer satisfaction. This process also explains why the number and volume of genuine consumer complaints have always remained relatively low.

Chapter II: The pressures build

(17) In the late 1960s and early 1970s the perception grew that European industrial policies favored producers over consumers. Consequently, the Council of Europe (COE) took up the issue of consumer protection in its 1967 – 1968 program, eventually resulting in 1973 in its "Consumer Protection Charter." Consumerist and political pressures also led to a commitment on the part of the EEC, when in 1972 Heads of State agreed that a consumer protection policy should be formulated by the Commission of the EEC in Brussels. Thus, consumer protection became an international political issue, which it has remained to date.

(18) Following the decision of the Heads of State in Paris in 1972, the Commission produced in 1975 a "Preliminary Programme of the European Economic

Community for a Consumer Protection and Information Policy," followed the same year by the Draft Directive on Misleading and Unfair Advertising.

(19) The Commission's preliminary program contained, among other features, five basic consumer rights. But to the surprise of many, the consumer "right to choose" was not included.

(20) The business world considered the Commission's program to be overly ambitious and heavily biased against business and advertising, especially regarding the exaggerated and unsubstantiated assertions about the negative influence of advertising on consumers.

(21) The Commission's program also went beyond the minimum requirements for harmonizing existing legislation. Instead of trying to find the lowest common denominator and achieve minimum harmonization, the Commission appeared to prefer to take leadership in the direction of maximum harmonization, thereby substituting its views on what would be good for consumers, for existing customs and regulations in Member States.

(22) Business did not take the preliminary consumer program as seriously as it should have, but when the Draft Directive on Misleading and Unfair Advertising appeared, the business world felt the Commission had undertaken a more complex task than it was ready to handle.

(23) The Commission made an unfortunate start with the Draft Directive on Misleading and Unfair Advertising by apparently "borrowing" from regulatory experience in the USA without considering the special problems in Europe that stem from the diversity of laws and jurisdiction, languages, cultures, and levels of economic, political and social development in Member States.

(24) As with the consumer protection and information program, the draft directive appeared to be biased against business and advertising, and it overstated at that time the significance of international advertising. The draft led to an atmosphere of confrontation and controversy rather than to cooperation and accommodation.

(25) During the consultative phase preceding the preparation of the draft directive, little contact existed between the Commission and advertising executives from multinational companies or agencies. This was regrettable, since the advertising business could have provided significant contributions to help understand the complex problems of regulating advertising on an international scale.

(26) Additionally, some countries were against the proposed changes in methods of settling disputes between advertisers and consumers; governments were not prepared to make changes in existing laws or voluntary regulations which were working satisfactorily in their countries. Harmonization for the sake of international tidiness was not acceptable.

(27) In view of the structure of the EEC organization and decision-making procedures – which include consultation with governments, advisory bodies and non-

governmental organizations (NGOs) – the approval of a directive is cumbersome and time-consuming. In the mid 1970s several committees recommended modifications of responsibilities and procedures, but they were never approved. As we will see later, similar efforts under way in the mid 1980s show greater promise.

Chapter III: Industry responds

(28) Following the introduction by the Commission of its first consumer program and the misleading advertising directive, the leaders of national and international trade associations in the field of advertising, together with a small group of advertising practitioners, decided on mutual action in defense of their legitimate interests.

(29) Initially this small group consisted mainly of representatives from advertisers and from advertising agencies; the advertising agency business is often called upon to take the initiative and the lead in certain activities, but it can do so only with the active support of advertisers who provide the funds on which the entire advertising business depends and who carry the ultimate responsibility for the advertising which is presented to the public.

(30) Consequently the International Union of Advertisers' Associations (IUAA), later renamed the World Federation of Advertisers (WFA), and the European Association of Advertising Agencies (EAAA), jointly formulated a response to the Draft Directive on Misleading and Unfair Advertising.

(31) Later this small group was augmented with representatives of international media organizations and later still, when the group became known as the European Advertising Tripartite (EAT), by outdoor advertisers and direct marketing representation. The International Advertising Association (IAA) becoming an observer in 1984. The Advertising Information Group (AIG) also became a member of the EAT and maintains contact with advertising organizations outside the Community within Europe, thus ensuring the widest possible representation.

(32) The EAT became the representative body for the entire advertising business at the international level, cooperating closely with supranational organizations, such as the Union of Industries of the European Community (UNICE), the ICC and others.

(33) Unfortunately international consumer organizations, in contrast to some of their national counterparts, were reluctant to participate in discussions with the business world. Apparently their lack of trust in the motivations of business prevented them from taking part in an active dialogue with advertisers and their advertising agencies.

(34) In its discussions with governmental bodies the EAT, which believes strongly in freedom of choice for the consumer, promoted self-regulation as the most effective and efficient way of controlling advertising in a market economy, with the

proviso that consumers should have access to courts of law if necessary.

(35) The advertising business also ensured that its points of view regarding the restrictions facing international advertising were made widely known. Its representatives of the business spoke at conferences, published articles in trade papers, and informed and involved a number of multinational corporations in the USA and in Europe. To counterbalance the reproach of being too defensive, existing literature on "The Case for Advertising" was updated in many countries. The self-evident strategy was to promote the view that government intervention was unnecessary and that voluntary controls of advertising could do an adequate job — better than could be done by governments.

(36) Unexpected support for the role of advertising in a market economy came also from Pope Paul the Sixth, who encouraged the advertising business to continue to contribute towards progress.

(37) Meanwhile discussions and debates continued on the Commission's misleading advertising directive. This book contains a Table comparing the four most important phases of this directive, which after more than a decade of drafting and revisions, was finally approved by the Council of Ministers on September 10, 1984. The Preamble of the final directive states that unfair and comparative advertising will become the subject of separate study. This has meanwhile been confirmed by Commissioner Stanley Clinton Davis, who has been responsible for consumer affairs since January 1, 1985.

(38) Apart from the controversial question as to what constitutes misleading advertising, there are other issues which involve important points of principle. For example, as long as it is legal to sell a given product or service, it should in principle be legal to advertise it. However, this freedom is not unconditional. There are some circumstances in which limitations on advertising of specific products or services are in the public interest. Discussions to limit such advertising should involve all interested parties, especially the advertising business, so that the fundamental freedom to advertise is not abridged in a way that is not in the public interest. Such limitations should adhere to the "least restrictive means" principle, that is, they should be only the minimum restrictions necessary to safeguard the interests of both producers and consumers. The advertising business should agree on international codes and close ranks on controversial issues before political considerations prevail.

(39) To cope with the many proposed or intended directives and with the great number of intergovernmental and other contacts with regard to advertising and its regulation within the Community, the advertising business appointed working groups that carried responsibility for specific advertising practices or product categories. These groups were composed of representatives from advertisers and advertising agencies with vested interests in the subject concerned.

(40) In any discussion about advertising regulation, it is important to take notice of the creative man's point of view concerning governmental restrictions imposed

on advertising. Generally speaking, creative people are not unduly worried by such restrictions. They are accustomed to working under the discipline of restrictions imposed by the client, the budget, the media, the time-factor, etc. However, most managements are of the opinion that there should not be any additional limitations on the creation of advertising which could impede the success of a brand in meeting consumer needs in highly competitive markets.

(41) In this connection, and bearing in mind the growing complexity of regulating advertising on an international scale, the business community also seriously questions whether or not the considerable costs of consumer protection in terms of money and manpower are justified by the benefits from these measures.

(42) Trends in regulatory activities in Europe and in the USA show a great deal of similarity. But the advertising business in the USA has more opportunities to enter into a formal dialogue on all aspects of the advertising process with the relevant authorities, such as the Federal Trade Commission (FTC), than is the case in Europe.

(43) While the direct results of Commission activity have not been impressive, the discussions and debates on consumer affairs have had a profound influence on the thinking of all parties concerned. This also applied to the Commission itself; it gradually changed its attitude and reacted more positively to comments from the business community. While at that time this new attitude did not yet lead to a fundamental overhaul of its consumer policy, the Commission modified its views with regard to the methods to achieve its objectives. For example, the role of self-regulation received greater recognition in the Second Consumer Protection and Information Program.

Chapter IV: Subsequent developments

(44) In addition to the actions by the business world and the critical comments from governments and consumer groups, there were other factors affecting the attitude of the Commission toward advertising: important external influences such as the economic recession, unemployment and inflation. The Commission wished to avoid restrictions on business that would unfavorably affect the trade between Member States, including those relating to advertising. Consequently, consumer affairs received lower priority from Commissioners. Budget cuts also made it more difficult for the Consumer Affairs Directorate to propose comprehensive and costly policies.

(45) Importantly, recent research indicates that the attitudes of consumers toward advertising have changed for the better. But most consumers continue to be relatively disinterested in the subject of advertising as such. There also is a growing appreciation of the positive role of advertising in the economic process.

These favorable attitudes have not altered the stance of a small number of consumer activists, who continue unabashedly their crusade against the perceived bad influence of advertising on consumers. Although these activities must not be overrated, it would be in the interest of all parties concerned if remaining uncertainties about the benefits of advertising could be reduced and ultimately dispelled, thereby pre-empting criticism.

(46) While at the national level a considerable amount of research is conducted to find an answer to these uncertainties, international advertisers have a special interest in learning more about similarities and differences in behaviors, tastes and preferences among specified groups of consumers in all Member States. Few facilities exist for such research.

Recommendation I

In view of the need for additional evidence about the effects of advertising on consumers, the economy and society – especially because of important market and consumer differences among the Member States – it is recommended that a European Advertising Research Foundation should be established. All segments of the advertising business from all Member States should support the foundation financially: advertisers, advertising agencies, advertising media and related research and service organizations.

The functions of the foundation should be to: (1) identify priorities for research on the effects of advertising and the effects of advertising regulation in all Member States, (2) administer funding to researchers for projects, or carry out such research directly, as appropriate, and (3) disseminate the acquired new knowledge to advertisers and their agencies, consumer groups, educational institutions, government agencies, legislators and media, preferably through the appropriate national associations in the countries concerned.

(47) In 1981 the Commission published its Second Consumer Protection and Information Program. It was more subdued in tone and content and less specific than the first one. It opened discussion on self-regulation and encouraged a positive and constructive "dialogue" between all parties concerned.

(48) The Commission's emphasis on dialogue was welcomed by the advertising business. But it remained difficult to enter into meaningful discussions with consumer groups at the international level, who seemed not to favor the Commission's apparent intention of resolving some of the outstanding issues by mutual agreement between all parties concerned.

(49) The dialogue with the Commission brought about greater cooperation between the Commission and the advertising business to defend the genuine interests of consumers.

(50) Despite improving relationships between the Commission and the advertising community, there remain many differces of opinion as to what advertising can and cannot do, and the propriety of the many different ways of conducting international advertising. These differences have to some extent arisen from lack of understanding of how advertising is produced and how it works in the marketplace. Both

regulators and representatives from the business world have from the start felt this to be an unfortunate situation but hardly surprising, considering the non-advertising background of many regulators and consumer representatives.

(51) Provided all parties would express interest and would be prepared to actively participate in preparations, the advertising business might well respond favorably to a request to organize a number of presentations at which all aspects of advertising would be presented and discussed.

Recommendation II

New initiatives should be taken to bring together representatives from supranational and inter-governmental organizations concerned with consumer protection and advertising regulation.

The advertising business should prepare informative presentations for this group on the most important aspects of producing, placing and measuring the effectiveness of advertising on an international scale.

(52) In its Second Consumer Program the Commission again raises the question of how to educate consumers for a better understanding of the economic process. A pilot test carried out at twenty-five schools within the Community did not result in any final recommendation. Consumer education has always been and will remain the responsibility of national and local governments. The COE's earlier educational activities and its Resolution of October, 1971 have not produced any concrete results. It would therefore seem appropriate for the advertising business to make its skills and experience available for the preparation of accurate materials to teach about advertising, to be distributed and used in a properly planned manner at elementary, secondary and advanced schools.

Recommendation III

It is recommended that the advertising business, in close cooperation with the teaching profession, offer assistance to private and public schools at primary, secondary and advanced levels, to draw up a plan for the preparation and distribution to schools, of responsible information about the role of advertising in a market economy. The contribution of industry could include making available existing information on tapes, cassettes, films, slides, etc., from which the right selection could be made. Such a program should initially be developed and tested in one or two countries in the Common Market, and then be revised, exported and adapted by other countries on the basis of experience gained.

(53) Apart from educating future generations of consumers at schools, it would seem equally important that those who want to make a career in advertising should have better opportunities to acquire basic knowledge about it; this would also ultimately benefit the buying public. There already exist a small number of reputable institutes in Europe which specialize in advertising education, some of which are part of the IAA educational program. However, relatively few opportunities exist in Europe for education in advertising, and especially too few universities offer an advertising curriculum.

Recommendation IV

It is recommended that the business community encourage universities in Europe to give greater prominence to the study of advertising as part of their curricula.

The study of advertising should preferably be included within one of the existing faculties, such as business administration or communication science, or both.

The successful completion of a course of study in advertising should entitle the student to a specialized degree. The development of such a program should take place in close cooperation with the business world to ensure recognition of the practical value of a degree to students who wish to make a career in advertising.

It would be important also for certain professors at European universities to have the opportunity to spend time at a company, agency or advertising medium to gain first hand exposure to the advertising business.

(54) Proper advertising education has been even more important since developments in the field of advertising regulation are being accelerated by the rapid growth and importance of advertising reaching homes via cable networks, satellites or other new technologies.

(55) The European Broadcasting Union (EBU), the Bureau Européen des Unions de Consommateurs (BEUC), the COE and the EEC have made their positions widely known. The Commission's green paper on "Television Without Frontiers" proposes a number of ground rules to support and stimulate international trade, but it also suggests certain restrictions with regard to the advertising of tobacco and alcoholic products and advertising to children. The advertising business welcomes the opportunity for a constructive discussion but is divided about the need for a directive at this stage.

(56) On the one hand existing legislation and voluntary controls in Member States appear to be helpful to ensure proper protection of the consumer from advertising via these "new media." On the other hand international advertisers would be well served with a framework of conditions enabling them to use advertising on television similarly in all European countries. Having considered all options, the Commission has proposed a directive that will also regulate advertising on television within the Community.

(57) While the new technological developments are phenomenal, their importance for the advertising business will largely depend upon the attraction of a great number of manifold programs for the viewing public. This of course will in turn determine if and to what extent advertisers will be interested in the use of these media. However, the long term potential of advertising via cable and satellite is unquestionable.

(58) The advertising business is not only concerned about the activities of the Community and its various institutions, such as the European Parliament (EP) which exercises increasing influence on consumer developments; but it also follows closely the activities of other supranational organizations that take an interest in

consumer affairs. Apart from the EEC, the "short list" includes as intergovernmental bodies, the COE, the Organization for Economic Cooperation and Development (OECD), the United Nations' Economic and Social Council (ECOSOC) and the UN's Educational, Scientific and Cultural Organization (UNESCO). Among the NGOs, and apart from members of the EAT, we count UNICE, BEUC, the ICC, the IAA, and the International Union of Consumers' Unions (IOCU). Some of these bodies cover territories beyond the Community, and their involvement in matters concerning advertising varies considerably, but they all have direct or indirect influence on developments under discussion in the European Community.

(59) The COE is of particular importance because of its European Convention on Human Rights, which concerns the freedom of expression for European citizens. Many believe that "commercial speech" is covered by this convention, but this view has not yet been confirmed by the European Court of Human Rights in Strasbourg. If commercial speech is covered, the consequences for advertising and its regulation throughout the Community and all of Europe are considerable.

(60) There are a number of other organizations with which the advertising business wishes to maintain contact, usually on an *ad-hoc* basis, concerning a multitude of issues that will, to a smaller or larger extent include aspects of importance to advertising. These contacts include the Commission of Family Organizations in the Community (COFACE), the Food Standards Program Codex Alimentarius Commission of the Food and Agriculture Organization (FAO) and the World Health Organization (WHO), both UN agencies, and many trade associations representing specific industries.

Chapter V: Preparing for the future

(61) Over many years the increasingly global economy has led to a greater variety of products and services and thereby greater consumer choice.

(62) In recent years European economies have no longer grown and expanded as rapidly as they did earlier. Stagnation has occurred in many industries. But there are signs of re-industrialization, growth of an information society, and increasing economic expansion in EC Member States. The economic situation, although still far from robust, shows signs of improvement. The worst of the political and economic uncertainty would appear to be over.

(63) Economic and political unity, as foreseen in the Treaty of Rome, is a long way off. Although some countries still follow a nationalistic and protectionistic policy, there is a glimmer of hope that earlier recommendations to encourage international trade and to simplify the structure, responsibilities and procedures of the Community's institutions, will at long last come to fruition.

(64) A new "Spaak Committee" under chairman Dooge from Ireland has made appropriate recommendations; president Mitterrand has taken initiatives for the development of European projects to counterbalance American and Japanese domination; the Commission has produced projects with a similar objective; President Delors at the start of his tenure in office expressed himself forcefully and convincingly in favor of a strong and united Europe; Lord Cockfield published a White Paper on "Completing the Internal Market," which shows vision and courage; and Commissioner Clinton Davis has announced a new approach to the subject of consumer protection and the need for directives.

(65) In this connection it is important to remember that in order to achieve the business climate in which advertising on an international scale will be most effective, the advertising business has on various occasions offered its expertise to the Commission to help to create acceptance and appreciation among European citizens of the EEC's efforts to achieve a unified Europe. The advertising business has felt that this goal is in the interest of both business and consumers. Initially the response of the Commission to these offers was not very encouraging, but it now appears to realize the need for professional help if it wants to overcome its serious communication problems within the Community. To this end the IAA, together with other international trade associations, now have a close working relationship with the Commission.

(66) In the market place itself two developments will be of crucial importance to future advertising regulation; on the one hand products and services marketed on a purely national scale will be facing greater diversification and polarization, while on the other hand technological developments in electronic media and the never-ending search by advertisers for new economies of scale, will lead to the increasing importance of advertising produced for use in a number of countries. Both developments will benefit from a minimum set of rules and regulations, applying equally to all Member States and the Europe as a whole.

(67) To finish this general background of the European scene, it is important to review consumerist activities, both in Europe and in the USA. On both continents militant consumerism is declining, but there still are threats to ban advertising in additional product categories. Pertschuk's ghost lingers and the need continues to monitor all developments carefully.

(68) In his policy document "A New Impetus For Consumer Protection," the new Commissioner for consumer affairs gave a number of reasons why previous Commissions have not been successful with their consumer programs. While agreeing with most of his points, there were other factors which contributed to the unsatisfactory results, especially the over-ambitious nature of the Commission's initial plans, the lack of experience in matters concerning advertising on the part of many members of the staff of the Commission, and the lack of informal contact between the Commission and experienced operators in the field of international

advertising. Most importantly, however, one vital question remains unanswered: *Was an international consumer protection program really necessary?* The new Commission and Commissions preceding it, have never produced convincing evidence of such a need, nor have large numbers of consumers expressed the desire for protection.

(69) The Commission's future consumer policy will concentrate on the health and safety aspects of consumer protection, but may also deal with a number of outstanding and new issues. These include unfair and comparative advertising; consumer credit; package tour contracts. The expected directive on television advertising will receive high priority. The existing directive on the labelling of foodstuffs will be revised. A recommendation has already been made for consumer education at primary and secondary schools.

(70) In addition to the planned program of the Commission, depending upon pressures from various sources, advertising of other products such as pharmaceuticals and alcoholic products, also may be the subject of proposed regulation.

(71) Apart from the Commission's future plans with regard to regulation of advertising, international advertisers are extremely interested in "negative" harmonization, or deregulation of existing rules and regulations, as part of the Commission's declared policy to remove barriers to international trade.

(72) The Commission has given up its desire to establish a dialogue between the business world and consumer groups on the subject of voluntary agreements as long as such agreements are not associated with Community legislation.

(73) The advertising business must not only monitor the Commission's plans and proposals but also those of other intergovernmental organizations that concern themselves with advertising regulation. This leads in Europe to considerable overlap and duplication of effort. The Commission, the COE, the OECD and the UN all have consumer programs which differ only in detail.

(74) This duplication and accumulation of regulatory activity has reached alarming proportions and would not appear to be in accordance with the objectives of the Treaty of Rome to break down barriers which prevent international trade. Also, this dissipation of resources would seem to be an extravagance hardly sustainable at a time when governments are pressed to seek new economies in their operations.

(75) In view of the political nature of consumer protection, it would seem unlikely that governments will reconsider their commitments in this respect. But the growing acceptance of self-regulation may gradually result in a better balance between statutory and voluntary advertising controls, with more emphasis on the latter.

(76) Self-regulation has become respectable and the new consumer policies of the Commission no longer disclaim the positive and satisfactory role which voluntary controls play in most European countries. Some argue that without acceptance of the positive role of self-regulation, the new policies of the Commission would hardly have been possible.

(77) The case for self-regulation has been and will continue to be a strong one, not necessarily as an alternative to statutory controls, but rather as an addition to the essential minimum standards and sanctions provided by government.

(78) The future stance of the advertising business should therefore be based on promoting a policy of deregulation within the European market economy, with freedom of choice and freedom of expression as indivisible components.

(79) Based on experience during the previous decade, when results achieved were largely due to a united policy pursued by the entire advertising business in defense of its legitimate freedoms, it would seem logical to continue this policy with singleness of mind and a strong sense of purpose. With effective and efficient systems of voluntary controls, governmental interference in communicating with consumers should be reduced to a minimum.

(80) Those associations that handle matters at the international level require close contacts and full cooperation from the national trade associations. Their support is vital to achieve common objectives and to defend the legitimate interests of the advertising business.

(81) In order to carry the burden of defending the interests of the entire advertising business, national and international associations also require full support in terms of money and manpower from international corporations, advertising agencies and media. Their senior managements must accept the responsibility to deal with consumer affairs by being available for consultation, corporately and individually. The success of the trade associations will depend directly on the input of the industries they represent.

Recommendation V

Following what is already being done by many corporations whose advertising within the Community is affected by regulation, it is recommended that these international corporations make such internal arrangements as will be necessary to keep abreast of relevant developments in the field of consumer protection, at both national and international levels.

Such arrangements often will include the appointment of an executive to act as the first point of contact with national and international trade associations, so that they can represent effectively the interests of the total industry at all levels.

(82) To enable the international trade associations to cope successfully with the many issues, the advertising business might like to consider the introduction of a scheme similar to the one introduced in the USA, under which young executives from advertising agencies are made available to the Washington Office of the American Association of Advertising Agencies (AAAA) on a temporary basis. They work on specific regulatory assignments of importance to the advertising business. The AAAA pays their out-of-pocket expenses, while their employers continue to pay their salaries.

Recommendation VI

It is recommended that the European advertising business consider the possibility of setting up a "Loaned Executive Assignment Program" (LEAP) along the lines of the US scheme.

Advertisers, advertising agencies and media would make young executives available on a temporary basis, to join the secretariats of international trade associations and accept specific assignments in the field of advertising regulation.

Such an arrangement would: (a) reduce the burden on the secretariats concerned, (b) contribute to a better relationship between the partners in the field of regulatory activity, and (c) contribute to a better understanding of the main issues by those who will later carry responsibility for their solutions.

(83) Despite the improved image of advertising among consumers and greater acceptance of it on the part of governmental bodies, the demands made upon the advertising business to advance its cause, to explain its role, and to defend its interests and those of consumers, will be considerable. Many erroneous views about advertising among many different parts of the population in Member States must still be dispelled. These activities will require the undaunted support of the entire business community and particularly of the small group of people who are seen by European citizens as the international business leaders, the captains of industry. The advertising business should make an appeal to these top men to make themselves available in greater numbers than to date.

(84) They should explain, in speeches and in writing, the advantages of an effective market economy, to the informed public and to the leaders of governments and of intergovernmental bodies. "Private enterprise" may seem to an overworked concept, but its basic merits remain indisputable to those who value the quality of today's society. The paralyzing influence of governmental bureaucracy must be removed. It is high time that the leaders of industry expose the extravagance of so many governmental activities. The costs do not appear to stand in any reasonable relation to benefits. Governments and intergovernmental bodies must listen to the opinions of those who have done so much to create today's society, attacked by some but cherished by most.

(85) Alongside the captains of industry, leaders in the academic world should feel responsible not only to criticize the market system, but also to explain its advantages to their students, who will in the future hold senior positions in our society. An accurate, balanced perspective is important.

(86) The saga of European regulation of advertising will continue. Commissioners will come and go. One consumer program will replace another. Directives will be proposed, amended, withdrawn or approved. Protagonists and antagonists of private enterprise and a market economy will continue their debate.

(87) Consumers throughout Europe will remain largely undisturbed, as they have in the past. They will continue to benefit from freedom of choice and advertising will help them to do so.

(88) This puts a great responsibility on the shoulders of industry and the advertising business to act as custodians of the freedoms that enable manufacturers to sell and advertise, and consumers to select and choose.

(89) If the leaders of the business community jointly continue their efforts to accelerate the positive economic trends that appear to be developing, to enhance the growing understanding and acceptance of advertising, and to support and develop self-regulatory advertising controls, they will benefit consumers and society as a whole.

(90) While the spirit of deregulation is gradually growing in Europe, there still is regulatory pettiness that can kill the hard-to-come-by entrepreneurial initiatives of imaginative business leaders. If a few European governments were to be replaced by ones that would reverse the deregulatory trend, the advertising business would be among the first to feel the effects.

(91) The job which the business community has done, is by no means finished. It will have to be continued with undaunted vigor. Pertschuk and his European counterparts are still with us. There is no room for complacency.

(92) During the last fifteen years the advertising business has gone through one of its most hectic periods. It has not only survived, but has emerged with greater strength and willingness to accept change and renewal as prerequisites for its future role and contribution to society.

(93) In his book *Self-Renewal* John Gardner says: "The renewal of societies and organizations can only go forward if someone cares" (Gardner, 1963: XV). Our book has been written for those who care enough to take part in the never-ending task of renewal. We hope that many will accept the challenge.

Introduction

"Idealism is the noble toga political
gentlemen drape over their will to power."
Aldous Huxley, British writer*

"Where there is patience and humility
there is neither anger nor vexation."
St. Francis of Assisi

This book contains a description and analysis of supranational regulatory activities affecting advertising. While the focus will be on advertising regulation as proposed by the Commission of the European Community (EC), and the response to it by the business world, the influence of other intergovernmental bodies, covering a wider area than the Common Market, cannot be ignored and will therefore be discussed. For a proper international perspective it is equally important to draw comparisons, whenever relevant, with other markets such as the United States, which still represents the world's largest advertising business, both in terms of expenditure per capita and in total. These considerations will therefore often lead to an extension of our discussion beyond the Community.

The origins of the consumer protection programs of the European Economic Community

Although the seeds of consumer protection activities are found in the economic and social conditions following World War II, early efforts to introduce measures for the protection of consumers reached a formal stage on April 14, 1975 when the Council of Ministers of the Community passed a resolution entitled "Preliminary Programme of the European Economic Community for a Consumer Protection and Information Policy" (See Appendix I). This preliminary program covered a number

---

* Sources of quotations at the beginning of chapters, can be found in the References under "Quotations."

of fields important to "health, safety and economic interests of the consumer," and required a consumer policy "to be implemented at Community level." Paragraph 48 of its Annex said that "in implementing its programme, the Commission will take full account of studies and other work already carried out by the Member States, international bodies and consumer organizations." It soon became evident that the Commission, in implementing the consumer protection policy, intended to go beyond harmonization of existing national legislation.

In November, 1975 the Commission of the European Communities released a Draft Directive on Misleading and Unfair Advertising. It recommended major changes in the way products and services should be advertised within the Community; these changes could result in serious limitations in the freedom of commercial enterprise. Many in business were concerned because they perceived the document to be biased not only against the interests of consumers, but also against business and advertising generally.

After prolonged discussions during the second half of the 1970s among officials of the Commission, other civil servants and representatives of consumer and trade associations, many changes and revisions of Commission proposals were made. The sharp edges of the Commission's initial recommendations to proceed with a "harmonious development of economic activities," as stated in Article 2 of the Rome Treaty, had been modified somewhat by the early 1980s.

The Commission which came into power on January 1, 1985, is indeed committed to a "down with the barriers" policy (Cockfield, 1985: iii), but its activities and those of others who wish to curb legitimate business and advertising practices, still give cause for concern.

Definitions

It is difficult to understand the various views on supranational advertising regulation because people define concepts and terms differently. This difficulty has two main components:

(1) The variability in translations and changes in the nuances of meaning when one language is translated into another. Misunderstandings attributable to nuances in translations are of vital importance, and we urge the reader to keep this problem in mind throughout the book.

(2) Different definitions for some of the same basic terms within a language. We can avoid this difficulty by stating our definitions at the outset and by reminding the reader to refer to them whenever there is any doubt about our intended meaning.

The consumer

Since most advertising regulations relate to consumers rather than to industrial customers, we shall limit our treatment to consumers, defined as private persons who acquire goods, services or anything of value mainly for their own use and not for resale or for use in business. This definition corresponds to the British or US term "ultimate consumer," and to the German term "Endverbraucher."

Consumerism

The representatives of consumers will play an important role in our discussions of advertising regulation. We define "consumerism" as the activities of those who are genuinely motivated in the promotion of consumers' interests and in protecting consumers from real or perceived abuses by sellers in the marketplace.

Advertising

Of the many definitions of advertising, the following is both comprehensive and precise, and it has long been widely accepted: "Advertising is any paid form of non-personal presentation and promotion of ideas, goods, or services by an identified sponsor" (Wright et al., 1971).

International advertising

The literature is somewhat confusing in its use of such words as "foreign," "multinational," "transnational," "cross-cultural," "intercultural" and "international," most of which are used more or less interchangeably.

In referring to advertising used in a number of countries, we choose, arbitrarily, to use the word "international" throughout, defining international advertising as that which is created at, coordinated or directed from one central point, for execution, with or without local adaptations, in a number of countries.

When referring to regulation of such international advertising, we shall use the term "intergovernmental" when it concerns bodies established by national governments to deal with matters affecting a number of countries within the Community, within Europe or within the entire world. The term "supranational" is a broader term and will be used to include intergovernmental as well as non-governmental organizations operating within the same regions.

The Community and its institutions

The EC was established on March 25, 1957.

> The Community traces its origins to the Treaty of Paris, signed on 18 April 1951, to create a European Coal and Steel Community (ECSC). The six founding Member States — Belgium, Germany, France, Italy, Luxembourg and the Netherlands — decided that this experiment, which proved an enormous success, should be deepened and extended to embrace their entire economies. On 25 March 1957 they signed the two Treaties of Rome, setting up the European Economic Community (EEC) and the European Atomic Energy Community (EAEC or Euratom) (*European File*, 1984b).

The ECSC, EEC and EAEC merged in July, 1967 as "the first step towards the setting-up of a single European Community to be governed by a single treaty" (Noël, 1982:3). However, agreement on such a treaty has not yet been achieved. Although progress on this matter was reportedly made at a meeting of the Heads of State in Milan on June 29 – 30, 1985, it seems unlikely that such a treaty will be concluded in the near future.

The ECSC and EAEC are relatively unimportant to this book, and will receive no further comment. We are primarily concerned with the EEC. The EC Commission is responsible for the development of consumer programs and proposals to regulate advertising within the Community. It is also the most important of all supranational bodies involved in consumer affairs in Europe.

Although we will discuss details of organization, procedures and the decision-making process later, we will introduce the major relevant institutions of the European Community in a general way now.

Since July, 1967 the aims of the Community have been carried out by "four institutions: the European Parliament (EP), the Council, the Commission, and the Court of Justice, with the support of the Court of Auditors" (Noël, 1981:3). Of these institutions the Council of Ministers is of greatest importance, since it is the only body authorized to make binding decisions for submission to the Member States of the Community for implementation.

The EEC is now comprised of 12 Member States* with a population of over 320 million. In addition to the original six nations, Denmark, Ireland and the United Kingdom joined the EEC on January 1, 1973 followed by Greece on January 1, 1981 and by Spain and Portugal on January 1, 1986.

Since this book deals primarily with the EEC, we shall use that abbreviation when appropriate. We will use the abbreviation EC for European Community when it is important to refer to the broader Community rather than to the EEC. Also, when referring to the institutions of the EC such as the "Commission" or the "Council," we shall follow normal EC practice and use each term without any descriptive label.

---

* Belgium, Denmark, France, Germany, Greece, Ireland, Italy, Luxembourg, Netherlands, Portugal, Spain, United Kingdom.

Over the years the Member States have formally transferred some of their sovereign powers to the EC. Legally the EC is a separate entity with powers of a sovereign State, within its fields of competence. For example, it has the power to seal contracts with third countries across a range of areas as set out in the European Treaties. More than 100 countries have diplomatic relations with the EC. It takes part in international conferences on trade, development and East-West cooperation. For example, the EC has taken over formal responsibility for representing its Member States in the General Agreement on Trade and Tariffs (GATT) and the North Atlantic Fisheries Organization (*European file*, 1984a:3).

There are also other important bodies active in the field of consumer affairs. The Council of Europe (COE), based in Strasbourg and comprising twenty-one European states, was the first intergovernmental organization to concern itself with the consumer, which it still does diligently. There are other intergovernmental and non-governmental organizations, which influence regulatory developments within Europe and the EC, and which especially deserve our attention. Some cover a much wider area than Europe.

The purposes and scope of this book

This is not a book dealing in detail with the advertising regulation in each of the EEC countries; other sources are available for such information. But there is no published comprehensive review of major regulatory developments at the supra-national level. This book contains such a review and it deliberately concentrates on one of the most visible and controversial aspects of intergovernmental regulation, namely on that of advertising.

This book begins with the conditions that led to the post World War II development of the consumer movement in Europe. Consumerists critized business in the 1960s and 1970s and indeed the prevailing economic system. These criticisms seemed to question the values of the market system, and especially those of "Advertising... [which was] an obvious scapegoat, for it is the most visible and immediate element in the process of production and distribution" (Green, 1976).

An important part of this book will be devoted to the reaction of the business world to these criticisms and the subsequent activities by the Commission and other intergovernmental bodies to regulate and restrict advertising as a tool for the marketing of products and services. We shall also deal with Non-Governmental Organizations (NGOs) such as the Union of Industries of the European Community (UNICE) and the International Chamber of Commerce (ICC) and their efforts to defend the interests of private industry.

The book covers the 1960s, when the criticism of advertising was gaining momentum, the 1970s, when the height of regulatory activity was reached, and the early 1980s when it subsided. We have followed events during that time closely, not because we believe that a chronological account is so important – in the light of history the details will soon fade away – but because these developments have led to the adoption of certain principles which guided united action by the business community. These principles, which we shall describe, will remain valid for many years to come.

This book therefore presents comprehensive information to assist readers in understanding the complexities of regulating advertising at the international level. It also explains the response of a united business community to the intentions of intergovernmental organizations. The authors have recalled and analyzed the past in order to help the reader to prepare for the future.

There should be no doubt at the outset where the authors stand. We believe that consumers should have the right to safety, to choose, to be heard, to be informed and to be educated; we also believe the preponderance of evidence indicates that industry should have considerable freedom to advertise. If advertising is accurate and truthful, as well as socially acceptable and responsible, it can contribute substantially to the welfare of a continuously changing society.

We recall the first sentence in Alvin Tofler's book *Future Shock*: "This is a book about what happens to people when they are overwhelmed by change. It is about the way we adapt – or fail to adapt to the future" (Tofler, 1970:3). We could have chosen the same introduction. We dare not fail to adapt to the developments that have evolved. They have by no means run their course. The process of finding a mature balance between the interests of all concerned parties will continue. In such a situation it is essential for all such parties to know what is at stake and how to react to new developments.

To achieve a balanced solution, the business world, consumer advocates and governments should attempt together to achieve the main objectives of the Treaty of Rome, namely "... a harmonious development of economic activities ..." and "... an accelerated raising of the standard of living ..." (*Rome Treaty*: Article 2:3).

It is hoped that in doing so, European governments will discontinue certain protectionist attitudes that can so easily undermine the business world's confidence in the future of Europe. New incentives to create a united Europe, both economically and politically, and less bureaucratic interference will be required if European nations are to compete successfully in the European marketplace. The principles of a free market economy should prevail, deregulation should replace regulation, the EEC and its institutions should not lose themselves in petty detail but should concentrate on bringing about the Common Market envisaged by its fathers.

Fortunately, recent signs indicate that the Commission is now set on a course to minimize obstacles for expansion of trade throughout the Community as the next step toward a fully united Europe. In fact, the Commission hopes to achieve "... completion of a fully unified internal market by 1992" (Commission of the EC,

1985a:4), an objective which the business world actively supports. Advertising can and will also make its contribution to the realization of this policy. In doing so, it will work toward the continuation of a society which counts freedom of choice and freedom of speech among its most cherished values.

Chapter I

Setting the stage

"Advertising is an evil service."
Aneurin Bevan, British politician

"Advertising is really a form of education."
King George VI

In order to understand the regulation of advertising on an international scale in Europe it is necessary to review briefly a number of conditions which form the background to consumer policy introduced by the Commission in 1975. In this chapter we will first discuss the economic importance of advertising. We then review certain essential European economic developments in the 1950s and 1960s, especially the nature of the market system as it operated in Europe, including EEC competition policy and the vision of a Common Market. We then discuss consumer behavior, the beginning of serious criticism of advertising and the development of "consumerism." Next we cover how governments reacted to criticism of advertising and introduced legislation and regulatory methods to bring advertising under control. Finally, we discuss the development of voluntary codes and controls, and their advantages and disadvantages. At this point we will have characterized the situation in which the EEC launched its consumer protection programs.

Introduction

The quotations at the beginning of this chapter indicate two essential opposite views of advertising, one negative and the other positive. While neither of these extreme views is held by a majority of Europeans, these opposing opinions provide the anchor points between which the opinions of most consumers fall. Almost everyone in the market economies of Europe is exposed to advertising regularly; and almost everyone has an opinion as to the proper (or improper) functions of advertising.

9

The range of opinions is broad, and advertising remains controversial. However, the majority view seems to be not only that advertising is an essential feature of a market economy, but also that there are times and circumstances under which at least some advertising needs to be controlled.

Advertising is an institution which has been with us ever since man attempted to "sell" a product or service to others. Advertising gives sellers a vehicle they need to do business; and it gives buyers information they need to make purchasing decisions. Its "staying power" as well as its numerous defenders illustrate well the need for advertising. Thus most criticisms and suggestions for change are intended to improve advertising rather than to abolish it.

For reasons which we shall discuss in this book, national governments as well as international governmental bodies such as the EEC, have felt the need to regulate advertising. In recent years the movement to do so has become more politically oriented, almost a self-perpetuating activity with a life of its own. And although some feel that too much attention has been given to regulating advertising, many others continue to feel that advertising is a very important economic and social force which must be given even greater regulatory attention.

Therefore we begin by addressing the importance of advertising as an economic activity.

The importance of advertising

According to Robert J. Coen, Senior Vice-President of McCann Erickson in New York and generally accepted as an authority on financial aspects of the advertising business, world advertising expenditures now exceed $150 billion (US), of which approximately 50% is spent in the USA, with Europe accounting for about 25% and the rest of the world for the remainder (Coen, 1984). To understand the significance of these expenditures it is helpful to look at advertising on a per capita basis, and as a percentage of Gross National Product (GNP).

Advertising expenditures on a per capita basis, and as a percentage of GNP are small. Therefore advertising seems to be of only modest importance economically. But there are great variations among European countries, indicating the different relative importance of advertising as an economic force in these countries.

Another way of judging advertising's importance is to look at the number of people employed. The American Association of Advertising Agencies (AAAA) estimates that in 1982, 111,000 people were employed by American agencies (*Advertising Age*, April 26, 1984). Since US advertising accounts for approximately 50% of world advertising, one might estimate that the total number of people employed in advertising agencies worldwide, may well be about 250,000. In comparison, in 1984 General Motors employed 746,000 people, Philips 343,000 and Unilever

Table I
Advertising expenditures per capita and as a percentage of GNP (1982)

Country	Per capita (in US$)	% GNP
USA	285.75	2.18
Canada	149.79	1.27
Belgium	49.47	0.40
Denmark	114.17	0.84
France	76.38	0.60
Greece	18.96	0.41
Ireland	36.61	0.86
Italy	55.40	0.77
Luxembourg	66.00	0.60
Netherlands	131.26	1.08
Portugal	6.08	0.23
Spain	43.77	0.74
United Kingdom	115.41	1.24
West Germany	87.22	0.63

Source: *World Advertising Expenditures*, New York: Starch INRA Hooper Group of Companies, and the International Advertising Association, 1984.

267,000 (*Fortune International*, August 20, 1984). Thus those employed in the advertising business will in any case constitute a small percentage of total industry employment worldwide.

It may also be argued that advertising contributes to the number of employed in manufacturing and other service industries. Advertising often is an important part of the marketing mix, helping to promote sales, thereby contributing indirectly to employment. Although the employment effect of advertising may be substantial, there is no available information on its size. Additionally, many people who are employed by the media owe their jobs directly or indirectly to advertising revenues. Perhaps the total employment due to advertising is approximately of the same order of magnitude as advertising's proportion of GNP – well under one per cent in almost all countries, and a very tiny percentage in many countries.

It should also be remembered that a substantial part of the approximately $150 billion (US) spent on advertising goes to the major media, such as newspapers, magazines, radio and television. Thus, advertising constitutes a major source of revenue for the mass media in most countries, and it makes news and entertainment possible. Also, media dependence on advertising not only makes them financially sound but also independent of political or government influence to a great extent. In democratic countries the long-term tendency in Europe and elsewhere seems to be toward increasing commercialization of the media.

In sum, advertising seems to be of comparatively modest economic significance. Therefore the great amount of attention focused on advertising has little to do with its economic impact. Advertising attracts attention and derives its importance mainly from its visibility in the marketplace and its alleged effects, directly and indirectly, on the combined cultural, economic, political and social life of nations.

Economic policies and developments in Europe

The different economic policies of European nations following World War II were in part a reflection of conditions in each country after the war, as well as the historical differences in economic development among nations. The history and development of economic thought in England, France and Germany, for example, were not identical. And, since economic policies of nations are shaped by prevailing economic thought, one should expect differences in the economic policies of these nations. Also, the differing types of dislocations and trauma of World War II, as well as the influence of US policies on some countries but not on others, contributed to diversity.

Yet there are also many similarities in historical perspective. European economies emerged from medieval times, gradually shedding local and national restrictions on trade, and in many cases adopting a philosophy of private enterprise and the market system. Although this philosophy was a repudiation of government control over business, it did not necessarily extend to prohibiting private monopolies, trade restrictions, or combinations. However, the position of the classical liberal economists in the nineteenth century nevertheless had a great impact, and the virtues of maintaining competition as a means of protecting society were widely recognized. Still, other views often prevailed regarding the efficiency of large-scale enterprise, especially the belief that private firms should be permitted to cooperate with each other, e.g. to form certain types of cartels, when it could be demonstrated that the public interest was served. For example:

> At the beginning of the [twentieth] century the British economy was the most competitive in the world; by 1945 it was minutely regulated. Tariffs had been erected before and after the first world war. During the depression of the 1930s the government had ecouraged manufactures to make agreements in order to share the available work. During the second world war the economy was regulated by rationing and price control. The government found it convenient to discuss supplies with a single, large firm, or with a trade association representing the interests of many. All this led to an atmosphere of fair shares for all — the antithesis of competition (Borrie and Diamond, 1973:289).

In 1948 legislation was enacted in the UK to prohibit monopolies, *if* an investigation should indicate that in a particular case of monopoly the public interest was not being served. In general a number of practices that restricted competition, such as fixing minimum prices and allocating market shares among firms, were also condemned, although there were some exceptions (Borrie and Diamond, 1973).

More recently monopoly and restrictive practices have been reduced in the UK, and policy has been to a great extent to foster increasingly competitive conditions; but the notion *fair trading* has been preserved.

The historical developments in continental countries were somewhat different. In Germany, for example, both the industrial revolution and political unification occurred somewhat later than in Britain. Also, the economic thought that guided economic policy tended to focus to a greater extent on prohibiting unfair competition so as to protect competitors, rather than on the preservation of competition in which the inefficient are expected to be driven either to change or to go out of business. Although combinations and cartels were more widespread in Germany than in some countries, the classical liberal tradition also flourished there; the Freiburg school, for example, produced Ludwig Erhard who greatly influenced German economic policies after World War II.

The influence of economic policies of the United States

It also seems appropriate to mention here certain US economic historical perspectives, sinde the USA by virtue of its economic assistance and recovery programs was deeply embroiled in European economic policy after World War II.

In the USA the market system, compared to that in Europe, evolved from different circumstances and acquired a different perspective. Historically the US government was relatively weak and few restrictions on business existed. Thus freedom of business from government was not an objective, but an existing condition. The government policy, then, was to maintain competition, especially to break up large monopolistic private enterprises as well as to restrict collusive arrangements among large firms. Whereas the market system in Europe arose as an alternative to state control, the competitive market system in the USA was considered as an alternative to private monopoly and private collusion. It is important to keep these distinctions in mind, since the US viewpoint on maintaining competition has had an impact on some European viewpoints on the nature of proper competition policy. The US perspective has by no means replaced the European perspectives that often focus more on fair competition than on free competition. In fact US emphasis on preserving competition has been widely regarded in European nations as extremist. Since World War II the relative indifference of Europeans to the problem of private monopoly reflects the greater prevalence of government restrictions in their countries, and the smaller size of their business organizations. Enclosed by national boundaries, markets were segmented and firms were smaller than those that evolved in the USA.

US/European differences and their implications

The differences in emphasis on conditions of competition in the market system of the USA and those in European nations has profound implications. In the USA competition is expected to keep prices down, to limit profits, to improve the quality of products and services, to keep opportunities open for the innovator, and to promote technical progress. Through the 1950s and beyond, when Americans said that competition was a failure, they meant that it failed to exist or that it failed to solve some important problems, such as the elimination of business recessions or the elimination of poverty, not that it failed to perform its consumer protective function. In Europe, in contrast, the private enterprise system has been regarded by many as rightfully permissive in allowing the concentration of economic power in the hands of business; the capacity of competition to protect the consumer interest has been widely denied. Thus, large numbers of people came to favor some form of state control of business to protect consumers as well as to protect competitors.

Another important difference in perspective is that European support for the market system historically has been from political conservatives. The private enterprise system has been regarded as protection for established business and property interests against reforms instituted by the state. But in contrast, in the 1950s and earlier, US support for the market system was from populist, liberal or radical groups. The competitive market system was seen as an instrument of reform.

Since World War II, however, the differences in viewpoint on the market system have changed greatly. In the 1950s, the importance of competition as the protector of consumers and society, won greater recognition in Europe. And in the USA, with the appearance of government programs for control of business, advocacy of the private enterprise idea was extended to include protection of private interests from government. Thus to some extent the US perspective was imported into Europe, and the European perspective was imported into the USA. These changes have muddled the political distinctions, and seemingly opposite economic groups may now be found on both sides of the Atlantic promoting private enterprise, or repudiating private enterprise, depending on whether they believe it leads to outcomes they desire or oppose.

Today on both sides of the North Atlantic those who defend the market system usually do so because they feel it benefits society. Competitive intensity is maintained, the incentives in the system lead to high levels of production, mass consumption and high standards of living; and the competitive market system has encouraged progress in technology at an unprecedented rate. The German Wirtschaftswunder (economic miracle) of the 1950s and 1960s is a frequently cited example. Nevertheless there are numerous skeptics who feel that the market system leads to serious inequities, especially among "disadvantaged" segments of society.

Today, most opponents of the market system say that it leads to monopoly, high prices, restrictions on output and consequently to unemployment, and to exhorbitant profits (see for example Lenzen, 1981:27ff). This viewpoint is supported by some economic analyses, but it is not widely accepted; little empirical evidence exists to support this view, and the reasoning behind it is largely hypothetical in nature; therefore it remains controversial.

On balance the market system seems to have demonstrated a far greater ability to meet the needs of society than any other system that has been tried. Thus, care should be taken that attempts to "improve" the system do not lead to destroying its virtues. If private enterprise market system is to continue to benefit individual consumers as well as society at large, it depends especially upon preserving effective competition among business firms.

This latter point is especially important because a significant feature of workable competition is that both consumers and sellers must have adequate information on which to base their purchasing and marketing decisions. In fact, consumer information and protection programs, as we will discuss later, are intimately related to competition policy.

EEC competition policy

A fundamental question facing the framers of the treaty that established the EEC was whether or not competition, in the long run, should be depended upon to bring about the best allocation of resources possible and to guarantee economic freedom. That question was not only answered resoundingly in the affirmative, but the answer was the inspiration "to establish for the EEC an economy based on free competition, undistorted by collusion between enterprises or by abusive use of power by enterprises with dominant market positions." To these ends, "Article 85, paragraph 1, deals specifically with restraints of trade resulting from collusion between enterprises ...' and "Article 86 contains prohibitions relating to ... the abusive use of power by enterprises with dominant market positions" (McLachlan and Swann, 1967:55 – 56). In Article 85 there are four main areas of *Competition/Restrictive Practices*:

(1) competitor collaboration (collaboration which divides markets, excludes non-collaborating suppliers, or regulates competition between suppliers);

(2) use of common/exclusive sales or buying agents

(3) bilateral exclusive dealing; and

(4) joint activities in research, production and distribution (adapted from Skinner, 1969:255).

These above-listed four areas are a continuum from almost per se illegality (#1), to great permissiveness (#4).

Article 86 has not been very important to subsequent development of EEC competition policy and therefore will be ignored here. Also, as a matter of direct interest to later material in this book, it should be kept in mind that there is nothing in Articles 85 or 86 that refers to advertising as a restrictive practice.

With respect to the features in Article 85, the point should also be noted that:

> Although the tendency to condemn all trade restraints can be discerned in the Common Market competition rules, it is tempered to a degree by conflicting policy considerations. [There was] the belief that the larger market created by European economic integration would work to the advantage of large enterprises capable of participating in the entire Common Market, and, conversely, would cause the demise of many small to medium size firms. To counteract this implicit threat of monopoly, or at least oligopoly, the drafters of the treaty desired ... to assure that consumers, as well as producers, would gain from the advantages of large scale production. [However, the] widely held opinion that the competitive threat posed by large non-Common Market businesses mandates cooperative effort among the generally smaller Common Market enterprises, [created] tension in the competition rules between strict enforcement of competitive standards and the permissive allowance of trade restraints if thought to be economically useful (adapted from Skinner, 1969:250 – 251).

This tension at the EEC level reflects a similar tension within EEC countries, namely, between that of preserving workable competition under which inefficient competitors rightly fall by the wayside, or protecting competitors from each other, which is the direct opposite of preserving conditions of effective competition.

Unfair competition or consumer protection?

The latter notion is sometimes imbedded in the idea of unfair competition. The call to prohibit unfair competition, especially to protect small firms from larger ones, may invoke the "protection of consumers" as a rallying cry; but if it does more to protect competitors than to preserve conditions of effective competition, it is not likely to benefit consumers.

The point is made in fuller fashion by a British writer (Fulop, 1977) who points out that the EEC tends to be producer dominated, and the laudable efforts to protect consumers may, if one examines them closely, protect traders and manufacturers from "unfair competition" as much or more than it protects consumers from false or misleading advertising. She points out that the concept of unfair competition may lead to legislation which is characterized by four features:

> First, it bans or diminishes the effectiveness of many marketing techniques, e.g. a free gift must be related to the product, or of insignificant value, or clearly marked with the name of the advertiser; legislation restricts clearance sales to certain periods and days of the year; the provision of free transport to a place of sale is not permitted, nor is it possible for a trader to put on a free fashion show with goods on sale at the end of it because it places customers under an 'obligation' in order to effect a sale. Yet such techniques ... can perform identifiable selling tasks more efficiently than other selling techniques. And this may be to the advantage of customers.

Secondly, the 'unfair' competition laws have been designed almost entirely in the interests of business, and in particular of the small shopkeeper who is an important political force in most EEC countries ... 'the desire to protect the individual interests of competitors has been first and foremost' (Schricker, 1969). Their purpose has been primarily to make sure that new or aggressive competitors do not disturb the status quo.

Thirdly, besides being often superfluous to modern day distribution and commerce the laws of 'unfair' competition are rigidly legalistic, and therefore cumbersome, slow and arbitrary.

Lastly, and contradicting the basic concept of 'unfair' competition which predominantly protects traders and manufacturers, this legislation has become intertwined with consumer protection measures. In Germany, for example the 1930s Act on Restriction on Premium Offers has been amended five times for this purpose. That the law against unfair competition and the law of consumper protection can be treated together is based on the idea of 'unlawful advantage' (gesetzwidriger Vorsprung), so that the 'unfair' action of a competitor is deemed to be ipso facto against the interests of consumers. In several EEC countries, consumer associations are now given the right, along with trade associations, to sue for injunctions against traders for acts of unfair competition. Thus, a situation has developed whereby two very different concepts are treated as one; it is a fallacy that measures designed to protect traders from so-called unfair competition from one another necessarily safeguard the interests of consumers.

... the law (on misleading advertising) has been geared far more to protecting the trader from unfair competition than the consumer from deception' (Schricker, 1969; Fulop, 1977:54 – 50).

The nature of competition

At this point it will be useful to make explicit some additional concepts of competition. The word competition unless qualified, ordinarily implies price competition. Yet economists have long included additional non-price variables in "industrial organization" models. In this regard, special note should be made of the constantly changing nature of competition and cooperation in business that occurred in the 1950s and 1960s.

Thus, the space between products in the marketplace is increasingly being filled by other new products. For instance, in music reproduction we may have our choice between TV, radio, high fidelity sets and tape recorders. We are gradually approaching a continuous spectrum of products. In some markets cross-product competition is probably even stronger than the rivalry between different brands of the same product.

New varieties of competition stem from new types of organizational arrangements among sellers. Examples include franchising and such other varieties of vertical systems as supermarket chains, representing a new type of competition next to traditional forms of distribution. Large retailers, such as Quelle in Germany, or Sears, Roebuck in the United States, inject a new element of competition by usurping from many manufacturers their old role of governing distributive relationships (Thorelli and Thorelli, 1977:45).

The above view of competition in the marketplace suggests that consumers view competing products along many dimensions in addition to price. Thus, a consumer oriented definition of competition would direct our attention to the alternatives consumers consider when making a purchasing decision. Such alternatives can include the entire range of benefits afforded by marketing — that is the set of activities known as the marketing mix — the time, place and possession utilities produced by decisions on pricing, product, promotion and marketing channels. These marketing activities become a part of the product offering and are important to consumers when they make purchasing choices among *competing products.*

Moreover, traditional ideas on economic concentration may be outdated. On the one hand we find analyses which deplore the rise of oligopolies and use this development to point out that consumers need protection from those with market power, as we shall discuss below. On the other hand, European competition policy has at times favored concentration.

> The ... expression of the belief that European business is at a competitive disadvantage *vis-à-vis* large firms from ... the United States, has come from J.J. Servan-Schreiber. His characterization ... reiterates a long felt fear on the part of many Europeans that the generally small firms which make up the bulk of European business activity have neither the size nor the financial ability to compete with large competitors from abroad. Whatever may be the objective validity of the theses ... its importance with regard to Common Market competition policy does not rest on its correctness, but in its wide acceptance and influence as a rationale for action. The Commission of the European Economic Community ... has indicated that it believes the response ... should be the encouragement of joint activities between enterprises ... To what extent competitors' cooperation and collaboration will be permitted ... is the source of the duality that exists within Common Market competition policy (Skinner, 1969:251 – 254).

Thus, a modified position on economic size and concentration of business is that

> ... sometimes competition between the few (oligopoly) can be more beneficial to society than competition between the many. Oligopoly ... has reigned in the chemical, drug and computer industries, all of which seem to have made rapid progress to the ultimate benefit of consumers. Conversely, the textile, shoe and saw mill industries in many countries are represented by scores or hundreds of firms — and yet the only major 'happening' in these industries often seems to be that they are becoming increasingly depressed relative to other parts of the economy. The point is that atomistic competition in the classical textbook sense seems less and less worthwhile as an ideal aim of public policy. On the other hand, there is certainly no guarantee that oligopoly will yield the type of competition we desire (Thorelli and Thorelli, 1977:45).

This modified view of competition seems hardly to have been noticed by those who argue that the European economic system has failed, and that government or EEC action is necessary to protect consumers. This consumer protectionist evaluation of the workings of the market economy will be discussed at length below, as we look to explain the rise of consumerism and as we examine consumerist views which led to the perceived need for consumer protection programs, and in particular to regulate advertising, especially that which some perceived to be misleading or unfair.

The rise of consumerism

In the 1950s and early 1960s there was in Europe no general recognition of consumer problems as a cause of special actions, and few obvious signs of a genuine consumer movement. But in retrospect it is clear that the conditions that occurred are those that are likely to lead to periods of consumer activism. Therefore we shall now examine the changing conditions in European nations between 1945 and the early 1960s, the period leading up to the consumerism of the late 1960s. This period was unusual in terms of the rates of economic change and levels of living. In affluent societies of the past, wealth and opportunities for advancement were restricted to a thin upper class.

> During the hundred years prior to World War II, the living standard of the bourgeoisie improved greatly in industrial countries, but very broad groups of the population remained at, or close to, the subsistence level. Today, [1970] in the affluent societies the great majority of households have not only gone far beyond the level of mere subsistence but indeed acquire and constantly replace an extensive variety of consumer goods. Many goods and services formerly unknown or considered luxuries available to but a few now represent necessities of life for the masses (Katona et al., 1971:7).

The major economic changes that occurred in Europe and the USA from 1945 to 1970 may be summarized as follows:

> (1) A high rate of economic growth: An annual rate of increase in GNP after World War II exceeding the rate of increase between the two world wars, and indeed during the first forty-five years of the century. No depressions and, in some countries, not even substantial recessions since 1945.
> (2) Considerable improvement in the standard of living: Improvement among practically all population groups with poverty persisting in certain sectors (the undereducated, the old, single women with children, and, in the United States, blacks).
> (3) Practically full employment: Continuous and substantial increases in the labor force. Shorter hours and fewer years spent working and greater security provided.
> (4) A decline in the proportion of farmers and blue-collar workers, and an increase in the proportion of white-collar, government, and professional workers. Occupational shifts and higher educational levels result in maximum incomes being earned at an ever-older age.
> (5) Increase in the net worth of broad population groups: Increase in home ownership, ownership of cars and households applicances, and also in financial assets.
> (6) Creeping inflation: Prices have increased continuously, albeit at a slow and gradual rate (Katona et al., 1971:17).

These conditions collectively, led not only to individual affluence, but provided the means by which nations could improve the social security system, health care, and welfare payments to the unemployed. The education level, in terms of the number of years of school completed, grew at least a little in most countries. Unemployment dropped as the demand for labor increased, leading not only to virtual full employment, but in some cases even to jobs for workers from other countries.

Changing consumer attitudes and values

One observer, noting the steady economic growth in France, Germany and Italy into the mid 1960s, suggested that the reasons for consumerism, consumer unrest and government reactions to them, can be found in behavior related to changing values, attitudes and conditions. He identified:

> The May, 1968 student/worker revolt in France, the hot autumn of 1969 in Italy, spontaneous strikes in 1969 and 1970 in Sweden and Germany.
> ... Student alienation from capitalism, viewing the goal of economic growth and affluence as a consumptionist trap, inducing the working population to spend up to the limits of their incomes, becoming consumption addicts in the process, and hence dependent on the system.
> ... [the] economic downturn in 1967, [which] spread dissatisfaction to workers, [and gave a] sense of unequal sharing, ... [of] powerful firms manipulating consumers in the interests of their own profitability, ... a climate of collective frustration.
> ... disenchantment with modern capitalism, includes some middle class professionals too ... an atmosphere in which ideologues and extremists are encouraged to espouse social change (Chamberlain, 1980:1 – 3).

The author went on to discuss the egalitarian drive to share authority and to remove class-based privilege, the desire to even out income and wealth, which derive from: (1) the liberal, individualistic free-enterprise tradition of the UK and USA, and (2) the humanist, socialist communitarian creed deriving especially from Marx and Engels. He added that the controllers of the principal industrial and financial institutions are relatively small in number, and that the limited access to education spawns an elite in Britain and France, via Oxbridge and the Grandes Ecoles, or limited access to higher education generally, such as the failure of Germany's secondary schools to provide equality of opportunity for advancement to higher education. These circumstances and behaviors are alleged to the associated with the consumer movement, along with other idealistic causes.

Relationships between affluence and consumerism

Another less conjectural view is based on research into the relationships between affluence and consumer behavior. Between 1950 and 1970 the improved standard of living made it possible for people to make any more choices about their spending and saving patterns. Such consumer decisions depend not only on what has happened, but on people's perceptions about what will happen. Although there were many differences among countries in people's attitudes and perceptions, a substantial proportion of Europeans perceived considerable progress in their personal financial well being. This confidence in one's progress and optimism for the future stimulated discretionary expenditures and led to higher and higher consumption aspirations (Katona et al., 1971:42).

Research in European nations in the late 1960s indicates an interesting relationship between consumer affluence and expectations. Such "progress or success makes for rising levels of aspiration . . . [and] the achievement of a higher income and an improved standard of living results not in saturation but in new wants" (Katona et al., 1971:12).

In general consumer affluence is beneficial to the human condition. But it also has a negative side. The affluent society was criticized as being overly materialistic, and increasing numbers of young men and women in the 1960s and early 1970s rebelled against it. Their own affluence, or more accurately that of their parents, gave them the time, the means and even the inclination to object. Affluence permits expansion from material to non-material pursuits − from "comfort and fun to cultural, artistic and spiritual pursuits . . . [Moreover] rapidly growing expectations easily lead to disappointment − the greater the aspirations, the greater the danger of frustration" (Katona et al., 1971:14). Also poverty, though reduced, was not eliminated. "The poor feel discriminated against and alienated," and the idealistic affluent felt the system needed change to correct these wrongs. In short, the institutions of society, especially a visible activity such as advertising, which has the obvious objective of influencing consumers, came under fire for allegedly meeting the needs of sellers rather than the needs of consumers. And, since advertising effects are at best difficult to measure, and in any event controversial, it was then only a small next step to demand protection for consumers from the "obviously powerful" force of advertising (Katona et al., 1971:14).

The above argument, however, is incomplete. Under conditions of effective competition and modern marketing, sellers ordinarily find it essential to meet or beat competition on the basis of price, quality, warranty, or others of the numerous characteristics by which consumers judge products. In fact, products in the same price category tend to become very much alike, and price differences tend to coincide with differences in the usefulness to consumers of different products or brands. The situation must always be somewhat imperfect, since it is dynamic, allowing for regular product improvement as sellers seek a differential advantage over their competitors. There is ample empirical evidence in the marketing research literature to support these propositions. Likewise it is easy to find exceptions in industries that operate under conditions in which competition is not effective, sometimes temporarily until competitors adjust or until a barrier (perhaps government regulation to protect competitors!) is removed.

In any event, advertising usually is under considerable pressure in most developed countries. Although the intensity waxes and wanes, the long-term pressures tend to be increasing; and advertising must adapt to the changing conditions brought about by such pressures. A common argument contends that consumers are (or should be) growing wary of the emotional persuasive terms of advertising, and are (or should be) turning toward more factual, rational information sources such as product test reports by organizations not connected with advertising — independent consumer associations or government supported organizations. Indeed this trend may be occurring on perhaps a small scale, since product testing organizations have been growing in both size and importance in North Atlantic countries, as a result of both government activity and private support.

Understanding consumer behavior

While some would argue simply that "the viewpoint of the consumer should be put forward vigorously" when considering advertising regulation (Fulop, 1977:45), others would demand that those who propose such legislation should base their recommendations on an up-to-date understanding of consumer behavior and market conditions. While at first thought one might expect these two viewpoints to be identical, experience has shown otherwise. Consumerists and consumer groups claiming to represent the viewpoint of consumers often have narrow, specialized biases, which may or may not be based on an up-to-date understanding of consumer behavior. Or they may wish to educate consumers in ways which are not consonant with the realities of consumer behavior. Information from consumer and market studies done by sellers all-too-often is proprietary, and not available to outsiders, including competitors or consumerists. In any event consumer behavior is exceedingly complex. One person alone can exhibit many different kinds of behavior, depending on the product or service he or she is buying as well as on the multitude of detailed circumstances surrounding the purchase and use of the product or service. For example, different criteria will be employed by a Mrs. Smith when buying clothing, cosmetics or household utensils; and likewise Mr. Jones will behave somewhat differently when buying clothing, household utensils or an automobile. Two people not only differ from each other, but each also exhibits different behavior under varying conditions. Since there are so many different kinds of consumers, the complexities of consumer behavior are one of the great difficulties which we face when trying to think about advertising regulation.

Can advertising manipulate consumers?

Can advertising be used to manipulate consumers to buy products they do not want? What are the cultural, economic and social effects of advertising on consumers, individually and collectively? How do consumers react to advertising?

In recent decades marketing researchers in the USA and other developed countries in Europe and elsewhere, have made great progress in identifying the nature of the process and effects of advertising. These results have been published, especially in the last twenty years in journals in the field of advertising, consumer behavior and marketing. These research results cannot be summarized briefly, since consumer information processing and advertising effects studies are complex and the literature is extensive. The point to be made here is that both critics and defenders of advertising often seem to be unaware of what is known. Critics therefore tend to appear superficial; and defenders who depend on their experience, while more often right than wrong (at least approximately) find it difficult to articulate their defense to those who are not advertising professionals.

Questions on the process and effects of advertising are at the very heart of the issue as to whether or not, or how, advertising should be regulated. And although the scientific literature on the effects of advertising is voluminous, it necessarily contains incomplete and mixed information. Nevertheless the world seems to be well populated by self-proclaimed advertising experts – people who have firm personal convictions on advertising's effects – and who use their convictions as a starting point for arguing that advertising should be regulated. Although such people generally criticize advertising as being too powerful, they do not agree on specifics. There is a full range or continuum of opinions and convictions about advertising, both negative and positive. Interestingly, *those who know most about advertising practices*, i.e. those who are employed in the advertising business, usually are relatively modest in their assessment of advertising's powers; based on their experience they tend to the viewpoint that consumers are able to make up their own minds independently, with or without advertising, and that consumers choose to use or not to use advertising as they see fit, and that advertising cannot manipulate consumers against their will. *Those who are not especially knowledgeable about planning and preparing advertising*, i.e. those without experience in the advertising business, tend to the viewpoint that consumers are not able to make up their minds independently when confronted by advertising, and that consumers cannot choose whether or not to be influenced by advertising, and that advertising can indeed manipulate consumers against their will. Thus, the advertiser is likely to assert that the first and foremost control of advertising is the power of the consumer; whereas the critic of advertising is likely to assert that since the consumer is often defenseless against advertising, some independent or government control is needed to protect consumers. Both could benefit from reading the scholarly literature.

We can start with the common ground that virtually everyone will concede: the validity of the need for producers and consumers to have at least the information they desire. Thus, some form of information transfer to consumers is essential. The question then becomes whether or not advertising can provide such information. Virtually all but a few extremists would agree that needed information and messages should be truthful, accurate, honest, decent and ethical. To be sure, it is difficult to define these terms, and it is difficult to measure whether or not specific messages deceive or mislead relevant persons; it is even difficult to define relevant persons. *But*, if the question of whether or not advertising ought to be regulated is framed in these terms, most would agree that we are on the right track, and it then becomes a matter of defining and measuring the effects of advertising. If advertising is not truthful, accurate, honest, decent and ethical, such "abuses" should be controlled. Thus, the question of advertising control shifts to advertising abuses, rather than focusing on advertising in general. And the question of whether or not to control certain advertising practices or techniques also shifts to controlling the use of those techniques rather than controlling advertising as an institution. This latter point is particularly important for considering advertising controls within and across the borders of the EEC nations, since the effects of some techniques vary across languages and cultures – endorsements or comparative advertising for example.

The above analysis is not complete, however, since it ducks the issue posed by critics who believe advertising is by its nature biased and thus cannot possibly provide information needed by consumers. They would argue that it is surely possible, and indeed likely for advertising to present biased and incomplete information that is useless to consumers for making objective purchasing decisions, yet without constituting an abuse regarding truth, accuracy, honesty, decency and ethics. Some critics argue also that much advertising has no informative characteristics apart from the name and packaging of the product, or that advertising consists only of persuasion rather than information. Such critics, although a small minority, are at times a potent voice in the marketplace of ideas sometimes influencing government out of proportion to their numbers.

If one has a low opinion of consumers' abilities to act in their own best interests, one is inclined to do things for the consumers, to give them only the products that are "good" for them, to limit their choices only to those items that are "good" choices, to limit their exposure to a few choices so that consumers do not become confused, and so forth.

If one has a high opinion of consumers' abilities to act in their own self-interest one is inclined perhaps to help consumers when they seek help, but in the main leave consumers to make their own choices and to accept both the beneficial as well as the adverse consequences of such freedom.

The information seekers

One research team reports:

> In view of the heated debate about advertising and its possible complements or antidotes, it is amazing that relatively little organized effort has been made to gauge the attitudes and perceptions of the consumer himself in this area, particularly with regard to product testing. Generalizations have been common; empirical studies few (Thorelli et al., 1975:4).

This team of researchers studied a special group of consumers in Germany and the United States, information seekers (IS), with most interesting results:

For better or worse, depending on one's viewpoint, advertising is the most important source of product and purchasing information available to consumers in industrial societies with open market economies ... Some consumers are much more concerned with information than others. As an identifiable group ISs represent a fairly homogeneous cross-cultural segment of the population in industrially advanced countries. Although constituting a fairly small group in most cultures, the European prosperity of the 1950s and 1960s increased their number greatly. ISs have significantly much higher income, education and occupational status than average consumers. A typical IS is a professional person at the upper middle income level with at least a four-year college degree ... He designates himself as an opinion leader ... his advice is sought by others ... Generally liberal in outlook, the typical IS nonetheless will often take a conservative stand on individual issues. He is, however, strongly in favor of governmental action in the consumer policy area. In the US he is more critical of advertising than the average consumer, while in Germany the reverse is true. The German IS ... [is the] most favorable to increased government control, followed by the average German consumer. The average US consumer is next, with the American IS the least favorable to increased government control. While a majority of metropolitan American and German consumers had an overall favorable attitude towards advertising, the Americans were more positively disposed than the Germans ... American metropolitan consumers believe more strongly than German that advertising is essential. Americans tend to believe that advertising results in better products, while Germans are only mildly positive in this regard. Americans also feel that advertising helps raise the standard of living, but Germans tend to disagree. Neither group believes that advertising results in lower prices ... American metropolitan consumers feel that advertising standards are higher 'now' [1970] than 10 years ago. German feelings are mildly in the same direction. Americans average out as about neutral in considering whether advertising 'insults the intelligence' and 'presents a true picture,' while Germans are disbelievers on both scores. Both groups believe that advertising 'often persuades people to buy things they shouldn't buy' ... Highly educated consumers tended to be less favorably disposed toward advertising than others [in both countries]. German businessmen were distinctly more favorable to advertising than German workers; in America no clear cut occupational differences were evident ... On both sides of the Atlantic, among IS as well as average consumers, the prevention of misleading advertising emerged as a key consumerist concern (Thorelli et al., 1975:xxiii – xxx).

While similar studies on other European nations are not available, it seems likely that information seekers have also increased in number in much of Europe. And, since they tend to be influential in a variety of ways, their views are likely to be felt by the leaders of consumer organizations in the consumer movement. In fact, many ISs probably are leading consumerists; but their greatest influence stems from the fact that they are active consumers rather than consumerists. "Although constituting a relatively small group in most cultures, the ISs apparently exercise a vital influence in the marketplace as opinion leaders, critics and proxy agents for other consumers" (Thorelli et al., 1975:xxii). They are a select group of active consumers who provide the driving force for market improvement, probably far in excess of their numbers, because they find and reveal shortcomings causing the market to work better for all.

The increase in the number of information seekers, along with increased scholarly interest among university researchers, among others, has led to perceptions that consumers need more information, better education and direct protection. This perception, with perhaps some stimulation by consumerists' ideas from the US, along with the favorable conditions for consumerism that had evolved in Europe, stimulated the rapid growth of the consumer movement in Europe.

The maturing of consumerism

Consumerism has come to mean the activities of those who promote or protect consumer interests from real or perceived abuses by sellers in the marketplace. The notion of conflict between consumer and business interests is inherent in the term. If business met the needs of consumers and society, there would be no need for consumerism. However, even if producers do their best, they cannot achieve perfection in meeting consumer needs individually and collectively. Therefore in the imperfect world in which we live, it seems likely that consumerism will be with us always, at least to some small degree. Moreover, the selfish motivations of those who produce or sell for self-gain, do not always coincide with the selfish motives of those who buy for consumption. And, being human, many marketers in the 1950s and 1960s engaged in practices about which they later had little reason to be proud. In a market economy the ethics of business tend generally to be in harmony with the ethics of society at large — neither substantially better nor worse.

However, business practices changed greatly in the 1950s and 1960s. The so-called marketing concept — a thorough-going customer orientation — gradually became more widely adopted, at least by large companies. And in other ways business became a little more sensitive to the needs of consumers and society in the longer run, as well as trying to meet the needs of consumers in the short run. But in retrospect it appears as if business adapted too slowly, and perhaps too defensively. In any event, the reaction of business was not satisfactory to consumerists. Of special relevance to advertising, consumerists called for more consumer information, better consumer education, and greater consumer protection. These three demands require explanation:

(1) *Consumer information* comprises data about products and services offered for sale — information to make specific buying decisions, especially comparative data.

(2) *Consumer education* is taken to mean the development of a knowledge base necessary to be an intelligent consumer — to know how the economy operates, how buyers and sellers interact, and how to deal with the people and institutions one encounters.

(3) *Consumer protection* refers to the actions of others (non-consumers) who seek to safeguard consumer rights, to protect against deceptive practices or to set standards for health and safety.

The intensity of efforts to inform, educate and protect consumers varies from time to time. At a simplistic level one might expect the intensity of consumerist activity to correspond to the levels at which consumers are misinformed, uneducated and unprotected. However, that does not seem to be the case. The intensity of consumerist activity seems to require explanation of a far more complicated nature. It seems sensible to begin with the size of the widely heralded information gap, and the degree to which consumers are said to lack education and are therefore unable to bridge the information gap when making buying decisions.

The information gap

The argument can be made that an information gap stems from:
(1) increased personal income and purchasing power;
(2) an expanded supply and greater diversity of goods and services
(3) increasingly sophisticated advertising, sales promotion and personal selling from many sources; and
(4) from modern retailing institutions such as self-service.

These circumstances have led critics to believe that today's consumers have increased difficulty in comprehending the ever-more complex and greatly diversified mix of available products and in making sensible purchase choices; additionally critics perceive that the risk of hazardous products has increased, and that sellers have drafted contracts and warranties to protect themselves rather than consumers. In sum, the argument is that consumers have increased difficulties in protecting their rights.

The consumer information gap has since long been identified and described in great detail by a number of writers. Going back to the 1960s and 1970s one writer observes:

(1) There is a product, brand and model proliferation of bewildering proportions. In Germany in 1969 there were 32 brands and types of "ordinary" 60 watt light-bulbs; in France there were 1,060 different types of refrigerators; and a big super-market stocks 6,000 – 8,000 different items; there are perhaps a half million different non-prescription drugs on the US market; there are many types and brands of synthetic fibers, some physically identical.

(2) The space between products is getting narrower as we look at the range of refrigerator-freezer combinations, or the recorder-amplifier-radio combinations, not to mention the range of new video equipment.

(3) Modern technology makes life not only easier and richer, but more complex, with a vast amount of equipment in the home. For example, a modern home may have a dozen or more electric motors – in the washing machine and dryer, record player, carving knife, razor, toothbrush and other appliances.

(4) Product characteristics are subject to rapid change, from eyeglasses to soft

contact lenses, from products made of wood to plastic; New York supermarkets added some 3,500 new items and dropped 3,900 in 1971.

(5) Mass distribution and self-service have increased the distance and made more anonymous the relationship between buyer and manufacturer. Mass promotion and advertising have increased, and people are forced to be primarily receivers rather than seekers of information that they lack.

(6) Nonmetro or rural markets are underprivileged in the sense that they lack comparative product information.

(7) Time is at a premium in our post-industrial society

(8) The rise in discretionary income and greater affluence brings all members of the family into the buying process, including children

(9) With the increasing diversity of buying criteria, the car is not just a means of transportation, but it must be sporty, reflect "my" youth, contain a radio and tape hi-fi center, have air conditioning and have extra strong rear suspension to handle the vacation trailer.

(10) Increasing social awareness means that not only must the product meet one's own needs, but it must be ecologically sound in design and packaging.

(11) Business ethics are perceived as lagging, especially increased deception in advertising

(12) Consumer expectations with regard to product performance seem to grow exponentially with the level of affluence (the above 12 points are based in large part on Thorelli and Thorelli, 1977:17 – 21).

There are a number of ways of looking at the information gap. First, the average producer is a specialist in his own particular products and is likely to be much better informed about them than the average consumer; but even though producers and distributors do not know everything about competitive offerings, the average consumer knows much less, and thus is at a disadvantage in the buying process.

Secondly, there can be no serious attempt to inform the consumer about all relevant competitive products; information overload would occur quickly, not to mention the demands on one's time or the astronomical cost of such an information program. As one writer put it: ". . . if it were seriously attempted to 'pump up' the consumer with enough information to close the real gap completely, he would probably burst at the seams in the process" (Thorelli and Thorelli, 1977:22).

Thirdly, it is interesting that most consumers perceive the information gap to be rather modest, or perhaps trivial, at least for convenience goods. The average consumer considers himself fairly well informed, and able to obtain adequate information when needed.

> That consumers think they are well informed about product markets is no more remarkable than the fact that most farmers in underdeveloped countries think they know whatever is worth knowing about agricultural practices. Yet the explanation of growing numbers of consumer complaints is likely to be found in part in underinformation (Thorelli and Thorelli, 1977:22).

Further,

> It would seem that consumers ... adopt a strategy of satisficing* with regard to information. That is, they care only for a certain level of market knowledge (varying by product, to be sure), without any greater ambition than achieving a reasonably satisfactory purchase in a plurality of cases. ... We ... think that this system, if left unimproved, is not likely to provide the market transparency base needed to maintain 'workable competition' in the still more complex markets of tomorrow (Thorelli and Thorelli, 1977:22 – 23).

Those who would make society better also note that because some groups of consumers have low incomes and insufficient education and knowledge of the market, they are less equipped than the average citizen to look out for their interests in making good consumer decisions. Thus, since they pay more for less adequate products and services, they are in special need of protection. Also, they are often dependent on expensive installment credit and they lack the means to take advantage of favorable purchase opportunities. Moreover, because of their relative lack of education they are more susceptible to pursuasive advertising or selling – or to deceptive or misleading sales information, and they have relatively little knowledge of their rights.

These considerations which led to the perceived need for expanded consumer protection are also connected with changes in the structure of the economy and in the forms of production and distribution. Consumerists argue that large-scale enterprises have led to oligopolistic conditions of competition in many lines of industry and commerce. Concentration has in some product lines weakened price competition, and product quality and performance. Therefore governments have adopted corrective legislation not only to avoid price abuses and restraint of competition, but also to provide for direct intervention to protect consumers from unfair or deceptive acts or practices.

In sum, the argument is that in an

> affluent economy based upon open markets, without sources of information that are both available and accurate, there is little hope that the buyer will find his way through the maze of proffered products and services toward purchases which best serve his wants and needs. As markets grow more complex, information accumulation, transmission and usage become increasingly critical determinants of marketing efficiency (Thorelli et al., 1975:3).

---

* Since consumers know they do not have the time or talent to seek and evaluate all possible information, they limit their efforts to that information which they consider adequate, given the importance and nature of the particular purchasing decision, and taking into account other demands on their time and energy. This compromise or trade-off is called satisficing.

Consumer dissatisfactions

Another way of assessing the welfare of consumers in society is to examine consumer dissatisfactions. Although consumer dissatisfaction is difficult to measure, and data on the matter are difficult to interpret, one researcher provides a solid beginning, reporting the following:

1. There is a positive correlation between consumer dissatisfaction and education, as well as between consumer dissatisfaction and standard of living. Thus, it is logical that as the educational levels and standard of living in EEC member nations rose during the 1950s and 1960s concomitant rising consumer dissatisfaction would create opportunities for consumerists and consumer organizations.

2. In 1978 in Sweden, when consumers were asked whether 'government regulation' or 'education and information' is preferable to help consumers in the purchase of goods, 8 out of 10 preferred the latter. While such information is not available in other nations, there is no reason to suspect that consumers in other nations are any more favorably disposed toward government regulation than the Swedes.

3. In general what little research is available indicates that consumer dissatisfaction is quite low in most countries. Many other matters are of greater concern than those relating to the purchase and use of products and services. Only a part of consumer dissatisfaction can be explained by market performance, i.e. how well consumers are actually served. Cultural variables and national characteristics seem to affect the consumer perception of the market supply considerably. In some countries it is more accepted and legitimate to complain; these cultures have more consumers who are price conscious (and it is not necessarily correlated with low incomes), and they are less content with whatever is offered; these cultures also have more people who are demanding and optimistic about what business should offer; and consumer dissatisfaction is higher in such nations.

4. Consumer dissatisfaction also tends to be higher in a market that is open and dynamic; it may imply a positive state of affairs. In a stable market with little interaction, low consumer dissatisfaction does not necessarily signify a desireable state of affairs. If there are few channels for voicing dissatisfaction, or if the market is highly oligopolistic, there is little for consumers to do but to adapt, and thus there is a lower level of consumer dissatisfaction (abstracted and adapted from Wikström, 1983:19 – 35).

Thus we can conclude that the enthusiasm for consumer protection may wax and wane over time, especially over the business cycle, or during alternate periods of liberalism or conservatism. But the evidence indicates that generally increasing education, income and consumer sophistication provide the main pressures for increased consumer protection and control of advertising. This conclusion is buttressed by evidence that the consumerism which prevailed in recent years has led to changes in consumer behavior, and concomitant changes in marketing and advertising policies, which in turn have made consumerism seem less urgent to many.

The consumer today

One study reported that consumers of the 1970s and 1980s are vastly different in their purchasing behavior from those of the 1950s. For example, the "little woman at home," of the 1950s has been in large part replaced by more highly educated women who work outside the home. The dutiful little *Hausfrau* who sacrifices herself by cooking, washing and ironing is dying out. The sense of duty, once a favorite German concept, is now left to the grandmothers over 50. A recent survey of 3,000 women carried out by *Market Horizons* in Germany shows that:

> ... like their counterparts elsewhere in Europe, German women have adopted a new sense of identity and fresh sets of aspirations — and that in turn has altered their attitudes towards advertising and the products they buy.
>
> For one thing ... women have become more intellectual. By 1982, more girls than boys were taking final school-leaving examinations and the number of female university students has doubled over the past 10 years, to account for 47.3% of the total.
>
> The biggest change has been in the goals of young women. Such traditional notions as having a family and keeping a nice house are no longer to the fore. The focus is now on themselves — in a desire for individuality, self-reliance and self-fulfilment.
>
> ... Today's women are likely to feel that housework is burdensome; there is a swing towards sharing the chores with men.
>
> In short, the family has become a working group. Accordingly, women dislike being depicted as compulsive cleaners or as 'just' housewives. The attitude towards cooking, particularly, has changed. Three square meals a day are out; snacks are in. Leisure time ranks ever more important.
>
> But there are also counter-trends. A reaction against the strident feminism of a decade age leads many women to profess allegiance to the family, without wanting to be housewives and mothers in the traditional way. Among the younger ones, too, there is a conservative group and another that may be called the 'no-future women': their motto is live for today rather than make sacrifices for the sake of the future.
>
> It is against that background that respect for brands was weakened. 'The younger women have grown up in an age of plenty and of TV; to them brands are something venerable and traditional.'
>
> The younger generation wonders whether branded articles really offer so much more quality, particularly as there is so little difference in their presentation and content, and that of the no-names, generics and house labels.
>
> ... Younger German women no longer have the same loyalty to brands that their mothers and grandmothers did. They consider it smart (as well as good financial sense) to patronise cut-price shops and stores, and regard generics, no-name and own-label products as more modern than the traditional 'names' (Mussey, 1984:31).

Since consumer purchasing behavior has changed, and since advertisers are adapting correspondingly, at least those who continue to be successful, it seems sensible to base current consumer policy and advertising regulation on current conditions. Many of the underlying assumptions of the 1950s and 1960s about consumers, advertising practices and market conditions are no longer valid. Nevertheless many of the proposals for consumer policy and advertising regulation still rest on such outdated assumptions.

Criticisms of advertising

Up to this point we have focused on changing conditions, concepts of competition, and the rise of consumerism, to provide the setting for understanding the increased criticisms of advertising and the demand for its regulation.

Now it is time to address directly the ways that advertising has been criticized, recognizing the reasons for such criticisms, including especially those which seem genuine and those which do not seem genuine; we shall attempt to distinguish the one from the other.

It should be kept in mind that criticism of advertising is not a recent phenomenon. What was new in recent years was how the increasing seriousness of criticisms led to efforts to regulate advertising, especially at the supranational level. Since EEC consumer programs that affect advertising are the principal focus of this book, we should identify more precisely just what the criticisms of advertising were that led to these programs.

The nature of criticisms

First, we should note that there is little point in preparing a long list of typical complaints against advertising. Such lists are available from many sources, for example, the prohibitions in the British Code of Advertising Practice (BCAP), or for that matter any economics text dealing with industrial organization, not to mention the numerous works of muckrakers. Criticisms fall into several major categories, namely: (1) advertising sometimes is unfair to or harms competitors (or at least is perceived as unfair by competitors), (2) advertising sometimes injures competition, or precludes the maintenance of workable competition and (3) advertising sometimes provides less than adequate, or even false, deceptive or misleading messages, and therefore harms consumers.

These three types of criticisms are inextricably intertwined. If we are to seek to understand successfully the many regulatory issues, we must keep all three of these categories of criticisms in mind. For example, as noted earlier by Fulop, criticisms of unfair competition are sometimes confused by incorrectly linking them to protecting consumers. Also, protecting competitors is not at all the same as preserving competition; the latter is of course one of the main means of protecting consumers, or avoiding harm to consumers. Moreover false, deceptive or misleading advertising may not only harm consumers, but may also injure competition, as well as harming honest competitors. And, very importantly these three categories are also recognized in a sense in the Council Directive on Misleading Advertising (Sepember 10, 1984) which refers albeit somewhat obliquely to the same three criticisms by stating that the purpose of the Directive is to protect consumers, business and the interests of the public in general.

In addition two general circumstances of the 1950s and 1960s have caused increased criticism of advertising: (1) the introduction of television which made people conscious of advertising in a way they had never been before, even in countries with no television advertising, and (2) the discovery by politicians just how fertile the issue of advertising regulation is. One observer in the UK says:

> A most important event in advertising occurred in 1955 with the advent of commercial television. The new advertising medium established itself quickly, since commercials had considerable impact on viewers and produced dramatic increases in sales of many products. In the 1950s and 1960s advertising in the UK was subjected to a greater volume of criticism than at any time in its history. In an increasingly affluent society, with much competition on the basis of advertising, consumers became more aware of advertising. Intrusive television commercials, and a wide variety of writers examining the ethics of persuasion and the possibilities of mass manipulation gave an opportunity to politicians. The Labour Party became particularly critical of advertising, setting up an independent body to seek 'all kinds of socially harmful advertising,' followed by an independent commission which produced the Reith Report in 1966 which, among other things recommended the establishment of a National Consumer Board. While not implemented, this recommendation was typical of the times, and coincide with similar trends in public opinion and political activities in other European countries. Thus, it is not surprising that at about the same time consumerists and their supporters would also create pressures for consumer programmes by the EEC (Nevett, 1982:199).

Implications for advertising regulation

Now, we shall try to provide some perspectives on the criticisms of advertising and the implications for public policy that flow from such criticisms.

One perspective is that truthful and accurate advertising which harms competitors ought *not* to be regulated. However, advertising that is false, deceptive or misleading ought to be regulated *not* only because it harms competitors, but first because it can harm consumers directly if they depend on such information to make poor purchasing decisions, and secondly because it can harm efficient competitors who serve consumers well, thereby interfering with the free flow of accurate information in the marketplace, which in turn can impair the ability of workable competition to protect consumers, to reward efficient producers and to benefit society in a larger sense. Thus false, deceptive or misleading advertising is to be condemned. But truthful and accurate advertising ought to be permitted and encouraged, even if it harms competitors. For example, comparative advertising once was not permitted in the UK, but now it is encouraged. Regulation should not protect those who do not serve consumers well.

Another perspective, from a consumer information standpoint, is that advertising which does not give as much relevant information as consumers desire, should also come under criticism. This matter is difficult, since sophisticated sellers ordinarily find it in their own best interests to give consumers as much relevant information as "most consumers" desire. However, a "correction" may be needed when the judgment of advertisers is faulty, or if collusion or some form of conscious parallel action by competitors leads to less than optimal information (from the consumer's standpoint). As pointed out above, however, consumers may not realize what is good for them, and there is always a possibility that they can be educated to require better advertising. Indeed this process seems to be constantly under way.

Objective versus subjective information

With this background, let us now look a bit more deeply into the criticisms of advertising. One source summarizes some additional useful concepts.

> In a fundamental sense, all communication conveys information. Thus, instead of saying that advertising typically furnishes both information and persuasion, we should rather say that it has an objective and a subjective information component. Discussions about product information often seem predicated on the twin assumptions that objective information is inherently superior to subjective, and that commercial sources − and notably advertising − are the only sources comprising a major subjective component. Throughout history and in all forms of human intercourse subjective information has played a critical role. All we can say, really, is that subjective information is different from objective information, (and that some of us might like to see the two more clearly distinguished in communication).
>
> In this discussion we are skirting at least two issues of some importance. It is well known that objective information tends to be subjectively interpreted by the receiver. Similarly, what is (or seems to be) represented as objective information is often subjective information; the borderline between objective and subjective may be vague. In addition, being advocates, many sellers display a strong interest in commingling the two (Thorelli and Thorelli, 1977:124 − 5).

From this perspective we can conclude that the critics of advertising who proclaim the virtues of objective over subjective claims are at best only partly correct. Communication effectiveness and the needs of consumers are too complex for such superficial criticism to be accepted as valid.

Our position is that as long as conditions of effective competition exist, we ought to let individual advertisers be the judge of the right mix of objective and subjective information. Previously discussed perspectives on consumer behavior suggest that we do not know enough about these matters to generalize in making reasonable judgments. Therefore we choose not to assume the arrogant position of one who will help consumers who may not need help, or who may not want to be helped.

Consumer sophistication

Although classical liberal economists have long held that consumers are (or should be) rational, there are many reasons to be skeptical. However, growing consumer sophistication, coupled with improved availability of information from advertising as well as alternative sources, may yet prove them closer to correct than current day critics believe. There is much evidence in the marketing research literature to this effect, for example:

It is clear that most consumers rely on more or less sophisticated strategies to govern their activity in the marketplace. Some of them involve very active conduct on the part of consumers. This may begin by a conscious setting of objectives – diagnosing needs and preferences and relating them to budgetary and other priorities. Analyzing what alternative types of products meet a given need may follow. After deciding on product type the consumer is faced with the brand information. He may have a strategy for search, e.g., the more 'important" or 'expensive' the product is for him, the more search. Or, 'the less prior experience I have of this product, the more search.' He may also have a strategy to avoid overload or stress, such as 'consider seriously only three alternatives.'

There are a great number of strategies to select from in order to arrive at the final choice of brand and supplier. Here are some illustrations:

You get what you pay for – price and quality move together. An old firm is reliable, or it would not still be in existence. If my prior experience of Brand X refrigerators (cars, etc.) is good, it is probably a good idea to buy Brand X again at this time (which may be five to ten years later).

General Electric refrigerators are good, so when I need a TV it is probably a good idea to buy a GE model.

These and similar strategies are drastic short cuts governing the conduct of millions of consumers. Both sober reflections and the fairly scant research on the subject indicate that these strategies are highly imperfect. Yet, in the absence of better alternatives, their superficial plausibility will continue to attract myriads of new followers. We submit that consumers will have little interest in applying more rational approaches to decision making (such as 'highest expected value') until the quantity, quality and comparability of product information has been considerably improved – a different way of saying that modern markets call for modern consumer information programs (Thorelli and Thorelli, 1977:43).

While one may agree or disagree with the last line of the above quote, the fact is that consumers indeed have gradually become more sophisticated and there seems to be no reason to suspect that the trend will not continue in modern "information societies."

Validity of criticisms: similarities and differences among nations

It is often assumed that criticisms of advertising which are valid in one nation also are valid in others. But if so, why do some nations have far more severe restrictions on advertising than others? A partial answer may be that the people of some nations differ in certain ways from those in others. By inspection we note that certain advertising practices that are considered false, deceptive or misleading in one language and culture, sometimes are not considered misleading in another. For example in a language such as German or Norwegian, consumers may be inclined to interpret equivalent statements more literally than they would in a language such as Italian or Spanish. Thus comparisons or the use of the superlative in some countries may be considered acceptable, but not in others. Also, in some cultures it may be entirely acceptable to "gild the lily," but unacceptable to do so to the same extent in others. Thus advertising regulation tends to be stricter in certain Northern European countries, than in some Southern European countries.

However, regardless of the differences, there are some broad categories of advertising criticisms that are similar across many nations. One of the most important of these is that claims that are not substantiated are considered deceptive or misleading, whether or not they ultimately turn out to be true or false. Thus it is widely accepted that advertisers should not use unsubstantiated claims. A second major area of agreement is that it is unacceptable to use misleading statements or visuals regarding prices, discounts, survey research results, product tests, warranties, testimonials or endorsements. But much more research is necessary to compare misleadingness on these issues across countries, before we will be able to generalize. At this point we can only sensitize the reader to these types of arguments.

National legislation and regulatory activities

An important part of the "setting" for a discussion of advertising regulation at the EEC level is the nature of legislation and regulatory activities within the several nations comprising the Community. The strengths and weaknesses of national legislation determine in large part the impetus for EEC regulation; they also determine whether or not proposed EEC actions are likely to be accepted by member nations and moreover, if accepted, whether or not they are likely to be implemented. Therefore, in this section, we will characterize certain salient features of national legislation and regulatory policies relating to advertising.

Although several important laws were enacted in the 1950s (and earlier) in most EEC countries, the main "flood" began in the 1960s. Often provisions relating to advertising were included in other legislation, or earlier laws were amended. Thus it is virtually impossible to count all of the laws, amendments and administrative rules (which have the force of law) that apply to advertising. We can only note that there are probably in excess of 50 or 60 pieces of relevant legislation in most EEC countries (see e.g. Dunn, 1974; Reich and Micklitz, 1980; Lawson, 1981; Painter, 1981).

In general in European countries, civil legislation or case law that relates to advertising originated from the idea of prohibiting "unfair competition (concurrence déloyale) and only gradually took account of the consumers' interests ... nowadays the consumers' interests have come to play a greater role than in the past, but are still not the primary aim of the law'' (Reich and Micklitz, 1980:42).

The principle of truthfulness

A common feature of modern advertising legislation in EEC countries is the principle of truthfulness. "The principle of truthfulness originates not only from the idea of concurrence déloyale (unfair competition) but also from criminal law, since false, misleading or fraudulent claims which are made recklessly or negligently by competitors in business and trade are contrary to the public interest and to public morals'' (Reich and Micklitz, 1980:49).

The principle of truthfulness in advertising legislation in France, Ireland and the United Kingdom is found mainly in criminal law; but in Belgium, Germany, Italy, Luxembourg and the Netherlands, it is found primarily in civil law. And in Denmark the system relies heavily on administrative law and the institution of the Ombudsman. Advertising law has many dimensions, covered in a variety of laws, and all three forms of enforcement (criminal, civil and administrative) can be found in most EEC countries.

The truthfulness doctrine embodied in legislation in all EEC countries is identical in the following respect:

> Advertising must have some factual content to be sanctionable by criminal or civil law. Messages without any factual content, puffs, hyperbolical claims and forms of suggestive advertising without any information at all, are not usually covered ... They must be regarded as being 'contra bonos mores' under the principle of unfair competition (Federal Republic of Germany, Belgium, Luxemburg, Denmark), but law is still uncertain about that point (Reich and Micklitz, 1980:44).

However, the standard of truthfulness adopted by the law varies among EEC countries as to what types of claims the courts will regard as false or misleading. In Germany and Denmark subjective tests of truth prevail, i.e. to catch ambiguous advertising statements, hints or indications likely to mislead the public. In most other EEC countries, varying combinations of subjective and objective tests are employed. The problem of varying interpretations of truthfulness has not yet been resolved satisfactorily by legislation in EEC countries.

It is quite common in EEC countries for the law to require advertising to provide minimum information, and to be decent and fair. But the truthfulness doctrine does not require an obligation to disclose information or to be objective. Thus in most countries there is some provision to introduce certain standards for informative and objective advertising. However, the varying approaches taken are difficult to compare.

Also, in most EEC countries there are additional specific requirements regarding decency, and on the adequacy of information in advertising of certain products −

especially medicines, foodstuffs, cosmetics, tobacco and alcoholic beverages. However, there is considerable diversity in the nature of such requirements and the method to enforce them.

"Truth in price claims" is a standard that is accepted unanimously in the legislation of EEC countries. On the other hand there is considerable diversity among EEC countries in the attitude of the law to comparison advertising, or how to deal with advertising that may be harmful to health (e.g. cigarette advertising).

Major pieces of national legislation

Along with economic, political and social changes in EEC countries in the 1950s and subsequently, there were numerous changes in the laws and their enforcement relating to advertising. It is impossible to mention all of the minor changes, but for the sake of illustration, Reich and Micklitz (1980:199 – 203) list a few of the major changes that arose during or out of those decades in the following Common Market countries:

Belgium

Act on the Control of Drugs, of March 25, 1964 (Loi sur le contrôle des médicaments)
Act on Commercial Practices, of July 14, 1971 (Loi sur les pratiques de commerce)
Act Concerning the Consumer's Health, of 1977 (Loi relative à la santé des consommateurs en ce qui concerne les denrées alimentaires et les autres produits)

Denmark

Act on Marketing Practices, of 1974 (Lov om markedsføring)
Medicines Act, of 1975
Price Marking and Display Act, of 1977
Consumer Sales Act, of 1979

Federal Republic of Germany

Act Prohibiting Unfair Competition, of 1909 (as amended in 1965 and 1969) (Gesetz gegen den unlauteren Wettbewerb)
Act on Foodstuffs and Consumer Goods, of August 15, 1974 (Lebensmittel- und Bedarfsgegenständegesetz)
Correspondence Course Protection Act, of August 24, 1976 (Fernunterrichtsschutzgesetz)

France

Act on Correspondence Courses, of July 12, 1971 (Loi sur l'enseignement à distance)
Loi Royer of December 27, 1973 (Loi d'orientation de commerce et d'artisanat)
Act on Consumer Protection and Information, of January 10, 1978 (Act No. 23) (Loi sur la protection et l'information des consommateurs de produits et de services)
Code on Public Health (Code de la Santé Publique)

Ireland

Consumer Information Act, of 1978
Sale of Goods and Supply of Services Bill, of 1978

Italy

Food Act, of April 30, 1962 (No. 283)

Luxemburg

Act on Unfair Competition, of December 23, 1974 (Règlement grand-ducal concernant la concurrence déloyale).
Drugs Act, of August 4, 1975

UK

Food and Drugs Act, of 1955
Trade Descriptions Act, of 1968 (as amended in 1972)
Medicines Act, of 1968
Fair Trading Act, of 1973

It should be noted also that at the time the above was written (1980) neither Italy nor the Netherlands had specific laws devoted to advertising control, although there were other means (e.g. regulations, court decisions) that can be brought to bear on advertising (Reich and Micklitz, 1980:42). In the meantime, in 1980, the Netherlands introduced a Law against Misleading Advertising and undoubtedly there has been additional legislation introduced and enacted in other Member States in the last five years.

Sanctions and enforcement

Although there are substantial differences among EEC countries with regard to legislation relating to advertising, there are even greater differences between them with regard to sanctions and enforcement — for example in the use of injuctions, claims for damages, penalties, and administrative proceedings. Likewise the competence of consumer organizations to participate directly in the control of advertising, ranges from substantial involvement in Germany and several other countries to no involvement at all in the UK, Ireland and Italy; in fact, comsumer organizations in Italy are prohibited by law from instituting actions against misleading advertising (Reich and Micklitz, 1980:59 – 60).

Systems of self-control also vary widely, from the extensive system which bears the primary burden of advertising control in the United Kingdom, to the relatively less powerful self-regulatory systems in most other countries, and to Denmark in which the system of self-control was in effect abolished by appointment of the Consumer Ombudsman in 1974.

In summary, although there are some common denominators, there are also remarkable differences in laws and their interpretation and application to advertising practices in the Common Market countries, In the midst of these national regulatory activities the first EEC Draft Directive on Misleading and Unfair Advertising was prepared. The law and its application in some EEC nations has a number of parallels with the EEC first draft directive, especially in Denmark, Germany, Belgium and Luxemburg, and to a considerable extent in France with regard to the concept of misleading advertising but not unfair advertising. On the other hand, if the first draft directive had been enacted, the law and practice in the UK, the Netherlands and Italy would have had to be changed substantially in order to comply. Since advertising standards in some European countries are stricter than in others, any attempt to harmonize standards at the EEC level is difficult. The relative high standards of some countries would not likely be acceptable to others; and using the standards of the less strict countries as the lowst common denominator would seem pointless.

Self-regulation of advertising within the Community*

Self-regulation of advertising has three basic objectives: (1) *To protect consumers* against false or misleading advertising; and against advertising that intrudes on the privacy of consumers through its unwanted presence or offensive content. In short, advertising must be controlled so that it is in harmony with the best interests of consumers who wish to be able to use advertising to guide their purchasing decisions. This objective of business might be called "enlightened self-interest," since if it is not achieved, consumers or their representatives in consumer groups or in government might take actions to control advertising, and such controls may not be in the best interests of all concerned. (2) *To protect legitimate advertisers* against false or misleading advertising by competitors. This objective dare not be oriented only toward the preservation of individual competitors, but must preserve the free flow of accurate information in the marketplace so that efficient competitors prevail over inefficient competitors. Such is the salutory effect of competition in a market economy. (3) *To protect the public acceptance of advertising*, so that it can continue as an effective institution of the market system.

The advertiser view of self-regulation often is that regulation by those who know advertising well, will have two characteristics: (1) it will be effective in identifying genuine abuses (it takes a thief to catch a thief) especially in the monitoring process

---

* The subject of voluntary self-regulation of advertising is far more complex than the material in this brief section suggests. Therefore the reader is advised to refer to the extensive literature on the subject. See for example Miracle and Nevett, forthcoming.

of self-regulatory agencies; and (2) it will encroach less (than government regulation would) on legitimate advertising activities.

The consumerist view of self-regulation often is that regulation by those who know advertising well, will provide a weak measure of consumer protection, since those in the industry would tend to preserve their freedom to the maximum they feel is possible. The motivation of members of the advertising business often is suspect. It is clear that it is in their self-interest to avoid regulation by legislators and by government officials who do not comprehend very well the nature of the advertising business and the effects of advertising on society. Motivations of politicians also are suspect as to whether or not they alone are a sufficient basis for regulating advertising in a way which genuinely serves society.

Advantages and disadvantages of self-regulation

We began by asking whether or not self-regulation will serve society well. Therefore, we present now a list of advantages and disadvantages that have been extracted from the literature on this subject. We ask the reader to evaluate these advantages and disadvantages from the standpoint of the two main objectives mentioned above (to protect consumers and to protect legitimate advertisers):

1. The case for advertising self-regulation

(a) Self-discipline and cooperation lead to full adherence to the spirit of the code or standards rather than only to minimal compliance because of the threat of prosecution by government. Self-interest compliance rather than coercion leads to a higher degree of commitment from advertisers than would be the case if a self-regulatory code became law. Moreover, if the system enlists the media to refuse to run questionable advertising, a self-regulatory system can be very effective.

(b) Self-regulatory systems handle matters more speedily, more simply, and with less "red tape" than governmental regulatory mechanisms or court processes.

(c) A self-regulatory code is more flexible in that it can be more readily updated than new or revised government legislation can be enacted.

(d) Self-regulatory systems are less costly than government regulatory measures, especially regarding less need for expensive legal fees or court costs.

(e) Self-regulation creates and maintains public confidence in advertising. If advertisers are seen to behave decently and considerately – in harmony with the generally accepted standards of the community in which they operate – they will be viewed as responsible and their advertising will be credible. Public confidence in advertising is essential to its continued effectiveness and even to its very existence as an important business activity.

(f) Self-regulatory codes and mechanisms do not interfere with the advertising business so that it cannot function effectively. Advertising as a legitimate business activity is preserved. The negative effects of over-regulation imposed by, or influenced by those who do not fully understand the way advertising works and its economic and social role, are minimized. Marketing and advertising costs are not increased by arbitrary rules/standards which do not really aid the consumer. Correspondingly the free flow of truthful and accurate information by advertising, properly understood by buyers and sellers, helps the free market to function effectively to accomplish the appropriate intended goals of an economy.

(g) Self-regulatory systems can have broader scope, to deal more easily with matters of taste and decency, especially since it can adapt to sometimes rapidly changing mores and social sources (see also #c above).

(h) A self-regulatory system can put the *burden of proof* (substantiation, or that a claim is not misleading, etc.) on the advertiser – which may not be appropriate for some legal systems.

(i) Finally, and perhaps with a bit of overlap with some of the above points, a self-regulatory system can help to achieve better understanding and cooperation with legislators, educators, students, consumers, and officials in government bureaucracies, which in turn help to stem unwise or unwarranted regulatory activity.

2. The case against advertising self-regulation

(a) It is difficult to get 100 percent voluntary cooperation, and to police the small number of unscrupulous advertisers.

(b) Enrolled members contribute different degrees of commitment in supporting the system and adhering to its established codes or standards.

(c) Open and responsive channels of communication between the self-regulatory body, consumers, and consumer groups, and agencies of the government are difficult to maintain. Disenchantment may occur and advertisers or consumer groups may become irate or cynical, and lose their enthusiasm for self-regulation.

(d) Self-regulatory systems do not have adequate powers, either to stop advertising quickly (as by temporary injunction) or to force compliance once an abuse has been determined.

(e) Self-regulatory standards are too lax for some social/advertising critics, especially when the real objective is to attack/destroy the market system, and to replace it with government ownership or control. Self-regulation of advertising thus perpetuates the market system.

(f) Self-regulatory systems are too parochial and self-serving when the codes are made and applied only by advertising people, without the benefit of "outside participation" by non-industry or public members.

(g) It is difficult to obtain adequate financing to provide a staff and resources that are able to cover more than the most egregious offenses; many complaints cannot be handled or resolved to the satisfaction of consumers, consumerists, consumer groups, and competitors.

Although there have long been industry initiatives to control advertising abuses, the first formal code that achieved widespread recognition in Europe was the ICC's "International Code of Advertising Practice," first published in 1937. The code was designed primarily as an instrument of self-discipline, but it has also been used as a reference for national self-regulatory codes, as well as "for court decisions in Belgium, Denmark, France, Germany, and Norway, and has been said to be integrated into Sweden's legal concepts relating to its Consumer Ombudsman" (Neelankavil and Stridsberg, 1980:8).

The development of self-regulatory codes, and mechanisms to apply such codes have led to several types.

(1) *Pure self-regulation.* In this type, advertisers, agencies and/or media determine what is acceptable. Sometimes public participation is included, which departs from the concept of pure self-regulation, but not significantly if the public members are used primarily for their input and perspectives and if they do no dominate the system to the point that the advertising business fails to cooperate fully with the code or rules. The National Advertising Division/National Advertising Review Board (NAD/NARB) in the USA, and the Deutscher Werberat (DWR) in the Federal Republic of Germany are examples of pure self-regulation. The Advertising Standard Authority (ASA) in the UK, with participation by independents is another example, albeit not "pure."

(2) *Negotiated codes of practice.* In this type, codes of practice are drawn up between an industry and a governmental body. Examples are industry codes drawn up with the Office of Fair Trading in the UK.

(3) *Agreements or conventions.* This type of self-regulation is suggested to, or imposed upon, the advertising business by an outside body. The World Health Organization "Code for the Marketing of Breastmilk Substitutes' is an example (adapted from EAT, 1983:6 – 8).

An evaluation of self-regulation of advertising within the Community

"Systems of self-control in advertising have . . . played an important role in all EEC countries" (Reich and Micklitz, 1980:61).

> Originally self-control is part of the idea of concurrence déloyale and does not primarily intend to serve the consumer's interests. It is directed at freeing the market from dishonest and deceptive claims and trade practices. It serves as a means of preventing state intervention. Only recently have we been able to note a trend of incorporating the consumers' interests into the standards of a self-control system or even of admitting consumer representatives to the bodies managing self-control (Reich and Micklitz, 1980:61).

Table II
Self-Regulatory Systems of Advertising Regulation in Europe

Nations	Year established, re-formed, revised or superseded**
*EEC nations**	
Belgium	1967 (1) (2), re-formed in 1974 (3)
Denmark	1971 (1), superseded by a Consumer Ombudsman under the Consumer Protection Law of 1974 (1)
Federal Republic of Germany	1972 (4)
France	1950 (1), re-formed in 1953 (1) and 1974 (5)
Ireland	1967 (1) (2)
Italy	1966 (2), re-formed in 1974 (1)
Netherlands	1948 (1), revised in 1963 (1) and 1967 (2)
United Kingdom	1962, revised in 1974 (6)
Other European Nations	
Austria	1971 (1) (2)
Sweden	1957, superseded by a Consumer Ombudsman under the Marketing Law of 1970 (1)
Switzerland	1966 (1) (2)

* Information on Greece, Luxembourg, Portugal and Spain is not available.
** Some of these are currently being revised and may be superseded by the time this book is published.

Sources: (1) Brandmair, 1977, (2) Neelankavil and Stridsberg, 1980, (3) Boddewyn, 1983a, JCP (6)3, (4) ZAW, 1979, (5) Boddewyn, 1984a, JCP (7)1, (6) Boddewyn, 1983b, JCP (6)1.

The influence of ICC guidelines on advertising appears in many ways, for example:

(1) within companies – self-control by advertisers, advertising agencies and media;

(2) in industry codes or guidelines, such as pharmaceutical products (and many others);

(3) as a partial base for governmental or quasi-governmental codes; and

(4) as a base for advertising industry centralized self-regulatory systems.

The influence of ICC guidelines has been especially important in the latter category, with centralized systems of self-control established and modified in European nations, as shown on Table II.

The UK system of self-regulation by the ASA for print media, poster and cinema is the best developed system among EEC countries. It was established in 1962 and reconstituted in 1974 with greatly expanded operations. It has not only the effective moral support of most of the advertising business, but a firm financial base and effective sanctions by media — which refuse to run offending advertisements. The somewhat similar government chartered but quasi-self regulatory operations of the Independent Broadcast Authority (IBA) and cooperating regional authorities also handle the regulation of broadcast advertising effectively.

The ASA handles over 7,000 consumer complaints per year and conducts more than two thousand investigations, of which more than a thousand deal with advertising copy run in print media. In addition the ASA's CAP Committee investigates more than 500 competitor complaints per year concerning print advertising. Taking into consideration the ASA media monitoring program, the number of advertisements that breach the code is a small fraction of one percent of all print advertising (ASA Annual Reports, various years). Similarly the IBA with its prescreening program, reduces the number of "improper" broadcast commercials to a very tiny number (ASA and IBA Annual Reports, various years).

In Belgium, France, Germany, Italy and the Netherlands, the self-regulatory codes are for the most part based on the ICC Code of Advertising Practice. The application and enforcement of codes in these countries is limited primarily to issuing recommendations, and asking advertisers not to continue "offending" advertising. In some cases it extends to "asking" the media not to carry offending advertisements. Although these systems enjoy considerable support from business, they are often criticized by others as ineffective. These self-regulatory systems handle fewer cases than in the UK, although the number is rising in some countries. (For details see Jean Boddewyn, 1983a, 1983b, 1984a.)

Another evaluative perspective is provided by Business International, a US consulting firm which argued that by 1980 most European governments did not have a political orientation that was sympathetic toward more consumer protection legislation. They pointed out that in some countries controls had already proceeded to the point at which the only question was thought to be how to implement the law. But, by 1980 it seemed as if in some cases a spirit of deregulation was creeping in, and the report suggested that certain "costly" parts of the law may in the future be enforced less vigorously than one would have expected some years ago. Also if there are to be major changes in the future, the report indicated that it seems likely that they will be at the self-regulatory level rather than more government regulation (*Business International*, 1980b:1 – 65/68).

On the other hand, there continue to be reports which provide material to support increased advertising control in Europe. For example, Professor Werner Kroeber-Riel and Gundolf Meyer-Hentschel of the University of the Saarland recently published the results of research dealing with the *coercive effects of advertising*. Based on empirical psychological findings regarding advertising's influence on human behavior, the book includes material on *"behavior control" (ideologically neutral)*, and *"behavior manipulation" (control which goes against societal standards)*. This book concludes with a section on consumer policy, especially with regard to what extent "well planned and rational consumer behavior" should be promoted (Kroeber-Riel and Meyer-Hentschel, 1982, as reviewed by Imkamp, 1983:101 – 103). This example illustrates vividly, that "scientific findings" are likely to be used by consumer activists to support future attempts to regulate advertising.

Since advertising seems likely to continue to come under attack, for specific abuses as well as for being an institution of manipulation, it seems unlikely that calls for effective self-regulation will still the clamor for state regulation. The self-regulatory anomaly in the UK is not likely to be exportable to other EEC countries, since an effective self-regulatory system requires a combination of circumstances which at this time do not seem to exist elsewhere. Nevertheless the self-regulatory systems that exist seem to be performing well in their national contexts, and self-regulatory mechanisms can be nurtured to handle an increasing proportion of problems as they occur.

Industry's internal controls

In the light of public criticisms of advertising and the ways in which abuses can be controlled and halted, we now examine how the advertising business reacted, and what steps were taken to improve internal controls on the content and presentation of advertising. The industry reacted to two interconnected criticisms: (1) of advertising generally, as a phenomenon of a market economy, and (2) of advertising for specific products or services.

These criticisms are interrelated because a negative image of advertising generally will influence adversely the effectiveness of advertising for specific products. Conversely misleading or untruthfull advertising for specific products or services creates a poor image of advertising generally.

We start where criticism of advertising hurts the industry most: if consumers are dissatisfied with the performance of a product or service, they often blame the unfulfilled promises of advertising. Therefore advertisers frequently monitor systematically consumer satisfactions and dissatisfactions with products and services and their relationships to advertising. Success or failure of their operations depend to a large extent upon reacting immediately, if the market barometer predicts bad weather.

However, opinions, habits and preferences of consumers change only slowly, not overnight. Thus, to these operators with their fingers on the pulse of public opinion, the adjustment of products and their advertising to prevailing consumer tastes and preferences is a continuous process, rarely requiring sudden or drastic changes.

With regard to general criticisms of advertising, the outcry in the 1950s and 1960s came mostly from consumerists rather than from consumers. These protestations, with their political overtones, hardly affected the attitudes and internal procedures of most advertisers; they knew only too well that the success of their business depended primarily upon satisfied consumers rather than on satisfied politicians.

Thus the general criticism of advertising, as part of the private enterprise system did not seriously affect the normal operations of advertisers, since they had little to do with consumer dissatisfaction. However, they had a lot to do with political dissatisfaction. Consequently industry rightly treated it as a political problem.

Does this mean that the advertising business did not take any internal steps to meet the general criticisms of advertising or, to put it more positively, to improve the quality of advertising? No indeed. The advertising business believed that the best way to combat criticism was to forestall it by a relentless search for ways to improve the creative product. Seminars and workshops were organized, an activity still pursued on a regular basis. Advertising executives from different parts of the world came together to discuss the latest trends in consumer motivations, tastes and preferences and to review developments, techniques and research methodology in the field of modern communication.

These seminars contributed to the production of advertising which was socially responsible, contemporary and relevant to the needs of consumers in a constantly changing environment.

Unilever for example ran its first Executive Advertising Course in 1953, followed by many others. It also organized a Creative Conference in New York in 1962, from which was published a list of "Ten Principles of Advertising Persuasion."

Nestlé has done likewise; it has run hundreds of seminars all over the world for its executives to learn and to share their knowledge on how to produce effective consumer oriented advertising.

These are just two examples of advertising training and education, by important multinational corporations, activities which have been repeated many times by other corporations in all parts of the western world.

Some advertisers go further; they produce product guidelines which contain managements' instructions on advertising do's and don'ts. An interesting example, albeit of a slightly different nature, concerns the *Reader's Digest* Corporation in New York, which instituted in the mid-1970s a consumer affairs department to advise on its direct marketing activities around the entire world. An Ethical Officer was appointed, with special responsibility for overseeing content and presentation of all direct mail activities for its magazines, books and records. This publisher's "Copy Guidelines" contains detailed instructions on all aspects of the product, the offer, the order form, formats, how to run sweepstakes and competitions, etc. It is a most comprehensive, consumer oriented document which is regularly modified and updated. *Reader's Digest* managers all over the world use it, in addition to taking account of national customs, laws and regulations which of course must be respected.

Key perspectives

The purpose of this chapter has been to provide information and perspectives which are important if one is to understand supranational consumer protection activities in Europe, especially as they relate to advertising regulation.

European nations followed substantially different economic policies during the 1950s and 1960s, with widely differing results, albeit leading to relative prosperity in most nations. Before and during the period in which the EEC was formed, grew and matured, the standard of living in the developed countries of Europe grew rapidly. The market system produced new technology, gains in productivity, increased consumer incomes, and a tax base to support greatly increased government services. During this period the generation responsible for such gains – which could still remember the hardships of war, the poverty, the drudgery and economic uncertainty of earlier times – was replaced gradually by a generation for whom material wealth was the norm. To the new generation, secure in relative affluence, the social costs in terms of pollution of the environment, the apparent depletion of natural resources, the vestiges of poverty, and the harshness of the competitive system in which the inefficient were forced out of business, were challenges to overcome.

Government, the economic system, and broadly "the establishment," came under attack. The new generation and their leaders held business largely responsible for the shortcomings of the economic system, and advertising which was one of the most visible aspects of business was an obvious scapegoat. Advertising was seen as the tool of business – the means to increase sales and profits by manipulating consumers to buy industry's products. The marketing concept – the consumer orientation that emerged in the 1950s and 1960s in leading firms – was widely but not universally accepted by business; and in any event it was not adequately understood by critics. Moreover, it was argued, correctly in some cases as subsequent experience has demonstrated, the satisfaction of the needs of each individual consumer was not necessarily in the best interests of consumers collectively, when environmental and other considerations were taken into account.

In view of the perceived deficiencies in the market system, there developed in the 1950s and 1960s fairly widespread, genuine belief that government planning was the wave of the future – that planning was necessary to "fine tune" and to improve the market system. The depth and breadth of this belief differed among Member States of the EC but it became an important force in each. Thus, although the EEC had begun with the goal of liberalizing trade as a means to achieve greater collective prosperity it seems to have evolved to focus to a great extent on protectionist and interventionist measures. Today it is concerned largely with redistribution of wealth among the member countries, especially with regard to protecting agriculture through subsidies. Another example of this focus is the development of proposals for consumer protection; a number of economic and social factors tended to lead to sentiment for increased consumer protection, and in particular, to the view that advertising regulation ought to be harmonized among EEC nations.

These pressures included especially the belief that the growing complexity of consumer decisions left consumers vulnerable to manipulation by unscrupulous advertisers; in particular the critics focused on misleading and unfair advertising, although the imprecise and controversial definitions of these terms caused considerable consternation.

Whilst these pressures resulted in restrictive measures being proposed regarding content and expression of advertising messages, there was substantial agreement among all concerned on the principles that underlie such measures. One writer notes that

> ... there is hardly anybody [in 1981] possessed of the most modest smattering of social conscience who is antipathetic to the essential requirements of a civilised society in its behavior in consumer affairs ... products, especially foods, should be pure, clean and safe and of no lesser quality than they purport to be. [he also feels that] we cannot ignore the essential requirement imposed by being a member of the human race: that there is a risk in living, a risk we face constantly as we progress from infancy to adulthood. There is a risk in matches, kitchen knives, roller skating, football, hockey, swimming, hang-gliding. We risk life and limb in crossing the road, and we cannot − and do not − expect protection against all eventualities (Shepherd, 1981:79 − 80).

This writer also reports about similar views regarding risks and responsibilities of consumers, being expressed by Molony, Chairman of the UK Commission whose report bears his name:

> The measures we recommend in aid of the consumer do not aim to relieve him of the duty to look after himself. No system of protection can avert all the consequences of folly or eliminate every possibility of hardship. We have not tried to achieve this, and we are sure it is neither possible nor desirable to do so. The law cannot guard against every wile or adjust every trifling injustice. The consumer's first safeguard must always be an alert and questioning attitude (Shepherd, 1981:80).

This attitude seems eminently sensible when one considers that available evidence from our review of the literature is at best inconclusive regarding the power of advertising to manipulate consumers, as well as the need of consumers for more or better information. The balance of evidence seems to indicate that most consumers are adequately sophisticated to make what *they* consider to be reasonably good choices, and they feel that they need little additional protection. Our review of the literature indicated that *consumer* dissatisfaction does not match *consumerist* dissatisfaction with the system. The basic requirement in a market economy for the free flow of truthful and accurate information is met by the interaction between business and the substantial numbers of reasonably alert and competent consumers. Some writers have noted the importance of such competent consumers, referring to them as information seekers. They exert influence in the marketplace far out of proportion to their numbers. The situation is far from perfect, of course, but it is also far more attractive than the alternative — an authoritarian economy in which decisions are made by "less than omniscient bureaucrats."

 If, however, consumerists should find some way to bring consumers to agree with their viewpoints, advertisers would need to adapt immediately, since they cannot ignore consumers if they wish to remain profitable. But, without consumer support, consumerists remain only in a potential position to bring about changes in advertising practice. Thus it seems that consumers must continue to depend on traditional concepts, such as truthfulness, which is a well developed and commonly accepted principle in modern legislation to control advertising in EEC countries. But even this principle is difficult to apply uniformly across countries. What is considered truthful (or misleading) in one language and in one culture is not identical to what is considered truthful (or misleading) in others — for example, the use of the comparative or the superlative.

In raising these many different viewpoints, some readers may feel that we have awarded too much space in our first chapter to the critics of advertising and that our enlarging on this subject does not stand in proper relation to its significance in the eyes of consumers. Indeed, the overwhelming and silent majority of the population has never failed to accept as useful an activity that has contributed to the standards of living which most people in Europe would like to maintain. This must to some extent be due to the increasing acceptance in many European countries of self-regulatory systems to control advertising and to prevent abuse in the marketplace.

However, readers should remember that an understanding of the origin and nature of criticisms of advertising, still topical and alive issues in Europe and the USA, are essential to an understanding of the events that are the subject of the rest of this book.

With these thoughts in mind we are now prepared to discuss and evaluate developments in the field of advertising regulation as they occurred in the mid-1970s.

Chapter II

The pressures build

This chapter covers the early attempts of the Commission to prepare a consumer protection program and focuses on that part of it relating to misleading and unfair advertising. It is designed to provide the necessary base of knowledge to understand the advertising business's reaction and activities, as well as subsequent developments.

The chapter also includes a brief review of the institutions and their complex decision-making procedures, especially the Commission and its relationship to other EC, intergovernmental and supranational institutions. Without such knowledge it is impossible to appreciate fully the reasons why the programs for consumer protection and regulating advertising evolved as they did.

Introduction

In July, 1974 in the American *Journal of Marketing* an article appeared which summarized the US legislative background on advertising regulation and the position of the Federal Trade Commission (FTC) on the meaning of "deceptive" and "unfair" advertising. The author identified and discussed the US criteria for defining deception, and pointed out that an advertisement will be considered false, misleading or deceptive when the following apply:

1. The claim is false,
2. The claim is partially true and partially false,
3. The claim contains insufficient information,
4. The claim may be true but the proof is false, and
5. The claim may be 'literally' or 'technically' true, but creates a false implication (Cohen, 1974:9 – 10).

Although the above stated US criteria for deception had been established over a number of years, the application of the "unfairness doctrine" was more recent. In Cohen's opinion the generally accepted US standards to protect consumers included the following criteria "for determining unfairness in advertising:"

1. The unsubstantiated claim – made despite lack of a reasonable basis for making the claim,
2. The special audience claim – which may motivate vulnerable groups to engage in conduct deleterious to themselves.
3. The puffing claim – which cannot be objectively disproved but offers promises unlikely to be fulfilled. Examples that may be subject to the unfairness doctrine are:
   a. the subjective claim – which is based on consumer perceptions of representations which are difficult to evaluate objectively, and
   b. the unconscionable claim – which contains elements of oppression and unfair surprise (Cohen, 1974:11 – 12).

A little over one year later in November, 1975 the Commission in Brussels published its First Preliminary Draft Directive on Misleading and Unfair Advertising, (Chapter III, Table III) containing in Article 4 the following statement of what would constitute "misleading advertising:"

(a) a claim is false; or
(b) a claim that contains insufficient information; or
(c) a claim that is partially true and partially false; or
(d) a claim that is true but creates a false implication; or
(e) a claim that is true but is falsely proved to be true; or
(f) a claim that is not adequately substantiated; or
(g) a claim that cannot objectively be disproved but makes offers unlikely to be capable of fulfilment.

The first five points above are virtually identical to Cohen's five points relating to deceptive advertising; the last two points in Article 4 are very much like two of Cohen's points about unfair advertising.

This striking conformity perplexed the business community. The Commission appeared to have used the American article as the basis for its own recommendations, adopting a substantial part of the US position without sufficient regard to the many differences between the USA and Europe. The industry felt that within the Commission there should have been a greater understanding of the problems arising from the diversity of laws and jurisdictions, languages, cultures and levels of economic and social development in the Member States.

Since the document contained the first recommendations from the Commission regarding advertising regulation, industry had to take it seriously. The industry made allowances for the fact that the Commission had been working under severe time pressure, and that many on its staff were not versed in the complexities of international advertising. Nevertheless, the apparent imprudence in producing this first important draft without more careful thought or consultation with experienced operators seemed inexcusable.

Additonally a statement in the Memorandum accompanying the draft directive added to the discomfort of business, namely that Article 4 set out "some of the commonest forms that deception takes e.g. providing inadequate information or making unsubstantiated claims and other abuses which it was considered important to regulate" (Appendix II:282). The Memorandum cited no evidence to support this paragraph, and indeed to support the need for other restrictions in the draft directive. These unsupported assertions were an unpleasant surprise to members of the advertising business. They felt that this attack on the role of advertising in promoting products and services to consumers was hostile to business and that the approach itself was misleading and unfair.

In any event, the reception of this draft directive by the business community was anything but positive. The fact that such a draft directive was prepared and published without adequate consultation with the advertising business, set the stage for confrontation rather than cooperation, for strife and controversy rather than accommodation.

We shall return to this draft directive in Chapter III, when we will deal with other objections to it and with further developments and new proposals from the Commission regarding the misleading advertising directive.

Consumer protection and the Treaty of Rome

In order to understand the situation described above, we need additonal background. Let us return to the Treaty of Rome which established the EEC on March 25, 1957. How did the EEC become involved in the subject of advertising in the first place? Did the Treaty of Rome make any reference to the consumer and the need for protection?

Although the Treaty contained a few minor references to the consumer, the language of the Treaty is of no help in answering the above question. The Treaty's main objective was to form a political union of Europe, beginning with the development of such a union on the economic front. Mr. Joseph Luns, who in 1957 was Minister of Foreign Affairs of the Netherlands and one of the signatories of the Treaty, said in an interview with one of the authors of this book: "I can say with certainty that during the preparation of the Treaty, considerations concerning the consumer and the need for a consumer policy, were never discussed" (Luns, 1983).

In a publication in the UK, G.L. Close gives us a similar perspective; he states:

> As is well known the EEC Treaty was drafted at a time when the consumer movement was in its early stages. Its prima facie orientation is moreover that, in general, consumer interests will be sufficiently catered for by an increase in production, free movement of goods and services, the increase of competition in the market and the development of the policies expressly envisaged. The result is that the Treaty does not lay down the basis for a consumer protection policy and there is a complete absence of any statement of the principles which should govern the development of such a policy (Close, 1983:221).

In a study published in Germany, Richard Lenzen gave a similar reason to explain why the EEC ignored consumer policy initially. He observed that a consumer policy was not included in the Treaty because free trade and full competition were expected to protect consumers, and special protection would be superfluous. Lenzen went on to point out that the subsequent need for a consumer policy apparently arose out of the perception that industrial policy fostered national and transnational concentration of companies, which in the course of the integration process, led to various power relationships which undermined the competitive system. It was felt that the resultant oligopolies led to disadvantages for the European consumer, especially lack of price competition, barriers to entry of small firms, barriers to competition, reduction in choices of products available to consumers from small independent companies, barriers to innovation, reduced quality standards, and so forth. Whether these beliefs were correct or not, will not be argued here. But they were sufficiently widely held to generate strong pressure for a consumer policy (Lenzen, 1981:27).

Authority in the Treaty

Gradually pressures from various sides forced the Commission to take the initiative in formulating a consumer policy. But how could this be done, one might well ask, without any provisions for such a policy in the Treaty?

The answer to this question can be found in the structure of the pact which Emile Noël, Secretary-General of the Commission called an "outline treaty," explaining, "The EEC Treaty ... confines itself to sketching out the policy lines to be pursued in the main areas of economic activity, leaving it to the Community's institutions ... to work out the actual arrangements to be applied" (Noël, 1981:15).

This interpretation of the Treaty, which was confirmed during a meeting of the Heads of the Member State governments in 1972, enabled the Commission to take the initiative in the field of consumer affairs.

Such an initiative had in fact already been taken in 1962 by Dutch Commissioner Mansholt, then responsible for Agriculture, who had arranged for a "Contact Committee for Consumer Questions" to be set up (*First Report Commission*, 1977:8). According to the Commission's First Report on its Consumer Protection Policy, the following organizations were represented on this Committee: the European Office of Consumer Organizations (BEUC), the Committee of Family Organizations in the Community (COFACE), the Confederation of European Trade Unions (CES), the European Organizations of the World Federation of Workers (OE-CMT) and the European Organization of Cooperative Organizations (EUROCOOP).

For advertising, one of the important members of this Committee was the BEUC, which had been established in 1962 and whose task it was "to liaise with the Community institutions in order to represent and defend consumer interests" (Commission of the EC, 1982a:6).

The BEUC is a consortium of consumer organizations. In 1984 it had 14 members in the then 10 countries of the Common Market and another 6 correspondent members in Portugal, Spain and the UK; its secretariat is in Brussels (BEUC, 1984:26 – 29).

The BEUC is involved in a wide range of activities. It is represented on the Consumers' Consultative Committee (CCC), many working parties and advisory committees, and on the Community's Economic and Social Committee (ESC); it also has close contact with the EP.

The BEUC also has contacts with other organizations and it administers within the Community the Consumer Interpol, which was established by the International Organization of Consumers' Unions (IOCU). The BEUC is mainly concerned with health and safety issues but it also takes an interest in the debate on future arrangements for satellite and cable television.

Let us then underline that with the formation in 1962 of Mansholt's Consumer Contact Committee, the first step was taken towards the development of an EEC consumer policy, which in ten years was to become such an important factor in matters concerning advertising.

Was it legal?

It is of interest to note that to this day legal experts differ as to whether or not there was "a sufficiently broad legal basis in the Treaty" (Close, 1983:221) to establish a consumer protection program under aegis of the EEC.

The authors of this book do not intend to join this debate; we simply note that at the time when the Treaty was prepared and signed, no provisions were made for the inclusion of a consumer policy. But the flexibility of the Treaty made it nevertheless possible to bring such a policy under its wings. This is precisely what happened and when the moment had come, its legality was simply – to use a German phrase – "hineininterpretiert" (interpreted as included).

Momentum for action

As discussed in the previous chapter, the consumer movement reached its peak in the 1960s and early 1970s; more consumer legislation was introduced throughout the world during this time than during any other period in history; consumer organizations flourished, political pressures were brought to bear on governments of Member States and also on the Brussels administration for steps to safeguard the interests of consumers against what were said to be serious abuses in the marketplace.

The EP, one of the institutions of the Community that will be discussed later in this chapter, also "called for more activity on the part of the Commission in the field of consumer protection" (*First Report Commission*, 1977:9); politicians saw opportunities for advancing their personal interests and the movement rapidly gained momentum.

It was not surprising therefore, that the concern for consumer welfare reached the ante-rooms of the Heads of Governments and that the subject was eventually put on the agenda of their meeting in Paris in 1972.

The "Summit" Meeting of October, 1972

Since 1972 the Heads of Governments have met at regular intervals to deal with Community issues. They now are officially referred to as meetings of the "European Council;" however, to avoid confusion with the Council of Europe in Strasbourg, a different body altogether, these meetings are also referred to as "Summit Meetings."

It is of interest to note in this connection that the Treaty of Rome contained no provisions for such meetings. They started as informal "fireside chats," and have since become occasions at which important matters are considered. In the opinion of some, this situation creates more problems than it solves, a point of view shared by historian Gordon A. Craig, who wrote:

> The summit conference is one of the most unfortunate diplomatic inventions of the modern area. It has increased, rather than relieved, misunderstandings between governments. There is much to be said for Frederick the Great's dictum that heads of state should, whenever possible, avoid meeting each other (Craig, 1984).

The summit meeting of October, 1972 was called at the initiative of President Pompidou of France. Many important issues were discussed, but it was also decided to call upon the institutions of the Communities "to strengthen and coordinate measures for consumer protection and to submit a programme by January, 1974" (Appendix I, p.257). Governments desired to improve the quality of life, to raise standards of living and "to show a more human face," an expression attributed to both Edward Heath, then Prime Minister of the United Kingdom and to Willi Brandt, then the German Chancellor. Consumer protection was formally recognized as a concern for study by the Commission in order to formulate a consumer policy for the Member States.

To their surprise the authors of this book have not been able to trace how this particular point came to be placed on the agenda of the Summit Meeting in Paris and which country put it there. Neither is it known how this matter came to be included in the final communiqué covering this meeting, since early versions of this document made no reference to it.

A spokesman for the Permanent Representation of the Netherlands at the EEC in Brussels, gave the following explanation in a letter to one of the authors: "... At such a last phase of discussions about the communiqué, much is left to the initiative and perseverance of the national civil servants who like to get a little more of their own intentions included in it ..." (Zwaan, 1983).

Our reason for elaborating on these matters of procedure and on the background of the Commission's early consumer protection endeavours is to point out that Heads of State did not place a high priority on this particular subject at that time. They felt that other issues were much more important, especially the establishment of an Economic and Monetary Union, the creation of a regional development fund, problems of inflation and price stabilization and, last but not least, the move to create relationships between Member States with a view to transform Europe into a European Union by the year 1980 (*Yearbook Winkler Prins Encyclopaedia*, 1972: 116).

However, lower level politicians, civil servants and consumerists were not discouraged by the somewhat low priority of a subject which they considered to be of prime importance. The Summit Meeting had after all decided that the Commission should deal with it, so deal with it they would.

Consumer protection had become a political reality, and henceforth would have to be treated as such by the entire business.

The Commission organizes for consumer protection

As an immediate consequence of the October meeting in Paris, in the spring of 1973 a Division for Consumer Protection and Information was set up, under Director-General Michel Carpentier, who answered to Commissioner Scarcascia Mugnozza. Consumer affairs became the responsibility of John Braun, whose main task was to draw up a consumer protection and information program.

The Consumer Contact Committee which had been established by Commissioner Mansholt in 1962, had not been effective and had been dissolved. But it was officially reinstated on September 25, 1973 as the Consumers' Consultative Committee. Its task was: "... representing consumer interests to the Commission and advising the Commission on the formulation and implementation of policies and actions regarding consumer protection and information, either when requested to do so by the Commission, or on its own initiative" (Commission of the EC, 1982a:12).

This mission was a very wide brief indeed, originally carried out by 25 members, but since the last amendments to its rules of procedure in 1980, by 33 members. The BEUC, COFACE, EUROCOOP, and the European Trade Union Confederation (ETUC) each provide 6 members; a further 9 seats are reserved for persons with special knowledge of consumer questions. In looking through the list of names on this Committee, representatives of business and industry were conspicuous by their absence.

Anticipating developments for a moment, after several years of great activity, Commissioner Richard Burke took over from Commissioner Mugnozza in 1977. Soon afterward a Directorate for the Promotion of Consumer Interests was formed. It consisted of three separate units, one each for (a) physical protection, (b) economic and legal interests, and (c) consumer information and education.

After the first director, John Braun retired from the Commission in 1977 and later became an independent consultant in European consumer affairs, Jeremiah Patrick Sheehan was appointed in March, 1978 as Director for Consumer Affairs.

Following the appointment of a new Commission in 1981, a Directorate-General for "Environment, Consumer Protection and Nuclear Safety" (DG XI) was formed, with Karl-Heinz Narjes as its Commissioner, Athanase Andreopoulos as its Director-General and Jeremiah Sheehan as head of the Consumer Affairs Directorate. Since January, 1985 Stanley Clinton Davis from the UK, has served as Commissioner for Consumer Affairs.

The preliminary consumer protection program

The Commission carried out the Resolution of the Paris Summit Meeting and produced a "Preliminary Programme of the European Economic Community for a Consumer Protection and Information Policy," which was formally adopted by the Council of Ministers on April 14, 1975 (Appendix I).

The document proclaimed five basic rights. "The principles stemmed from President Kennedy's consumer message of 15 March 1962 and the objectives from the Consumer Charter of the Council of Europe" (Braun, 1981:19 – 20).

We shall discuss the COE and its activities in the field of consumer protection more fully in the following chapter. But we should note here that two years before the publication of the EEC preliminary consumer program, the Assembly of the COE adopted on May 17, 1973 a European Consumer Protection Charter, which included the same five basic rights found in this EEC program. This correspondence is not surprising since the same man, John Braun, had a hand in writing both documents.

The following is a comparison of the Kennedy list with that of the European declarations:

Kennedy's message to the US Congress:	*EEC's program and the COE's Charter:*
The right to safety	The right to protection of health and safety
The right to choose	The right to protection of economic interests
The right to be heard	The right of redress
The right to be informed*	The right to information and education
	The right of representation (the right to be heard)

Kennedy specifically mentions "The right to choose — to be assured, whenever possible, access to a variety of products and services at competitive prices." But this right does not appear on the Commission's consumer program.

It should be noted that the rights on both lists are interrelated and not mutually exclusive. For example, the right to be heard suggests the desirability of an informed and educated population. Likewise the right to information and education is important if one expects consumers to use information and education intelligently to make good choices when buying products and services. Thus the omission of "the right to choose" in the EEC's program appears incongruous. Why stress the right to information and education if consumers are not to be guaranteed the fullest opportunity to use such information and education to make purchasing decisions? Incidentally, "free choice" is mentioned in one place in the Commission's Preliminary Programme (Appendix I, par.8 on p.260). But such brief mention hardly makes up for its omission as a right.

This omission was certainly not intended by the author of the EEC program; he recommended in a proposal submitted by the Commission to the Council of Ministers on December 5, 1973 that in addition to the five basic rights, the following statement should be added: "These rights are seen within the context of a general consumer right to the primary satisfaction of basic needs and freedom of individual choice for the expenditure of discretionary income" (Braun, 1983a).

There is no doubt that the diversity of viewpoints within the Member States made it difficult to agree on a common set of desirable consumer freedoms. However, the right to choose is especially important to the efficient operation of a market economy. Perhaps those who believe in state ownership or control of the factors of production see little need to depend upon consumer decisions as important to the

---

* In 1976 President Ford proclaimed the additional "right to education," which is closely allied with the right to be informed.

efficient allocation of resources, since the state is presumed to be able to allocate resources more efficiently and more fairly than the market mechanism. However, it would be a great understatement merely to point out that such a presumption has not yet been demonstrated to be correct. The remarkable economic and social progress of private enterprise market economies of Western Europe stand in stark contrast to the malaise in socialist states. Compare, for example, the quite different levels of living in what once were roughly equivalent economies, the Federal Republic of Germany and the German Democratic Republic.

So while it can be argued that the right to choose is inherent in the rights of consumers in our western society, it remains difficult to understand why, when adopting a document of this significance, such an important right was not included in the final program adopted by the Council. One would be tempted to believe that leaving out specific reference to consumers' right to choose reflected the belief that it is not an important right. Such a view can only stem from a low opinion of the ability of consumers to make good choices for themselves. It is in any case regrettable that the additional wording recommended by John Braun was not included.

Topics covered

The Commission's preliminary consumer program dealt with the five basic rights in great detail; it stated many fields of importance, requiring study or immediate action; it identified specific product categories and practices relating to services; it covered in total no fewer than 51 fields of interest, but it also contained the following more general provision:

> Facilitaties should be made available to children as well as to young people and adults to educate them to act as discriminating consumers, capable of making an *informed choice* of goods and services and conscious of their rights and responsibilities (Appendix I, p.269) (italics added).

The final paragraph of this ambitious program read as follows:

> This text should be regarded as the first stage of a more comprehensive programme which might need to be developed at a later date. The aim is to complete this first stage within four years (Appendix I, p.271).

When asked about this final paragraph, John Braun read the following from his original draft of August, 1973:

> ... But whatever blueprint is laid down in advance, sudden events or discoveries ... may call for a revision of the program. Similarly, existing plans may need to be modified or enlarged in the light of experience. Subject to these qualifications an action program has been drawn up based upon a short term two years, medium five years and long term eight years or more forecast (Braun, 1983b).

In addition, Braun made the strong recommendation that relevant studies should be made before concrete proposals should be formulated and presented. But his recommendation was ignored. After a long process of negotiations, the Council of Ministers shortened the proposed document to twelve pages and reduced the time-table for implementation of the first stage from eight to four years.

Sources of issues

At this point it is important to recall who suggested, recommended or insisted that certain consumer interest issues should be covered by the program. The avalanche of proposals for action came from many different sources: consumer organizations, the CCC, the Commission itself, the EP, and the governments of Member States. There was also considerable influence from the governments of the non-EEC Scandinavian countries; the Organization for Economic Cooperation and Development (OECD), with 24 countries throughout the world, provided ideas developed from its Australian, Canadian and US members. The recommendations of these bodies were for the most part in harmony with the prevailing trend towards greater regulation of business activities and advertising in the supposed interest of consumers. Countries such as Denmark and the UK were leaders in the development of consumer issues, which probably explains why John Braun, an Englishman, was selected as Head of the Division of Consumer Protection, and Karen Muller, a Dane, was selected as his number two. Together with Ludwig Krämer from the Federal Republic of Germany, and Michel Carpentier from France as the Division's Director-General, this cosmopolitan team set out to combine the many proposals into a workable program.

Were Member States prepared?

Another point to be considered is whether or not Member States were prepared for the introduction of a program as comprehensive as this one. In a study conducted for the Commission, Professor Norbert Reich observes:

> Rights are more easily proclaimed than translated into the practice of legislative acts. In order to implement such an ambitious programme, several requirements have to be met. Firstly, there has to be an organisation safeguarding the consumer's interests. Secondly, there must be a government policy taking up the consumer's interests. Thirdly, a new body of law has to be developed by legislation, court practice and other means which in the following we shall call *consumer law*. Finally, collective representation of consumers' interests is required in private and public bodies responsible for the implementation of consumer policy and consumer law (Reich and Micklitz, 1980:2).

These conditions have not to this day been fulfilled. In its First Report on Consumer Protection and Information Policy the Commission stated that "The administrative set-up in the member countries for the defence of consumers' interests is quite different in each country" (*First Report Commission*, 1977:20). In its Third Report the Commission mentions a number of provisions that Member States made to deal with the administration of consumer affairs. Among these were also a few retrograde measures, for example:

> France suppressed the post of State Secretary for Consumer Policy and replaced it in June, 1978 with a Directorate within the Ministry for Economic Affairs ... Following the general election of 1979, the new UK government abolished the Department of Prices and Consumer Protection, and transferred responsibility for consumer questions to the Department of Trade (*Third Report Commission*, 1980:14).

In discussing the four requirements mentioned above, Reich explained that the situation leaves much to be desired. He stated: "Unlike the labour movement the consumer's interests are not yet sufficiently organized" (Reich and Micklitz, 1980:2 – 3). And with reference to consumer law he observed: "It is still a question in EC countries whether a special consumer law has been developed or is in the process of evolution" (Reich and Micklitz, 1980:10). He added that in his "survey of consumer organizations in the EC, there is still only a small representative element in the existing bodies that formulate and further consumer interests. This is the main reason why consumer representation is still in its infancy" (Reich and Micklitz, 1980:12).

Reich does not analyze the reasons for these shortcomings. But they probably stem from the fact that there has been insufficient political pressure to bring these conditions about. Consumerism and consumer protectionist sentiments are cyclical. Usually only a small group of activists promotes the issues while the majority of consumers are not deeply concerned.

Another negative factor affecting the development and implementation of the consumer protection program in those days was the worldwide recession in Member States that forced governments to economize. While financial considerations were not the main reason for slow action on the consumer program, the serious economic situation had an arresting effect.

The initial reaction of business

When the First Preliminary Consumer Program was introduced, the business world perceived it as a most ambitious, indeed somewhat extreme document. Many people regarded it as a statement of intent which they did not expect to lead to concrete proposals and action. Therefore they did not take the proposal especially seriously, choosing instead to wait for concrete proposals. This industry reaction was understandable but unfortunate. The program represented after all a serious political development and the business community should have realized its important implications earlier. Political decisions by Heads of Governments should not be treated lightly.

The consumer program's biases

Building on the consumerist ideas that we discussed in Chapter I, the Commission stated its reasoning in the first paragraph of the General Considerations of the Preliminary Program as follows:

> While consumer protection has long been an established fact in the Member States of the Community, the concept of a consumer policy is relatively recent. It has developed in response to the abuses and frustrations arising at times from the increased abundance and complexity of goods and services afforded the consumer by an ever-widening market. Although such a market offers certain advantages, the consumer, in availing himself of the market, is no longer able properly to fulfil the role of a balancing factor. As market conditions have changed, the balance between suppliers and consumers has tended to become weighted in favour of the supplier. The discovery of new materials, the introduction of new methods of manufacture, the development of means of communication, the expansion of markets, new methods of retailing — all these factors have had the effect of increasing the production, supply and demand of an immense variety of goods and services. This means that the consumer, in the past, ususally an individual purchaser in a small local market, has become merely a unit in a mass market, the target of advertising campaigns and of pressure by strongly organized production and distribution groups. Producers and distributors often have a greater opportunity to determine market conditions than the consumer. Mergers, cartels and certain self-imposed restrictions on competition have also created imbalance to the detriment of consumers (Appendix I, p.259).

Industry was puzzled: What abuses? What frustrations? What pressures? What opportunities to determine market conditions? Experienced businessmen saw things differently from those who had produced this document. Business felt that its language expressed strong biases against marketing and advertising. Not only did these statements contradict directly the experience of knowledgeable advertisers, but they demonstrated lack of respect for the intelligence and the power of the consumer. The document was long on unsupported assertions and short on evidence.

The above "general considerations" imply that the immense increase in the variety of goods and services somehow operated to the detriment of consumers. In fact, however, such variety could not be produced and sold without consumer demand for it. And there is no question that such variety is a move in the right direction to satisfy the many different needs of increasingly sophisticated consumers.

Had the opening paragraph in the Preliminary Program been written in the early 1960s, one might have felt some sympathy with it. Not all marketing and advertising activities in the 1950s and 1960s would have passed the standards of the 1970s, by which time much had been done to eradicate earlier abuses and misrepresentations, perhaps partly as a result of consumer activist criticisms. But more important were the self-correcting tendencies in the operation of the competitive market. Changing conditions led to a greater sense of responsibility on the part of manufacturers and their advertising agencies. Improved internal systems of control had reduced the justifications for criticism. This is not to suggest that advertising had become perfect. A few abuses inevitably continue to occur, as they do in any line of endeavor. Ronald Beatson, Director-General of the European Association of Advertising Agencies (EAAA), explains the view of the advertising business:

> We have come a long way since the times of the mountebank and the hucksters, whose aims were trickery and fraud. We can claim today to be far more disciplined as a profession, exercising far greater respect for the public's intelligence, than many politicians in this world who certainly do not always advertise in a way that is decent, honest and truthful (Beatson, 1983a:11).

The business viewpoint is that in the 1960s and 1970s consumers developed into better informed citizens who could discriminate more carefully and intelligently, and shop with increasing precision. Allowing for the few exceptions, most consumers could differentiate between what is patently untrue or misleading and what could be accepted with a smile as a salesman's harmless hyperbole, "speaking well of himself," as we quoted Samuel Johnson at the beginning of this chapter.

First endeavors to regulate advertising

The subject of advertising and its significance to the consumer for making his or her decisions, was only part of the total package of issues covered by the Preliminary Consumer Program. Yet advertising became one of the first subjects to receive full attention from the Commission. In November, 1975 only a few months after the publication of the consumer program, the Commission published its Draft Directive on Misleading and Unfair Advertising.

It would have been difficult for the Commission to select for one of its first major efforts in the field of consumer affairs a more complex and controversial subject than this one. Under pressure from various sides, the Commission clearly underestimated the task it was taking on, and plunged into what soon turned out to be a hornet's nest: How to regulate on an international scale this complex combination of emotion and intellect known as "advertising."

As James O'Connor, then European Adviser, Independent Television Companies Ltd. (ITCA) has said:

> Why initiatives about advertising? It is a moot point and one that often puzzles me. But it is clear that we attract by the very nature of our work those who are dazzled by the apparent glamour of communication, the way we do it, and who see some of its style rubbing off, while at the same time doing them a bit of voting good! (O'Connor, 1981)

The short answer to O'Connor's question is that the CCC, government experts from Member States and Commission gave priority to the subject of advertising because they had no choice. The Commission simply had to respond in some way to pressures from many different directions. We shall discuss this particular draft directive more fully in our next chapter when we also review other Commission activities with regard to consumer affairs. But before doing so it is essential for a proper understanding of the work of the Commission, to describe in some detail its authority and how it is structured.

Authority and structure

According to Article 189 of the Rome Treaty

> The Council and the Commission shall, in the discharge of their duties and in accordance with the provisions of this Treaty, issue regulations and directives, take decisions and formulate recommendations or opinions. (Rome Treaty, 1957:60).

Since "directives" are of most importance to advertising regulation, we will explain the various phases through which they pass from inception to adoption.
Article 100 of the Rome Treaty states:

> The Council shall, by a unanimous decision, on a proposal of the Commission, issue directives for the approximation of such legislative and administrative provisions of Member States as directly affect the establishment or operation of the Common Market.
>
> The Assembly* and the Economic and Social Committee shall be consulted in the case of directives the implementation of which would involve amending legislation in one or more Member States (Rome Treaty, 1957:38).

Before discussing procedures in detail, we should explain that neither the Commission nor the Council can introduce legislation in the Member States; as Emile Noël puts it:

> ... the Community is not a federation; it does not have a 'federal government' to which national parliaments and governments are subordinate in certain areas. Our best course may be to leave it to future historians to find an appropriate label and simply describe it as a 'Community' system (Noël, 1981:1).

The Commission cannot legislate but it can and does take the initiative to develop and formulate directives, which then form the basis for legislation in Member States. This process is often long and laborious. The directive on misleading advertising was in the Brussels pipeline from 1975 to 1984, and Member States have two more years to implement it. The long time from inception to implementation is due not only to the fact that the "Community" system requires the twelve Member States to approve the directive and eventually to introduce legislation in their respective countries; it is also because of the complicated organizational structure and the

---

* The term "The Assembly" is no longer used; this body is now called the "European Parliament," which is how we shall refer to it.

time consuming decision-making procedures of the Brussels administration. Quick decisions are almost impossible.

The fact that documents must be translated into many languages, does not make the process any easier or quicker. As noted in the *Eighteenth General Report of the EEC,* for the year 1984 the Translation Division translated a total of 684,826 pages, excluding revisions, while the "terminology bank" now contains 345,331 entries of equivalent terms in most of the Community languages, as well as 85,042 abbreviations and acronyms (*EC General Report*, 1984:38).

In Article 100 of the Treaty, initiation of policy and the formulation of proposals concerning consumer protection, which may develop into a directive, lie with the Commission, which is the main administrative body.

Apart from a Secretariat-General for the Commission as a whole and a number of Service Departments (Legal; Statistics; Interpreting; Publications; etc.), as of January 1, 1986 President Jacques Delors and sixteen Commissioners are responsible for the following twenty Directorates-General:

External Relations	DG I	Willy De Clercq/Claude Cheysson/Grigoris Warfis*
Economic and Financial Affairs	DG II	Alois Pfeiffer
Internal Market and Industrial Affairs	DG III	Lord Cockfield
Competition	DG IV	Peter Sutherland
Employment, Social Affairs and Education	DG V	Manuel Marin
Agriculture and Forestry	DG VI	Frans Andriessen
Transport	DG VII	Stanley Clinton Davis
Development	DG VIII	Lorenzo Natali
Personnel and Administration	DG IX	Henning Christophersen
Information, Communication and Culture	DG X	Carlo Ripa de Meana
Environment, Consumer Protection and Nuclear Safety	DG XI	Stanley Clinton Davis
Science, Research and Development	DG XII	Karl-Heinz Narjes
Information Market and Innovation	DG XIII	Karl-Heinz Narjes
Fisheries	DG XIV	Antonio Cardoso e Cunha
Financial Institutions and Taxation	DG XV	Lord Cockfield
Regional Policy	DG XVI	Alois Pfeiffer
Energy	DG XVII	Nicolas Mosar
Credit and Investments	DG XVIII	Abel Matutes
Budgets	DG XIX	Henning Christophersen
Financial Control	DG XX	Henning Christophersen

* Within one Directorate-General Commissioners can share responsibilities with other Commissioners. For a complete list of Commissioners, their responsibilities and their staffs, see the *Directory of the Commission of the European Communities*, published by the Office for Official Publications, Luxembourg.

The key DGs for advertising regulation are: (1) DG III under Lord Cockfield, who in June, 1985 produced an important White Paper "Completing the Internal Market," (2) DG XI, now the responsibility of Mr. Stanley Clinton Davis who produced a paper "A New Impetus for Consumer Protection Policy," which also appeared in June, 1985 and (3) DG X, now under Mr. Carlo Ripa de Meana. DG X is important not only because of proposals in the field of pan-European television programming, but also because of its efforts to create greater involvement of European citizens in the objectives of the Community, leading to a "People's Europe." All these matters will be discussed in subsequent chapters.

The phases of a directive

Against the above background, let us now look at the various phases through which a directive will pass before it becomes law in Member States. These are:
(a) the preparatory phase,
(b) the consultative phase,
(c) the decision-making phase, and
(d) the implementation phase.
The four bodies inside the circle in Figure 1 are the EC institutions which have responsibility for the first three phases in the process. The Commission is responsible for initiating the directive, in the preparatory phase. Both the Commission and the Council engage in extensive consultations in the next phase. They are influenced by many others, especially the five bodies outside the circle. The decision-making phase includes the Commission's decision to send a proposed directive to the Council, but the main decision-making responsibility to approve a draft directive for implementation rests with the Council. Responsibility for the implementation phase rests with individual Member States.

The five bodies outside the circle in Figure 1 influence the process at numerous points in the first three phases of directives. But these bodies are only advisory. Although they may agree or disagree with a draft directive or a proposal for a directive, the Commission carries the responsibility to initiate a proposed directive and to submit it to the Council. However, since the Council will also consult with official advisory bodies, the Commission will need their advice. Thus the Commission will act reasonably, although it obviously cannot accommodate all points of view in one directive.

The consultation steps in the process are not mutually exclusive. There must be considerable overlap between them, since consultation in all of the first three phases is a key-element in each step of the process. To emphasize this point, we have deliberately omitted from Figure 1 any lines between the Commission, or the Council of Ministers and the various advisory bodies.

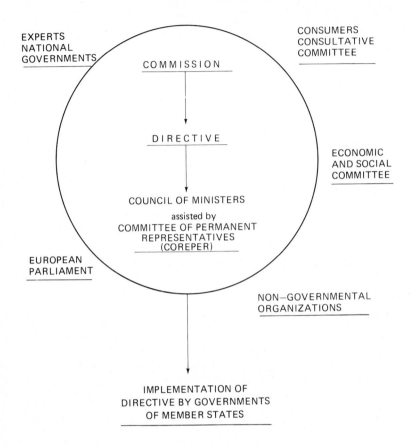

EXPERTS
NATIONAL
GOVERNMENTS

CONSUMERS
CONSULTATIVE
COMMITTEE

COMMISSION

DIRECTIVE

ECONOMIC
AND SOCIAL
COMMITTEE

COUNCIL OF MINISTERS
assisted by
COMMITTEE OF PERMANENT
REPRESENTATIVES
(COREPER)

EUROPEAN
PARLIAMENT

NON−GOVERNMENTAL
ORGANIZATIONS

IMPLEMENTATION OF
DIRECTIVE BY GOVERNMENTS
OF MEMBER STATES

Figure 1. The draft directive process − from initiation to implementation.

The preparatory phase

In preparing a proposal, the Commissioner concerned, aided by his staff, will first study carefully all existing and relevant material, especially legislation in the Member States. These studies depend upon cooperation from experts appointed by their governments.

Once a proposal has been formulated, the lobbying starts. There will be a great number of purely informal discussions among many people, organizations and bodies at many different levels. The reason for this informality is to prepare drafts of proposals which, once presented formally, will not meet with serious resistance from those who have already been involved. At this point the Commission is ready for the consultative phase.

The consultative phase

This phase is the most important of all, because a number of advisory bodies will now be asked to give a formal opinion on the proposal which emerged from the informal discussions in the preparatory phase. Many of the same bodies will now be consulted officially at this stage.

The previously mentioned experts of national governments are vital in this phase because of their specialized knowledge of the situation in their respective countries. For example, they know what can and cannot be done without having to change existing national laws. If the proposed directive requires changes in national legislation, problems of serious proportions can arise, particularly if national existing legislation, or other forms of control are perceived by a country to be functioning perfectly satisfactorily. The Draft Directive on Misleading and Unfair Advertising was a typical example of such a situation.

What bodies are consulted?

Michel Carpentier, then Director-general of DG XI, said in this connection at a Colloquium in October, 1978:

> I should like to point out that the Commission brought together no less than four groups of national specialists before sending the Council a draft directive on Misleading Advertising and that it carried out consultations on this same directive over a period of nearly three years (Carpentier, 1978).

Apart from national experts, the Commission will seek the opinion of the CCC and a number of so-called Non-Governmental Organizations (NGOs), such as the ICC and various trade associations, depending upon the nature of the directive and the particular topics it covers. In the case of the Draft Directive on Misleading and Unfair Advertising, these included the World Federation of Advertisers (WFA), formerly the International Union of Advertisers' Associations (IUAA), the EAAA and a number of international media organizations.

The "them and us" syndrome

Many in the advertising business believe there was, and still is, an important gap in communication between the Commission and the relatively small but experienced group of advertising "professionals" working for multinational advertisers and advertising agencies in Europe. Admittedly the Commission received a considerable amount of information from some parts of the advertising business to assist in preparing "technical" directives. But there has been relatively little direct contact between the Commission and this small group of operators who carry special responsibilities for consumer advertising on an international scale.

This group of men and women is unquestionably the best informed, most experienced and knowledgeable source of information about advertising that crosses national borders. They have been practicing their trade for decades within the Community and Europe as a whole. Through the multinational companies and agencies they represent, they possess unparalleled information about differences and similarities with regard to habits and motivations of consumers in the many European cultures and languages. They can give advice as to when advertising can be the same in multiple countries and when it has to be different. Their consumer research is more comprehensive and complete than that of any government or intergovernmental body. Success or failure in the markets in which they operate depend on this knowledge and its application.

One would have thought that if the Commission had really been interested in expert opinion on a subject which was – and to a large extent still is – "terra incognita," the Commission would have found a way to get more out of these international specialists. And yet, this resource went largely untapped by regulators and legislators. If there had been a regular dialogue, much time and money could have been saved.

It has been said that the Commission welcomes initiatives of the business community to discuss problems of mutual concern. In fact, the influence of industry on the Commission may be greater than many people assume. But one must wonder nevertheless why the Commission itself has so rarely taken the initiative for discussions. One hears the argument that consumerist pressures have been responsible for the low profile of the business world, and for the infrequent mention of advertising business viewpoints in the Commission's official publications. The CCC for example, has been rather hesitant to enter into an ongoing dialogue with business representatives.

This is most regrettable and the advertising business has therefore made efforts not only to establish good relationships with the Commission but also with supranational bodies representing consumer interests. These latter contacts have been retarded by lack of trust in the true motivations of the business world. We shall come back upon this point later, but it is remarkable to note that while the advertising business felt the Commission acted without adequate input, consumer organizations thought otherwise. John Braun said: "During the whole of my period in Brussels all consumer organizations, without exception, felt that EEC legislation generally was industry dominated and that it seemed to them that trade associations had limitless resources to lobby and influence the Community institutions" (Braun, 1985).

The advertising business has indeed made progress in its relationships with the Commission. But the question remains why the Commission and its staff members, in spite of the wide range of their portfolios, did not at an earlier stage avail themselves of the opportunity to acquire professional insights into the complexities of the subject with which they were dealing.

The decision-making phase

After the Commission concludes its consultations, and after drafts have been amended, corrected or rewritten, the Commissioner concerned will submit a proposal to the Commission as a whole, which must approve it before it can go to the Council of Ministers.

At this point one would expect that the individual members of the Commission would have accumulated a great deal of detailed knowledge about each draft directive before it is forwarded to the Council for a decision. But Lord Thomson, who was a Commissioner at one time, indicates otherwise:

> During the five years of development in the European Commission of the Proposed Directive on Advertising, which would fundamentally alter the British control system, it was never once debated by the Commissioners collectively. It remained during most of that time within the private province of the Directorate-General responsible for consumer protection. And when it was finally formally sent to the Council of Ministers for a decision binding member Governments most of the thirteen Commissioners did not know of its existence. Directives of this kind are approved by the 'Procédure Ecrite' under which they are circulated in written form round Commissioners' private offices – the 'Cabinets' which are such an important feature of the Commission system. Only if one of the private secretaries objects does it come to the Commissioners themselves for decision. Most Directives become official Commission policy without individual Commissioners being aware of them. Of course it is impossible for Commissioners to be aware of all acts that are taken in their name, but the fact that the procedure inevitably works in this way with limited political guidance, is a strong reason for being highly selective and discriminatory about the number of policy proposals suitable to become Directives (Thomson, 1981:42).

Thus, the decision to forward a proposal for a draft directive to the Council of Ministers is not a carefully considered proposal from the standpoint of the entire Commission. It is instead largely the result only of work done by the responsible staff members of the Directorate-General concerned.

With regard to decisions concerning consumer affairs, an improvement in this situation was achieved in 1983, when

> ... Greece took the initiative to organize, for the first time, a Council meeting of Ministers responsible for consumer affairs, which was held on 12 December 1983. Thereafter, ministerial meetings were planned on a more regular basis ... (Commission of the EC, 1985b:16).

The Council of Ministers and COREPER

According to Article 146 of the Rome Treaty, the Council shall consist of representatives of the Member States. "Each government shall delegate to it one of its members. The Office of the President shall be exercised for a term of six months by each member of the Council in rotation following the alphabetic order of the Member States" (Rome Treaty, 1957:52).

The Council of Ministers has the authority to decide and send a directive to the Member States for implementation. But after the Council receives the proposal from the Commission, much still remains to be done before the Council will take such a decision. If a directive requires "amending legislation in one or more Member States" the Council must submit the proposal for formal comments to the EP and to the ESC.

The Council of Ministers delegates its consulting responsibilities to the Committee of Permanent Representatives (COREPER), which organizes and coordinates all contacts on the subject of a directive. COREPER is made up of representatives with the rank of ambassadors. This committee was created because the membership of the Council of Ministers varies over time and according to the subject under discussion. It is COREPER's task to ensure continuity and to take all necessary steps in preparation for a final decision by the Council. It will be COREPER then, which will send a proposed directive for comments to the EP and to the ESC. We shall now provide basic information on these two bodies, so as to clarify how a proposed directive might be handled by them, as well as to indicate the importance of their views in shaping the final directive.

The European Parliament

The EP has 434 members, of which France, Germany, Italy and the UK each provide 81; the Netherlands contribute 25, Belgium and Greece 24 each, Denmark 16, Ireland 15 and Luxembourg 6. Because of the entry into the Common Market of Portugal and Spain on January 1, 1986, total membership will become 518, with 60 members joining from Spain and 24 from Portugal. The members from these two countries will be elected in the course of 1986 and until then, delegations of national MPs will take their seats in the EP.

In June, 1979 the then 410 members from nine States (Greece joined in 1981), were for the first time directly elected by the citizens of Member States. Article 138 of the Treaty of Rome specified that the elections should be held ". . . in accordance with a uniform procedure in all Member States." But in view of the failure to agree on such uniform procedures (which at the end of 1985 had not yet been agreed upon) the elections were held instead in conformance with the national voting practices of the Member States.

The total voter turnout in 1979 was not impressive; only 61% of the Community's 270 million people went to the polls. The figures for the individual countries varied greatly: Belgium 91.4%, Luxembourg 85% (voting is compulsory in these two countries), Italy 85.5%, Germany 65.9%, Ireland 63.6%, France 61.3%, Netherlands 57.8%, Denmark 47% (Greenland 33%) and the UK 32.6% (Commission of the EC, 1981:58).

In June, 1984 the second European Parliamentary elections were held, with a voter turnout of only 60%, even lower than in 1979. In early 1984 the economic situation in Member States was grave; agricultural subsidies in the EEC caused internal strife; and the UK sought to have its contribution to the EEC budget reduced.

Although French President Mitterrand and others managed on the eve of the election to bring about a solution to these problems, the European public remained largely disinterested. The EEC in concept, as well as the EP in particular, were to most people uncertain entities, impersonal, remote and of no particular consequence in their daily lives.

An additional confusing factor was that the EP operates out of three different locations: Strasbourg, Brussels and Luxembourg. One week per month the Parliament meets in Strasbourg; this city is also the home of the COE, contributing to the confusion. The remaining three weeks of the months members of the Parliament and accompanying civil servants are in Brussels. But part of the Parliament's Secretariat remains in Luxembourg.

On April 21, 1982 the EP approved a report criticizing these arrangements and their excessive costs. But, although great savings could be achieved if the Parliament met in one location, Belgium, France and Luxembourg are unlikely to agree, since they do not want to give up the lucrative revenues and the prestige of hosting the Parliament (*De Telegraaf*, April 22, 1982).

The Grand Duchy of Luxembourg even instituted legal proceedings against the Parliament, requesting the annulment of its resolutions of this body by which governments of Member States will decide mutually about the seat of the Institutions of the Community. The EC Court of Justice dismissed both appeals (Case No. 230/81, Court Decision of 10 February 1983 and Case No. 108/83, Court Decision of 10 April 1984). Thus this strange and inefficient situation is likely to continue indefinitely.

Nevertheless the EP wants to be seen as a coherent, efficient body with a clearly defined sense of purpose. To accomplish this end, as well as to bring out the voters, an advertising campaign was launched prior to the 1984 election. However, it was unrealistic to expect, as many members of the Parliament did, that this last minute advertising campaign would overcome voter inertia. The failure of the campaign was no surprise to advertising professionals who know only too well that advertising's power is limited.

While background on the EP is important to help us understand its functions and powers, it is even more important to remember that this Parliament is not a legislative assembly, although many of its members would like it to become one. As one of the leading international magazines said recently: "Few legislative bodies in the Western world have less real power than the European Parliament" (*Time Magazine*, May 20, 1985:6). However, the Parliament has many important powers that permit it to exert influence on the legislative process; for example, it has the power to dissolve the Commission.

Regarding Council directives, however, Parliament's role is only advisory. Nevertheless a Council directive cannot be adopted until the EP has delivered its opinion, which it may withhold.

After the Council of Ministers sends a proposed directive to the EP for advice, the Secretariat of the Parliament will submit it to the appropriate Committee. In the case of consumer issues, this will be the Committee on Environment, Public Health and Consumer Protection. This committee consists of a Chairman and 27 members of Parliament, selected from various Member States and political parties.

The influence of this Committee's activities on shaping consumer policy should not be underestimated; it may not have executive authority, but it can exert considerable pressure. A typical case in point was the Public Hearing on the Commission's Second Consumer Program, which this Committee organized in 1980 and which we shall discuss in our next chapter.

It is of interest to note that the various advisory bodies have different perspectives on proposals from the Commission and the Council. Since the EP is a political body it therefore expresses primarily a political point of view. In contrast, the CCC is concerned mainly with the impact of a proposal on consumers; and the ESC represents the interests of employers and employees.

The Economic and Social Committee

The ESC is the other main consultative body whose opinion must be sought before a directive can be approved. This Committee is sometimes referred to as ECOSOC, which is wrong and causes confusion with a United Nation's (UN) Committee entitled the Economic and Social Council, rightly referred to as ECOSOC.

The ESC according to Article 193 of the Rome Treaty, consists "... of representatives of the various categories of economic and social activity, in particular, representatives of producers, farmers, transport operators, workers, merchants, artisans, the professions and representatives of the general interest." This committee consists of 189 members, one third representing employers, another third representing employees, and the final third representing various other interests such as agricultural and farmers' organizations; associations of smaller industries, banks and crafts; governmental departments; and consumer organizations. Very few of the members of this committee have any substantial marketing or advertising experience. The limited representation of the marketing and advertising community on this and other advisory governmental bodies, leads to an unfortunate adversary or confrontational situation from the standpoint of the business community – the "them and us syndrome," as described above.

Voting procedures

After all requirements in Article 189 have been met the Council of Ministers is in a position to make a decision. Article 148 of the Rome Treaty stipulates: "Except where otherwise provided for in the Treaty, the Council's resolutions shall be reached by a majority of its members."

However, in 1966 President De Gaulle insisted on an agreement that in all cases in which a country's national and vital interests were at stake, a unanimous vote would be required. This so-called "Luxembourg Agreement" put the responsibility on the shoulders of the Council of Ministers to determine what is of "vital" interest. In practice it meant that virtually all council decisions must have unanimous approval. This situation existed until December, 1974 when the Heads of Government "decided that the practice of insisting on the unanimous agreement of Member States on every issue should be dropped" (Noël, 1981:20). Although since then some decisions can be taken on the basis of a majority or "quasi-majority" (the Member State who disagrees abstains), delays in decision taking of important matters persisted. As the enlargement of the Community on January 1, 1986 would only aggravate this situation, formal discontinuation of the "Luxembourg Agreement" was part of Senator Dooge's recommendation for simplified procedures, made to the Council of Ministers in March, 1985 (see final chapter).

The implementation phase

After COREPER completes the coordinating activities described above, there is one more important hurdle before the Council of Ministers will approve a directive. Article 189 of the Rome Treaty provides ". . . Directives will be binding, in respect of the results to be achieved, upon every Member State, but the form and manner of enforcing them shall be a matter for the national authorities . . ." In practice this means that not only must full agreement be obtained on the policy laid down in the directive, but there must also be agreement about the "form and manner" of enforcement.

Although Article 189 leaves the implementation of the directive to the governments of the Member States, there would be little point in agreeing on the content of a directive if at the same time there was uncertainty about its implementation. The proposed directive on Misleading and Unfair Advertising was a typical case in point. Its final approval by the Council of Ministers was held up because the UK had made it known that it could not accept some of the consequences of the directive, especially the methods of legal control. The voluntary control system for advertising in the UK was working well. The British Advertising Association expressed the prevailing viewpoint of many in the UK:

> . . . we feel that it is most important that the proposals made should respect Article 189 of the Treaty of Rome and should not attempt to override each Member State's right to settle in what form and by what means the agreed result is to be achieved. This principle is flouted by the proposal (AA, 1978).

It is in this respect instructive to refer to the 38th Report of the House of Lords Select Committee in the UK concerning the Draft Directive on Misleading and

Unfair Advertising. The Report contains the full text of all written and verbal statements made by the Department of Prices and Consumer Protection, the ASA, the AA, the National Consumer Council (NCC), the Incorporated Society of British Advertisers (ISBA), and others (House of Lords, 1978). For our purposes the salient points in the Select Committee's Report are in the final paragraphs in the Summary of Conclusions:

> (iv) The special court procedure provided for in the draft Directive should not be accepted, since it cannot be made to fit into the existing system of the United Kingdom, and makes an attempt to replace our existing method of preventing misleading advertising which is consonant with our current legal system and which, on the evidence, appears to be more efficient than those of other Member States.
>
> (v) The Committee, though they recognise that there are loopholes in the United Kingdom's self-regulatory system, are of the opinion that, in general, it is efficient and economical and that it would be unwise to set up alongside it the legal system called for by the Directive which might supplant the self-regulatory system, and not work as well.
>
> (vi) In view of the present state of evidence, and of the fact that contrary to Article 189 the draft Directive goes on to deal with the form and methods of achieving the results for which it provides, it seems to the Committee that the draft Directive does not fall within the powers conferred to the Community by Article 100 of the EEC Treaty (House of Lords, 1978:X).

Although the above point of view stems from one country only, it is typical of governments generally who are unwilling to change existing laws and regulations when the system seems to be working satisfactorily. However, once the Council approves a directive, governments are expected to make arrangements ensuring proper implementation of it within a certain time period, usually 18 to 24 months. Some Member States implement directives faster and more accurately than others, but concern is sometimes expressed that some countries will postpone implementation almost indefinitely. By way of illustration, the new Commission appointed in January, 1985 reported in one of its first documents that the UK, Ireland, Luxembourg and the Netherlands had almost completely fulfilled their obligations with regard to 17 directives (on cosmetics, textiles and the labelling of foodstuffs); Germany, Denmark and France were lagging behind but the matter was being put in order, Belgium, Greece and Italy had considerable backlog, with Italy even ignoring a decision of the Court of Justice which found this country at fault in 1982 for failure to incorporate the directive on cosmetics, which still has not been implemented.

> Generally speaking, the Commission notes that Member States tend to forward the implementing provisions late, with the result that it is obliged to initiate infringement proceedings for failure to notify. Most of the 47 infringements recorded come under this heading, for the Commission received only a few complaints for incorrect incorporation or inadequate application of the directives (Commission of the EC, 1985b:56).

The Court of Justice

The institutions of the EC include a Court of Justice which has its seat in Luxembourg. It is "composed of 13 judges appointed for six years by agreement among the governments" (Noël, 1981:3). The judges can be and frequently are reelected; they are assisted by six Advocates-General.

"The Court of Justice shall ensure the observance of law in the interpretation and application of this Treaty" (Rome Treaty, 1957:55).

The first cases that came before the Court were brought by the Commission against governments for infringement of the Treaty, but later governments or individuals brought action against decisions of the Commission. The Court also has an important function in giving clarification of the Treaty and guidance with regard to its implementation.

An official publication of the EC reports as follows:

> The European Court of Justice is faced with an increasing number of cases relating to the proper functioning of the internal market, including a number referred from national courts, and has made several judgements of great importance to the consumer. Among the most notable of these has been the Cassis de Dijon judgement, where the Court held that a product which could be legally traded in one member state could only be denied access to the market in another member state on genuine health or safety grounds; and the recent decision against Ford Motor Company of Germany, which upheld a Commission decision that challenged Ford's right to refuse to supply right-hand drive cars in certain European markets (*Europe 85*, 1985c).

Why problems and delays are normal

The decision-making process on draft directives is exceedingly lengthy, cumbersome and time consuming. Some people have no objections to delays, arguing that the longer decisions can be postponed, the better. They feel that unwise Commission proposals are thus permitted to sink into oblivion. Others say they would prefer quick decisions. On balance the business world feels it is better served by prolonged and productive arguments with the Commission, than by quick decisions which may not be in the best interests of either business or consumers.

Alastair Tempest, a director of the EAAA in Brussels, summarizes the basic reasons why it is difficult for the Commission to obtain Council approval and adoption of directives that relate to advertising:

> ... there are great national differences in the products and services which are banned or restricted; in the media which can carry advertising; and in the forms of advertising which are allowed. The way in which advertising content is controlled nationally depends upon traditions and customs which are based on entirely different precepts in each country. Transgressors may find themselves facing either civil or administrative law in some countries, or even criminal law with penal sanctions.

Apart from the body of law and case law that is to be found in all European states, some countries, like West Germany, concentrate marketing under competition laws, allowing consumers to take class actions to question disputed advertising claims. Under the postwar Federal constitution the freedom of information in Germany is absolute. Any product legally manufactured may be advertised, and exceptions can only be made with specially sought agreements (e.g. for cigarettes on television). Even the operations of the self-regulatory body (the Werberat) have to tread carefully through the minefield of anti-censorship and competitive laws (Tempest, 1984b:18).

After describing how the advertising self-regulatory system operates in the UK, Tempest continues:

It should also be noted that a substantial part of advertising falls outside the control system, whether legal or self-regulatory. Most countries do not permit control bodies to consider public service advertising, and of course that most misleading of all advertising, political messages, are sacrosanct!

These examples reflect fundamental structural differences in the legal and quasi-legal operations of the EEC countries which cannot be thrust aside without considerable political will on every side (Tempest, 1984b:18).

However, it is not surprising that efforts have been made to simplify the procedures and structure of the EEC and EC institutions. Such initiatives have been made not only to improve efficiency and speed, but also to achieve more quickly the EEC's ultimate objective of creating a united Europe. For example, in November, 1976 Mr. Leo Tindemans, then Belgian Prime-Minister, presented a report on the subject of European unity to the Summit Meeting in The Hague. He recommended the formation of a European Union and he proposed a series of measures to prepare for it; they included a common external policy, an economic and monetary union, and uniform European social and regional policies. Another recommendation was made by a Committee of "Wise Men," nominated in 1978 and chaired by Mr. Biesheuvel, past Commissioner and past Prime-Minister of the Netherlands; his Committee studied how the organizational structure could be simplified and how decision making could be accelerated and improved. The Committee recommended giving greater responsibility to COREPER and a more important role to the Commission. A more limited study was carried out by yet another Committee, consisting of five independent experts under the chairmanship of past Dutch Ambassador Spierenburg; this Committee concentrated entirely on the activities of the Commission, recommending that it be given greater authority and that its procedures should be streamlined (*Yearbook Winkler Prins Encyclopaedia*, 1980:105).

At the time, none of these recommendations were accepted. Thus, on balance it is clear that in the 1970s, despite the efforts of a number of prominent politicians, Europe was still far from united. The idealism of the founding fathers of the Community to build a politically and economically united Europe were far from realization. Gone were the days, when the Queen of the Netherlands would ask her Minister of Foreign Affairs, Mr. Joseph Luns, when he would expect that Holland would have to give up some of its sovereign rights (Luns, 1983). Instead, protection-ism and nationalism prevented the formation of a politically and economically unified Europe.

But there are some encouraging signs. In the mid-1980s renewed and serious efforts were made to achieve greater economic unity and to simplify the Community's complex procedures. These efforts will be further discussed in the final chapter, but if successful, the future of the Common Market and of Europe as a whole will be more promising.

Key perspectives

Many of the activities of the Commission in the early and mid-1970s seemed to set the stage for confrontation between business, consumerist groups and government. The first consumer protection program and the Draft Directive on Misleading and Unfair Advertising were prepared in response to criticisms of the functioning of the market economies of Europe. These proposed programs were based in part on bor-rowed ideas rather than on careful analysis of the European scene. To some they seemed politically motivated rather than seeking the genuine welfare of society. Both consumer groups and the advertising business felt that the other tended to do-minate the Commission.

The Commission's authority and structure are difficult to evaluate because they are so complex and they are influenced by so many pressures. The phases through which a directive must go from inception to implementation necessarily require the contribution of many. The process is lengthy and comprehensive, not only because of the several locations of the participating bodies, but especially because of their complex structure, policies and procedures. In spite of endeavors to bring about the necessary reforms, these facts are not likely to change very much in the foreseeable future.

The Preliminary Consumer and Information Program and the first Draft Directi-ve on Misleading and Unfair Advertising received little acceptance from the business community. Although members of the advertising business did not react strongly against the preliminary consumer program itself, their attitude changed when the draft directive appeared. It was felt to have overly ambitious objectives, to be biased against advertising, and to go beyond harmonizing existing legislation. As a writer for the Wall Street Journal said: "Any program of consumer interest legislation is bound to leave some group sputtering mad, but the Common Market seems to have done the impossible with its consumer program: it has offended just about every-one" (Kronholz, 1979).

The Commission's Directorate for Consumer Affairs had made an unfortunate start. But these events vitalized the advertising business, forcing it to reassess its role in the economic process and to evaluate its function in communicating with consumers throughout the markets of the Member States. Some members of the advertising community even called the Commission's activities a blessing in disguise.

Chapter III

Industry responds

"No men can act with effect who do not act in concert;
no men can act in concert who do not act with confidence;
no men can act with confidence who are not bound together
with common opinions, common affections and common interests."
Edmund Burke, English statesman and writer

In this chapter we will describe how industry reacted to the Commission's first consumer protection program and to the draft proposal for a directive on misleading advertising. The formulation of the European Advertising Tripartite (EAT) and other defensive measures will be discussed, followed by comments on the various phases of the misleading advertising directive. A Table is included, comparing the original draft, proposed, amended and final directive. We will also cover controversial issues in the field of advertising regulation and discuss advertisers' rights to promote legitimate products and services. We will comment on the effects of advertising regulation on the creative product and on the cost/benefit aspects of consumer protection. This will be followed by a comparison between advertising regulation in Europe and in the USA. The Commission's evolving attitude and the indirect effects of the Commission's activities on regulation of advertising in the Member States will conclude this chapter.

Introduction

Initially the business world did not react vigorously to the first proposals from the Commission. But when the serious nature of these proposals became more apparent, some in the business community and particularly the advertising business realized that action had to be taken. Yet, even then it was not easy to mobilize quickly the necessary forces for the defense of their interests. A number of conditions help to explain the somewhat relaxed business attitudes.

First, in the eyes of the senior management of most corporations, advertising is not the only or even the most important factor to successful operation of a business. It is more important to some companies and industries than to others, depending especially upon the percentage of sales that a corporation devotes to advertising. In exceptional cases advertising will amount to as much as 25% or more of a company's net sales revenue; in other instances it will be well under one percent. Manufacturers of consumer products with relatively high advertising-to-sales ratios are more concerned and involved in advertising regulatory matters than manufacturers of heavy industrial products who spend little on advertising.

Second, despite the early activities of the COE, the subject of advertising regulation on an international scale was new. There had of course been earlier efforts to develop international codes of a purely voluntary nature, such as the ICC Code of Advertising Practice. But the notion of harmonizing the existing legislation of Member States came as a surprise to the advertising business, and it took some time for the serious nature of this development to register.

Another reason for assuming a somewhat passive attitude was that some industry people found the first proposals from the Commission so unrealistic that they were not taken seriously. This was of course unwise because irrespective of the qualities of these proposals, they were the direct consequence of a political decision taken by the Heads of Governments in 1972. Thus it should have been clear that this matter would not suddenly disappear.

Joining forces

After the adoption of the preliminary consumer protection program in 1975, a number of representatives from business emerged to join forces and to develop a common strategy to meet the challenge. They comprise three categories:

(a) Purely *local companies* who did no business outside their own countries and to whom the Commission is relatively unknown and non-threatening. It would take a long time before the consequences of any EEC decisions would affect them, so as one could expect, with one or two exceptions these companies were not greatly interested in the business world's organized defense.

(b) *International companies or advertising agencies*, operating from their headquarters or through their offices or selling agents. Some took an immediate interest in these developments which could seriously affect their business, but most did not. Those who were serious about actions were mostly of European origin. They found it difficult to make American corporations operating in Europe understand the seriousness of the problems. To most American multinationals the Brussels beehive was a rather mysterious and inscrutable phenomenon, vaguely reminding them of their own FTC but fortunately not as near. Generally, the attitudes of both

European and American based companies, with a few exceptions, was that surely it would not be as bad as all that. But anyway, was this not something the trade associations should handle? And what about the advertising agencies — was this not really their responsibility? Thus most managements of these companies kept themselves reasonably well informed but left it to others to participate actively in these discussions.

However, it was quite another matter with a small number of European multinational advertising agencies and advertisers who regularly commited considerable expenditures to advertising. These few became very active, especially making senior executives available to monitor and represent them on all appropriate occasions. The executives made speeces at meetings and conferences and wrote magazine articles to defend the importance of free communication to the interests of business and consumers alike. They felt that if the Commission had paid more attention to their points of view the positive developments which eventually occurred could have been achieved much sooner, to the benefit of all parties concerned.

(c) The *international trade associations*, who knew from the start that advertisers, advertising agencies and the media eventually would expect them to take the lead in dealing with these problems. Supported by their members, as well as by national trade associations and executives of multinationals, these forces turned out to be quite strong, representing the total advertising business (advertisers, agencies and media) and doing everything possible to avoid a collapse of consumers' basic rights that were so aptly described in President Kennedy's message to the US Congress on March 15, 1962. We shall discuss the activities of the trade associations in more detail later, but at this point suffice it to say that the entire business world owes a great deal to the professionalism, loyalty, perseverance and sheer energy of this small force.

The International Chamber of Commerce

In Chapter I we mentioned the important impact the ICC Code of Advertising Practice had had on the development of national self-regulatory codes, even on government regulation and as a reference for court decisions. There were many forces at work in defense of the freedoms of the marketplace, but we should pay special tribute to the role of the ICC for its significant contribution.

The ICC was founded in 1919 in the USA and Europe by leading figures in the business world. Its initial objectives after World War I were to build an organization to establish contacts between the business community and governments in order to stimulate trade.

According to its Annual Report for 1984, the ICC is represented in 106 countries and territories. It has National Committees or Councils in 57 countries, and groups or direct members in 49 others. It claims 1,570 organization members and 5,281 individual members. The ICC has developed into the most important non-governmental, independent and global organization to represent the interests of international business, especially to defend private enterprise and the market system. It has a large number of separate Commissions on a variety of issues. Its Commission on Marketing, Advertising and Distribution, under the chairmanship of Unilever's Ken Fraser, is of particular importance to the advertising business.

The ICC has published an impressive list of special studies on marketing and advertising. Its 1937 Code of Advertising Practice has been thoroughly revised at regular intervals. It was extended in 1982 with special guidelines for advertising to children, a clear indication of the importance which business has long attached to achieving proper advertising standards through voluntary codes (ICC, 1983). The ICC has NGO status at the UN's ECOSOC and has had a most positive influence on the UN discussions of Consumer Protection Guidelines.

Although the ICC as a worldwide organization does not confine its activities to the EC, the advertising business in Europe sees this organization as an important ally in the defense of private enterprise and the freedoms of choice and speech.

Issues at stake

In the above mentioned "joining of forces," we include the ICC as one of the precursors of the small but potent industry group that responded to the need for action. This group perceived a number of threats to business and consumers which we now summarize to clarify the main reasons for industry's concerns, at both the national and the international levels. What issues were at stake and what tasks had to be accomplished to deal with them?

As the Commission's activities often are a reflection of developments in Member States, it is useful to describe a debate about advertising controls in one country in the early 1970s, which to our knowledge was representative of similar discussions taking place at about the same time in other countries. We have selected Norway for this purpose, first of all to illustrate that this debate was not confined to EEC countries, second, because Norway was at the time run by a social democratic government which had recently introduced an "Ombudsman" and third, because we have on record a public debate between representatives of the Norwegian government and private industry that took place in Dublin in June, 1973 on the occasion of the 23rd World Congress of the International Advertising Association (IAA).

The IAA had invited Mrs. Eva Kolstad, then Minister for Consumer Affairs in the Norwegian government to be the keynote speaker during a session called "Government Control and Free Enterprise – are they Compatible?" Other speakers presented the points of view of the advertising business.

In listening to Mrs. Kolstad's address, delivered at the conference in her absence by the Director-General of her department, Mr. Lars Oftedal Broch (who would later become Executive Director of the IOCU), one could clearly sense the direction in which government positions were moving. Mrs. Kolstad's presentation included a number of statements similar to the arguments we evaluated in Chapter I and which were to be used later by the Commission, for example:

> The balance existing previously in the market between seller and buyer is no longer working ... The number of product varieties is increasing all the time, making it more and more difficult for the consumer to form a well-founded opinion as to which products will best meet his requirements ... It has become increasingly evident ... that modern marketing methods have given a relatively much more powerful position for the seller than for the buyer because of their great potentialities to influence the buyer's choice ... Control of this choice process, and influencing it in a desired direction, means that the supreme power is transferred from the buyer to the controller ... It is a general opinion that the marketing process *must* seek to influence the consumers to buy ... If it were absolutely neutral and objective, its *raison d'être* would by and large disappear ... Today the consumers, through their purchasing, must pay for a marketing process which often weakens their own position in the market (Kolstad, 1973:1 – 6).

Mrs. Kolstad concluded:

> Where we ought to place the borderlines between what is regarded, on the one hand, as natural regulation and balancing of social interests and, on the other hand, 'governmental dry-nursing mentality,' *will depend to some extent upon one's political opinion.* Industry and trade on the one side and the Government on the other may have a tendency to be at variance with regard to where the control of marketing practices should be vested (italics added) (Kolstad, 1973:15).

Needless to say the industry speakers responding to Mrs. Kolstad's presentation challenged her statements vigorously. Madame Hélène Burollaud, then Chairman of the cosmetic house of Harriet Hubbard Ayer in Paris, said:

> What rather surprised me, when listening to the Minister's paper, was her apparent underlying lack of confidence in the consumer. Is the average consumer really so naive, uneducated, gullible, weak and ignorant of what he wants and what is good for him, that he has to be guided like an infant? (Burollaud, 1973:2).

Mr. Paul Griffin, then Vice-President of the advertising agency FCB International added:

> I find no evidence [in Mrs. Kolstad's paper] to show why the Norwegian Government, or any Government for that matter, has taken control of what can or can't be said in advertising. But let's face it. Governments are taking and have taken over. And I worry, because I don't think that Governments know what they are doing ... Instead of Government control, I believe we should do our own policing (Griffin, 1973:1 – 3).

Mr. Murray Evans, then the principal executive of an advertising agency in Australia, looked at the problem from a different point of view:

> Mrs. Kolstad ... is convinced that false and misleading advertising emanates mainly from major advertisers ... With this I fundamentally disagree because in my experience ... the most flagrant and repeated cases of misleading advertising and communication come *not* from long established, prestigious advertisers of products and services. It comes from individuals and many retail organizations selling and advertising such goods and services as real estate, appliances, furniture, second-hand motorcars and others (Evans, 1973:2).

Finally, Mr. Jimmy Williams, then Director-General of The Advertising Association in the UK pointed out that:

> The great advantages which successive governments have seen in self-regulation of advertising are speed of action in applying the sanction of non-publication by media, the quick adaptation or extension of the voluntary Code to cover new or dubious marketing practices, and the fact that no cost whatsoever falls on the poor over-burdened taxpayer ... To my mind, Norway has slammed the door on responsible associations of manufacturers and traders ... I would have thought that Mrs. Kolstad's legal chastity belt should have gone out with the medieval dark ages of the huckster and the trickster, but it is an anachronism in today's more enlightened era of marketing (Williams, 1973:3 – 4).

An important point of controversy in Mrs. Kolstad's presentation was the role of political opinion in determining the nature of advertising regulation. As a practical matter there is no doubt that political opinion is an important determinant. But legislators and regulators should pay attention not only to the political opinion that reflects the will of the people at the moment, but should also base their decisions on clearly reasoned business, economic and social principles that guide the will of the people in the long. It is unfortunate that public servants often stress immediate political opinion at the expense of the sound analysis that will prevail eventually. The main issue should be to determine what regulatory policies maximize the collective benefits to business, consumers and society – ideally it should be viewed more as a consumer issue than a political issue, and consequently advertising regulation should be based more on sound business, economic and social principles.

It is also of interest to note, that none of the speakers commented on the Ombudsman type of control as such. It is of course clear that its acceptance and effectiveness depends largely on the prevailing political climate and the personality of the person holding such an important office. In Norway the business community has criticized the Ombudsman for going too far, whereas consumer organizations have criticized the same Ombudsman for not going far enough. Whether advertising is controlled by an Ombudsman or by other administrative legal procedures will largely depend upon different cultures and levels of consumer sophistication in the countries concerned. What is good for one country need not be good for another. It is also important to note that in the Dublin debate the representatives of the business world attacked government controls per se, irrespective of the type of governmental control, while supporting industry self-regulation. Such debates were at the time taking place in practically all European countries.

In Brussels, this same kind of debate, with similar arguments and counter-arguments, was taking place at the international level. The initial outcome of this debate was laid down in the two documents that have been mentioned: the first consumer protection program and the draft of a proposed directive on misleading and unfair advertising. In the previous chapter we have already commented on the anti-advertising character of both documents. This bias was a serious concern for the advertising industry, especially because (contrary to the COE's Recommendations embodied in its Consumer Protection Charter) the Commission was in a position, through the Council of Ministers, to take action leading to binding decisions for all Member States. It appeared to be quite prepared to do so in this most difficult field of advertising.

In this connection it is also surprising how lightly the Commission talked about the existence of a "European Consumer;" this fact made the Commission's proposals for international consumer protection especially suspect and unrealistic in the eyes of the advertising business that knew only too well that there were many millions of consumers in Europe but only a very few "European consumers," whatever that term might mean.

One writer, in discussing obstacles to creating the Community's goal of free trade pointed out:

> The concept of a European consumer is largely an abstraction: the behavior of consumers in Europe is intricately — perhaps inviolable — connected with their countries of origin. Language differences, vastly divergent cultural and political organizations, the discrepancies in the various Member States' stages of economic and social development, not to mention long-standing prejudices and antipathies between the nations and peoples all directly and indirectly affect the nature of the consumer, and hence trade, in the EEC (Shaw and Grayson, 1980:3).

Since the concept of a European consumer was unrealistic, except for narrow market segments, the concept of harmonizing existing consumer laws in all Member States — of changing those laws without any other justification than to achieve European uniformity — is illogical. However, to remove trade barriers, to open up frontiers, to allow business to sell and to advertise a range of goods and services across national borders, in short to achieve one of the main objectives of the Rome Treaty, would of course necessitate that conditions for selling and advertising within the Common Market should be sufficiently similar to make it possible to achieve these goals. A delicate balance had to be struck between the needs of international trade to be able to operate successfully, and the sacrifices required from governments in making the minimum number of necessary changes in existing laws or control systems, to allow for and encourage the development of such international trade — a difficult task indeed for the Commission.

At the time the Commission had struck anything but a delicate balance to advance international trade. It had in the opinion of the business community gone far beyond the minimum requirements for harmonizing existing legislation, thereby restricting rather than enlarging opportunities to advertise products and services on a national and international scale.

Thus, the advertising business found itself in a position that at all levels it had to defend and explain the role of advertising in a market economy, the function it fulfilled in informing consumers, and the contribution it could make to growth and expansion. All this had to be done with regard to consumer groups, governments and intergovernmental bodies, convincing all parties at the same time that industry was capable, through codes of conduct and other self-regulatory controls, of avoiding harmful abuse in the marketplace.

To add to industry's discomfort, the entire subject had moved away from strict business considerations. It had become a political issue, and arguments which were perceived by many as practical and sound, did not impress an ideologically inclined audience.

Consequently, there was a compelling and urgent need to take a strong stand against what were believed to be serious threats against the future of the advertising business and what it stood for. In addition, and to avoid criticism in this respect, the advertising business should not only be seen as defending itself. It should at the same time revive and revitalize the positive case for advertising and make it known to the widest possible audience.

Against this background the advertising business had to prepare itself for action.

The advertising business prepares for action

Initially the number of advertising practitioners who became involved in the defence of the advertising business was very small indeed. They were a handful of people who had identified the danger signals and who had decided that action was required.

There was for example Nils Färnert, then Director-General of the EAAA, an organization whose members depended entirely upon the production and placing of advertising; their very existence was at stake if advertising were to be seriously curtailed. It is no wonder that the EAAA was very much alarmed. There was also James O'Connor, then head of the Institute of Practitioners in Advertising (IPA) in the UK, representing the interests of advertising agencies in that country, which was and remains one of the most advanced advertising centers in the world. O'Connor was painfully aware of the possible consequences for advertising in the UK and in the Community as a whole, if the Commission's consumer program were to be carried out to the letter. The IPA was a member of the EAAA which made mutual cooperation and consultation easy. The same comments applied to Roger Underhill, Director-General of the AA, representing the entire advertising business in the UK. Although the AA was not a member of the EAAA, Underhill was able to involve in the informal discussion other European countries, which had "umbrella"-organizations similar to the AA. He thereby widened the circle of people and organizations that could make a contribution to the common cause. Together with people like Dieter Schweickhardt, Director of the Gesellschaft Werbeagenturen (GWA) in Germany, and other so-called Senior Paid Officers (SPO's) of national advertising agency associations, a nucleus was formed whose objective it was to avoid governmental interference in matters concerning advertising reaching unacceptable proportions. Close cooperation with advertisers was sought and found: Paul de Win, Director-General of the IUAA, later renamed WFA, became an active participant in all discussions concerning the general principles affecting the advertising business. The support of advertisers was of course of decisive importance for success or failure of any joint action. While advertising is the only pillar on which the existence of advertising agencies rests, it is only one of many pillars supporting the business of advertisers; yet, without their support advertising agencies by themselves could do very little. Although the EAAA took many initiatives that were appreciated by the entire business world, it could only do so in close cooperation with the IUAA, representing advertisers. Fully realizing this, the presidents of the EAAA and the IUAA met in Londen on August 5, 1975 to discuss how to speed up mutual consultation and action (London Meeting, 1975). This meeting led the two organizations to formulate a joint point of view with regard to the proposed directive on misleading and unfair advertising. It also led the media to join the group. They were a little hesitant at first, but later took an active part in the discussions to arrive at common viewpoints concerning all aspects of advertising regulation.

It is thus of interest to remember that the action which was generated and the success which was ultimately achieved, largely go to the credit of a handful of committed people who decided that joint action was called for. It has remained like that ever since. Some of the names have changed and have been replaced by others, but the spirit of cooperation between a few professional and dedicated specialists, most of them running national and international advertising trade associations, still prevails and puts its stamp on all debates and discussions at which joint solutions are sought and found.

One would have expected that as a first priority and in accordance with the customs of the advertising business, a "brief" would have been written and an official action plan would have been drawn up. However, the issues were felt to be so straightforward and so self-explanatory, that such formality was not deemed necessary. Industry's stance was to be in defense of consumers' freedom of choice and the business community's freedom of speech as vital components of a market economy, coupled with effective and efficient controls of advertising based on codes and other voluntary agreements. The positive contribution of advertising to the market system was to be presented to relevant audiences at national and international levels.

The informal group mentioned above used its influence, individually and collectively to convince all concerned in the advertising process that uniformity of action would be required. Consequently, closer consultation and cooperation was sought. Each association using only its own arguments would have weakened the desired total impact on the Commission and others. The advertising business chose to speak with one voice at the international level, thus maximizing the strength of agreed arguments in the defense of its interests and indirectly those of consumers.

Formation of the European Advertising Tripartite

In the late 1960s and early 1970s, under the able and inspired leadership of John Hobson, the EAAA took many initiatives in the face of growing anxiety about the intentions of governmental and intergovernmental bodies in Europe. In 1975 Rein Rijkens succeeded Hobson in the chair of the EAAA. The years of his chairmanship were marked by a climax in proposals for international advertising regulation. But this period was also characterized by great cooperation between all international trade associations in the field of advertising.

In the late 1970s this "coalition" of associations became such an important force in discussions with international authorities, that the "European Advertising Tripartite" (EAT) was formed, unofficially representing the total advertising business in Europe. It followed the example of similar groupings at the national level, such as the AA in the UK and the Zentralausschusz der Werbewirtschaft (ZAW) in Germany that represented the interests of the total advertising business in their respective countries.

The EAT consisted initially of the following members:
(1) World Federation of Advertisers (WFA) – which until December, 1984 was called International Union of Advertisers' Associations (IUAA),
(2) European Association of Advertising Agencies (EAAA),
(3) Communauté des Associations d'Editeurs de Journaux de la CEE (CAEJ),
(4) Fédération des Associations d'Editeurs de Périodiques de la CEE (FAEP),
(5) European Group of Television Advertising (EGTA),
(6) Advertising Information Group (AIG).

The last mentioned partner, the AIG under Chairman Roger Underhill, operates not only within Member States but also maintains close contacts with advertising organizations in other European countries. In 1983 the outdoor advertising organization, the Fédération Européenne de la Publicité Extérieure (FEPE) joined the EAT. In April, 1985 the European Direct Marketing Association (EDMA) also became a member. In 1984 the IAA joined on an informal basis. The purpose of including so many groups was to widen the representative nature of the EAT. It was agreed that the EAT and its corporate membership would carry out all lobbying functions at European institutions; the IAA on the other hand would continue its work to promote understanding of advertising and to provide information to intergovernmental bodies outside Europe.

At this stage, a word of explanation about the IAA and its unique position in the world of advertising is in order. The IAA is the only worldwide organization that represents individuals and corporate members across the advertising business – advertisers, advertising agencies and media. It has Chapters in more than 45 nations, with about 3,000 individual and more than 50 corporate members. On the one hand the IAA defends advertising against attacks from governments and consumer groups; on the other hand it promotes high advertising standards, especially through its worldwide education programs. Since 1984, the IAA has NGO status at the UN's ECOSOC and at the UN's Education, Scientific and Cultural Organization (UNESCO). This organization is now taking an active interest in the education program of the IAA. Because of successful public service advertising conferences, held in Brussels in 1979 and 1983, the EC officially approved the appointment of the IAA to counsel on advertising. The IAA does this function in close cooperation with its sister organizations. The IAA also conducts studies and publishes a wide range of information on topics of interest to the advertising business.

The EAT has not confined its contacts only to EC institutions and to the COE. As it represents all aspects of the advertising business, it has established working relationships with bodies such as the ICC in Paris, the UNICE in Brussels and the European Broadcasting Union (EBU) in Geneva. It has become an influential body in discussions with these parties at the supranational level.

The EAT is not a formal body. It likes to describe itself as "an alliance for concerted action by advertisers, agencies and media on matters affecting the advertising business where their views on such matters coincide" (EAAA, 1984:3). While the role and contribution of each constituent member is significant, the initiators of this unique informal organization still form the nucleus for most activities. Advertisers and advertising agencies work hand in hand through their organizations, and of course in close cooperation with the other members of the EAT, to defend the interests of the entire advertising business and to help improve the quality of advertising and its regulation.

The "inactivity" of consumer organizations

It may come as a surprise that there still had been little dialogue between consumer leaders and the advertising business. This was not because business did not want such a dialogue. On the contrary, it was prepared to go out of its way to bring it about. The reason was that leaders of consumer organizations had shown little willingness to enter into a discussion with the representatives of what they considered to be the manipulators of consumers and their interests.

In the previous chapter when discussing the CCC we pointed out how difficult it has been (and still is) to come to meaningful and constructive discussions on subjects of mutual interest. There are a number of reasons for this problem.

With the exception of countries such as the UK and Holland, where the positive
contacts between the advertising business and consumer organizations are mostly of
a non-political nature, the rise of many consumer organizations happened at a time
when criticism of advertising attracted consumer advocates with motivations that
were not always devoid of political and selfish interests and therefore did not see
any personal advantages in dialogues with their main opponents. Roger Underhill,
Director-General of The Advertising Association in the UK, said in November, 1981:

> We in industry recognise the need for dialogue and applaud the intention. But it is going to be quite
> a challenge to make it happen.
>
> In many instances, organised consumerism is an end in itself. In some cases it is a business by
> which people earn money. If there is no conflict, or no battle to be fought and won, then those
> who set out to be the consumer's champion lose their jobs . . . But, whatever the problems, business
> interests must grasp this opportunity of dialogue with consumer bodies, and lean over backwards
> to make it work. In doing so we must take the legislature along with us, be it the British Govern-
> ment, European Commission or Council of Europe. Their influence for good or ill is too important
> for them to be allowed off the hook (Underhill, 1981b:59 – 61).

Another factor that undoubtedly inhibited the activities of consumer leaders is
that consumers are only marginally interested in advertising as such. Research has
confirmed time after time (see Chapter IV) that consumer priorities focus on more
important issues, such as looking after the family, bringing up children, earning a
living, etc. Thus consumer leaders receive little backing from those they seek to protect, and must depend instead on those few who approach consumer problems with
idealistic zeal. Since the leaders of consumer movements have no mandate from
large numbers of consumers, they often have only modest financial and human
resources and are ill-equipped to deal with well informed and experienced operators
in the field of consumer advertising. They often seem to shy away from direct confrontation with opponents who have greater knowledge and resources to enter into
dialogues and to debate the issues.

Let us elaborate. On November 15 – 16, 1983 at the "Zentrum für Europäische
Rechtspolitik," University of Bremen, Germany, a seminar was conducted at which
the subject of voluntary controls as an alternative for legislation, was discussed.
Many of the participants in this seminar were members of the European Consumer
Law Group (ECLG), an independent body consisting mostly of legal representatives
of consumer organizations and others who contribute a legal point of view on subjects of interest to consumer groups. The group had been formed in London in 1977.
Its main purposes were to strengthen the links between practitioners and researchers
in the field of consumer affairs, to coordinate research projects and to exchange experience. The group meets on a voluntary basis about twice a year and issues reports
on consumer subjects. The BEUC in Brussels furnishes the secretariat for the group.

The ECLG in 1983 reiterated the frequently expressed views of consumerists
about their problems:

The European Consumer Law Group is of the opinion that normally the bargaining power of consumer organisations is not sufficiently strong in order to be able to successfully conduct negotiations. This relative weakness of consumers' bargaining power has many reasons, e.g. the general character of consumer organisations, which are confronted with highly specialized sectors of trade and industry, the lack of money, manpower, resources and research facilities compared with professionals; and the small degree of organisation of the individual consumer who likes being protected but does not like to be an active member of a consumer organisation (ECLG, 1983a:217).

As already indicated, consumer organizations from different countries do not all hold the same attitudes toward the advertising business. As John Braun pointed out: "Denmark, the Netherlands, Belgium and France were in the forefront of consumer activism, with Germany and the UK being more moderate" (Braun, 1985). In the UK the Consumer Association, for example, has long been receptive to listening to the viewpoints of business.

Ironically consumer organizations and the advertising business have the same ultimate objective in mind – to serve consumers. There is little argument about this goal; there is only argument about its practical implementation.

It is regrettable therefore that the advertising business had to accept that while all concerned put the interests of consumers first, including the Commission, the reasons for doing so differed so much between industry, the advertising business, consumer organizations and the Commission that common plans to achieve the objectives were not possible.

Thus, the business world embarked upon a program of defending and explaining the role of advertising in the economy and society, taking the position that advertisers ought to have the freedom to operate without excessive restrictions, so that the market system throughout the Community could work effectively to preserve competition and to operate to the benefit of consumer and industry alike.

One of the first steps the advertising business took was to arrange for meetings with the Commissioner and his staff that were responsible for the implementation of the consumer protection program.

Meetings with the Commissioner for consumer affairs

When the first draft on misleading and unfair advertising was published in November, 1975 the informal group that preceded the formation of the EAT started meeting more frequently and also had its first encounters with the Commission. Such discussions initially took place with the Directorate for the Internal Market, where responsibilities for consumer protection resided. But, when a new Commission was appointed on January 1, 1977, Commissioner Richard Burke and Director-General Michel Carpentier became responsible for the development and implementation of consumer protection proposals. Mr. Carpentier had already been involved in consumer affairs under Commissioner Scarascia Mugnozza.

Richard Burke was genuinely sincere in his efforts to bring the parties together to reach agreements. He would listen attentively and formulate his thoughts carefully. He did not side with any of the parties, but instead emphasized his desire to bring about a proper balance between producers and consumers. He felt that producers were in a better position to make their case than consumer representatives, so he supported the CCC. However, in discussions with the advertising business he remained fair and objective. His term of office finished on January 1, 1981 when a new Commission was appointed with Gaston Thorn as its President. Commissioner Narjes from Germany became responsible for consumer affairs but he did not give this portfolio the same priority as his predecessor.

Director-General Michel Carpentier was a sharp, quick, intelligent Frenchman, whose ambition seemed to be to get as many directives approved as quickly as possible. He was an exacting man for his subordinates, but realistic and prepared to compromise as long as directives were completed regularly.

In January, 1977 the advertising business took an initiative which the Commission appreciated, and which helped to create better future relationships: the EAAA invited Richard Burke and his senior colleagues to an informal meeting in Brussels on April 18, 1977 (Brussels Meeting, 1977a). This meeting offered the advertising business and the relevant members of the Commission a good opportunity to get to know one another and to exchange views on the consumer program and the Draft Directive on Misleading and Unfair Advertising. It was the start of a relationship which, despite many conflicting interests, proved to be effective in the years to come.

A typical example of how the parties gradually grew together came at a meeting on February 24, 1978 when Commissioner Burke, Michel Carpentier and two of their senior advisors were invited to discuss informally not only the Draft Directive on Misleading and Unfair Advertising, but also a number of other important issues such as: (1) a then intended directive on tobacco advertising, (2) the problems regarding advertising and children, (3) research into consumer attitudes towards advertising, (4) a report on the industry's experience with methods of self-regulation, and (5) the need to agree on an early consultation procedure.

This impressive agenda illustrated the readiness of both the Commission and the advertising business to listen to each other's points of view, a particularly important attitude during these early days of Commission activities in the field of advertising. It was a positive development that would pay off in later years (Brussels Meeting, 1978).

Meeting with the President of the Commission

The EEC and its activities were not well known by the citizens of Member States, a situation that the advertising business felt to be to the detriment of accomplishing

EEC aims. Therefore it was decided to offer to help the Commission to improve its image and to increase public awareness of the EEC and its activities. Such help would at the same time be in line with the interests of the international business community and its desire to expand trade.

In his first address to the EP on January 11, 1977, Commission President Roy Jenkins had referred to "giving greater weight to the protection of the consumer," concluding his remarks as follows:

> We must never forget the size of the stakes. The value of justice for all, individual freedom and intellectual integrity, which were the norms of a civilised society, and to which can now happily be added a sense of social fairness, are now genuinely at risk. There are not many countries in the world which can be counted upon to sustain them. We represent about half that number. If our Community cannot be made to work, what can? If we, among the richest and certainly among the most favoured and talented of the populations of the globe, cannot learn to work together, what prospect is there for humanity? These are the stakes and these are the issues. Let us approach them with an awesome sense of responsibility, but also with a courageous and determined optimism (Jenkins, 1977).

Consequently the EAAA invited President Jenkins and his senior colleagues to a meeting, which took place in Brussels on June 13, 1977 (Brussels Meeting, 1977b). Although the consumer program and the Draft Directive on Misleading and Unfair Advertising were discussed, the emphasis was on the general objectives of the EEC and its image in the eyes of the public. The EAAA offered to try to help the Commission to achieve its objectives. In a note prepared for this meeting the EAAA stated: "Anything our Association can do, either directly or through indirect influence, to help the Commission in achieving its overall aims for a happier and more united Europe, will certainly be done" (EAAA, 1977b).

Mr. Jenkins was most appreciative. He agreed that communication experts could make a considerable contribution toward developing a better understanding of the EEC among the population of the Member States. He felt such understanding was very important, in view of the direct elections for a EP which would take place in 1979. There was mutual agreement that people should be made aware of the EC and what it meant to European citizens in their daily lives. Mr. Jenkins said he would discuss with his colleagues the help offered to the Commission and the advertising business would hear from him again soon on this matter.

Much to the advertising business's regret, it did not hear from Mr. Jenkins. The advertising business felt that the Commission's lack of interest in what really motivated the people of the Community was unfortunate. This situation continued to exist until the early 1980s when a closer relationship started to develop between the Commission and the advertising business on matters of general importance to the Community.

Disseminating the viewpoints of the advertising business

To alert advertising executives to the dangers threatening their businesses, activities were not confined only to the work of the trade associations, either directly or through the EAT. The subject of advertising regulation also appeared regularly on the agenda's of many industry meetings, conferences and workshops. For example, the publishers of *Advertising Age*, a prestigious and widely read US publication in the field of advertising, held four conferences: (1) in Amsterdam in November, 1976; (2) in London in November, 1977; (3) in Paris in November 1978; and (4) in Frankfurt in November 1979. Under the name of EurAm 1, EurAm 2, EurAm 3, and EurAm 4, these conferences were attended by a mixed European and American audience, and the first three of these conferences offered an interesting chronicle of Commission activity in the field of consumer protection.

EurAm 1's first session in 1976 was held under the title: "Need for Advertising in Today's Environment." The conference was opened jointly by the Chairman of the AAAA and the President of the EAAA. The latter addressed the recently introduced EEC proposals and the changing conditions in marketing and advertising in Europe, saying:

> We ourselves, the professional communicators, created today's consumers . . . more critical because less dependent, more discerning because better educated . . . It is a pity that there has not been a closer professional cooperation between consumer organizations and manufacturers . . . the activities of consumer organizations sometimes show a tendency to over-react, losing a sense of perspective and becoming a vehicle for the promotion of selfish, often political, interests . . . It may be a harsh thing to say, but governments are beginning to show contempt for the marketplace, contempt for business, contempt for the intelligence of the consumer, contempt for our free society . . . Clearly everything we can do to turn the activities of the Commission into a more positive contribution should be done (Rijkens, 1976).

At the next EurAm Conference, held in London in November, 1977 a session was devoted to the subject of "New Directions – Government and Public Policy," presented by a panel of which Commissioner Burke was a member, together with Miss Ann Burdus, then Research Director of McCann Erickson International in London and Mr. Keith Monk, then responsible for Nestlé's international advertising. Mr. Rein Rijkens chaired the panel.

Mr. Burke first gave an outline of the Commission's Consumer Program and then continued:

> Vast resources of expertise and finance are devoted to advertising and marketing . . . The result is that the consumer is faced with very sophisticated advertising and marketing operations . . . The average consumer is not in a position fully to appreciate the real meaning and value of what is being presented to him. Thus, the forces that work are unequal. It is this imbalance which leads public authorities to intervene. A further reason for intervention is that the consumer is faced with a growing number of products which can present unsuspected dangers to his health or to his environment (Burke, 1977a).

He continued by referring to existing codes, saying that "it is not our intention to substitute state control for regulation by industry, [but] in the final analysis, however, public authorities have a duty to provide a firm basis for standards and sanctions." He added: "I would go even further and say that it is neither fair nor reasonable to expect the industry alone to adopt and implement rules in an area which is of public importance" (Burke, 1977a).

The advertising business was upset by Commissioner Burke's uncompromising, almost arrogant tone. Neither in this speech, nor in any other speech or official document was evidence produced by the Commission to support its strongly worded statements. The advertising business repeatedly asked the Commission to produce convincing reasons why controls, as developed on a voluntary basis, would not work satisfactorily, but no reply was ever received.

Nevertheless, business continued its efforts to create a better dialogue with the Commission. After the Commissioner's presentation, an industry magazine in December, 1977 reported:

> Rein Rijkens ... said that a lot of progress had been made towards achieving a dialogue with the EEC Commissioner. His suggestion was that industry should make contributions to future directives, not try to ignore them in the hope that they might go away. 'An early consultation is essential for the efficiency of future directives,' he stressed (*Media International*, 1977:58)

Eventually these efforts paid off. In 1978 contacts between the Commission and the advertising business were fairly frequent. When EurAm 3 was organized in Paris in November, 1978 Mr. Burke was asked to give the opening address. It had been suggested that he should:

> present views and experiences of yourself and your colleagues regarding the consumer programme, future developments in this connection, your opinion about the cooperation between the business world and the Environment and Consumer Protection Service and − last but not least − drawing a parallel between the way in which the US and Europe are approaching the question of consumer protection (Rijkens, 1978a).

In his opening speech Mr. Burke referred to proposed or draft directives on: (1) misleading and unfair advertising, (2) labelling of domestic appliances and energy, (3) amendments to directives on unit pricing, and (4) doorstep sales and correspondence courses. He made the point that "the consumer movement is becoming increasingly aware of the role which it can and should play." With regard to results achieved Mr. Burke commented:

> It has been said that, in the three and a half years since its approval, our 1975 programme has not produced any results. Strictly speaking, this is true if we look at the legislative record. As with many simplifications, however, this statement misses the point. As Europeans present here will know, the Commission carries out what I would call exhaustive consultations with all the interested parties before finally approving proposals for Community legislation. This was the case, as many of you will know, with our proposal on misleading and unfair advertising.

> If we look at the record of proposals produced rather than legislation adopted, we will find that the degree of activity following the adoption of the 1975 programme has been very substantial indeed. This is all the more so when we consider the small numbers of staff involved in our consumer protection directorate and the considerable number of other areas in which they have to be involved (Burke, 1978a).

Talking about the Commission's contact with the business world, Mr. Burke stated that he was happy that much progress had been made and that his contacts "have taken on the character of extremely fruitful cooperation." On the subject of comparing US and European approaches to consumer policy, he said:

> In the US there is a Federal Government structure. It is fair to say that there is a constantly shifting balance between Federal and State Governments in a number of areas of public policies. Consumer policy is one of these. It seems to me, however, that there is a fairly clear idea as to which parts of consumer protection policy are properly within the competence of Federal Government and which parts can more effectively be carried out by the States.
>
> The situation in the European Community is rather different. We do not have a federal government. You will have inferred from some of my earlier remarks that we are still arguing about the balance between actions to be taken by the Community and those which are best carried out by the Member States. It is clear to us that there are some areas in which Community involvement is necessary in order to ensure the results we aim for. It is equally clear that there are some areas which are inappropriate for Community intervention. We still have quite some distance to go before we can say with any confidence that we have marked out the appropriate boundaries (Burke, 1978a).

Comparing Mr. Burke's 1978 EurAm speech with the one he had delivered in 1977, the industry sensed that Mr. Burke seemed to feel that since progress with the Commission's program had been disappointing, he hoped that a conciliatory approach to consumer organizations and to the advertising business would accelerate progress. As we will see later, a better dialogue between all parties concerned would be a prominent feature of the Second Consumer Program. But meanwhile the industry felt the realities of the situation were not as benign as Mr. Burke made them appear. There still seemed to be a considerable need for progress to close the gap between conciliatory speeches and the hard facts of Commission proposals.

Other actions

Conferences, meetings and workshops, were not the only means by which the industry could inform the Commission and a larger audience about its viewpoint on the issues. Those in the advertising business produced a stream of articles for national and international trade papers and magazines to draw the attention of their readers to the subject. For example, *Advertising Age* in the US carried articles by Rein Rijkens with the following headlines and points of view:

AD FORCES RALLY TO REPEL THEIR EEC CRITICS
Listening to US admen rant and rave about the increasing regulatory mood in Washington would make a European feel right at home, or at least at home in Brussels where the eurocrats of the European Community (EC) have turned their Berlaymont headquarters into a FTC-like fortress (Rijkens, 1978b).

MARKETERS AND ADMEN CHALLENGE DIRECTIVE
Industry believes the Commission should only seek harmonization of objectives and should allow flexibility when it comes to the means of achieving these objectives in the member states (Rijkens, 1978c).

TOUGH GLOBAL CHALLENGE CONFRONTS AD INDUSTRY
With advertising under attack in most Western countries, the time may well have come for agency associations in the US, Canada, Europe and others to combine forces to combat those at work against us (Rijkens, 1978d).

EUROPE ADMEN MUST DEFEND THEIR INDUSTRY
It is easier to play ostrich and hope the criticism will blow away or someone else will come to the rescue. But as most of us know, the threats don't fade. They, indeed, turn malignant if left unattended (Rijkens, 1979).

European publications such as *Campaign Europe* also carried articles. A typical example was a contribution by Phil Geier, then CEO of the Interpublic Group of Companies, who attacked excessive controls on advertising as follows:

I am deeply concerned about the effects of these controls on our business, on economies and on the democratic system. The reality of the marketplace is that the consumer wants to be told product advantages, and advertising is necessary to accomplish that. I would go one step further. What the consumer wants to know is what the manufacturer thinks his product's advantages are. Industry – any industry – puts new technology to work and responds to new consumer needs – but the manufacturer must be able to tell the consumer about those developments. Preventing that process does not spare the consumer from his own folly: it may keep him from the benefits of product improvements. Advertising is the vehicle for the consumer in his or her right to know. It cannot be withheld from selected legally manufactured and sold products, or a form of censorship results ... The people who really commune with the consumer are those whose products must be voted for over and over again – perhaps daily, weekly, monthly or at most every few years. Legislators do not commune with consumers but with voters.
   That's not the same. The feed-back loop for the manufacturer is short. That goes for the advertising agency, too. In the country of business, the consumer is king (Geier, 1978:30 – 31).

Last but not least, the following American corporations with interests in Europe were informed in detail on the program of the Commission and particularly of its Draft Directive on Misleading and Unfair Advertising. The President of the EAAA visited the top managements of these corporations in the US and encouraged them to draw the attention of their European managements to these developments and to instruct them to support the common efforts of the European advertising business as forcefully as possible.

Avis	Johnson & Johnson	Scott Paper
Avon	Kodak	Seagram's
B.A.T.*	Miles Laboratories	Sterling Drug
Bristol Meyers	Mobil Oil	Texaco
Caltex	Newsweek	Time Inc.
DuPont	PanAm	Union Carbide
Ford of Europe*	Pepsico	Wander
General Electric	Pfizer	Warner Lambert
Gillette	Polaroid	Wrigley
I.T. & T.	Quaker Oats	

* Visited in Europe.

The discussions with these corporations, the presentations during national and international conferences, and the publications in the many well known and widely read trade papers and magazines, led to an encouraging unanimity of opinion among those concerned with selling and advertising goods and services in Europe. It provided the support needed for the industry representatives on the frontline to be forceful and singleminded in handling problems in the name of the entire advertising world.

The positive case for advertising

While representatives of the advertising business participated in long arguments with the Commission, there were those who asked what the advertising business was doing to put the positive case for advertising to the world at large. They argued that it is not enough only to be against something. That attitude is too negative. They pointed out that the advertising business has little to be ashamed of, and therefore it should explain in a positive and convincing way the role of advertising in a market economy and its contribution to consumers' opportunity to select and choose. Others who were more complacent argued that the best way to present the case for advertising was simply to produce good advertising. They felt that little more should be done. While the merit of this argument cannot be denied, it was not good enough at a time when advertising came under severe attack from many different directions. Not only was advertising subjected to the continuous probing of consumerists, it also felt the direct consequences of the even greater demands of affluent consumers. It could not just sit back with an air of misplaced superiority.

So in addition to taking a stand against the restrictive nature of some of the Commission's proposals, the advertising business also revised its "Case for Advertising," to be presented to different and much larger audiences. However, efforts such as public exhibitions to explain to the public at large the importance and the techniques of advertising misfired. Few people were interested. It was quite a different matter when the IAA organized its first Public Service Conference in 1981 in Brussels, repeated with great success in October, 1983. The advertising business demonstrated on both occasions how advertising can help to solve society's problems such as forest fires, drug abuse and illiteracy. Campaigns were run in public media, produced and placed gratuitously by the advertising business. In the USA the Advertising Council had done this kind of advertising for many years. Now, through the initiative of the IAA this exemplary activity is also making progress in Europe.

In addition, the advertising business in many countries revamped their brochures on advertising and made them available to schools and universities, opinion leaders, civil servants, and to the public at large. Probably the best example of such a brochure is the one published in 1979 by the EAAA under the title "Ten Points of Public Concern About Advertising."

Conferences, meetings and workshops were also conducted to present the positive case for advertising. In the UK the AA led the way with a conference in 1970 entitled "A Positive Approach to Advertising in Society." The AA invited distinguished speakers from business, consumer associations and government to address the subject from their respective points of view (AA, 1970).

Advertising and the Vatican

Quite unexpected support came from the Vatican. The views of Pope Paul the Sixth on advertising received considerable publicity around the world. A party of 45 members of the EAAA visited Rome in April, 1976 and a small delegation was received in private audience. Pope Paul on this occasion made a statement about advertising, part of which was:

> You are not without merit in your efforts to try and reconcile what is often difficult: how to make the available products better known and more widely known in a convincing way to stimulate progress while respecting the value of goods and the truth in the elements submitted to the judgment of consumers.
>
> It is evident that one could not talk of progress if people were abused or, in spite of themselves, deceived by flattery or simply pushed towards desires, they could not or should not satisfy. Your responsibility is that much heavier when it is exercised towards unsophisticated peoples or when European agencies address countries in other continents which have other habits and other needs. We want rather to encourage all the members of your agencies to have a true sense of educational techniques which respect a universal ethic, so that advertising shall be neither misleading nor unfair. These are the things your profession should be proud of. We thank them for their efforts and bless them wholeheartedly (EAAA, 1976).

Directive on misleading and unfair advertising

"There is no more misleading advertising," said Raymond Haas in Paris (Haas, 1983b). "Certain people want to be misled because they are desperate," said Jeremy Bullmore in London (Bullmore, 1983).

Both statements contain an element of truth but shouldn't be taken literally. There is misleading advertising; there always will be. The UK's ASA reported that in May, 1985 "... Ten complaints about misleading advertising were ruled to be unfounded ... but forty one advertisers did manage to mislead their readers in one way or another" (ASA, 1985). Mail-order firms and local retailers are especially noticeable among those few who still sometimes sin against truthfulness in their advertising. While regrettable, it is on the other hand fortunate that there are not many cases of misleading advertising that harm consumers. Moreover the advertiser sometimes cannot foresee that certain messages will mislead consumers. All too frequently people who have problems can "read into" an advertisement a ray of hope or a possible solution to their predicament, which the advertisement does not claim. "The receiver of an ad is just as creative as the submitter," says Jeremy Bullmore; the receiver may mislead himself rather than being misled by the advertising.

Yet, back in the 1950s and 1960s there was advertising which, even in the context of then existing values and criteria, could be criticized on grounds of untruthfulness or gross exaggeration. Such abuses led to resistance among the buying public against forms of advertising which were thought to be tricks of manufacturers to convince consumers to buy products which would not live up to the claims made for them. This also led in 1973, as we have seen, to the COE's Consumer Protection Charter, which called on nations to

> ... take, in such manner as is compatible with their legal concepts, all measures necessary to introduce into their national legislation, comprehensive provisions ... which have the effect of prohibiting in any form or medium advertising which directly or indirectly is likely to mislead consumers of the advertiser's goods and services in such a way as to influence their decision to avail themselves of those goods and services ... (Greer and Thompson, 1985:25).

The Charter also recommended that "self-regulation by industry groups as well as cooperation between industry and consumer organizations be encouraged by the States" (Greer and Thompson, 1985:25).

Unfortunately, these excellent recommendations were soon overtaken by events; the first Draft Directive on Misleading and Unfair Advertising, which went considerably further than the Council of Europe's Charter, appeared in November 1975. It surprised the business community by its uncompromising character.

Let us at this point remind the reader that in principle, the advertising business is not against an approximation or harmonization of laws affecting the marketing and advertising of products and services throughout the Common Market, or for that matter throughout Europe as a whole. On the contrary, international trade and commerce will prosper if trade barriers are removed since the flow of products across borders is made easier by uniform conditions for the production, distribution and advertising of products in all markets.

No fewer than 20 "technical" directives, dealing with harmonization of laws in the Member States were approved between 1964 and 1974, prior to the introduction of the consumer program, and 39 of such directives were approved between 1975 and 1981 (Braun, 1981). These directives dealt primarily with easily definable factual subjects such as colouring substances, preservatives, fibre mixtures, dangerous substances and motor vehicles. There is little reason for business to complain or argue about them. On the contrary, they were a necessary job, well done.

But the subject became more complicated when the Commission left the realm of facts and relatively simple subject matter and moved into the world of moods, emotions, fantasy and imagination! This is a very real world just the same, a world in which people sometimes attach more importance to what they believe to be true than to what actually is.

In Chapter II we gave a brief introduction to the first draft directive, especially Article 4. Now we will look closely at the complete texts of the first draft, the Proposal for a Directive and the proposed amendments, which were the forerunners of the final Council Directive of September 10, 1984 (See Table III). This table is set up so that the reader can examine the full document by reading down each column so as to understand each document separately. The reader can also read across, by articles, to trace the evolution of principal features during the several stages of development.

We will also examine the Commission's Memoranda that accompanied the published documents. An explanatory "Memorandum" normally accompanies each stage of a proposed directive to give background and reasons why the directive is being proposed, to explain the present situation in individual Member States, to describe work undertaken in preparation for the directive, and to give a detailed explanation of each article in the directive.

The first draft

For this first draft of a directive in the field of advertising, the Commission prepared an unusually lengthy "Memorandum" (See Appendix II). The nature of what business could expect quickly became clear on the first page of this twenty page document. After refering to the important role which advertising had played in the development of modern European economies, it continued as follows:

> ... However, with the development of mass markets, modern advertising techniques, and the competitive drive within a society, there is a temptation for a producer of goods to base his advertising less on the inherent qualities, price, usefulness or differences of his product but on false or misleading information.
>
> This has important repercussions on the competitive character of the market. The consumer who is subjected to misleading advertising is prevented from making the right consumer choice and the producer who employs such methods acquires an unfair advantage over his competitors.
>
> The essential needs of a society are not well served by such distortion of the truth of competition and it is therefore essential to regulate such abuses (Appendix II, p.274).

Table III
Comparison between first draft – proposed directive – amendments – final version of misleading advertising directive*

First preliminary draft directive November, 1975	Proposal for a Council directive 1 March, 1978

<table>
<tr><td align="center">ARTICLE 1</td><td align="center">ARTICLE 1</td></tr>
</table>

ARTICLE 1

Member States shall adopt the measures necessary to prohibit misleading and unfair advertising.

ARTICLE 1

The objective of this Directive is to protect consumers, persons carrying on a trade, business or profession, and the interests of the public in general against unfair and misleading advertising.

ARTICLE 2

1. 'Advertising' means any communication of a commercial or professional character, which is made through any medium about goods or services, or about the supply of goods and services, offered to the public or any part thereof.
2. 'Goods' includes all property, real or personal, and any rights therein, and any other rights, licenses or franchises provided for consideration.
3. 'Services' includes facilities provided for consideration, whether by way of entertainment or otherwise.
4. 'Medium' includes publications, broadcasts by television, radio or other means, leaflets, posters, points of sale material, window display, direct mail material, records, tapes and models.

ARTICLE 2

For the purpose of this Directive:
– 'Advertising' means the making of any pronouncement in the course of a trade, business or profession for the purpose of promoting the supply of goods or services.
– 'Misleading advertising' means any advertising which is entirely or partially false or which, having regard to its total effect, including its presentation, misleads or is likely to mislead persons addressed or reached thereby, unless it could not reasonably be foreseen that these persons would be reached thereby.
– 'Unfair advertising' means any advertising which:
    (a) casts discredit on another person by improper reference to his nationality, origin, private life or good name; or
    (b) injures or is likely to injure the commercial reputation of another person by false statements or defamatory comments concerning his firm, goods or services; or
    (c) appeals to sentiments of fear, or promotes social or religious discrimination; or
    (d) clearly infringes the principle of the social, economic and cultural equality of the sexes; or
    (e) exploits the trust, credulity or lack of experience of a consumer, or influences or is likely to influence a consumer or the public in general in any other improper manner.
– 'Goods' means property of any kind, whether movable or immovable, and any rights or obligations relating to property.

* The Commission's comments are included in its explanatory memoranda in the Appendices.

Amendment to proposal for Council directive 10 July, 1979	Council directive 10 September, 1984

ARTICLE 1

Unchanged.

ARTICLE 1

The purpose of this Directive is to protect consumers, persons carrying on a trade or business, persons carrying on a trade or business or practising a craft or profession and the interests of the public in general against misleading advertising and the unfair consequences thereof.

ARTICLE 2

For the purpose of this Directive:
- 'Advertising' means the making of a representation in any form in the course of a trade, business or profession for the purpose of promoting the supply of goods and services.

Unchanged.

- 'Unfair advertising' means any advertising which:
    (a) casts discredit on another person by reference to his nationality, origin, private life or good name; or
    (b) unchanged;
    (c) abuses or unjustifiably arouses sentiments of fear; or
    (d) promotes discrimination on grounds of sex, race or religion; or
    (e) abuses the trust, credulity or lack of experience of a consumer, or influences or is likely to influence a consumer or the public in general in any improper manner;

- Unchanged.

ARTICLE 2

For the purpose of this Directive:
1. 'advertising' means the making of a representation in any form in connection with a trade, business, craft or profession in order to promote the supply of goods and services, including immovable property, rights and obligations;
2. 'misleading advertising' means any advertising which in any way, including its presentation, deceives or is likely to deceive the persons to whom it is addressed or whom it reaches and which, by reason of its deceptive nature, is likely to affect their economic behaviour or which, for those reasons, injures or is likely to injure a competitor;
3. 'person' means any natural or legal person.

Table III (continued)

First preliminary draft directive November, 1975	Proposal for a Council directive 1 March, 1978

ARTICLE 3

1. 'Misleading advertising' means any advertising, whether in specific or general terms, which by one of the means specified in Article 4 or otherwise or by omission and on a reasonable understanding thereof, misleads or is likely to mislead persons about the goods or services advertised, or in particular about:

   (a) the characteristics of the goods and services, such as the nature, composition, method and date of manufacture or provision, fitness for purpose, range of use, quantity, extent, geographical or commercial origin, and the results to be obtained from use;

   (b) the conditions of sale, lease, or provisions of the goods or services, such as the value and final price, the conditions of delivery of the goods or provision of the services and the conditions of guarantee;

   (c) the status, nature, qualifications and rights of the advertiser, such as the ownership of intellectual property rights, the identity, capabilities or solvency of the advertiser and the awards and distinctions of the advertiser.

ARTICLE 3

1. In determining whether advertising is misleading or unfair, pronouncements shall be taken into consideration concerning in particular:

   (a) the characteristics of the goods or services, such as nature, performance, composition, method and date of manufacture or provision, fitness for purpose, usability, quantity, quality, geographical and commercial origin, properties and the results to be expected from use:

   (b) the condition of supply of the goods or services, such as value and price, conditions of contract and of guarantee;

   (c) the nature, attributes and rights of the advertiser, such as his identity, solvency, abilities, ownership of intellectual property rights or awards and distinctions.

2. Advertising shall in particular be regarded as misleading when it omits material information, and, by reason of that omission, gives a false impression or arouses expectations which the advertiser cannot satisfy.

ARTICLE 4

The means referred to in Article 3 shall include:

(a) a claim that is false; or

(b) a claim that contains insufficient information; or

(c) a claim that is partially true and partially false; or

(d) a claim that is true but creates a false implication; or

(e) a claim that is true but is falsely proved to be true; or

(f) a claim that is not adequately substantiated; or

(g) a claim that cannot be objectively disproved but makes offers unlikely to be capable of fulfilment.

ARTICLE 4

Comparative advertising shall be alowed, as long as it compares material and verifiable details and is neither misleading nor unfair.

Amendment to proposal for Council directive 10 July, 1979	Council directive 10 September, 1984

ARTICLE 3

1. In determining whether advertising is misleading or unfair, representations shall be taken into consideration concerning in particular:

   (a) unchanged;

   (b) unchanged;

   (c) unchanged.

2. Advertising shall in particular be regarded as misleading when it is not readily recognizable as an advertisement or when it omits material information, and, by reason of that omission, gives a false impression or arouses reasonable expectations which the advertised goods or services cannot satisfy.

ARTICLE 4

(In its Explanatory Memorandum to the proposed Amendment, the Commission stated:

"This Article concerns comparative advertising, which the Economic & Social Committee requests should be authorised for a trial period. It is not proposed to adopt this request. Comparative advertising is already legal in a number of Member States. The question of authorisation only for Member States which do not recognise comparative advertising as legal would be inappropriate in a Directive for the approximation of laws.")

ARTICLE 3

In determining whether advertising is misleading, account shall be taken of all its features, and in particular of any information it contains concerning:

(a) the characteristics of goods or services, such as their availability, nature, execution, composition, method and date of manufacture or provision, fitness for purpose, uses, quantity, specification, geographical or commercial origin or the results to be expected from their use, or the results and material features of tests or checks carried out on the goods or services;

(b) the price or the manner in which the price is calculated, and the conditions on which the goods are supplied or the services provided;

(c) the nature, attributes and rights of the advertiser, such as his identity and assets, his qualifications and ownership of industrial, commercial or intellectual property rights or his awards and distinctions.

Table III (continued)

First preliminary draft directive November, 1975	Proposal for a Council directive 1 March, 1978

ARTICLE 5

1. 'Unfair advertising' includes advertising which:
    - (a) (i) without justifiable reason plays on fear; or
        - (ii) plays on superstition; or
        - (iii) contains anything which might lead to or lend support to acts of violence or crime; or
    - (b) without prior permission
        - (i) portrays or refers to any persons in a private or public capacity; or
        - (ii) depicts or refers to any person's property in a way likely to convey the impression of a personal endorsement; or
    - (c) is so presented that it is not readily recognised as an advertisment; or
    - (d) motivates specially vulnerable groups to engage in conduct deleterious to themselves or to others.
2. Unfair advertising also includes denigratory advertising which, whether true or false, casts discredit on the commercial reputation of any other person
    - (a) by unfairly discrediting his firm, the goods he produces or the services he provides; or
    - (b) by any other unfair means; or
    - (c) by making personal attacks concerning in particular his family origin or nationality.

ARTICLE 6

1. 'Comparative advertising' means any advertising which draws a comparison between the goods, services, reputation or character of the advertiser and the goods, services, reputation or character of any other person.
2. 'Comparative advertising' shall be prohibited
    - (a) where it constitutes 'misleading advertising' within the meaning of Article 3 of this directive; or
    - (b) even where it does not constitute 'misleading advertising' within the meaning of the said article; in all cases where it is based on facts which are unfairly selected.

ARTICLE 5

Member States shall adopt adequate and effective laws against misleading and unfair advertising.

Such laws shall provide persons affected by misleading or unfair advertising, as well as associations with a legitimate interest in the matter, with quick, effective and inexpensive facilities for initiating appropriate legal proceedings against misleading and unfair advertising.

Member States shall in particular ensure that:
- the courts are enabled, even without proof of fault or of actual prejudices:
    - (a) to order the prohibition or cessation of misleading and unfair advertising; and
    - (b) to take such a decision under an accelerated procedure, with an interim or final effect;
- the courts are enabled:
    - (a) to require a publication of corrective statement; and
    - (b) to require publication of their decision either in full or in part and in such form as they may judge adequate;
- the sanctions for infringing these laws are a sufficient deterrent, and, where appropriate, take into account the financial outlay on the advertising, the extent of the damage and any profit resulting from the advertising.

ARTICLE 6

Where the advertiser makes a factual claim, the burden of proof that his claim is correct shall lie with him.

Amendment to proposal for Council directive 10 July, 1979

Council directive 10 September, 1984

ARTICLE 5

Member States shall adopt adequate and effective laws against misleading and unfair advertising.

Such laws shall provide persons affected by misleading or unfair advertising as well as associations with a legitimate interest in the matter, with quick, effective and inexpensive facilities for either:

(a) initiating appropriate legal proceedings against misleading or unfair advertising; or

(b) bringing the matter before an administrative authority with adequate powers.

Member States shall in particular ensure that

- the courts or the administrative authority, as appropriate, are enabled, even without proof of intention or negligence or of actual prejudice:

  (a) to order the prohibition or cessation of misleading or unfair advertising; and

  (b) to take such a decision under an accelerated procedure, with an interim or final effect;

- the courts, or the administrative authority, as appropriate, are enabled

  (a) to require publication of a corrective statement; and

  (b) to require publication of their decision either in full or in part and in such form as they may judge adequate.

Member States shall ensure that the consequences of infringing laws and decisions in the field of misleading and unfair advertising take into account the extent of the harm.

Where the above mentioned powers are entrusted to an administrative authority, the authority shall not be controlled by advertising interests, shall be obliged to give reasons for its decisions, and shall be under a duty to exercise its powers so as effectively to control misleading and unfair advertising; and procedures shall exist whereby improper exercise by the authority of its power or improper failure by the authority to exercise its powers or to apply reasonable standards can be reviewed by the courts at the request of the parties.

ARTICLE 4

1. Member States shall ensure that adequate and effective means exist for the control of misleading advertising in the interests of consumers as well as competitors and the general public. Such means shall include legal provisions under which persons or organizations regarded under national law as having a legitimate interest in prohibiting misleading advertising may:

   (a) take legal action against such advertising; and/or

   (b) bring such advertising before an administrative authority competent either to decide on complaints or to initiate appropriate legal proceedings.

   It shall be for each Member State to decide which of these facilities shall be available and whether to enable the courts or administrative authorities to require prior recourse to other established means of dealing with complaints including those referred to in Article 5.

2. Under the legal provisions referred to in paragraph 1, Member States shall confer upon the courts or administrative authorities powers enabling them, in cases where they deem such measures to be necessary taking into account all the interests involved and in particular the public interest:

   - to order the cessation of, or to institute appropriate legal proceedings for an order for the cessation of, misleading advertising, or

   - if misleading advertising has not yet been published but publication is imminent, to order the prohibition of, or to institute appropriate legal proceedings for an order for the prohibition of, such publication,

   even without proof of actual loss or damage or of intention or negligence on the part of the advertiser.

   Member States shall also make provision for the measures referred to in the first subparagraph to be taken under an accelerated procedure:

   - either with interim effect, or

   - with definitive effect,

Table III (continued)

First preliminary draft directive November, 1975	Proposal for a Council directive 1 March, 1978

ARTICLE 7

Member States shall adopt the measures necessary:

(a) to provide adequate civil and criminal remedies for persons injured by misleading or unfair advertising and against persons responsible for that injury whether advertisers, advertising agents or persons in control of the advertising media;

(b) to confer on persons injured or aggrieved by a breach of the prohibition of misleading or unfair advertising and on any other persons representing the state, a public authority, a consumers association, or a trade association, the right to initiate the penal and civil proceedings flowing from (a) above;

(c) to confer on persons injured or aggrieved by a breach of the prohibition of misleading or unfair advertising and on any other persons representing the state, a public authority, a consumers association, or a trade association the right to initiate proceedings for an injunction on the sole proof that it is likely the public will be misled, and without proof of negligence or intention on the part of the defendant;

(d) to confer on persons injured or aggrieved by a breach of the prohibition of misleading or unfair advertising and on any other persons representing the state, a public authority, a consumers association or a trade association the right to apply for a correction or apology to be made by those responsible for the breach of the above mentioned prohibition.

ARTICLE 7

Where a Member State permits the operation of controls by self-regulatory bodies for the purpose of counteracting misleading or unfair advertising, or recognizes such controls, persons or associations having a right to take legal proceedings under Article 5 shall have both that right and the right to refer the matter to such self-regulatory bodies.

Amendment to proposal for Council directive 10 July, 1979	Council directive 10 September, 1984

on the understanding that it is for each Member State to decide which of the two options to select. Furthermore, Member States may confer upon the courts or administrative authorities powers enabling them, with a view to eliminating the continuing effects of misleading advertising the cessation of which has been ordered by a final decision:

— to require publication of that decision in full or in part and in such form as they deem adequate,

— To require in addition the publication of a corrective statement.

3. The administrative authorities referred to in paragraph 1 must:

(a) be composed so as not to cast doubt on their impartiality;

(b) have adequate powers, where they decide on complaints, to monitor and enforce the observance of their decisions effectively;

(e) normally give reasons for their decisions.

Where the powers referred to in paragraph 2 are exercised exclusively by an administrative authority, reasons for its decisions shall always be given. Furthermore in this case, provision must be made for procedures whereby improper or unreasonable exercise of its powers by the administrative author ity or improper or unreasonable failure to exercise the said powers can be the subject of judicial review.

ARTICLE 6
(See left Article 7)
Unchanged.

ARTICLE 5
This Directive does not exclude the voluntary control of misleading advertising by self-regulatory bodies and recourse to such bodies by the persons or organizations referred to in Article 4 if proceedings before such bodies are in addition to the court or adminsitrative proceedings referred to in that Article.

Table III (continued)

First preliminary draft directive November, 1975	Proposal for a Council directive 1 March, 1978

ARTICLE 8

Nothing in this Directive shall be taken to mean that self-disciplinary controls on misleading or unfair advertising shall necessarily be excluded from the means employed by Member States to implement this Directive: provided, however, that where Member States permit the operation of voluntary controls, persons on whom a right of action is intended to be conferred by virtue of Article 7 shall, in such ways as Member States consider appropriate, be entitled to exercise that right as an alternative to self-disciplinary control and by way of appeal from a decision reached by the self-disciplinary system.

ARTICLE 8

The present Directive does not prevent Member States taking or maintaining other measures for the protection of consumers against misleading or unfair advertising to the extent that these measures are in conformity with the Treaty.

ARTICLE 9

Member States shall bring into force the measures necessary to comply with this Directive within twelve months of its notification and shall forthwith inform the Commission thereof.

ARTICLE 9

Member States shall bring into force the measures necessary to comply with this Directive within 18 months of its notification and shall forthwith inform the Commission thereof.

Member States shall communicate to the Commission the text of the main provisions of national law which they adopt in the field covered by this Directive.

ARTICLE 10

Member States shall communicate to the Commission the text of the main provisions of national law which they adopt in the field covered by this Directive.

ARTICLE 11

This Directive is addressed to the Member States.

ARTICLE 10

This Directive is addressed to the Member States.

Amendment to proposal for Council directive 10 July, 1979	Council directive 10 September, 1984
ARTICLE 7 Where the advertiser makes a factual claim, the burden of proof that his claim is correct shall in civil and administrative proceedings lie with him.	**ARTICLE 6** Member States shall confer upon the courts or administrative authorities powers enabling them in the civil or administrative proceedings provided for in Article 4: (a) to require the advertiser to furnish evidence as to the accuracy of factual claims in advertising if, taking into account the legitimate interests of the advertiser and any other party to the proceedings, such a requirement appears appropriate; (b) to consider factual claims as inaccurate if the evidence demanded in accordance with (a) is not furnished or is deemed insufficient by the court or administrative authority.
ARTICLE 8 Unchanged.	**ARTICLE 7** This Directive shall not preclude Member States from retaining or adopting provisions with a view to ensuring more extensive protection for consumers, persons carrying on trade, business, craft or profession, and the general public.
ARTICLE 9 Member States shall bring into force the measures necessary to comply with this Directive within 24 months of its notification and shall forthwith inform the Commission thereof. Member States shall communicate to the Commission the text of all provisions of national law which they adopt in the field covered by this Directive.	**ARTICLE 8** Member States shall bring into force the measures necessary to comply with this Directive by 1 October 1986 at the latest. They shall forthwith inform the Commission thereof. Member States shall communicate to the Commission the text of all provisions of national law which they adopt in the field covered by this Directive.
	ARTICLE 9 This Directive is addressed to the Member States.

The advertising business felt the statement in the first paragraph to be outrageous; it was unsupported by evidence and it was manifestly incorrect. The above paragraphs also underlined the conceptual problem the Commission was facing, illustrated by the title of the Memorandum: "Memorandum on approximation of the laws of Member States on fair competition – Misleading and Unfair Advertising." It is difficult to combine the promotion of "fair competition" with the "protection of consumers against unfair advertising," since "fair competition" implies protecting competitors, which is not necessarily the same as protecting consumers (see also Chapter I). At a later date when the responsibilities for consumer protection became part of a separate Directorate-General, this strange situation would be corrected by focusing on consumer protection only. However, the 1975 Memorandum combined the two concepts and frequently refered to the rules of unfair competition within the Member States, based upon studies ordered by the Commission in the mid-1960s "to ascertain the differences between national rules on fair competition liable to affect the development of the Common Market and to find precisely what disadvantages resulted from the divergence in legislation" (Appendix II, p.280).

Consequently, the Commission's Memorandum went to great lengths to explain why common rules about advertising – especially misleading advertising – would be essential for a proper functioning of the Common Market. Having stated how advertising campaigns are "increasingly planned outside a national context," the Commission continued:

> The adoption of common rules on advertising will reduce distortions of competition which the differences in national rules at present bring about.
> These distortions arise because an advertiser in country A will be able to use his campaign in another state B with similar rules. But an advertiser in country C will not if the rules in country C are substantially different from those in B. The advertiser in country A will have an advantage over the advertiser in C who will have to invest in more than one advertising campaign if he is to advertise successfully abroad.
> It is true that conditions (cultural, linguistic, etc.) in B may dictate a different kind of advertising campaign from the kind which would be appropriate in A; but here again our premise has been that in fact there is a great deal of scope for common advertising campaigns. This is borne out by the actual increase in such campaigns and the general increase in interstate trading.
> ... Distortions of competition also arise however from the failure to regulate misleading advertising at all or the present inadequacies in such regulations. Deception of the consumer will in all probability lead him to make the wrong choice in his purchase of a particular product; and the producer who employs deception acquires an unfair advantage over his competitors who may be producing better quality goods. The distributive function of advertising is distorted and the proper functioning of the market is upset (Appendix II, p.277-8).

The business world was upset about the entire Memorandum but felt particularly unhappy about the Commission's views as quoted above, which were considered artificial and lacking understanding of advertising. It also seemed incorrect and improper to assume that misleading advertising was frequently and widely used by advertisers to give them an unfair advantage over others, thus distorting competition and upsetting the proper functioning of the Common Market.

The Commission was also wrongly informed about the number of advertisers employing similar advertising in several countries. This number was small and most advertisers still used country-by-country advertising for their international brands. There were many international advertisers but there was little international advertising. It was not until the late seventies and early eighties that increasing numbers of advertisers seeking economies of scale became convinced that much advertising could in fact be used on an international scale.

The Memorandum also assumed that increasing numbers of advertisers using uniform advertising in several countries, would be more successful and would have a competitive edge over others using advertising on a national basis. This assumption was incorrect. Greater effectiveness of international advertising versus locally produced advertising is difficult to prove and the debate about the greater effectiveness of the one or the other, is as topical and controversial today as it was in 1975 or 1965. The Commission's view that there was a need for uniform controls on "uniform" advertising throughout the EEC was an idea whose time had not yet come.

Most importantly however, as the Commission did not produce any evidence to give a qualitative or quantitative indication of the frequency of misleading advertising in Member States, the justification for the introduction of the directive was unclear. It gave the impression that the Commission was using a sledge-hammer to crack a nut.

The advertising business responds

Following the appointment by the Commission of a Working Party of Government Experts, which in 1972 decided that misleading advertising represented a topic which should be given priority, the EAAA produced in June, 1973 a Memorandum on the subject of "Misleading Advertising: Harmonisation or Legislation." It contained a presentiment of things to come:

> In the new social conditions in Europe, the practice of advertising, like the practice of so many other things, is gradually evolving. Consumerist pressures of the right kind − the kind that is really based on consumer interests as opposed to intellectual or political motivation − are accepted by the advertising profession as valuable, and there should be no need for antagonism between the profession and this kind of consumerism. What the business is anxious to avoid is sudden imposition of new, untried, and often unsound, restrictions on the traditional operation of honest advertising, proceeding from some external and often elitist preconception of consumer interests.
>
> We believe this concept of gradual healthy evolution will best be served by ensuring that the local attitudes to, and practices of, advertising should be left to develop without any attempt to force them into a rigid harmonised pattern of procedures (EAAA, 1973b:9).

The presentiment turned out to be correct, so when the first Draft Directive on Misleading and Unfair Advertising appeared, this prompted advertisers and advertising agencies to draw more closely together. Their international trade associations, the IUAA and the EAAA, produced a joint reply in April, 1976 (see Appendix III). The main points in this reply were:

(1)   The draft and related documents contained little or no evidence for the criticisms of advertising.

(2)   "... the effect of the detailed provisions of the Directive , if it became law in each country, would almost certainly be to raise doubts about almost any advertising."

(3)   Regarding Article 4: "We have strong objections against this article" and "... In our view [it] should be omitted."

(4)   While the Commission had repeatedly said that it would only propose "minimum rules" the proposed rules "represent a considerable sharpening of the legislation about advertising as it now exists in the Community as a whole."

(5)   The Commission should avoid detailed harmonizing legislation, since the occasions when identical advertising campaigns would cover all countries were few.

(6)   Self-regulatory controls would be perfectly adequate and should receive more support.

(7)   Legal measures of enforcement should be left to Member States.

(8)   Defining misleading advertising in terms of what was omitted could create serious difficulties for virtually all advertising.

(9)   Under certain conditions, comparative advertising should be allowed.

(10) Corrective advertising was rejected emphatically.

The concept of misleading advertising had been prominent in earlier discussions and documents in the early 1970s, and it was to be expected that the advertising business would focus on this continuing issue rather than on the relatively less familiar concept of unfair advertising. Thus little was said about unfair advertising in the reply. In spite of the fact that the concept of unfairness was an important part of competition policy in most European countries, many tended to see the unfairness issue as relatively unimportant and did not make a clear distinction between "misleading" and "unfair." However, it is interesting to note that the issue of unfair advertising soon received as much negative comment in the UK as the issue of misleading advertising (Select Committee, 1978 and 1979).

John Braun explains in a letter to one of the authors: "The concept of unfair advertising was ... one that had to be developed as it had not appeared before in concrete terms. Carpentier insisted that such a concept had to be introduced and it was very much a French ... concept" (Braun, 1985). Braun added that the idea may also have come from a paper by Dorothy Cohen presented at the "First Workshop on Consumer Action Research, held by the International Institute of Management in Berlin in October, 1974" (Braun, 1985).

It should be noted also that the advertising business was not the only source of objections to the first draft, or to the proposed directive and proposed amendments. The UK government sustained objections throughout, "... pressed consistently by the advertising business supported by commerce and industry. As the self-regulatory aspect was only a minor one in all countries other than the UK, the main weight of opposition to the directive fell on its other two constituent parts, misleading and unfair advertising" (Braun, 1985).

With hindsight it seems regrettable that at that time a consultative document, such as the green paper entitled "Television Without Frontiers" had not been prepared by the Commission. It published the draft directive without stating that it was supposed to be a discussion paper. The advertising business recipients of this first draft directive and its accompanying Memorandum therefore erroneously accepted these documents as the formal opinion of the Commission. The Commission's reproach that the vehement reactions against the draft directive were very much overdone, did not resolve the industry's fears.

During the years that followed, Commissioner Burke, who had assumed responsibility for Consumer Affairs in early 1977, saw as one of his most urgent tasks to reopen the entire subject for new discussions with representatives from governments, consumer organizations and the advertising business.

The draft diretive becomes formal

In March, 1978 the initial period of discussion of the draft directive came to a close with the publication of a Proposal for a Council Directive on Misleading and Unfair advertising (see Table III), again accompanied by an extensive Memorandum (see Appendix IV).

The opening paragraphs of the Explanatory Memorandum accompanying the Proposed Directive were remarkable:

> Advertising is an integral part of the system of mass production and distribution serving the general public. Manufacturers of goods and providers of services need the opportunity to inform and remind the public of what they have to offer. Such a system of information is useful to the economics of production. Consumers need information on goods and services so that they can make their choice between the many alternatives.
>
> Advertising has the additional effect of stabilizing employment by ensuring the steady disposal of production, it provides the basis for competition in the markt-place and encourages product development and innovation and the provision of low-cost goods and services previously regarded as too expensive for the mass market. In addition advertising makes a vital contribution towards the cost of the media (see Appendix IV, p.297).

Compared with the introductory remarks in the first Memorandum, the content and tone of these two opening paragraphs showed improvement. It is perhaps of interest that the author of these paragraphs was John Hobson, who had joined an

EAAA delegation to visit Michel Carpentier in November, 1977 to discuss the draft directive. Commenting on the still prevailing negative attitude towards advertising within the Commission, Carpentier quite unexpectedly offered to start off the Memorandum which would accompany the proposed directive with a positive statement about the role of advertising, but he asked if someone would write it for him. John Hobson volunteered and sat down at Carpentier's desk to write the two paragraphs then and there. Our reason for relating this little anecdote is to illustrate the gradual change of heart of the Commission and its desire to make a gesture of goodwill toward the advertising business. But there remained other passages in the Memorandum which industry still found hard to accept because they gave a distorted picture of what was actually hapenning in the European marketplace.

Stating that differing degrees of legal protection were hindering a harmonious development of economic activities, the Memorandum said:

> Moreover, in view of the development of media techniques, advertising increasingly reaches beyond the frontiers of individual Member States and directly addresses consumers in other Member States. This is particularly true with the products of large firms. Laws which differ from country to country therefore jeopardize the effective protection of those involved in the economic process.
>
> The different laws also affect the free movement of goods and services. Differences in the laws make it impossible to plan and conduct advertising campaigns beyond the frontiers of a Member State. If certain advertisements are allowed in one Member State but banned in another it is difficult, particularly in border areas between two or more Member States, to operate a uniform marketing system for goods or services. The greater expense of planning and conducting several advertising campaigns simultaneously also affects the advertiser's competitive position. Furthermore, a skillful salesman may be able to secure competitive advantages over his competitors by exploiting differences in the laws. Equality of competitive opportunities, however, is one of the prerequisites for the common market (see Appendix IV, p.300).

It was understandable that the Commission again used the argument of increased international trade as a justification for proposing the directive. But in 1978 the Commission's proposals were not sufficiently different from those made in 1975 to change the business world's opinion of them.

The Select Commission of the House of Lords in the UK did not accept the Commission's position either. In its meetings in April, 1978 it stated:

> The evidence given by the representatives of the Department of Prices and Consumer Protection was that 'we have no evidence whatever that there is any impediment at all to inter-Community trade as a result of differing practices as now conducted.' The representative of the Advertising Standards Authority, asked whether the differences between the national laws lead to inadequate levels of consumer protection and affect the free circulation of goods and provisions of services, said that he had no evidence of it at all and did not believe the Commission had either (House of Lords, 1978).

In July, 1979 the Commission proposed further amendments to the directive (see Appendix V), following requests from the EP and the ESC which had studied the proposed directive in detail. The most significant point was that the Commission now accepted self-regulation as a means of controlling misleading advertising, as long as consumer recourse to a court of law was not ruled out.

The main changes in the proposed directive and in the proposed amendments to the directive were:

(1) The criticisms of the definition of "misleading advertising" in the first draft directive had been taken into account and Article 4 had been deleted.

(2) Advertising would not only be regarded as misleading when it omitted material information, but also when it would not be readily recognizable as an advertisement.

(3) Comparative advertising would now in principle be allowed.

(4) The burden of proof that a claim is correct would lie with the advertiser.

(5) Member States could now either initiate legal proceedings against misleading advertising, or bring the matter before an administrative authority. But at the request of either party, the case could be reviewed by the courts.

(6) Member States sanctions for infringing the laws against misleading and unfair advertising should be a sufficient deterrent, and should take into account the extent of the damage or harm resulting from such advertising.

(7) The courts or administrative authorities of Member States "are enabled" to require corrective statements.

The amendment was an important step forward and particularly pleased those representatives of the advertising business who had been pleading strongly for the acceptance of self-regulatory bodies. But this was not the end of the story. Other aspects of the proposed directive, such as the concepts of "unfair" and "comparative" advertising, on which Member States could not agree, caused further delays.

After several more years of debate a rather unusual step was taken. For the first time ever, the EAT and the BEUC, representing the advertising business and consumer organizations respectively, wrote jointly on June 30, 1982 and again on February 15, 1983 to the President of the Council of Ministers urging him to do everything within his power to bring about an early decision on the directive.

In their letter of June 30, 1982, the two organizations pointed out:

> The principles which underlie the Directive are ones to which both advertising practitioners and consumers whole-heartedly subscribe. Their application is necessary both to protect consumers' purchasing power against misleading or unfair claims and to avoid distorting of competition. The advent of satellite and increasing transnational advertising, will make the directive particularly relevant as a basis for agreeing on practices in Member States ... We would both welcome a practical and workable solution and are writing to ask you to use your influence to ensure that the subject is given urgent attention (BEUC/EAT, 1982/1983).

Gradually, however, through many informal discussions, because of the wish to accommodate and in recognition of cable and satellite developments, a compromise solution was reached. On September 10, 1984 the Council of Ministers finally adopted a directive on misleading advertising.

The Council directive on misleading advertising

As the title indicates, the regulation of "unfair advertising" was deleted from the final directive (see Table III). Member States simply could not agree on its definition and interpretation. However, the preamble to the directive contains the interesting announcement that

> ". . . at a second stage, unfair advertising and, as far as necessary, comparative advertising should be dealt with, on the basis of appropriate Commission proposals;"

The main points in the final directive were summarized by James O'Connor:

> The Directive defines misleading advertising as "any advertising which in any way, including its presentation, deceives or is likely to deceive the persons to whom it is addressed or whom it reaches and which by reason of its deceptive nature is likely to affect their economic behavior or which, for those reasons, injures or is likely to injure a competitor."
>
> The Directive sets out the matters to be considered when determining whether advertising is misleading, such as product characteristics, origin, uses, price and conditions, as well as the rights of the advertisers. Consumers having a legitimate interest in an advertisement which they consider misleading, may bring an action before the Courts or before a designated administrative competent authority. It has been left to the Member States to decide whether these actions can be brought directly or via Court procedures. The Courts or the designated administrative authority will be given the power to order the withdrawal of misleading advertisements, or to prevent the broadcasting of these for the first time even without proof of actual damage to the complainant or of negligence on the part of the advertiser.
>
> Member States can also confer on the competent authorities the power to require publication of their decisions and to order the publication of rectifying statements with a view to correcting misleading effects. Voluntary or self-regulatory means of control are permitted, provided the obligatory procedures are also available.
>
> Advertisers will have to furnish proof of their statements and, in the absence of any proof, the statements can be regarded by the authorities as misleading.
>
> Member States have two years in which to implement the terms of the Directive through national legislation (O'Connor, 1984).

When comparing the final Council Directive with previous versions, it is of interest to note:

(a) not only was "unfair" advertising deleted, but "comparative" advertising, at first prohibited then in a later version allowed, was not even mentioned in the final directive; however, both are intended to become the subject of separate directives;

(b) the provision was deleted that referred to advertising as being misleading "if it is not readily recognizable as an advertisement or when it omits material information" (Article 3 of the Amended Proposed Directive);

(c) the final directive no longer required Member States to take into account "the extent of the damage" (Article 5 of the Proposed Directive), or "the extent of the harm" (Article 5 of the Amended Proposed Directive);

(d) the option to require corrective statements remained.

The deletion of any mention of unfair advertising, omission of material information, or extent of damage or harm was necessary because no agreement could be reached on the definition of these terms.

Member States have until September, 1986 to bring their national laws into conformance. A number of countries will not need to make any changes. Others that do not have the principle of reversal of the burden of proof, will have to introduce it; in the UK and in Ireland additional legal recourse will have to be added to their self-regulatory systems. In Germany, according to the *ZAW Service* Nr.121/122 of August 1984, the advertising business assumes that the directive will not necessitate any changes in the interpretation and application of the "Gesetz gegen den unlauteren Wettbewerb (UWG)."

After the considerable upheaval over a number of years, the somewhat lukewarm, even indifferent reaction to this directive is not surprising. Virtually all controversial elements have been deleted or made optional, leaving a somewhat truncated version of the previous documents. Some described the final directive as a non-event, others called it a victory of moderation.

The positive side of reaching agreement on this complex issue should not be overlooked. New developments regarding electronic media necessitate a "horizontal framework for the regulation of advertising, at a time when the need is far greater than it was ten years ago," as Roger Underhill wrote in a thoughtful article in *Europe 84.* Underhill takes the opportunity to recall past difficulties in the relationships between the Commission and industry, but hopes that in the future there will be closer relationships between them, saying:

> Now that the difficulties and misunderstandings of the Misleading Advertising Directive are out of the way, we in the advertising industry would like to see further improvements in the various "dialogues" that are so important to the regulatory process. On the one hand we would like to establish a more effective dialogue between consumer and advertising interests at the Community level. The partnership between producer and consumer is all-important in the field of commerce: it needs much more nourishment at the political level (Underhill, 1984:15).

We agree with Underhill's desire for a better dialogue between all parties, a subject to which we shall return in our next chapter. But the basis for many misunderstandings and frustrations in the past must surely be attributed in large part to the complexities of regulating what can and what cannot be permitted when communicating with consumers in the twelve different countries that constitute the EEC. Advertising is a myriad of complex activities requiring great flexibility and judgment if it is to be regulated so that the legitimate interests of both business and consumers are to be protected. Experience has shown that reasonable uniformity in the regulation of advertising is exceedingly difficult even within one nation (consider for example the differences between the North and South of Germany). But it is even more difficult among several nations. Moreover, although consumers in Europe today are in many respects more alike than different, these differences are precious to them. Thus, international advertising must take them into account. Any uniformities in advertising must conform to the basic values and requirements of the several local cultures. The task of preparing effective and appropriate advertising is already difficult enough, without arbitrary legal requirements for uniformity. Yet, considerable time, energy and money was devoted by governments, consumer organizations, the business community, and indeed the Commission itself, in finding an acceptable solution to a problem which in the opinion of many did not really warrant such extraordinary effort.

As far back as 1964, John Hobson, then Chairman of Hobson, Bates & Partners in the UK put the subject of misleading advertising in the following perspective:

> My own appraisal therefore of this whole issue is that the balance of strength between the drive of the seller for more sales, and the natural caution and resistance of the buyer (which is in fact the current balance, and which has grown up in a free society over many centuries), is still the best system and cannot be replaced by externally imposed limitations on either the buyer or the seller. In this balance of strength, salesmanship and advertising, which is mass salesmanship, play their part on behalf of the seller; and caution, inertia and habit as well as judgment, play their part for the buyer.
>
> No one should ever underrate the capacity of the British public to define and assess the true values of what is offered. It is erroneous as well as patronizing to think it can be easily fooled. The public is very adult and can be treated as such. This is not to say that within this pattern there is not a case for every reasonable limitation on unfair selling and every possible protection for incautious or ignorant buying — and these precautions are being more and more devised by all concerned in the business. But we know this pattern works; all the alternatives are untried (Hobson, 1964).

Hobson's comments made more than twenty years ago not only apply to the situation in the UK, or indeed only to the subject of past misleading advertising. They should also be remembered when future advertising regulation is considered. For example, if horizontal frameworks for the regulation of international advertising are required, Hobson's "balance of strength" should weigh heavily when new advertising controls are prepared. This raises the point that some of the many issues the advertising business faces are sensitive and controversial. Because they affect the principles underlying all advertising and its regulation, we will deal with them first.

Controversial issues

It is not appropriate in this book to discuss whether or not consumers should or should not use certain products or services. This book is concerned only with the regulation of advertising for products and services that consumers can buy within the Common Market or Europe as a whole. In this respect it seems reasonable that as long as it is legal to produce and sell products and services, it should in principle also be legal to advertise them. However, this freedom is not unconditional. There are circumstances under which it is in the public interest to place certain limitations on advertising or even to prohibit advertising of certain products in one or more of the media. Moreover, when such actions are in the public interest, it is in the best interests of the advertising business to agree to them. It is not in the best interests of the advertising business to resist restrictions on advertising when the public believes there is sufficient evidence to warrant such restrictions. Business must not only serve the public interest, but it must be seen to do so.

It is impossible to generalize on what advertising should be prohibited or restricted. The sale and advertising of feminine hygiene products, lottery tickets, pharmaceuticals, alcoholic beverages and other products may be perfectly acceptable in some countries but not in others. But it is most important that discussions and debates should consider the genuine well-being of the population of the country concerned. In the past, political interests and conflicts have sometimes caused irritations and frustrations. Issues have been blurred, causing the parties to be obstinate and unprepared or unwilling to arrive at a reasonable compromise. This point is very important when considering the growing internationality of the marketing and advertising of products and services throughout Europe. If governments are to implement the new policies of the Commission, breaking down barriers that resist a rapid expansion of international trade, they will have to bury some of their prejudices with regard to what advertising should be allowed in which media. International expansion of trade depends in large part on international advertising carried out in accordance with international rules and regulations.

All this highlights the urgent need for early consultation between industry and the advertising business, particularly on codes of self-regulatory agreements for controversial product categories or services where such international agreements do not yet exist. Such agreements could then serve as the basis for discussions with intergovernmental bodies, preventing such categories becoming the victim of unilateral governmental legislation.

Consultation between parties concerned should be subject to one indefeasible condition only: the freedom in principle to advertise legitimate products or services should neither be disputed nor denied. Any abridgement of this freedom should be in accordance with the "least restrictive means" principle, that is governments should employ only the least restrictive means necessary to safeguard the interests of both consumers and producers.

We shall come back upon this important subject when we discuss the Human Rights Convention in our next chapter; let us now explain how the advertising business and its trade organizations organized themselves at the international level to deal with the many issues that arose and how they can cope with the numerous future initiatives that can come from many different sources.

The formation of working groups

When the possible consequences of the Commission's consumer program became apparent, the EAAA formed special working groups for each of the areas or categories concerned. These working groups were to formulate a proper response for presentation by its "rapporteur" and to represent the group in all discussions at the international level.

International Advertising Agencies with a client in the product category concerned, were asked to make executives available to serve on such groups, thus ensuring informed opinion on the subject. Such involvement was important both to the agency and to its client, therefore justifying the commitment of time and money.

As the EAT developed into a representative and prestigious body and after representatives from advertisers and the media joined these EAAA working groups, some of them came under the auspices of the EAT. In addition, the WFA also formed specialized committees that usually handled short-term rather than the long-term issues that were already covered by the EAT. While EAAA and WFA working parties dealt mainly with specific problems of advertising agencies and advertisers, the EAT concentrates on the more general areas, such as tobacco, alcoholic beverages, advertising and children and more recently, the Commission's green paper on television advertising.

For example, the EAT's Working Group on Advertising and Children contributed to the development of the ICC Guidelines for Advertising Addressed to Children, adopted by the ICC on March 22, 1982. Another example of EAT activity is of an even more international nature. On January 8, 1980 the AAAA organized an International Meeting on Alcoholic Beverage Advertising in New York. This meeting was attended by members of the particular EAT working group, as well as by US representatives from the Brewers Association, the Wine Institute and the Distilled Spirits Council. The interests of the combined alcoholic beverage producers were discussed and plans for their defense were made. Additionally, the EAT Working Group on Tobacco Advertising assisted in the preparation of the IAA document "Tobacco and Advertising."

Thus, these working groups with their balanced and professional composition formed the spearheads of the industry's response to threats to advertising. These threats came from many different sources. The response was therefore necessarily complex and difficult. The EAT's efforts are now respected by all concerned.

The EAT's activities are important even though the interests of its members sometimes do not coincide, for example in the case of the expected directive on television advertising, which we shall discuss in the next chapter. Nevertheless the business world must try to present a united front to be effective. Let us therefore hope that divergent opinions can be resolved.

The effects of advertising regulation on the creative product

Up to this point we have discussed many of the main areas of concern to all parties involved in the regulation of advertising, except those of creative people who are at the very center of the advertising business. Do they share the concerns of their commercial colleagues?

We wish we could report on the effects of advertising regulation on the creative product. But unfortunately, there does not yet exist any conclusive evidence to indicate how regulatory restrictions influence the quality, content and presentation of creative advertising messages.

It is one of the strange phenomena of the advertising business, and perhaps one of its attractions, that in this age of computerized technology, it is not yet possible to predict accurately if an advertising message, irrespective of the restricted or unlimited character of its component parts, will work in the marketplace. Personal judgment, supported by available marketing and consumer research data, is still the major factor in creating successful advertising.

This fact would not seem to make the industry's case against restrictions a very strong one. Lack of concrete evidence that restrictions impair results in the marketplace could encourage the Commission to introduce them.

Before expressing a point of view on this point, one should listen to the opinions of those who actually create the advertising the business world tries to defend and whose opinions may well differ from its own.

During the years that the debates about advertising controls and restrictions were taking place between business and governments of Member States, there was a school of thought among creative people, that governmental restrictions on advertising would not really make much difference. It was argued that creative people are accustomed to restrictions, albeit of a different nature, and will always find a satisfactory solution; in fact, restrictions might even have a stimulating influence on the creative man's mind. So why should one take so much notice of these restrictions, as long as they apply equally to all manufacturers within a given product category; in the end the only thing that matters is the bottom line, the "Chairman's Corner."

There was a great deal of evidence to support this school of thought. Indeed the creative staffs of advertising agencies usually were not unduly worried. They had learned to live with all sorts of restrictions, such as money, time, and the demands in the client's briefing. They agreed that as long as they knew exactly the framework within which they were supposed to create advertising, they didn't really mind.

In 1978, Dennis McDonnell, then Group Creative Director of Charles Barker ABH International in the UK, wrote an article on the subject in *Campaign*, from which we quote:

Don't go thinking that creative people are discouraged by constraint. It's true that heavy regulations provide a handy excuse for *not* being creative but the person who needs such an excuse is probably not too much troubled by creative urges anyway ... If anyone gets my sympathy, it's the regulator, the unfortunate person who has to write rules which seek to control some of the most imaginative, highly paid and highly motivated people in the country ... Agency managements could do a great deal by making more contact with the rules and the regulations, *before* the work is done and confrontation is inevitable ... Best of all, agency managements could arrange for the creative people to meet a real live censor from time to time. They would get on very well together (McDonnell, 1978).

In a presentation at an IAA conference in Amsterdam in May, 1979, Bob McLaren, then International Creative Director of SSC&B:LINTAS International said:

Creative people in advertising work to "controls" all the time. Controls imposed by the limitations of the product itself, the market, the budget, the brief, the copy strategy (a self-imposed control), research, space, the printed page, the time slot. But there is a very real difference between intelligent controls, however imposed, and unintelligent restrictions imposed by legislation ... Advertising is too important to be left to legislators, but we feel that having legislators leaning heavily on the advertising profession is going to accelerate that profession's cleaning up of its own house. We are going to be forced to examine our motives and to regulate the advertising we make; this will not cause us any real hardship (McLaren, 1979),

Advertisers tend to take a similar attitude; Mr. Keith Monk, then International Advertising Adviser to the Nestlé Company in Switzerland wrote:

In general terms, I believe it's true to say that, given normal creative ingenuity levels in top agencies, a good creative man, today, can still produce very powerful advertising ...

He or she will have to take into account the ever-changing situation in the local market, as it affects the product they are trying to advertise. This will, logically include legal and regulatory considerations. Nothing new in this. It's always been so (Monk, 1983).

Although creative people may not be unduly worried about restrictions imposed upon them by laws and regulations, and may even look upon them as a challenge to their creativity, account managements of advertising agencies and advertisers themselves should take a different perspective. Once one accepts restrictions that are dictated by governments rather than by the competition in the marketplace, where will it stop? By limiting content and presentation of advertising ideas, so hard to come by, a product's competitive edge in the marketplace can easily suffer.

An illustration of what can occur if advertising restrictions are not removed comes from the J. Walter Tompson advertising agency that produced a television commercial for Kellogg's Cornflakes, intended for use internationally.

The starting point was a commercial of Kellogg's cornflakes that has proved successful in the UK. Before re-recording the soundtrack in the different languages and putting it on the air throughout Western Europe, the advertising agency asked their representatives in several countries to watch the commercial and say whether there were any parts of it that would not be allowed by their national laws. There was very little left of either pictures or soundtrack after they had each had their say.

Statements about vitamin content were the first to be axed. In Belgium it is not permitted to say "extra" vitamins of those that were not contained in the first place. The Dutch had to rule out all mention of extra vitamins and also added iron. (In Switzerland you may claim the presence of vitamins only if they are present in constant quantities.)

The use of children also caused trouble. In France they may appear but not endorse a product. In Austria children may not appear. Instead Austrian advertisers have taken to using dwarfs over the age of 16.

The Germans insisted that the statement "Only Kelloggs make their cornflakes the best there's ever been" was reduced to "Only Kelloggs make their cornflakes" as no proof was provided for either a competitive claim or a claim stating that their own cornflakes had been improved. What could have been a substantiation, namely the addition of vitamins, had been deleted by the Belgians and the Dutch. Finally, though not a matter of regulation, the Italian office refused to have a mother portrayed with anything other than dark hair (*Unilever Magazine*, 1983).

A senior executive of a European confectionery company puts the problem of advertising restrictions in a more general context:

Italy has restrictions on the number of times a brand name can be mentioned in a commercial ... Austria forbids tobacco, spirits, loan services, political parties, religious groups, pharmaceuticals, intimate products ... France forbids alcohol, jewelry, tobacco, tourism, retail stores, building societies, publishing and computers ... Holland only forbids tobacco, but has strict regulations for pharmaceuticals and − as we know − sweets. Even the UK, often considered liberal, does not permit cigarettes (and cigarette tobacco) − although cigars and pipe tobacco are permitted. Other products [and services] prohibited are political organizations, religious bodies, matrimonial agencies, betting shops and feminine hygiene products. Alcohol is permitted, but the spirit manufacturers have agreed not to advertise their products (Bottomley, 1985).

The story of the Kellogg commercial and Bottomley's comments carry a serious warning for the advertising business and for legislators at national and international levels. Quick and effective harmonization of rules and regulations affecting advertising are a matter of great urgency. Unless the necessary steps are taken, expansion of international trade supported by advertising is unrealistic. How can an international campaign be competitive if it has to take into account the idiosyncrasies of twelve Member States of the EC. If little is allowed, little can be said or shown. This cannot be in the interest of international trade and of the consumer's freedom to choose.

By the same token, and while accepting that the good creative man holds in reserve considerable talent and imagination, managements of agencies and companies should do everything within their power to avoid curbing the legitimate exercise of that all-too-rare creative talent. A key word in this last sentence is the word legitimate, which implies activities which benefit consumers − such as accurate and truthful information presented creatively, interestingly and usefully. Since demonstrable product differentiation is difficult to achieve, the "added value" created by advertising can be easily eroded if stringent restrictions are placed on advertising.

Fortunately, the Commission under president Delors has announced steps to be taken to simplify the process of harmonization in order to achieve quicker expansion of international trade. These steps will be discussed in the final chapter of this book. Suffice it to say that the business world welcomes this policy which should also lead to creativity in the development and placing of international advertising not being unduly hampered.

Costs versus benefits

Another serious issue arising from proposed regulation of advertising, whether at the national or international level, is the increased cost to the advertiser, governments and ultimately to the consumer.

It would be unthinkable in well managed business enterprises to spend arbitrarily considerable resources on insufficiently considered projects. It is not surprising therefore, that the question of relationships between the cost and the expected benefits of advertising regulation and the apparent lack of thought given to this aspect, has frequently been raised. For example, the ICC has prepared a booklet on the subject of costs and benefits, in which is stated:

> Consumer protection is a legitimate concern for business as for governments. But in the last decade the volume of consumer protection legislation and regulations has considerably increased, without adequate attention being paid to the costs involved. Implementation costs for business will ultimately be borne by consumers in the form of higher prices, and administration and enforcement costs for governmental bodies are ultimately charged to the taxpayers.
>
> Therefore, the International Chamber of Commerce (ICC) strongly urges that particularly in the present difficult economic conditions, much more attention should be paid to cost/benefit analyses of existing and future consumer protections measures, and formulates, with that in mind, specific recommendations for action by business, governments and intergovernmental organisations (ICC, 1981a:5).

The business world applauded the thoughts in this document, as echoed by Lord Thomson in remarks on the Draft Directive on Misleading and Unfair Advertising:

> Some earnest researcher might profitably do a study of what it has cost in expensive official man-hours to produce the present stage of the draft Advertising Directive, which is arguably ultra-vires, demonstrably lacking in evidence, and of debatable value in developing the EEC. Highly paid Community officials have beavered away in the backrooms of the Berlaymont or toured the national capitals. Less highly paid national officials have laboured in the depths of their own departments before dutifully going back and forwards to Brussels to man the working-parties — first of the Commission, then of the Council of Ministers. Apart from the labours of the British Parliament already discussed, both the European Parliament and the Economic and Social Committee have set up their own Committees and summoned their own experts. Throughout these seven years senior people in industry and their Trade Association officials have spent countless hours fighting for common sense and practical reality. A thorough cost-accounting of all this activity

would be fascinating and would produce a formidable bill. And to what end has all this energy been spent? Would a Directive on Misleading and Unfair Advertising make any contribution to the growth and success of the European Community commensurate with the time and treasure spent on it? (Thomson, 1981:45).

The ICC report on costs and benefits admits the many problems and difficulties in arriving at a proper cost/benefit estimate of any consumer protection law or regulation. But the ICC nevertheless strongly recommends the use of this tool before embarking on any regulatory program. The ICC suggests a number of checkpoints to be used by governments, business and intergovernmental organizations, which, if applied properly, would at least eliminate measures of obviously questionable benefit to consumers from being seriously considered.

In referring to its checklist, the ICC points out that more development work should be done "by business and governments possibly in cooperation with academic institutions and/or consumer organisations, to perfect the techniques of cost/benefit analysis in the socio-economic sphere" (ICC, 1981a:14).

As could be expected, the ICC also comes out strongly in favour of self-regulation which in general "can constitute a faster, more flexible and more effective way to protect the interests of the consumer" (ICC, 1981a:8).

It is in this connection of interest to mention the point of view of the new Commission wich took office in January, 1985. In one of its first documents, which we shall discuss more fully in our final chapter, Commissioner Clinton Davis, responsible for Consumer Affairs, says:

> ... the Commission rejects arguments attempting to bolster up the idea that in a period of crisis efforts to improve consumer protection are a luxury. Surely the prevention of serious hazards, a more frugal use of natural and human resources, and more effective competition are likely to facilitate the necessary structural changes within the industrial economies of the Member States? Furthermore, no proof has been advanced that additional costs which might derive from the application of consumer protection regulations represent a determining factor in the reduced competitivity of European industry, for rival non-community industrialized countries have achieved a high level of protection (Commission of the EC, 1985b:60).

While there may be no proof that the cost of consumer protection reduces the competitivity of industry, neither is there any proof that such consumer protection as has been introduced, has made any noticeable improvement in existing standards of consumers' well-being throughout the Community.

We therefore believe that the Commission should give much more serious thought to the cost/benefit aspects of consumer protection before embarking on the preparation of new directives.

Mayo Thompson, an ex-Commissioner with the FTC in Washington, also strongly endorsed the need to apply economic considerations to the regulation of advertising, combined with effective self-regulatory controls; he put it as follows: "Government regulation of advertising is justified when — and only when — two conditions are satisfied: (1) the alleged misrepresentation must be causing economic harm to the consumer, and (2) the alleged misrepresentation must be one that cannot be corrected by the market itself" (Thompson, 1975).

A comparison of advertising regulation in Europe and the USA

Although our focus is on European advertising regulation, it is useful to examine advertising regulation from the broad perspective of both European and US developments; it would be unrealistic to consider the situation in Europe in isolation from developments in the USA.

There are of course important differences between the two continents. But the size of both markets, the similar level of advertising sophistication and the growing importance of American business in Europe and vice versa, make it useful to compare trends in advertising regulation and the reactions they provoke in business circles in both Europe and the USA.

In the USA in the 1950s and the early 1960s there was increased resistance to forms of marketing and advertising which were perceived to be exaggerated or misleading. Critical publications by authors such as Vance Packard, Ralph Nader and John Kenneth Galbraith led the way, with relatively little reaction by consumers or the business community. It was not until the late 1960s when the gradual growth in the number of concerned consumers became significant that business became increasingly alarmed. Numerous pieces of federal legislation affecting advertising were enacted in the 1960s, and the FTC had become "activist."

As discussed in Chapter I similar events occurred in Europe. Most Member States passed substantially stricter legislation and instituted stronger enforcement policies relating to the control of perceived business abuses. Self-regulatory systems were established in most Member States. In both the USA and Europe such controls were "justified" more on the basis of negative opinions about advertising than on the basis of solid information on the impact and power of advertising.

But there was an important difference between the USA and Europe. The European advertising business felt that interaction between the Commission and the advertising business was not adequate in the 1970s. The business had wanted to lend its expertise but the Commission did not seek it.

Hearings in the USA

The situation was different in the USA. In July, 1971 the US FTC announced that it was interested in obtaining information that would enable it to function more knowledgeably in its activities relating to the advertising business. Therefore in October, 1971 the FTC held informational hearings to learn about modern techniques of advertising, especially:

(1) To consider advertising addressed to children.

(2) to determine whether television advertising may unfairly exploit desires, fears and anxieties.

(3) To determine whether technical aspects of the preparation and production of TV commercials may facilitate deception.

(4) To consider consumers' physical, emotional and psychological responses to advertising as they may affect the standards by which advertising is judged (Moskin, 1973:8).

The FTC invited senior executives from advertisers, advertising agencies, media, and trade associations, along with distinguished professors who were especially knowledgable in such fields as consumer behavior and marketing, to testify on specific subjects in their areas of particular expertise.

Among the more than 40 experts who testified were 26 advertising business leaders, organized into a joint task force by the AAAA and the ANA to present eighteen hours of testimony over a four and one-half day period. They testified on "the advertising process, its theory and practice . . . [which they believed] was the most coherent, cohesive and comprehensive analysis of the use of advertising – from research to execution to placement to post analysis – ever assembled" (AAAA, 1973).

Since the average tenure of FTC staff is only a few years, and in view of the continued activist nature of the FTC in the early and mid-1970s, one may question whether or not the FTC hearings had much influence on advertising regulation. But at least the industry had the opportunity to express its views, along with those of others. It is probably safe to venture that the subsequent activities of the FTC were indeed predicated on a somewhat more sophisticated understanding of advertising than would have been the case if there had been no hearings. Even those FTC staff who were added subsequent to the hearings had available to them the 700 pages of original printed testimony, as well as a number of analyses of the hearings published in the months following the hearings.

To illustrate how the advertising business in the USA and in Europe were facing similar problems, we quote from the presentation given by Alfred Seaman on the occasion of the FTC hearings. His testimony was entitled: "The Power of Words:"

> . . . If advertising is to remain a vital force for the development of our economic system and help spread the benefits throughout our society, it must have access to the vigorous use of words.
>
> . . . If you ask advertising leaders where we stand, it's solidly in the corner of good taste. Contrary to what many "experts" say, I believe that there *is* a consensus in any society at any given time with clear ideas of what good taste – or at least bad taste – really is. But in judging advertising, let us be sure we represent good taste and not an unwordly piety.
>
> . . . It must be clear to any perceptive observer that people buy products and services for more than physical performance. . . . Psychic satisfaction is just as important as mechanical satisfaction – often more so.

... Please do not make the rules required to stop the excesses on the periphery so broad and general
that they smother enterprise and excellence at the core (Seaman, 1971).

Nevertheless in the early 1970s the US consumerist momentum of the 1960s continued; a decade of consumer legislation had yielded more than 25 major federal
laws affecting advertising directly; the FTC assumed what came to be called the role
of a "national nanny," and Chairman Pertschuk tried to make the FTC into the
greatest "public-interest law firm" in the country.

Although consumers themselves did not lead the way, they became increasingly
aware of advertising abuses; and there was widespread sentiment for corrective
action. Consumer organizations held well publicized meetings and those in government reacted. President Kennedy formed the first Consumer Advisory Council in
the federal government; President Johnson named a Special Assistant to the President for Consumer Affairs. President Nixon proposed a Buyer's Bill of Rights and
a new Division of Consumer Protection within the Justice Department, along with
several pieces of new legislation and a new Office of Consumer Affairs in the Executive Office of the President.

Meanwhile in Europe the Commission in designing the 1975 draft and the 1978
proposal for a directive on misleading advertising as well as "regulators" within the
Member States, did not seek the kind of input from the European advertising community that the FTC had sought in the USA. Consequently the advertising business
felt that the information base for these documents was deficient.

During these years the voices to support business perspectives were neither frequent nor widely heard. Yet, such voices existed in both Europe and in the USA.
The advertising business in the USA had an ally in FTC Commissioner Mayo
Thompson, although he was outnumbered and outvoted on the Commission. Before
he resigned in protest against the FTC's activist regulation of advertising, which in
his opinion was "both too much and of the wrong kind," he made a presentation
to the Annual Meeting of the Association of National Advertisers in Palm Beach
in 1975. Ironically, his speech contained ideas which were later to become more
widely accepted in the USA. His comments could also have been relevant to the situation in Europe. He said:

... Forcing the business community to hire a small army of lawyers to parse every word of every
ad disseminated in the country and thus pushing up the price of virtually every item the poor consumer buys, is not a program that can be sensibly defended in terms of the *consumer's* interest any
more than saturation bombing can be explained in terms of the interests of the inhabitants of that
particular village. Something else is involved and that 'something else,' to repeat, is the fact that
the people doing the regulation are not *economically* oriented. They don't think the way economists
and businessmen think. They don't know how difficult it is to write an ad that *sells*, one that gets
the consumer's attention long enough to persuade him to just *try* the product. They don't really
understand the role of advertising in promoting economic effeciency. They aren't comfortable with
such ideas as the relationship between production volume and unit costs, between the cost of

production and the price to the consumer, between prices in individual industries and the inflation-unemployment problem in the economy as a whole. The economic sophistication of the government's regulatory personnel is very low and that is a shame. It imposes a very high cost on the business community and, ultimately, on the consuming public (Thompson, 1975).

Commissioner Mayo added toward the end of his speech:

I'd like to see the FTC ... directed and staffed by men and women who don't just *tolerate* free enterprise, but have a deep and abiding affection for it, who serve it with the same loyalty and passion that the citizen is expected to feel for his home, his country, his flag (Thompson, 1975).

However, support for consumer protection regulation in the USA, as in Europe, depends very much on the leadership of the ruling government, which in turn depends on the government's support from voters and from pressure groups. During the first years of President Carter's administration, the FTC under Chairman Pertschuk continued new consumerist initiatives (Pertschuk, 1982). But on several occasions members of the US Congress criticized the FTC severely. Congress, by employing the "power of the purse," finally made it clear to the FTC that broad sentiment for deregulation had developed, and that the FTC was out-of-step with the prevailing climate which had turned against more and more government regulation. President Reagan in 1981 replaced Pertschuk with a new Chairman of the FTC, James Miller, who in turn appointed FTC personnel who were more "in-tune with the times," and more responsive to the views of business.

On April 21, 1982, the advertising business in the USA made another presentation to the FTC on advertising self-regulation to explain: (1) the application of internal standards by advertisers and their agencies during the process of producing advertising; and (2) how a number of organizations created the mechanisms for self-regulation, how it works and what its results have been (AAAA, 1982).

In 1983 the FTC again held hearings to learn industry viewpoints on a number of advertising regulatory issues. For example, in response to the many questions relating to "advertising substantiation" the AAAA submitted comments in a 144 page document (AAAA, 1983).

It would be useful if such an explanation of internal company and agency controls on the production of advertising in Europe, could be given to the EEC institutions and other interested parties at the supranational level and we shall come back to this point later in the chapter.

Hearings in Europe

We do not know if the example from the US played a part in the decision of the European Parliament to organize the public hearings held in Dublin in 1980, shortly after the second consumer program had been introduced, which we shall discuss in our next chapter. In any case, the "Committee on the Environment, Public Health and Consumer Protection'' of the European Parliament organized the event and invited the following organizations to send representatives to participate: Commission of the European Communities, Economic and Social Committee, European Bureau of Consumer Organizations, European Trade Union Confederation, Union of Industries in the European Communities, Association of Family Organizations in the European Communities, Euro-Coop, European Association of Advertising Agencies, Council of European Municipalities, United Nations Educational, Scientific and Cultural Organization, European Mail Order Traders' Association, International Chamber of Commerce, Organization for Economic Cooperation and Development, and the Committee of Professional Agricultural Organizations of the EC (Public Hearing, 1980).

The purpose of the meeting was to discuss the second consumer program. Participants had received in advance a questionnaire, listing what the Committee felt were the most important and relevant questions about the new consumer program, as well as some broader issues on the activities of the Commission generally, on services needed by consumers, and on policies regarding information, education, prices, and so forth. There was also the question of the advantages and disadvantages of voluntary agreements compared to government regulation.

In view of the replies to this questionnaire, the BEUC took the position that it would not dispute the claimed advantage of voluntary codes; but it saw problems with monitoring and enforcing such codes at an international level. In contrast to this view, Mr. Peter Gilow, then President of the EAAA, said on this occasion:

> Nobody knows better than the consumer goods industry and the advertising industry how quickly and unpredictably public opinion about new products or market trends can change. And every change can mean a new need for regulation. The adaptability of a regulatory system is a basic requirement for its effectiveness. And we have already seen that voluntary controls can adapt to a given situation much more quickly than legislation. But voluntary controls can only flourish where there is a high standard of freely imposed discipline. If there is too much legislation self-imposed disciplines will weaken. In our opinion that would be very much to the consumers' disadvantage (Gilow, 1980).

It is difficult to say what precise influence this public hearing had on the Commission. But it is interesting to note that gradually the idea of centrally organized advertising self-regulatory systems in individual European countries, strongly supported during the public hearing in Dublin by the advertising business, received greater acceptance among European governments.

As outlined in Chapter I, between 1948 and 1974 eight out of the ten Member States introduced or reinforced centralized systems of self-control; in 1972 the US did likewise.* In that year:

---

* There were of course many earlier and relatively unsuccessful examples of non-centralized self-regulatory activities in the US and in EC Member States.

... four associations, the American Advertising Federation, the American Association of Advertising Agencies, the Association of National Advertisers, and the Council of Better Business Bureaus joined forces to establish the National Advertising Review Board (NARB). The primary purpose of this body of industry executives and representatives from the public sector is to sustain high standards of truth and accuracy in national advertising (NARB).

It is not appropriate here to describe in detail how the US system functions and how effective it has been. But there is considerable evidence to indicate that this self-regulatory mechanism, as similar systems operating in many European countries, works to the advantage of the buying public and to the satisfaction of the business community. FTC Chairman James Miller sent the following message to the 1981 Annual Meeting of the NARB, commemorating the tenth anniversary of advertising self-regulation in the USA:

It is an honor to congratulate this organization (NARB) on its tenth anniversary. You have been extraordinarily successful in your efforts to ensure accuracy in advertising. As members of the business community, you have first-hand knowledge about advertising. You can stop false ads quickly and informally. With your efficient self-regulation, the Federal Trade Commission does not have to intervene in the marketplace as would otherwise be necessary (*Better Business News and Views*, 1981:4).

Whatever the similarities or the differences between the USA and Europe with regard to consumer protection and advertising regulation it will always be to the credit of John Crichton, who as President of the AAAA in 1976 at the association's annual conference arranged for an informal meeting between the representatives of the European, Canadian, Australian and US advertising associations. Topics of mutual importance were discussed, such as advertising of tobacco and alcohol, and advertising to children. Experiences were exchanged and plans were made to maintain these global contacts on a regular basis. Not only did John Crichton and his successor Leonard Matthews come to Europe, but representatives from the European advertising business frequently visited the USA. They established important useful exchanges that continue to this day.

Interchange of information between Brussels and Washington

We have made a number of comparisons between the situation in the USA and in Europe with regard to advertising regulation. Both continents have, broadly speaking, gone through the same waves of regulatory activity and a subsequent lessening of tensions. Although there has been no need for formal interchanges or agreements between the two administrations, there have been many informal contacts between civil servants on both sides of the ocean. They have similar interests and can learn from each other, just as is the case with representatives of private industry in Europe and the USA.

The press is also an international conveyor of information. The *Washington Post* and *The New York Times* have an international readership and the same can be said of the *Financial Times* and the *Economist*, all four of which follow regulatory developments.

Against this background of the most important developments with regard to international advertising regulation in Europe and in the USA, it is useful to examine how the Commission responded to the many concerns and reactions from the business world.

The Commission's evolving attitude

According to Article 39 of the first consumer program, the Commission is supposed to publish an Annual Report, describing progress in the field of consumer protection. To date only three such reports have been published. Anticipating for a moment future developments within the Commission that will be discussed later in this book, it appears as if such annual reports will no longer be published. It also is most unlikely that there will be a third consumer program. However, in its first report, released in March, 1977 Commissioner Richard Burke who had been responsible for Consumer Affairs since January of that year, said in his Foreword:

> ... it is evident that the Commission − in the interest of its citizens and in keeping with the need for coherent and mutually reconcilable policies within the Community − must take the initiative with policies to promote the interests of consumers. Only in this way can the Commission have a role of its own in shaping and directing the movement towards better organization of society in the service of the citizen (*First Report Commission*, 1977).

His remarks were a firm statement with an ambitious objective, clearly reflecting the Commission's early intentions to carry out the agreed consumer program with speed and determination.

The first report contained a description of how the Commission operates and the role of the various advisory bodies. The report also listed a large number of directives, approved during the period from June, 1974 to December, 1976 covering subjects and products such as colorants in foodstuffs, honey, preserved milk, health problems affecting trade in fresh poultry meat, additives in feeding-stuffs, cosmetic products, aerosol dispensers, measuring instruments, braking devices for motor vehicles, speedometer equipment, and reflex reflectors for motor vehicles. These directives were important to the industry concerned, but they do not touch directly on advertising.

In the first report there was no reference to contacts with the business world, unless they were covered by the final paragraph of the "Conclusions" of this first report, which read: "In the years to come, the Commission will continue its efforts in liaison with work undertaken in the Member States, the European Parliament, the Economic and Social Committee, the Consumers' Consultative Committee and international institutions" (*First Report Commission*, 1977:60).

It is interesting to note the change of emphasis and tone in the Foreword to the second report, released in March, 1978 exactly one year later. It listed another seventeen "technical" directives approved in 1977 and it expressed satisfaction with progress. In his Foreword Mr. Burke this time said: "Such satisfaction, however, as may be derived from progress thus far is tempered by the realization of how much remains to be achieved before comprehensive consumer protection is accomplished throughout the Community" (*Second Report Commission*, 1978:3).

This tempered optimism was obviously caused by the considerable resistance the Commission was facing. This development was even more clearly expressed in the third report, released in October, 1980, about eighteen months after the second one.

It contained a Foreword, again written by Commissioner Burke, appearing to convince the reader of the Commission's enlightened interest in consumer well-being. He said:

> The passage of legislation, however, is by no means the only important index of progress in consumer welfare. On the contrary, the most powerful instrument consumers have for the protection of their interests is their own active participation either in the exercise of judgement and choice prerogatives as individuals in the marketplace or in joint action through their representative associations.

And in referring to the second consumer program which would replace the preliminary one, Mr. Burke said:

> ... in making my proposals for a second programme to the Commission, which adopted them in June 1979, I laid particular stress on participation, on dialogue, on mutual recognition by producer and consumer of their interdependence, never more evident than in the present conjuncture of economic difficulties.
>
> My perception of the promotion of consumer welfare has been in those terms ever since I assumed responsibility in that area of Consumer Policy. The translation of these terms into credible and practicable working arrangements and the judicious blending of legal and voluntary measures resulting from enlightened and realistic negotiations by all interests concerned, both public and private, will be the tasks for accomplishment in the next five years (*Third Report Commission*, 1980:Foreword).

Compared to the previous reports, the Commission had made an almost complete volte-face. It now recognized the "powerful instrument" of consumer "judgment and choice," and stressed not only "participation," "dialogue," and "mutual recognition by producer and consumer of their interdependence," but also the need for "judicious blending of legal and voluntary measures." Its objective was now "enlightened ... negotiations by all interests concerned, both public and private."

Placing the three reports side by side, it is quite clear that the Commission had made progress not so much in the actual results it had achieved, which were far from impressive, but in its realization that as far as directives in the field of advertising are concerned, it had been counterproductive to rush matters unrealistically.

In looking back upon these years, an outstanding fact is that the concerted action of motivated advertising business representatives prevented their worst fears from materializing. Gradually, the activities of the business community to influence governments and supranational bodies showed results in terms of better cooperation between the national and supranational authorities and representatives of the advertising business. There was a greater acceptance of practitioners' points of view and experience. There was also a great deal more openness in the Commission's attitude, and a willingness to debate rather than dictate – a desire for better mutual understanding.

For example, when Michel Carpentier, then Director-General of Business Environment and Consumer Protection Department of the EEC, addressed the meeting in Brussels in October, 1978 to which we have referred before, he spoke frankly on that occasion about the problems the Commission was facing and the changes he believed to be necessary in the way the Commission was operating. He said that this particular meeting was held

> ... at a time when a consumer programme, whose adoption in April, 1975 was hailed with such hope and enthusiasm, is now, after it has been put into practice, the subject of nothing but recrimination, grievances and criticism and when people are now saying 'too bad' about a policy considered to be on its last legs (Carpentier, 1978).

He continued, dealing with organizational matters, progress achieved, obstacles and criticisms, the legality of the consumer program and a few recommendations for reshaping it. In this connection he said:

> First of all, it would be a good thing to be even more selective in the choice of work which the Commission is asked to carry out. This will mean that it will sometimes have to refuse to follow up certain tasks of marginal importance which it might be asked to carry out, either by the consumer associations or by certain institutions.
>
> Secondly, we should doubtless try to be much more imaginative in order to find new formulae which will make it possible to effectively attain the desired goals without causing too many complications for the national administrations and yet without removing any of the Community legislation's specific character.
>
> Thirdly, the Commission should try to make the Member States understand the importance of the preparatory work for a draft directive before this is submitted to the council.
>
> Of course, the Commission should also try to be more active as regards its attempts to distribute information on the consumer policy, both vis-à-vis the man in the street and the economic and social forces which are active in the various countries (Carpentier, 1978).

In this speech Mr. Carpentier dealt with a number of points which the advertising business had raised on numerous occasions. It is interesting to note that these comments were made by the same person who was known for wanting to push through as many directives as possible. If he had accepted earlier the "green paper" approach and procedure as later practiced by the Commission, some of the obstacles Carpentier mentions could have been overcome.

Indirect effects of the Commission's consumer activities

Although it cannot be denied that the Commission was disappointed that so few directives were approved under the first consumer program, we should remember Commissioner Burke's comment: ". . . the passage of legislation . . . is by no means the only important index of progress in consumer welfare." While demonstrable results were indeed few, the indirect influence of Commission activity on governments, the business community, trade associations, and consumer organizations was considerable. Commission activity not only helped to shape consumer policies by Member State governments, but it also influenced the policies and practices of business. Although the advertising business fought many battles with the Commission, there can be no question that the pressures from Brussels and the threat of governmental intervention played a significant role in making the business world even more aware of its responsibilities toward consumers throughout the Community.

Key perspectives

In this chapter we have chronicled the business world's response to the conditions described in Chapters I and II, especially the way industry organized itself to react to the Commission's consumer protection and advertising regulatory initiatives. One of the most important features of this response was that the industry had a worthwhile goal — to resist what was perceived as excessive government interference with some of the basic freedoms of consumers and commercial enterprise. Industry and the advertising business achieved considerable success when they joined forces to crystallize the issues, to organize and to act.

But success was not complete in all respects. The advertising business attempted unsuccessfully to achieve a meaningful dialogue with consumer organizations. However, it did bring about a positive dialogue with the Commission and other intergovernmental organizations. The advertising business also succeeded in large part in getting greater involvement from US and European multinationals to defend the interests of industry and the advertising business.

The organized activities of the business community had a significant impact on achieving less restrictive consumer programs than those originally planned, and on reversing what at times seemed to be an inevitable trend to excessive restrictions.

There is no doubt that at the beginning of the 1980s, the most serious threats had been avoided.

The details of these successes hold important lessons for future action by industry and the advertising business: (1) the need to be strongly united and well organized in order to be able to speak with one voice, (2) the necessity of continued support from the entire business world, both in terms of money and people, to enable appointed business representatives, such as grouped in the EAT, to cope with present and future issues, and (3) the realization that as the world grows smaller, it is necessary to compare what is happening in European nations with what is happening in other nations with similar problems, and to share information on actions and reactions to changing conditions.

Against this background, and with the first three chapters providing the factual information needed to assess further developments in the field of advertising regulation, we will in the next chapter turn our attention to the second consumer protection program. As we will see, the desire to protect was still stronger than the wish to offer opportunities for expansion of trade. The Commission was not yet ready to order the complete reappraisal of its earlier programs and future objectives, as would be done by the new Commission which was appointed in January, 1985. But the first signs of such a reappraisal were clearly visible.

By way of bridging past and future Commission activities, we add some additional perspectives and reflections of an ethical nature, to guide our evaluation of the issue at stake. We find the words of F.P. Bishop, written almost forty years ago, especially revealing and appropriate:

> Advertising, then, is not unethical because it is biased, nor is it necessarily dangerous because the information it gives is partial and highly coloured. Truth is absolute, but ethical standards are relative; they exist to meet the practical needs of people in varying situations and circumstances. The ethical standard for advertising cannot be "the truth, the whole truth and nothing but the truth," simply because such a standard is impossible and the attempt to attain it would reduce advertising to complete ineffectiveness and prevent it fulfilling its legitimate and necessary function.
>
> The ethical standard for advertising must be a utilitarian, not an ideal, one. The advertiser must, that is to say, conform to the rules of conduct which a developing public conscience establishes as proper in matters of business persuasion. These rules are unlikely at any time to meet the perfectionist requirements of the most rigid moralists. But that is not the question. The question is whether they meet the practical requirements of society at a given stage of development (Bishop, 1949:87 – 88).

Chapter IV

Subsequent developments

In this chapter we shall look back on the first consumer program, review trends in consumer attitudes toward advertising, and consider how research can help to fill gaps in knowledge in this respect. Next we will discuss the Commission's second consumer program and the need for a proper dialogue between all parties. Then we will deal with education to increase the understanding of advertising by non-industry groups, the younger generation of consumers and advertising professionals. The need for such knowledge will become clear from our review of new media technologies, especially advertising via cable and satellite. Activities of other inter-governmental bodies and the involvement of non-governmental organizations will conclude this chapter.

The preliminary consumer program in retrospect

With hindsight one might argue, that the furor and agitation of the 1960s and 1970s were grossly exaggerated, that they were not in proportion to the number and seriousness of abuses, or to the actual harm done to consumers. Some did not accept that the benefit of the free market system far outweighed the relatively minor disadvantages. Moreover, many of the alleged evils had already been eliminated, as normally occurs in effectively operating market systems. Advertisers had become more conscious of the changes in consumers' life-styles and attitudes. The introduction of voluntary systems of self-regulation had made it possible to correct harmful excesses quickly and effectively. However, the clock could not be turned back. The Commission's first program was in place.

One should not necessarily blame politicians in a free society for taking the opportunity to champion a cause – to be seen by voters as defending their interests against business moguls, such as the multinationals. After all a free marketplace of ideas is as essential to the political well-being of free people as effective competition in business is to its economic well-being. In fact, the two are inextricably intertwined. Economic freedoms are a necessary condition for, and corrollary of, political freedoms. In any event politicians rode the wave of prevailing resentment against big business. The pendulum swung from what had been seen as extreme freedom for advertisers, toward the desire and intention to introduce strong controls.

In the meantime recession and growing unemployment were forcing governments to be cautious in introducing measures that would restrict the development of international trade. Tax revenues declined and government budgets came under pressure. The Commission's limited budget prevented it from carrying out many plans made in better times.

The advertising business has in the past criticized the Commission for not providing evidence to substantiate its criticism of advertising. The main reason such evidence was never produced, we would venture to suggest, was not so much the Commission's unwillingness to accommodate its critics, but rather its inability to obtain such evidence. Yet, much information on the impact of advertising on consumers and on their attitudes towards advertising existed. Such information could have been made available to the Commission if it had expressed an interest in it. But the Commission apparently did not have confidence that the business world could provide information to contribute to a better understanding of consumer opinions, preferences and priorities throughout the Community.

On the following pages we now present some research findings on trends in consumer attitudes towards advertising. Consumers had in the 1960s and 1970s been exposed to much publicity and propaganda from consumer organizations and others on the negative role of advertising in today's society. So it is important to know if and to what extent, events during those years would be reflected in consumers' opinions. This information also serves as a useful background to our discussion of the Commission's new consumer program, introduced in 1981 as the result of pressures from outside, coupled with those exerted from the business world. As we shall see later, it was a typical product of compromise.

Consumers and advertising

The topic can be divided into two parts: (1) are consumers deeply interested in the subject of advertising generally? and (2) do they express opinions or make complaints about specific advertisements? Our reading of the evidence indicates that the answer to the first question is no; they are not deeply interested. Our answer to the second question is yes, just as they complain about any other aspects of their economic and social environment.

How do consumers express opinions about advertising?

It is convenient to begin by discussing the second of the above questions. Consumers express their opinions, approval or complaints about advertising and products: (1) to the advertiser, or (2) to some independent authority (e.g. government, a self-regulatory organization, or one of the media which carry advertising).

The first of these is most important to advertisers. As Armand de Malherbe, then President of Ted Bates International, said during a presentation to an EAAA meeting in Brussels on March 22, 1979:

> ... Yet, like every advertising professional, I carry the scars of campaigns which ended in failure ... not by ramping reproaches of professional advertising enemies ... but by the gentle hand of the housewife who, in front of the supermarket shelf, by moving her hand ten inches to the left or fifteen to the right, decides whether I shall have a job in six weeks' time or not (Malherbe, 1979).

In fact, the consumer is not only prepared to move his or her hand to the right or to the left, but will sometimes register complaints directly to the seller if an advertisement is thought to be misleading, unlawful or in bad taste. However, it is in the interest of all parties if independent bodies exist to which consumers can complain. Thus, in Belgium, France, Germany, Holland, the UK and many other European countries, bodies have been set up which receive and deal with complaints from consumers about specific advertisements or advertising practices. The advertising business welcomes the formation of such bodies and encourages consumers to use them. In spite of this the number of complaints that deserve attention is relatively small. Opinions differ with regard to the importance that should be attached to actual numbers of complaints. Most will agree that consumers' attitudes toward advertising cannot be measured accurately this way. Some will argue that complaints only represent the top of the iceberg and that consumer discontent with advertising is greater than indicated by the number of complaints. Nevertheless it is useful to explain in some detail the experience of one country where a comprehensive system of handling complaints is in use.

Dealing with consumer complaints

A good example of an effective body to which consumers can complain is the Advertising Standards Authority (ASA) in the UK, which administers the self-regulatory control system for print, cinema and poster advertising. The ASA receives complaints, makes decisions regarding their validity, publishes monthly case reports, and makes recommendations to the advertising business as to how to improve the content and presentation of advertising. It also instructs its media members not to cary an advertisement that is found unacceptable. The IBA, a quasi-governmental body, not only performs similar functions for broadcast advertising, but also prevets most commercials before they are aired.

Importantly, a system for competitors to complain is also available through the CAP Committee, which is administered by the same secretariat as the ASA. Competitors are sometimes the best able to identify advertising abuses, and the opportunity for them to do something about such cases increases the effectiveness of the competitive market economy.

Although the ASA/CAP was established in 1962, it was not until the mid-1970s that changes in financing and organization led to an increase in the number of complaints from a few hundred to several thousand per year. The ASA advertises nationally and receives a great deal of free publicity so that just about any Briton who has a complaint about advertising can easily determine how to lodge such a complaint properly and effectively. In 1983 and 1984 the complaint volume exceeded 7,000 per year. Many of these were frivolous, directed to the wrong authority (e.g. broadcast complaints should go to the IBA), duplications of previous complaints, or otherwise not actionable. But in 1983, 1,473 complaints were relevant to advertising in the print, poster or cinema media, and the ASA upheld 70% of them wholly or in part (ASA, 1984).

The ASA also monitors advertising; in 1981 the Authority scanned some 352,000 newspaper advertisements, finding 137 (or 0.03%) in breach of the British Code (ASA, 1982).

In 1983, the ASA "spoke out on its objectives for advertisers in 1984 by listing six areas where it wants to see an improvement:"

> Above all ... it looks forward to a cut in the number of copy claims advertisers make but which they cannot substantiate and so have complaints against them upheld. And naming specific groups of advertisers it identifies as prime sources of trouble, the Authority says how much it would welcome 'better and clear advertising for computers.'
>
> Among other improvements it hopes for is a fall in the number of complaints involving sales promotion schemes that, from the public viewpoint, so often go awry.
>
> Finally, the ASA will be happy if next year it has a lot less need to look into complaints about car, car component and homework schemes advertising.
>
> The inability of advertisers to demonstrate the truth of many of the claims made in press copy and printed material generally is seen by the ASA as 'perhaps the most worrying trend of the year.'

The ASA says it is concerned that claims are still being made with 'little or no regard' as to whether they can be proved. As the Authority sees it, 'too many advertisers appear only to begin to dream up a hasty substantiation after a complaint has been made' (*Campaign*, 1983).

A sampling of issues mentioned in ASA Case Reports in 1984 gives additional impressions regarding the number and type of complaints against advertising:

1. For a number of reasons, ranging from non-availability of product to unsubstantiated claims, nine complaints about computer advertisements are upheld in the following pages (ASA, 1984b).
2. The British Code of Sales Promotion Practice affords useful Guidelines to those about to mount competitions and promotions. It also sets out the rules to be observed – but six advertisers this month shut their eyes to both guidelines and rules (ASA, 1984c).
3. Readers' fears were raised by six advertisers with widely divergent interests this months. Companies offering agricultural products and insulation systems joined security and insurance organisations in adopting unjustifiable appeals to fear (ASA, 1984e).
4. ... an advertiser claiming that specific amounts of weight could be lost in a given period of time was found to be in flagrant breach of the Code and the publishers were censured for accepting it (ASA, 1984d).

Happily, there were also lighter moments in the life of the ASA:

The Authority was unable to share the sensitivities of the forteen complainants who were offended by one particular advertisement, featuring a reproduction of a Van Gogh self portrait, together with the headline 'The one person who wouldn't appreciate what we're selling ... these days you need more than a good ear to appreciate ITT products. You need two' (ASA, 1984b).

As is well known, the famous Dutch painter Van Gogh during a fit of insanity cut off one of his ears, which fact can be seen clearly on the self-portrait shown in the advertisement. Although the complaints against this advertising were not upheld, the Authority considered the advertisement to be inane and in poor taste.

The experience of the ASA and that of other countries, clearly indicates that large numbers of consumers who are offended or upset by a particular advertisement, will express their opinions forcefully and unreservedly. This healthy phenomenon should be encouraged. As we said earlier the number of annual complaints is not especially important, since such complaints are not necessarily representative of total public opinion. The importance of bodies such as the ASA lies in the fact that they exist, that consumers know where to go if they have a complaint, and that advertisers know that their advertising can be challenged.

Having thus described consumers' reaction against specific advertisements, let us now turn our attention to consumers' opinions about advertising in general. Although the available studies have some limitations, they provide useful perspectives.

Trends in consumer attitudes toward advertising

The advertising business has never won a first prize in a popularity contest. It is accepted by many as an activity which performs an essential role in our economic system — to help consumers in making purchasing choices. But the environment in which advertising operates today seems to be less hostile than in the 1970s. There is a trend towards a more positive image of advertising among the buying public. The advertising business has every reason to be pleased about this gradual change, which it has earned by its efforts to reform itself as well as by its endeavours to educate others about the nature and proper functions of advertising.

There is substantial information to indicate that consumers consider advertising relatively unimportant compared to other activities and institutions in their lives. In the UK for example, the AA has studied public attitudes toward advertising since 1966. Several surveys have been conducted by the same independent market research agency, making meaningful comparisons over a number of years possible. Fortunately, it was possible to include Canadian and Australian figures in the following tables. This is particularly important because both countries have severe advertising controls. "Canada, I'm embarrassed to say, is also a country that may lead the world in the amount of advertising regulations, with the threat of more always on the horizon," said Keith McKerracher, President of the Institute of Canadian Advertising (McKerracher, 1984). The voice from Australia is even more alarming:

> The advertising industry has failed so badly to defend itself against ill-informed and vexatious prejudice that it now faces only two alternatives: a major reorganisation of its public representation, or failing that, the near prospect that within a few years the process of advertising in Australia will be so emasculated as to render itself useless to many marketers and unrewarding to its practitioners (Whitington, 1985).

It may be of some consolation to the advertising business in both countries that the figures in the following tables do not reflect great differences in consumer attitudes between these countries and the UK. The evidence in Table IV indicates that in both the UK and Australia consumers consider advertising to be relatively unimportant as a topic of conversation.

The remarkable similarity between the UK and Australian data suggest that it is not unlikely that similar results would be obtained from surveys in other economically advanced nations. This conclusion is buttressed by similar responses to a question about salience of advertising to consumers in Australia, Canada and the UK, as reported in Table V. Few hold strong opinions about advertising, compared to other subjects.

When asked whether or not a major change is needed with regard to the subjects mentioned in Tables IV and V only a small minority in the UK, two percent, feel that a major change is needed in advertising, much lower than most other categories (Beatson, 1984a:28).

Table IV

A comparison of UK consumer attitude changes 1972 – 1980, with Australian consumer 1982 data

Most-talked-about subjects	1972 (%)	1976 (%)	1980 (%)	Australian consumers' important "topics of conversation," 1982 (%)
Advertising	8	6	8	9
Big business	9	6	9	9
Bringing up children	45	43	41	28
Clothing and fashion	39	41	36	12
Family life	57	54	53	32
The government	48	36	42	34

Source of UK data: Advertising Association, as reported by Beatson, 1984a:21.
Source of Australian data: Australian Advertising Council, 1983:3.

Table V
Salience of consumer opinions

Strongest opinions on	UK 1980 (%)	Australia 1982 (%)	Canada 1978 Women	Canada 1978 Men
Advertising	4	4	7	7
Big business	5	4	4	13
Bringing up children	25	16	53	31
Clothing and fashion	9	3	16	8
Family life	26	20	40	28
The government	31	21	21	46

Source of UK data: Advertising Association, as reported by Beatson, 1984a:22.
Source of Australian data: Australian Advertising Industry Council, 1983:4.
Source of Canadian data: Institute of Canadian Advertising, as reported by McKerracher, 1984:2.

There is a great deal of additional information on attitudes toward advertising. Beatson reports, for example: (1) a majority of consumers in Germany in 1983 felt that advertising is helpful and that it gives useful information to consumers. (2) Over 80% of Norwegian consumers in 1983 believed not only that advertising is necessary in a modern society, but that it is interesting and useful. (3) In Finland in 1981 over 75% of consumers feel advertising is at least a somewhat positive thing.

(4) In the UK in 1980 over 75% of consumers approved of advertising at least a little, as contrasted with only 10% who disapproved a little, and only 6% who disapproved a lot (Beatson, 1984a:2,3,5,6).

Attitudes toward advertising in certain other countries seem to be not as favorable. Beatson reported: (1) Only 48% of Danes in 1982 believed that advertising was of benefit to consumers. (2) In France in 1983, only 41% held a favorable attitude toward advertising, 33% were to some extent opposed, while the remainder were indifferent or had no opinion. However, 64% of the French felt that advertising was useful, and 56% felt it was well done (Beatson, 1984a:4,7,8).

Beatson also reported Italian data, which he felt "is fairly typical" on what he called the "me:them" phenomenon. Only 45% of Italians in 1983 felt that advertising influenced *their own purchases* a lot (11%) or quite a lot (32%), while 89% believed that advertising influences *other people's purchases* a lot (39%) or quite a lot (50%). "In other words: Others are more susceptible, fragile, and gullible than I am" (Beatson, 1984a:10).

The attitudes of young people are not only important now, but will become even more so since they are the consumers of the future. Keeping in mind that other matters are much more important than advertising, it is still disturbing to note that the youth of some nations harbor many negative opinions as well as positive opinions about advertising (Table VI). Cultural differences apparently are great, for example: "In contrast to the mercantile traditions of anglo-saxons, people in southern Europe have been culturally programmed for centuries to despise filthy lucre, associate profit with usury, and consumption with vice, and to mistrust traders" (Beatson, 1984a:16). Nevertheless one finds far less strict advertising regulation in Italy compared to Denmark, and generally a more tolerant attitude toward commercial freedoms. Obviously more research is needed to clarify our understandings of these contrasts.

As we have seen, attitudes of consumers towards advertising appear to follow a more or less similar pattern throughout Europe. This is surprising because of the cultural, historical and social differences between European nations. One might have expected that the image of advertising in European countries would differ far more than it does.

Beatson comments on this point as follows:

> The Europe that concerns us consists of two major grouping of States. The Council of Europe is composed of 21 states. Within that group is the European Economic Community which [until January 1, 1986] consists of five Republics, four Kingdoms and one Grand Dutchy: 10 states in all, with others waiting to join. These two politico-economic groups, the Council of Europe and the EEC are what make Europe greater than the sum of its parts.
>
> At different points in our history, each of our nations has been the ally and the enemy of each of the others. We still speak 19 different languages in 16 major markets. So what can we possibly have in common? (Beatson, 1984a:1).

Table VI
Attitudes of young people toward advertising; all 15 – 25 year olds agreeing

	Austria (%)	Greece (%)	Italy (%)	Nether-lands (%)	Spain (%)	Sweden (%)	UK (%)
1. Overall, advertising is more good than bad							
15 – 19	62	57	37	28	22	36	66
20 – 25	54	50	27	31	17	29	65
2. Advertising is mostly quite entertaining							
15 – 19	56	49	53	57	49	61	75
20 – 25	57	43	41	49	28	54	76
3. Advertisements are useful in giving me ideas about what to buy							
15 – 19	63	54	48	46	47	79	68
20 – 25	58	40	39	53	38	80	68
4. Advertising makes people buy things they do not want							
15 – 19	88	88	75	89	89	74	69
20 – 25	86	85	80	91	92	83	84
5. Advertisements have made me buy things I did not want							
15 – 19	31	46	44	23	51	33	38
20 – 25	35	46	42	29	50	33	38

Source: McCann-Erickson, as reported by Beatson, 1984a:16 – 18.

Nevertheless, the main attitudes toward the relatively "unimportant" subject of advertising, are more similar than dissimilar, which makes it seem reasonable to suppose that the Advertising Association's conclusions on attitudes toward advertising in the UK apply to all Europe:

> The general conclusion from the weight of scientifically-conducted and published research (by the Advertising Association and others) must be that 'advertising' as a general concept remains extremely low on most people's list of concerns. Few people talk about it, fewer still hold strong opinions on the subject, and only a tiny majority (2 percent) feel that any major change is needed. Even the critics of advertising do not disapprove wholeheartedly, are aware of the legal and other constraints, and few of them see any need for further restrictions (Bullmore and Waterson, 1983:370).

A TV commercial for Samsonite in France

In addition to the above brief review of consumer attitudes toward advertising, an important signal comes from France – a court decision on advertising for *Samsonite* luggage. It illustrates what is permissible in advertising today.

A TV commercial for this product showed a pair of bulldozers, playing with a *Samsonite* case on a soccer field, throwing it in the air and pushing it across the field. The suitcase at the end of the commercial came out undamaged and completely intact; not a word is said.

A competitor claimed that this commercial was misleading, that in fact many *Samsonite* cases had been damaged during the shooting of this commercial and that the use of it should be forbidden because of its misleading character.

In the first court case the competitor won the suit. But *Samsonite* won when it appealed to a higher court. The "Cour d'Appel" argued that advertising techniques had gone through an important evolution and that the average consumer was perfectly capable of differentiating between what really would be misleading and what would be seen as perfectly acceptable exaggeration that would not be misleading ("la loi n'étant pas destiné à protéger les faibles d'esprit" – the law was not designed to protect the feeble-minded). Nobody in his right mind would believe that a *Samsonite* case could actually endure such a game undamaged; believing the opposite would deny the average consumer any critical ability and intelligence ("estimer le contraire reviendrait à nier tout sens critique et intelligence de la part du téléspectateur"). The Court pointed out, furthermore, that the particular law had been designed to protect consumers, that no complaint from consumers had been received, and that a competitor had registered the complaint. Consequently the Court reversed the first decision and decided in favor of *Samsonite* (Samsonite, 1983). To the delight of the advertising business this 1983 verdict was confirmed in May, 1984 by the "Cour de Cassation, Chambre Criminelle," in Paris.

Of course, one must be cautious not to overgeneralize from one case. This judge's opinion in France might not be the same as the opinion of judges on similar situations in other countries. However, ten years ago it would have been less likely for a French judge to decide that consumers have matured and that they have become accustomed to the attention-getting creative fantasies, exaggerations and hyperbole of modern advertising. Perhaps in the future judges in other countries will also demonstrate increased respect for the intelligence of today's consumers, which would be a refreshing departure from the patronizing attitude of so many regulators and legislators in recent years.

However, despite these happier moments in the lives of advertising men and women, there remain many topics that require research to add to our knowlegde. Particularly we need to learn more about communicating effectively with consumers about products and services sold in many different countries. When can advertising be the same and when will it have to be different?

The European Society for Opinion and Marketing Research (ESOMAR) conducts seminars and publishes papers, reports and a journal dealing with many aspects of market research as the basis for effective decision making in separate European countries. But the advertising business today needs more than that. In order to decide on the use of one advertising idea or theme and on the need to create variations of its presentation in many different countries, the advertising business must learn more about similarities and differences between consumers in these countries. It is also important to compare legislation, administrative law and court decisions which illustrate the rules under which advertisers must operate in Common Market countries.

These types of studies, covering the entire Common Market, require active participation and financing by advertisers, advertising agencies, media and commercial research organizations.

The Advertising Educational Foundation in the USA

In this connection it might be of interest to examine the research funding program of the Advertising Educational Foundation (AEF) in the USA, which is supported by the advertising business.

The AEF describes its objectives as follows:

> Our goal is threefold: first, to educate ourselves through research in order to understand and practice our profession better; secondly, to build a bridge of understanding between advertising and the academic community so that teachers and students at the college and university level may better understand the role of advertising in contemporary life; and thirdly, to raise the general perception of advertising as a beneficial force, socially and economically, among thought leaders and the general public (*Advertising Educational Foundation*:37).

The interesting point about this program is that its three main objectives are interrelated: research will not only help to improve the quality of advertising, but it will also contribute to "build a bridge ... between advertising and the academic community," which in turn will influence the "thought leaders."

While this program relates to the situation in one country, one might consider such a program for Europe. It would certainly be possible to identify topics in a number of European countries about which the advertising business or others would like to have more knowledge. An international research foundation might well be the answer to acquire such knowledge, and indeed to use the findings of research for the same purposes and in the same way as is done in the USA, provided that in Europe the newly acquired knowledge should be disseminated through existing channels of national organizations in the countries concerned.

An example of research funded by the AEF was a study on the comprehension and appreciation of television commercials, entertainment programs and news reports. Similar studies in Europe would be of considerable interest not only to advertising professionals, but also to consumer organizations and intergovernmental bodies. Other useful studies could be done on the cost/benefit aspects of consumer protection programs, a topic of which the ICC says: "It is recommended that more objective studies should be made comparing the effectiveness and efficiency in practice of self-regulation in providing consumer protection" (ICC, 1984:18).

With this in mind, we would like to formulate the following

Recommendation I

In view of the need for additional evidence about the effects of advertising on consumers, the economy and society — especially because of important market and consumer differences among Member States — it is recommended that a European Advertising Research Foundation should be established. All segments of the industry from all Member States should support the foundation financially: advertisers, advertising agencies, advertising media and related research and service organizations.

The functions of the foundation should be to: (1) identify priorities for research on the effects of advertising, and the effects of advertising regulation in all Member States, (2) administer funding to researchers for projects, or carry out such research directly, as appropriate, and (3) disseminate the acquired new knowledge to advertisers and their agencies, consumer groups, educational institutions, government agencies, legislators and media, preferably through the appropriate and relevant national associations in the countries concerned.

Against this background of trends in consumer attitudes and how further knowledge of consumer behavior, tastes and preferences could be obtained throughout the Community, we now turn our attention to the second consumer program of the EEC which appeared in May, 1981.

The second consumer protection and information program

In view of the many reactions of consumer groups, the advertising business and governments to the Commission's first consumer program, the Commission set out to produce a new program. It reflected the gradually changing public opinion about advertising, the decreased attention being given to the subject in the public media and a growing awareness among the Brussels administration, that consumers were more capable of looking after their own interests than was assumed when the first program was drafted.

Producing a second consumer program was in line with the final paragraph of the first one, in which the Commission had stated: "The aim is to complete the first stage within four years." The Commission only managed to complete the second program four years later, (on June 20, 1979) and sent it to the Council of Ministers for approval. The Council took two years for its deliberations, finally passing a Resolution on May 19, 1981 (see Appendix VI).

Analysis of the new program

The Commission said in its third progress report on the consumer protection and information policy:

> In essence, the second programme retains, in their entirety, the basic rights and the principles governing their implementation as enunciated in the first programme of 1975 as being invariant elements in the policy structure of consumer protection. It lays stress, however, on the importance of the dialogue between producer and consumer interests which should be carried out in full mutual recognition of their functions as partners in the operation of the Common Market. As counterpart to the acknowledgement of that role by consumer representatives the draft programme takes the positive attitude of promotion of consumer interests and not merely their protection. This would be realised, in practical terms, by the encouragement and facilitation of producer/consumer dialogue, leading in certain instances to specific agreements between their representatives on matters of common concern. This dialogue process is seen as complementary to legislative action which will continue to be necessary at Community as well as at national level (*Third Report Commission*, 1980:8).

The Commission had concluded that it had to adapt itself to the realities of the situation. It therefore struck a more conciliatory tone in its second program, without in any way officially withdrawing from the ambitious plans laid down in its first program.

The new program was characterized by the following points:

(1) It formally confirmed the original program, as introduced in 1975, albeit adapted to new and different circumstances.

(2) It referred to the "current difficult economic situation" emphasizing the need to pay special attention to the price and quality of goods and services, both public and private.

(3) It appealed on the one hand to the consumer movement to "progressively take into account the economic and social implications of the decisions on which it might wish to be consulted;" on the other hand it urged political and economic decision-makers to "be willing to take consumers' views into account ... when preparing and implementing decisions which are likely to affect consumers' interests;" the latter recommendation was one that the advertising business had long desired.

(4) It especially recognized the need for dialogue and consultation, which the business world had repeatedly been asking for, stating explicitly: "In particular the Community should try to encourage a dialogue and consultation between representatives from consumers and representatives from producers, distributors and suppliers of public and private services with a view, in certain cases, to arriving at solutions satisfactory to all the parties in question" (Appendix VI, p.320).

(5) It made a gesture towards voluntary controls by stating:

> Although legislation both at national and Community levels will still be needed in many cases in order to ensure that the consumer may exercise the fundamental rights listed above and that the

market operates properly, the application of certain principles might also be sought by other means, such as the establishment of specific agreements between the various interests held, which would have the advantage of giving consumers additional assurances of good trading practice (Appendix VI, p.320).

(6) It reiterated that a number of products and practices required further action, for example: foodstuffs, cosmetics, textiles, toys, pharmaceutical products, misleading advertising, product liability, consumer credit, and unfair contracts.

(7) It contained an interesting point with regard to alcohol and tobacco. The Commission stated that it would only "assess to what extent divergencies in measures taken by Member States in regard to these products affect the Community market and, where necessary, make appropriate proposals;" it would also support actions taken by governments, associated "with the use or abuse of such products by consumers;" but the Commission itself clearly was not going to take any initiatives on the regulation of these products (Appendix VI, p.325).

(8) It restated the principle laid down in the first consumer program, that with regard to education "Facilities should be made available to children as well as to young people and adults to educate them to act as discriminating consumers, capable of making an informed choice of goods and services and conscious of their rights and responsibilities." But the second consumer program no longer recommends specific actions to achieve this aim and confined itself to say: "... Community action will consist in continuing the wide-ranging exchange of views on national experience and joint consideration of the aims and methods of consumer education in schools" (Appendix VI, p.334).

(9) It referred to the need for dialogue and consultation, especially to encourage "closer cooperation between associations which would defend and promote consumers' interests and play an active part in trying to achieve the necessary balance between consumers and producers/distributors," going on to reaffirm its offer of "more aid to organizations which represent consumers" (Appendix VI, p.335).

(10) Finally, in its introduction to the new program, the Commission stated that this program "will ensure the continuity of the measure already undertaken and enable new tasks to be undertaken in business years 1981 to 1986" (Appendix VI, p.318).

When studying the Second Consumer Protection and Information Program, one could easily come to the conclusion that it did not really offer anything new, that it was a kind of watered down version of the first program and that apart from openly admitting the apparent weakness of consumer representation the Commission was simply giving itself another five years to accomplish what it had previously intended to do.

We do not necessarily share this somewhat negative view. One should not go only by the Commission's words, but also by its deeds. There were a number of positive changes in the Commission's stance, such as the call for dialogue and consultation, and the willingness to accept in principle some form of voluntary agreements. But there was more to it than that. The importance of the second program should also be judged by what it did not say. Considerable pressure had for example been exerted on the Commission by the EP's Committee on the Environment, Public Health and Consumer Protection; this committee urged the Commission to go much further in restricting the marketing and advertising of products and services. A draft motion for a resolution from Rapporteur John O'Connell said among other things that the Commission should "introduce, as a priority measure, a proposal for a directive prohibiting the advertising of tobacco and alcohol;" the Commission should also "introduce Community measures to control the advertising of medicines" (European Parliament, 1980).

An earlier document of the same committee had also proposed a ban on advertising to children on television, but this was not included. Thus, while past experience led to a certain amount of industry skepticism about the Commission's intentions, there now were signs that the Commission would not go along with some consumerist demands which fell outside its competence, or for which the need could not be demonstrated.

Commission recommendations for dialogue between all parties

The Commission expressed the desire to give industry and consumer representatives a chance to sort things out between themselves, but it insisted that it be a part of this dialogue. Some felt that by encouraging dialogue and consultation, the Commission was shifting its responsibility to others, a standpoint taken by the BEUC.

Pessimists believed that this process would not be successful and that the Commission would prevent other bodies from exercising any real influence. Others felt that industry and consumer representatives could work closely together to prepare agreements sufficiently complete that they would be ready for the Commission's official approval. As we shall see later, the pessimists were right. In practice, these intentions did not work out.

A dialogue is more than two monologues

Earlier we expressed doubts that consumer organizations represent consumer opinion adequately. Moreover, most representatives of consumer organizations are at best only mildly interested in the professional views of those in the advertising business. Therefore one might ask why business should try to create a working relationship with consumer organizations. There are two reasons: (1) many consumer organizations have a genuine interest in advancing the welfare of consumers and therefore it is sensible to consider their proposals carefully, and (2) governments of

Member States as well as intergovernmental organizations will insist that "official" consumer representation be consulted on all matters concerning consumer affairs. If therefore the advertising business wants to be part of discussions on consumer affairs, it must be prepared to sit at the table with formally recognized consumer groups.

However, to achieve this working relationship is easier said than done, and the experience to date has not been entirely positive. For example, on November 16, 1982 a meeting was held between members of the Bureau of the CCC and a delegation of the EAT, under the auspices of the Consumer Affairs Division of the EEC. In the absence of any proposals from either the CCC or the Consumer Division, the EAT proposed four points as a basis for discussion. Four papers had been prepared by members of the EAT delegation on the following subjects and were presented during the meeting:

(1) "What is the influence of advertising on prices, product quality and ultimately the level and quality of consumers' lives?" by Jean-Natthieu Hellich, Legal Counsel of the Colgate Palmolive Company in France.

(2) "Are innovations launched with large advertising campaigns often without real substance?" by Patricia Mann, Vice-President of J. Walter Thompson International in the UK.

(3) "Does the emotional nature of advertising impede consumer organisations' attempts to make the purchasing act as rational as possible?" by Patricia Mann.

(4) "What are the effects on the freedom of information of the assumption of control of media by industrial and financial groups?" by Stefen Gullmann, Director of the *Politiken* Newspaper in Denmark.

Six representatives from the Commission attended. Among them was the Chairman of this meeting, Jeremiah Sheehan, the Commission's Director for Consumer Affairs. Seven members from the CCC also attended, three of whom represented the Coop movement, one represented trade unions and three represented consumers. The EAT sent a delegation of eleven people, led by Roger Underhill, Director-General of the Advertising Association in the UK (EAT, 1982).

All elements to make a good meeting were there: the will to get together, proper delegations, and an interesting selection of subjects with carefully prepared written papers on each of them. And yet, the meeting was not as successful as the advertising business had hoped. A genuine dialogue in which participants exchanged ideas and tried to move toward a better understanding of each other's position, was still absent.

The Bremen meeting

On November 15 – 16, 1983 a meeting was held in Bremen to discuss "soft law," i.e. self-regulatory codes of practice or agreements within industry to "regulate" advertising voluntarily. This meeting was attended by representatives from the ECLG, the Commission and the BEUC. Tony Venables, director of the BEUC addressed the subject of "European Codes: A Red Herring." The title indicated the direction of his thoughts. He began by pointing out that "After two years of 'dialogue' with the Union of Industries of the European Community (UNICE), the European Advertising Tripartite (EAT), the distributors, and manufacturers, this experiment has been an embarrassing failure . . ."

In his presentation, Venables accepted the usefulness of informal meetings with industry, which ". . . can occasionally lead to joint positions on EEC directives and policies," but he questioned the practical value of voluntary codes.

> 'Codes" are not the best answer to the legislative impasse with the EEC consumer programme. 'Soft' law co-exists with the 'hard' variety. If there is no threat of legislation, no one is obliged to negotiate seriously. In the last four years, as a result of this tactical error, there have been neither any European codes nor any EEC directives under the consumer programme (Venables, 1984:297).

In a more general way, the BEUC had expressed its dissatisfaction with the Commission's consumer program and its lack of progress long before the Bremen meeting. In 1980 the BEUC had said in a document prepared on the occasion of the public hearing in Dublin that it attributed the slow development of the consumer program to insufficient cooperation from Member States which were not giving great priority to consumer affairs, particularly in those countries where there is already significant legislation in this field. Consumer organizations also believed that industry had considerable influence on blocking or watering down proposals from the Commission, for example on product liability and misleading advertising.

Regarding the desirability of legislation versus voluntary controls, the BEUC agreed with the CCC which had reservations about voluntary agreements:

> There is no guarantee that a dialogue can be carried out on equal basis between consumer organizations and commercial interests and that there will be full access to information; there is the difficulty of ensuring that all branches of industry are correctly represented; the Commission has neither provided machinery for monitoring and ensuring the inforcement of such agreement or any complaints, arbitration or judicial procedures; in no case should voluntary agreements replace Community instruments (BEUC, 1980).

In Bremen, these objections were repeated and the ECLG, in a paper which had been distributed to the participants, took a strong stand against voluntary controls, arguing that: ". . . the primary motivation for codes on the part of producers and traders is self-interest, particularly the avoidance of legislation which would be more restrictive (or more rigorously enforced) than the code accepted" (ECLG, 1983a:210).

After dealing with many aspects of codes, the ECLG paper commented on codes at the international level:

> .. the elaboration of international codes raises specific problems. At the international level, both consumers and traders are differently organized; the imbalance of resources and bargaining power between traders and consumers is certainly not palliated. Enforcement of international codes seems all the more complicated when there is no public officer who could be responsible for disseminating information. The European Consumer Law Group therefore recommends that individual consumer organisations should not, in isolation, embark upon the negotiation of international codes (ECLG, 1983a:221).

In its Conclusions, the ECLG said:

> The European Consumer Law Group is aware that in some countries and in certain circumstances, codes have proved that they could effectively raise standards. From the consumer viewpoint, the essential and most important point is the existence and effective implementation of protective rules. It does not matter to consumers whether this protection is ensured by virtue of statute law or in any other way. Thus the European Consumer Law Group has, in principle, no objection to non-legislative means of consumer protection, nor against codes in particular. In most cases, however codes have been unsuccessful, at least in promoting the consumer interest. The main reason for codes is indeed the interest of traders, particularly the avoidance of legislation (ECLG, 1983a:222).

The ECLG continued by saying that codes do not generally provide a valuable alternative to legislation and that their advantages do not balance their drawbacks. The ECLG therefore recommended that codes should only be considered when there is no prospect of legislation to achieve the same objective. It also summed up a number of requirements which codes must meet before they can be considered as a potential means of improving consumer protection:

> *Negotiation.* Up to now unilateral codes (which have proven not to be useful to consumers) have been elaborated by traders themselves, in the interest of traders and not of consumers. Codes should always be negotiated, be it with consumer organisations and/or with a public officer. Negotiations with a public officer should be preferred when consumer organisations do not have adequate resources to engage in negotiations with various branches of trade.
> *Consultations.* Whenever the negotiation of a code is considered or initiated, consumer organisations and the public should be informed. Consumer organisations should have the opportunity of making their views known; they should however not be committed to the results of the negotiations.
> *Content.* Issues of health and safety should be regulated by statutory provisions.
> *Information.* The public officer in charge of the negotiation of the code should also be responsible for disseminating information on it. Specific attention should be paid to means of complaining about breaches of the code; such information should in particular be printed on contract forms.
> *Outsiders.* Any code should provide for a mechanism by virtue of which the code is made applicable to all traders concerned with the subject matter of the code.
> *Monitoring.* The public officer in charge of the negotiations of the code should also be given adequate means to enable him to monitor the actual implementation of the code.
> *Complaints.* An independent body, where consumers and traders should be equally represented, should be entrusted with handling the complaints under the code.

Sanctions. Codes should provide for sanctions that act as a real deterrent, including information to the media and pecuniary fines (ECLG, 1983a:223 – 224).

Finally, the ECLG stated:

> The European Consumer Law Group is of the opinion that the EC Commission has a mandate and a duty to make proposals for the effective implementation of the principles laid down in the Second Consumer Action Programme. Where EC legislation cannot be achieved, it would be better to adopt national legislation (ECLG, 1983a:224).

It is interesting to note that against these negative opinions from the ECLG about "soft law" and a dialogue with industry, the Commission introduced in the proceedings a refreshing note of optimism.

The Commission's Director for Consumer Affairs, Jeremiah Sheehan, first of all defended the Commission's recommendations for a dialogue by saying that "... the Commission was ready to experiment with dialogue, particularly in certain fields, as an additional element of strategy in pursuit of consumer welfare, but not as a substitute for law-making activities. Quite clearly, one had to proceed with caution and not hope for too much too soon" (Sheehan, 1984).

More importantly, he also said:

> We also have a process of 'negative' harmonisation, whereby national laws which purport to protect consumers, can be tested in the Court of Justice and either rejected as unnecessary for that purpose, in which case they should be struck out, or upheld, in which case Community action would be strongly indicated to bring other member states' laws into line, so eliminating, in one sense or the other, the technical barrier to trade created by the national law in question (Sheehan, 1984).

This comment indicates a growing awareness within the Commission, that a kaleidoscope of different laws and regulations to control the many factors that comprise a brand and its meaning to consumers, seriously inhibits the quick and effective development of a succesful national brand into an international one, and that such controls retard the development of trade among nations and the benefits therefrom. The advertising business felt that a combination of minimum harmonization of existing legislation, and improved systems of self-regulation would appear to be the solution. If, therefore, "negative" harmonization were put into practice, the highly desirable expansion of international trade throughout the Community would be stimulated.

While this would be a great step forward, the fact must not be overlooked that at the Bremen meeting no hand was offered to those favoring self-regulation. At the risk of becoming repetitious, we must once again point out that neither in Bremen, nor anywhere else for that matter, was evidence produced to support the allegation that voluntary controls of codes do not work to the best interest and to the satisfaction of consumers, as well as to those of the advertising business.

The criticism of voluntary controls depends on the assertion that the industry acting in its own interest must necessarily act to the detriment of consumers. The critics ignore the fact, that advertising control systems in several countries demonstrate that a minimum legislative basis provides a foundation on which a successful voluntary system can be built — a system that goes far beyond what a legal system could do to protect and improve the position of consumers in the marketplace. Naturally, the effectiveness of voluntary controls depends upon the active support of the media, that are in a position to withhold space for advertising, and on the policing of the advertising by an independent body. As in many countries these conditions exist, the advertising business feels that unsubstantiated claims about the weakness of voluntary regulations are unfair, misleading and counter-productive.

Since the early 1980s relationships and mutual understanding between the business world and intergovernmental bodies fortunately have improved. But meaningful and constructive discussions with consumer groups have not yet materialized. Perhaps the comments of BEUC's Director-General towards the end of his presentation can be seen as a positive indication for this group's willingness to take contacts with the business community more seriously. Venables pointed out that in areas where the chances of new EEC legislation are small, there are other useful approaches:

1. Greater emphasis on enforcing [existing] legislation by the EEC.
2. Better choice of priorities and more latitude for national authorities to achieve common objectives by different means.
3. Coordinate and approximate legislative progress at national level, rather than seek to harmonize at all costs (Venables, 1984:299).

In trying to summarize the factors that still appear to influence adversely the relationships with consumer representatives, the main points are:

(1) Some representatives of consumer organizations suspect the real motivation of industry and assume that multinational advertisers are able to manipulate consumers into buying things they do not need; this myth is still believed by many critics of advertising.

(2) Representatives of the advertising business resent unsubstantiated criticism of the effectiveness of codes and other voluntary controls of advertising that protect the interests of both consumers and advertisers. They not only protect consumers from advertising abuses, but they ensure that advertising is not debased; they also protect advertising against unwieldy bureaucratic and costly state intervention. Many of these controls have proven their value in practice and are increasingly accepted by consumers and governments in European countries.

(3) If an experienced group of practitioners in international advertising debates controversial questions with consumer representatives who do not have the same

experience and professional background, the latter group can easily be caught off balance and be forced to depend more on questioning the motives of the business world than on facts about consumer behavior.

(4) According to the ECLG, the poor participation of consumer organizations in the dialogue is due in part to their lack of money and resources. It is difficult to accept this argument. If consumers felt strongly about the issues at stake, they could easily contribute the necessary money and manpower for consumer organizations to enter into a dialogue with industry. But the average consumer just is not very interested.

Since the dialogue concerning the interests of consumers and industry is important, it is regrettable that efforts to bring about such a dialogue have not yet had any demonstrable results. As the Commission said in June, 1985: '[this] hope has not yet been translated into reality" (Commission of the EC, 1985c:21).

What can be done to improve relationships?

The French saying *"la critique est aisée, mais l'art est difficile"* is fully applicable to the situation. What should be done about the disappointing relationship between consumer representation and industry and how can the improved relationship between industry and the Commission be further stimulated?

This task is not made any easier by the fact that consumer protection is not about "firms which ... carry out a respectable policy towards consumers ... but it is about the problem areas, or the problem firms which will probably remain outside voluntary arrangements" (Venables, 1984:298). Since most firms belong to the category of "respectables," consumer protection activities seem necessary only because of a small minority of problem firms. Yet consumerist attacks and proposed programs seem to be aimed broadly at the entire advertising business. Perhaps the main reason for the differences of opinion that still exist between parties concerned, can be traced back to misunderstandings on the part of civil servants and consumer groups about what advertising can and cannot do. But also there are relatively few advertising practitioners who understand the complexities of the bureaucratic machinery in the Berlaymont Building in Brussels, which houses more than ten thousand officials.

Educating non-industry groups

Both regulators and advertising practitioners have from the start felt this lack of knowledge to be an unfortunate situation. But consumer groups have not expressed their concern in this respect; the majority of them simply have not been accessible. Yet, it must be clear to all concerned that without their cooperation little will be achieved that consumers can appreciate. We would suggest that it is more in the interest of consumer groups than in anyone else's, to seek closer contact with the business community. Maintaining a negative attitude toward such contacts cannot very well be interpreted by anyone to be in the interest of those that consumer organizations claim to represent.

It has often been suggested that the advertising business should organize a number of planned presentations on the functioning of advertising, and offer them to an international audience of officials of the various EC departments, the COE, the OECD and most important the BEUC and other groups concerned with consumer affairs. The media, and particularly its editorial staff, should also be invited to attend such presentations and participate in the discussions that would follow. It may come as a surprise to many that the editorial staffs of newspapers and magazines sometimes belong to advertising's most severe critics. Public criticism is of course to be welcomed in a democratic society, but it should be informed and objective criticism rather than an expression of personal prejudices.

The advertising business has on several occasions discussed running such meetings. But more urgent priorities prevented the preparation of a detailed plan for action. It would seem that the time has come to carry out this task, which is even more appropriate today than it was a few years ago. However, it would be unrealistic to expect that the advertising business would make available the necessary funds and talent without some clear indication that such a series of meetings would be acceptable to all parties concerned. In fact, since the advertising business has already tried to take the initiative for a dialogue with consumer organizations, it would now appear to be their turn to do so. This leads us to:

Recommendation II

New initiatives should be taken to bring together representatives from supranational and intergovernmental organizations concerned with consumer protection and advertising regulation.

The advertising industry should prepare informative presentations for this group on the most important aspects of producing, placing and measuring the effectiveness of advertising on an international scale.

Consumer education

The subject of educating consumers for a better understanding of the economic process is not of central relevance to the subject of this book. However, it is important to the business community that the European citizens should be prepared for their role as informed and demanding consumers in society. Individual governments, the EC Commission, the COE and a number of supranational organizations are also rightly concerned. The advertising business believes that objective information about advertising as a vital part of the economic process, should be given to children and students in their primary, secondary and advanced education.

The consumer education program of the EC

It is interesting to note that although the Rome Treaty gives the Community institutions no more than a limited jurisdiction in the field of education, the Commission nevertheless saw fit to include the following statement in its first consumer program:

> Facilities should be made available to children as well as to young people and adults to educate them to act as discriminating consumers, capable of making an informed choice of goods and services and conscious of their rights and responsibilities. To this end, consumers should, in particular, benefit from basic information on the principles of modern economics (Appendix I, p.269).

The Commission soon realized the complexities of such a broad program. In its second report on its consumer program, the Commission no longer mentioned "adults" but referred to "the incorporation of consumer education into the normal curriculum of young students"; it planned to take measures to:

> – establish a network of pilot schools covering all Member States through which initial experience will be gained and exchanged in teaching a course of elementary consumer education to students in the final years of primary, and the early years of secondary education
> – set up a group of teachers who will develop resource material and appropriate pedagogy for such courses (*Second Report Commission*, 1978:22)

In its second consumer program, the Commission wisely reduced the breadth of its earlier ambitions:

> Given the power of the Member States with regard to education and the work the Commission has already undertaken, Community action will consist in continuing the wide-ranging exchange of views on national experience and joint consideration of the aims and methods of consumer education in schools (Appendix VI, p.334).

Apparently the Commission had come to the conclusion that its desire to educate adults was unrealistic and that instead it should concentrate on consumer education in schools.

We subscribe to this view, since we are skeptical about the need for such adult education. We believe that adults need

(a) proper general education;

(b) knowledge about products and services, acquired through personal experience and the competitive situation in the marketplace;

(c) advice from friends, neighbours, relatives, etc.;

(d) to have access to the multi-media situation, informing them about the qualities of products and services; and

(e) the availability of consumer advice centers.

We feel that the above listed resources are ample to help most citizens in our developed western society to be intelligent, discriminating, indeed demanding consumers, who will not need, nor be interested in, special studies or courses about the economics of the marketplace.

However, the situation with regard to young people is entirely different and deserves our full attention. In December, 1977 the Commission sponsored a symposium in London on Consumer Education in Schools. During this symposium a number of reports were discussed, which the Commission, in cooperation with national governments, had initiated in 1976. In April, 1983 Jeremiah Sheehan, made a presentation in Washington on the subject of "The Market Pacemaker ... Consumer Education." At this conference, sponsored by the US Office of Consumer Affairs and AVON Products, Inc., Sheehan described how Member States jealously guard the delicate sphere of young people's education and government's rights in this respect. Referring to the symposium in London, Sheehan summarized the findings of that meeting as follows:

> Firstly, ... all member states subscribe in principle to the value of consumer education in schools, but rather few take really affirmative action as a matter of planned policy. Secondly, ... wherever it exists, consumer education is usually integrated in other subjects rather than standing as a subject in its own right. Thirdly, it tends not to be given the highest levels of ability streaming in schools because more traditional subjects are critical, for example, for college admission. Fourthly, ... it can be given to very young children providing it can be related closely to their personal experiences as consumers, but ... parents should be closely associated at the young age groups with the program and try to give it support away from the school environment in cooperation with teachers. Fifth, ... one should allow for and harness the parallel education experiences that children inevitably get from the media outside the school – an obvious point. Sixth ... as far as possible, children should assimilate consumer education in a larger context consumption policy and its consequences for others, including the less developed nations in terms of trade, in terms of conservation and scarce resources, environmental pollution and other global considerations of that kind without which consumer affairs tends not to assume its proper place and proper context (Sheehan, 1983a:26 – 27).

Meanwhile the Commission conducted a pilot project from 1978 to 1983. The purpose was to develop and test teaching methods which can be used for consumer education in schools. Mr. Hans Rask Jensen of the Institute of Marketing at the Århus School of Business Administration and Economics in Denmark, was business project leader. Twenty-five schools established in Ireland, Italy, Holland, Denmark, Belgium, France, Germany and the UK, participated.

Since all schools involved wished to use their own methods in testing consumer education, the project leader had to accept a particularly heterogeneous network. In his report, he said:

> ... The various factors to which I had to adapt included a large number of different subjects and age groups, a large number of different teachers with a wide range of differing views relating to the principal content of consumer education and the method of teaching, and a large number of different national expectations with regard to the main findings of the research work (Rask Jensen, 1983:12A).

Consequently, Mr. Jensen concluded that in view of the considerable differences between educational systems, the absence of any training for teachers in problems of consumer education, and the non-compulsory nature of the subject of consumer education in most Member States, he was unable "... to provide any answers as to whether the existing standards and regulations in the educational field may be regarded on the whole as being an acceptable base on which to organize up-to-date instruction in this field" (Rask Jensen, 1983:140). Mr. Jensen continued:

> What the pilot project has shown, then, is that the consumer education provided within the existing network of pilot schools has been aimed to an overwhelming degree at enabling the pupils to solve their own problems in close contact with the social, economic and political reality of which they, as consumers, are a part ... (Rask Jensen, 1983:141A).

The writer finally asks a number of questions to which an answer will have to be given if the Commission wishes "to satisfy existing and future national needs in this area." These questions refer to the resources of the Commission to offer know-how and expertise: (1) Can the Commission call on resources from other areas involved in consumer policy? (2) Can the level of cooperation between Member States be increased? (3) Are there permanent channels of communication with the national authorities? (4) Is the Commission in a position to recommend or define what futher research must be undertaken before recommendations can be made?

The project leader of this difficult study stopped short of saying that the Commission should shelve the entire project. But that seems to be the message when one "reads between the lines."

The new Commission which took over on January 1, 1985 made several statements on the subject in its review of consumer policy over the last ten years. It now fully accepted that it could not hope to achieve anything like its earlier ambitions with regard to consumer education, when it stated: "... in no circumstances ... [is] Commission work designed to establish standard European programmes for consumer education at school and teacher training for this purpose in the Member States" (Commission of the EC, 1985b:49). But the Commission did not fully shelve the project either. During the first half year of 1985, it forwarded to the Council of Ministers a draft resolution on consumer education in primary and secondary schools. The Commission stated that the resolution:

> ... recognizes firstly the need to systematically provide such education for all pupils during the period of compulsory education ... it invites the Commission, in cooperation with the competent authorities in the Member States, to organize experimental seminars on teacher training, and to continue to study the inclusion of consumer affairs [or] carrying out, with the Commission's assistance, the translation, adaptation and publication of documents for teachers, and the production of teaching materials (Commission of the EC, 1985b:51).

The role of the Council of Europe

The COE has a clearly defined role to improve cooperation between its Member States in matters of education, and has been active in this area long before the EC became involved.

In one of its brochures, the COE says:

> The Council of Europe's work in this field is aimed at the gradual replacement of traditional educational structures by a system of permanent education better suited to present-day individual and social needs and at enabling everyone to develop his creative potential. The Council is accordingly seeking to promote a European education policy which will bring the different education systems more into line with one another through a greater convergence of curricula (Council of Europe, 1979:33).

In pursuance of this policy, on October 15, 1971 the COE adopted a Resolution (doc.B(71)98), calling for the integration of consumer education in the educational systems of member countries. It was an ambitious plan and the number of themes to be included in courses at all levels from primary school to university, included:

1. Consumers' needs;
2. consumers' resources;
3. planning and budgetting by consumers;
4, taxes, duties and fixed consumption costs;
5. variable consumption costs;
6. short- and long-term consumer goods;
7. services;
8. goods distribution;
9. advertising and other sales-promotion measures;
10. market mechanisms and various types of markets;
11. state intervention as a means of regulating market mechanisms;
12. consumer information;
13. leisure time and opportunities for cultural development;
14. the role of the consumer in society and in the economy.

It is not surprising that both the COE and the Commission eventually came to the same conclusion, namely that the subject of consumer education would always remain the primary responsibility of national governments. Little can be expected from intergovernmental programs. Consumer education does not lend itself to international coordination or harmonization and we believe that this also applies to education about advertising.

This fact was confirmed in November, 1981 when the COE ran a five-day seminar in West Germany devoted entirely to the subject of advertising. It was attended by teachers from eight European countries. The theme was "Advertising and its Effect on Youth" and Professor Dr. Herbert Mittag from Austria, representing the EAT, gave a keynote address. He explained the function of advertising, what it wants to achieve, methods to be applied and the necessity of advertising in our present social and economic structure. Professor Mittag made a particularly strong plea that prejudices against advertising and its influence on the young should be removed and that much should be done to convince those teachers who sometimes had a negative attitude toward advertising, of their responsibilities to give objective information to their students. Unfortunately, in the already overcrowded curriculum of most schools, there was little opportunity to include information on advertising's role in society. But it seemed important that accurate material about advertising should be distributed to schools and that teachers and their classes should be invited to visit advertising agencies and advertising departments of companies (EAAA, 1985b:5).

Mittag's presentation was both revealing and disturbing. It pointed to the many problems and to the colossal task the advertising business faces to achieve better advertising education in schools within the Community.

The views of the advertising business

The EAT has been alert to these matters and in 1984 published a statement entitled "Consumer Education within the Market Economy." The statement concentrated primarily on the young person:

> As the economy has developed, coupled with technological advance, the consumer has been offered much more choice, and many more benefits. General education is arguably no longer sufficient on its own to prepare young people for their roles as consumers. The principal aim of consumer education should be to help modern consumers to identify their needs and wants, to make an informed assessment of what goods or services will best fulfil those needs and wants, and then to make judicious purchases based on availability, satisfaction and price.
>
> No commercial system will ever be perfect. Consumers therefore also need to be aware of their rights, and how to invoke them should they be misled or deceived into making a wrong choice (EAT, 1984a).

The statement also points out how important it is that "students learn something of the 'how' and 'why' of industry, to broaden their knowledge of the economy and society in general." It draws attention to advertising as part of the total marketing process and indicates that consumers should understand how the process works and how it should be used. It makes the following additional points:

> All sides of the advertising business should participate in consumer education, both to ensure that advertisers and consumers benefit fully from advertisements, and by education to ensure that people are not misled by lack of knowledge. The advertising industry is aware of its responsibilities in consumer education. It is willing to contribute both on its own, and jointly with the consumer movement and educational organizations (EAT, 1984a).

This last point takes us to the heart of the matter: How can the advertising business contribute to a better understanding among young people, of the role of advertising in society and in the economic process?

It is gratifying to note that encouraging progress is already being made in many countries. In some cases responsible literature for use at schools already exists, or active plans are under way to produce and disseminate sound information and materials. Many national trade associations have produced special material for schools and a number of multinationals in the USA and in Europe have done likewise. But more has been done. For example: (1) the Department of Education of the University of Manchester in the UK is running a project "Understanding Economics," for young people aged 14 – 16, (2) the Scottish Consumer Council and the Scottish Curriculum Development Service have jointly produced a "Consumer Education Bibliography" to help young people to learn about the purchase of goods and services, both in the public and private sectors, and (3) the Zentralausschuss der Werbewirtschaft (ZAW) an industry sponsored body in Germany that is in many respects similar to the AA in the UK, has through its members also supported advertising education in German schools (Boettcher, 1979).

While these and many other national activities should be warmly encouraged by the entire business community, the following factors may well stand in the way of real progress:

(1) the preconceived opinions and anti-advertising mentality of a great number of teachers, on whose cooperation industry depends for the successful introduction of an advertising educational program, that stresses the need for freedom of choice for the consumer and freedom of speech for the manufacturer;

(2) the technical problem of getting the message about the role of advertising in the economic process across to children at schools with different educational levels, either through special or integrated courses, or through the distribution of responsible information and materials.

Professor Mittag noted that many teachers are prejudiced against advertising. As long as such prejudice exists, it retards better education about advertising. It will therefore have to be a priority of the advertising business to find in every Member State a core of teachers who already have a realistic understanding of the role of advertising in our economy and society. Then, in cooperation with these teachers the advertising business can determine what educational materials will be useful at primary, secondary and advanced levels. It would be unrealistic to expect that industry can do much more than make available to teachers and their pupils the wealth of information about advertising that already exists on tapes, cassettes, films, slides, etc. Nevertheless, advertisers, advertising agencies and the teaching profession should decide jointly on the right materials for the right level, and develop a plan for its distribution and proper usage.

One would hope that such a plan could be drawn up first in one or two Common Market countries. After testing it could be revised, exported and adapted by other countries. Even allowing for differences between various educational systems in Member States, the basic information about advertising and its role in the economic process will be similar.

A project to prepare and execute an educational program of this kind is time consuming and complicated. One would hope that an international organization in the field of communication would be prepared to volunteer to do it, since adequate and responsible information about advertising for the future generation of consumers should rank among the highest priorities of the advertising business and its international associations.

Recommendation III

It is recommended that the advertising business, in close cooperation with the teaching profession, offer assistance to private and public schools at primary, secondary and advanced levels, to draw up a plan for the preparation and distribution to schools, of responsible information about the role of advertising in a market economy. The contribution of industry could include making available existing information on tapes, cassettes, films, slides, etc., from which the right selection could be made. Such a program should initially be developed and tested in one or two countries in the Common Market, and then revised, exported and adapted by other countries on the basis of experience gained.

Educating advertising professionals

Apart from educating the future generation of consumers in the role of advertising in the economic process, we should also pay attention to the education of those who may select the advertising business as a career. It may be argued that this subject falls outside the scope of this book, a point of view we would share if there were ample opportunities in Europe to obtain the right kind of qualifications at business schools, institutes or universities. Although there are a number of reputable schools and institutes which teach advertising in a responsible and professional manner, very few universities in Europe include advertising as an important component in their educational programs. This is most regrettable. Although practical experience is indispensable to success in advertising, a sound theoretical and problem-solving education is also essential. In recent decades many European universities provide appropriate education for careers in business administration, with some opportunity to specialize in marketing. But compared to the USA there is very little advanced education in advertising, communication science and mass media, with an appropriate business orientation, suitable for those who will seek careers in advertising and related fields.

Advanced education is particularly important for those who wish to find careers in international advertising. The complexities of understanding human behavior in several cultures are great – not to mention the variety of other economic, legal, political, social and technological circumstances that must be analyzed, interpreted and utilized to produce successful international advertising.

Moreover, with the arrival of cable and satellite television transmission and other new technologies, international advertising will gain in importance, as will the need for mutually agreeable controls. There is thus a great need to educate future advertising men and women to prepare them to produce advertising that is appropriate to meet the needs of business and consumers.

Recently the IAA, under the leadership of one of the authors, established an international advertising qualification. This "Diploma in International Advertising," builds upon the "Basic Certificate" and "Advanced Certificate" which the IAA had previously established in cooperation with a number of local institutes in several nations offering advertising courses. In spite of the success of this educational scheme, students at universities who would consider a career in the advertising business, should have more opportunities in Europe for the study of advertising, communication science and the mass media before obtaining the indispensable practical experience needed.

Recommendation IV

It is recommended that the business community encourage universities in Europe to give greater prominence to the study of advertising as part of their curricula.

The study of advertising should preferably be included within one of the existing faculties, such as business administration or communication science, or both.

The successful completion of a course of study in advertising should entitle the student to a specialized degree. The development of such a program should take place in close consultation with the business world to ensure recognition of the practical value of a degree to students who wish to make a career in advertising.

It would be important also for certain professors at European universities to have the opportunity to spend time at a company, agency or advertising medium to gain first hand exposure to the advertising business.

We have dealt at some length with the question of advertising education for future consumers, and for those who will produce tomorrow's advertising, because in our view such education could help to avoid a repetition of what happened in the 1960s and 1970s. A well informed public and properly prepared advertising executives would be of great benefit to both the advertising business and the consuming public. Particularly, the future generation of advertising women and men who want to make a career in international advertising should be properly prepared for their future. They require not only experience and knowledge of how to communicate effectively and efficiently with consumers in Europe and their many different cultures, habits and motivations; they should also know about the different forms of advertising control as they exist in European countries, particularly in view of the rapid development of new technologies. They should therefore acquire insight in the way in which not only the Commission but also other supranational organizations can influence advertising and its regulation within the Community and the rest of Europe.

For these reasons the last sections of this chapter are devoted to the new technologies and the activities of a number of supranational organizations.

Satellites and new technologies

When the Soviet Union launched Sputnik 1 in 1957, the world entered a new era. Today international communication is heavily dependent on satellites. Banks, air travel, telecommunication and many industries could not operate without them. But this new technology did not attract the serious attention of the advertising business as soon as one might have expected. Many in the business world felt that it would be a long time before satellites would be exploited for advertising purposes and there seemed to be no reason for haste in thinking about the consequences for advertising regulation.

But the pessimists were wrong; technical developments continued to progress rapidly, adding a new dimension to the discussion of international advertising and its regulation. For this reason we now describe and highlight technical developments in this fast moving scene, in so far as such information is needed for a broad comprehension of the commercial situation and its impact on advertising regulation. For futher information the reader is advised to consult our References, especially EAAA, 1983; Wood, 1983 and 1985; *European File*, 1984c; Beville, 1985; and Bernard, 1985).

As background for the discussion of new technology and its application for international advertising purposes, it must be kept in mind that international advertising has been with us almost as long as advertising itself. Brands such as Lux Toilet Soap, Coca Cola and Marlborough, have used advertising ideas on an international scale for many decades. In the early 1980s when the excitement surrounding satellite developments caused a revival of the discussions about opportunities for what then was called "global" marketing and advertising, it was as if it were something new rather than a recurring theme. The question of when to use the same advertising for the same product was again debated by increasing numbers of advertisers and advertising agencies. For example, in 1980 Kenneth Miles, Director of the Incorporated Society of British Advertisers (ISBA) said:

> ... there is only one Coca Cola, but there are a lot of companies today that are able to advertise the same product with more or less the same message in several countries. Not necessarily in every country, but ... it is not too difficult to see 50 or a hundred companies representing two or three hundred brands able to use the same message and the same product story [in] several countries (*The Battle for Eyeballs*, 1980).

Commenting on the point made that companies at that time were selling products with national images, Kenneth Miles replied: "They will have to change, but you must not assume that they are so hide-bound that they won't change – they will change. If the media and communications opportunities encourage them to do so they will change. Believe me!" (*The Battle of Eyeballs*, 1980).

His prediction was only partly correct. In spite of an almost euphoric mood among some advertising people that very soon broadcasts via satellite and carrying commercials would cover the entire continent, these changes did not come quite as rapidly as some expected. Apart from organizational, financial and technical set-backs, governments became aware that transnational television could violate some of the diverse national laws. Also the national media worried about competition. But most importantly, the number of international brands with a sufficiently similar profile and market situation in European countries that could overcome language problems, was still small.

This is not the place to prolong the discussion about opportunities for advertisers to exploit the new electronic media to advertise brands that already are international or that can be made international. However, it should be said at this stage that availability of new media has by itself never been a sufficiently compelling reason for advertisers to use them. These new media will first have to have an audience of adequate size before many advertisers will be interested. This in turn requires the right kind of programs to attract such audiences.

Be this as it may, the magnitude of electronic developments was such, that the advertising business soon referred to it as a "media-explosion," giving new life to discussions on perceived opportunities for "global" marketing and advertising.

The globalization of media

The 1984 – 1985 debates about global advertising took place at a time when a media revolution was beginning – the globalization of media. We refer not only to television, but also to radio, which has long had global capability, and especially to newspapers and magazines, many of which are becoming increasingly important global media with large audiences. Print media are making use of facsimile transmission by satellite, thereby permitting almost simultaneous production capability in multiple world locations. They are still in the early stages of exploiting this new technology. But they are growing so rapidly that their future is difficult to over-estimate ("Global Media," 1984:45 – 61).

Among those who are looking for future media developments important to advertising, it is currently popular to point to the many variations and combinations in cable and satellite television transmission. The two that are mentioned most frequently in Europe are Direct Broadcast Satellite (DBS) and Fixed Service Satellite (FSS).

Increasingly Europeans are able, through local or national cable networks, to receive a range of "broadcast" programs. A small number of people are able to pick up DBS signals with special "dishes," which at present cost well over $1000 (US). DBS seems to have great potential for reception of television programs and its advertising in much of Europe, especially since the price of dish antennae is expected to decrease considerably. Additionally there may be the cost of decoders for one or more channels.

Another possibility is FSS, which is lower powered than DBS and at present not suitable for direct home reception. Transmissions are received on a large dish antenna for redistribution via a cable network.

But we should not forget that new technologies also make possible many other developments that are important to advertising – improvements in existing systems, as well as unimagined new media. Beville (1985) foresees that soon television receivers will have the ability to give viewers "zoom shots," "stop motion" and "split screen effects." Multichannel sound with a decoder will make available foreign language translation. Already (1985) in Japan bilingual television news and programming in Japanese/English and Japanese/Chinese are in frequent, routine use by at least five stations each in Tokyo and Osaka. Vertical blanking intervals in the television set, now used for captions for the deaf or for teletext, have the potential for carrying other kinds of information. Remote control devices to switch channels are in wide use in some countries, giving birth to the practice of zapping – changing channels during the commercial, or to find out what is on other channels without consulting the printed guide.

Beville (1985) continues with the observation that some possible but as yet less popular services include: (1) household teletext, a one-way information service receivable on TV sets – for news, sports, weather, shopping data, theaters and many other items, and (2) videotext and two-way cable – both featuring two-way transmission of information-based services, with considerable potential for in-home shopping services.

Satellite transmission of television signals offers several major substitutes for cable TV, for example: (1) Satellite Master Antenna Television (SMATV), (2) Multichannel Multipoint Distribution System (MMDS), and (3) DBS. There are also variations of these systems. All depend on line-of-sight reception.

SMATV is the most like existing cable systems, requiring a master antenna. For cost and technical reasons it is usually limited to apartments of over 200 units. David Wood reports:

> It now looks likely that SMATV will be approved in a number of European countries. This will mean that a dish receiver of approximately 1.8 metres in diameter can be erected on a block of flats and a cable connection run to individual apartments. Systems can also be installed in hotels, pubs or clubs. Once this happens, the potential universe of homes able to receive satellite channels may start to increase rapidly (Wood, 1985:31).

MMDS operates by picking up a satellite signal and distributing it by microwave; normally MMDS covers homes within a 25-mile radiation area, much like a "wireless cable." MMDS is low cost and can handle six or eight channels (Beville, 1985).

DBS is well established in the USA with at least a million homes receiving cable network signals on two-to-three meter dishes. However, it is the most complex of the new technologies and it is doubtful if the costs of DBS will enable it to compete with SMATV and MMDS, let alone with cable. However, once the small dish receivers will be available at reasonable cost, cable reception will come under severe competitive pressure. Nevertheless, the future of DBS remains speculative (Beville, 1985).

Another development with great consumer potential is the video cassette recorder. Its penetration in the USA and in Europe is considerable; 40% of British households, 20% of German, Swiss and Swedish households, and 10 to 15% of Belgian, Danish and French households have a VCR (Bernard, 1985:10). The great advantage of the VCR to consumers is the ability to record a program, or rent pre-recorded cassettes, with or without its advertising, and play it back at any convenient time.

The other side of the coin

While technological developments have been breathtaking, the question arises to what extent the ultimate beneficiaries of these developments, the viewers at home, share this exciting progress. André Bernard, a director of SSC&B:LINTAS World-wide, pours oil in the waves when he says:

> ... Although the pace of technological development is accelerating, it takes much longer to convince consumers to replace their household equipment or change their personal habits. Moreover, we constantly run the risk of technological myopia, of believing that if we can dream of it we can make it, and if we can make it people will want and will use it (Bernard, 1985:1).

Referring to the situation in the USA, he says:

> ... we must conclude that US television remains a mass medium, that commercial TV continues to attract a vast majority of viewers even in the cable universe, that the technology is merely a means of delivering the programming to the market and that the consumer is not looking at cable or satellites but at programmes. This lesson was learned at great cost in the US (Bernard, 1985:2).

While firmly believing that television has the potential to become the greatest international medium, with regard to Europe, Bernard observes:

> In Europe today, the excitement over new technologies is very similar to what happened in the US 5 years ago. However, many people forget that consumers are not buying chips, fibre cables or satellites, but entertainment and information. Many also underestimate the barriers which continue to exist in Europe (legal, copyright, languages, etc.) (Bernard, 1985:7).

Finally, in his concluding remarks, Bernard says:

> ... I also believe that the pace of change will accelerate. However, I think that much of the current excitement about the new electronic media will fade away, as many of the projects will fail or be abandoned. We shall have to adopt a pragmatic approach to media developments. As our television systems change over the next decade, we shall need to test each possibility by closely scrutinizing the economics and, most importantly, the real consumer benefit which until now has always been quality programming at a reasonable price and not technology (Bernard, 1985:14).

Cable and satellite in operation

A number of cable and satellite projects are in operation or under preparation throughout Europe; some are national, others involve several countries. One of these projects was initiated by the EP, which asked the Commission on March 12, 1982 to study and eventually propose the introduction of "a European television programme, to be broadcast throughout the continent by direct broadcast satellites" (*Euro Forum*, 1983:iii). The EBU will play an important part in this international project, but not all its member broadcasting organizations are equally enthusiastic. Some see the project as a threat to their national programs, but the organizers of this pan-European project have high expectations. They believe its potential audience to be somewhere between 16 and 20 million households and the EP has even set up an all-party "Intergroup," promoting the creation of a European television channel (EAAA, 1985a:4).

Table VII
European satellite channels which currently carry advertising

Channel	Language	Homes universe	Countries of reception
Sky Channel	English	4,051,178	Netherlands, Switzerland, Germany, Finland, Norway, UK, Austria, Sweden, Luxembourg, France, Denmark, Belgium
Music Box	English	2,544,000	Netherlands, Switzerland, UK, Finland, Germany, Sweden, Austria, Denmark
TV-5	French	2,000,000	Belgium, Finland, France, Germany, Netherlands, Norway, Sweden, UK, Switzerland
SAT-1	German	460,000	Germany
Children's Channel	English	110,000	UK
Screen Sport	English	100,000	UK, Sweden from Sept. 85, Finland from Jan. 86
RAI	Italian	N/A	Belgium
New World Channel	Multi-lingual	–	–

Source: *Campaign* August 30, 1985:35, as reported by David Wood.

From a receiver's point of view, the Commission sums up this exciting development:

> Tens of millions of Europeans already receive up to a dozen national or foreign television channels by cable daily. A few million tune in to programmes broadcast by satellite, such as Sky Channel, an independent British undertaking, or TV 5, a joint inititative by francophone national television stations. But this is only a beginning. It has been estimated that by the end of the decade, viewers in most European countries will be able to watch, apart from their usual stations, up to five satellite TV channels, 30 national stations transmitted by cable and a host of other programmes broadcast from countries throughout the continent. By the 1990s, at the touch of a button, millions of Europeans may be able to choose between an English soccer match, a French news programme or an Italian documentary, with translations into their own language, either on sound or through teletext subtitles (*European File*, 1984c:3).

A snapshot of the satellite channels that now [1985] carry advertising is shown in table VII.

By way of explanation, David Wood reports:

> Points to note are that the biggest channels in terms of homes connected (Sky and Music Box) are English language; TV-5 is a channel run by the public broadcasting authorities in Belgium, France, Switzerland and only accepts sponsorship; SAT-1 is a commercial TV channel owned by a private consortium in Germany: RAI is the public broadcasting in Italy and New World Channel is owned by an American company, uplinked from Norway but which, as yet, has not been granted permission to be relayed on any cable system (Wood 1985;31).

It is of interest to note that according to Wood's latest forecasts, the popular Sky Channel programs transmitted from the UK via satellite and cable operators to European homes, may by the beginning of January 1987 be received in 17 countries in more than 9 million homes. Wood also reports that in 1986, an average of 5% of all European homes were receiving satellite channels via cable. He estimates that by 1990 this percentage will have more than doubled (Wood, 1986).

The parties involved

Understandably most of the organizations which we discussed earlier in this chapter take an interest in these important developments. Those most immediately concerned are the EBU, the COE, the Commission, EAT and BEUC.

The General Assembly of the EBU adopted on July 15, 1983 a "Declaration of Principles Regarding Commerical TV Advertising Broadcast by DBS," referring to the ICC Code of Advertising Practice, which the EBU was "desirous of following, with all the adaptations necessary for the operation of DBS advertising broadcasts." The EBU also called on its members to comply with domestic laws applicable in the countries concerned and to strengthen, where necessary, internal rules in order to avoid the broadcasting of advertising for cigarettes and alcoholic beverages. The

Declaration also called for a review of rules on advertising for pharmaceutical products, medicinal treatments and advertising affecting children (EBU, 1983:7 – 8).

The COE's Committee of Ministers, adopted on February 23, 1984 a recommendation to its 21 Member States on the principles which should guide all television advertising, including satellite advertising. The guidelines were of a general nature, leaving it to governments to take any necessary specific steps; they included provisions on advertising of tobacco, alcoholic and pharmaceutical products and on advertising to children.

On December 7, 1984, the Committee of Ministers adopted another recommendation, dealing with "The Use of Satellite Capacity for Television and Sound Radio," which set down a number of points with regard to responsibilities and standards of satellite programs, including: (1) news should be presented fully and accurately; (2) programs should not contain pornography, nor give undue prominence to violence or invite race hatred; and (3) programs should respect the sensitivity and the physical, mental and moral personality of children and young persons. We mention the latter recommendation because it represents an effort to curb serious potential harm to children, and goes far beyond innocent toy advertising. The purpose is to avoid the filth and violence which a few makers of television programs pour out unhindered – under the mask of their right to the freedom of expression.

Another important party is the BEUC which in August, 1983 produced a comprehensive report entitled "The Impact of Satellite and Cable Television on Advertising." In this report the BEUC criticized the documents from the EBU and the COE as weak and very general. The report contained a joint submission from the IOCU and the BEUC to the COE in March, 1983 under the title "Direct Broadcasting by Satellite (DBS) and the Consumer."

The report also discusses the various forms of advertising regulation, including self-regulation and codes of practice, saying that they "have a useful part to play" and are "a marginally helpful aid to raising advertising standards." But on the subject of DBS, the report does not go any further than to state the need "for an international framework," whithout indicating the nature of such a framework. Interim arrangements should be made, "ensuring that the DBS advertisements . . . meet the legal and other regulatory requirements of all the countries which receive the signal" (BEUC, 1983:Annex 1:97 – 98 – 103). In its Conclusions the BEUC report recommends that the Commission prepare a directive on television advertising, which leads us to the activities of the Commission in this respect.

The Commission's green paper: "Television without Frontiers"

The above described activities were mere skirmishes prior to the appearance of the long awaited green paper "Television without Frontiers." This document was published by the Commission as a discussion paper on May 23, 1984 (Commission of the EC, 1984).

The Commission should be congratulated on the procedure it followed. The subject is almost as difficult and complex as "misleading advertising." By opening up the subject for general discussion and encouraging dialogue between all parties concerned, the Commission may have avoided the irritations and frustrations of the past.

The green paper acknowledged the "positive contributions that broadcast advertising is able and indeed entitled to make in accordance with the fundamental provisions of the Treaty on the free movement of goods, persons, freedom to provide services, and undistorted competition." But at the same time it called for a draft directive, and a number of limitations on advertising, especially: (1) a ban on all tobacco advertisements, (2) restriction guidelines on alcohol advertisements, (3) a limitation on the amount of total broadcasting time for advertisements, and (4) a number of restrictions on braodcasts likely to impair seriously the physical, mental and moral development of children or young persons.

On December 12 – 13, 1984 the Commission organized in Brussels a public hearing on the subject of its green paper, attended by representatives of the Commission, industry, the advertising business and consumer groups. The Commission made it clear on that occasion that it considered it necessary to draft a directive.

Interestingly, the Commission gave as its main reason for a directive the need for all Member States to move toward a common market, which would allow television advertising throughout the Community, including two countries which at the moment do not have commercial television – Denmark and Belgium.

The Commission also explained that while it was in favor of liberalization, certain limitations on advertising would have to be imposed. During the discussion consumer bodies stressed their desire to limit the amount of time permitted for advertising; they also demanded "upwards" harmonization of rules and regulations concerning advertising.

Speakers from the advertising business did not agree and asked for a deregulatory policy instead of one that standardized the most restrictive rules in the Community. They also pointed out that the phrase "common market" not only emphasized "common" but also "market" and that markets were places where buyers and sellers were brought together and where competition existed.

The advertising business also had difficulty in accepting the Commission's statement that "A degree of flexibility could be maintained by providing that national legislatures would remain free to impose stricter rules for broadcasts originating within the national territory" (Commission of the EC, 1984:par.38). Industry asked: If countries would be free to make more stringent rules than foreseen in a directive, what would be the purpose of a directive to harmonize all legislation?

An interesting case in point is the "Debauve" Case in Belgium. The Commission's green paper is to a large extent based upon Articles 59, 60 and 62 of the Rome Treaty; Article 59 specifically states: "... restrictions on the freedom of provisions of services within the Community shall be progressively abolished ..." (Rome Treaty, 1957:25).

Consumer organizations in Belgium had lodged a complaint against cable operators on the ground that these operators "... had infringed a prohibition on the transmission of television broadcasts in the nature of advertising ..." (Debauve, 1980:93). Cable operators covering a part of Belgium, had indeed provided subscribers with foreign broadcasts containing advertisements from outside Belgium. Belgian legislation prohibits national radio and television broadcasting organizations from including advertising, but cable operators have disregarded this prohibition and have transmitted foreign programs which include advertising; the Belgian government had tolerated this practice. Following the complaint from consumer organizations, the "Tribunal Correctionnel" (Criminal Court) in Liège, Belgium had brought this case before the Court of Justice in Luxembourg, which ruled on December 13, 1979, that in absence of any approximation of national laws, "... a prohibition of this type fell within the residual power of each Member State to regulate, restrict or even totally prohibit television advertising on its territory on the ground of the public interest" (Debauve, 1980:94).

Faced with this situation, in which on the dubious grounds of "public interest" a Member State can prohibit the total relay of a foreign broadcast by cable on the grounds that the broadcast carries commercials, the EEC, which is dedicated to the free flow of goods and services, had no option but to take up the Court's challenge and attempt to standardize rules on advertising, copyrights and other contentious matters. This led to the green paper on "Television without Frontiers."

With regard to advertising of certain product categories on television, it is of interest to note that the documents we have discussed (the EBU declaration, the recommendation of the COE, the IOCU/BEUC submission and the Commission's green paper), all contain special references to the need to restrict the advertising of specific categories such as tobacco, alcohol and pharmaceuticals, and advertising directed at children. This highlights the necessity for the advertising business to be on its guard all the time in defense of its legitimate interests.

After two days of public hearings in December, 1984 the Commission committed itself to drafting a directive. It is expected that the draft will by and large follow the Commission's recommendations as included in its green paper. Meanwhile the usual round of consultations with various consultative bodies has started and will continue well into 1986.

Of these, the EP has already expressed an opinion. In the autumn of 1985 it voted in favor of such a directive. Interestingly enough, its aims are to keep TV regulations and rules to harmonize TV advertising to a minimum. Charles Dawson, then Vice-President of Young and Rubicam Europe, reports:

> [The European Parliament] have called on the EEC Commission ... 'to harmonise certain aspects of national regulations concerning advertising' ... the Commission is instructed to ... 'submit framework proposals only'; and, sensibly, 'to resist the temptation to tender perfectionist solutions.' ... It is not often we get treated to the spectacle of the European Parliament taking up the cudgel on the part of the advertiser, and against its own member governments. But that is exactly what is happening (Dawson, 1985a:52).

The MEPs also expressed their desire for a directive to ensure:

> − that advertising continues to be controlled at national level, but that there also be European codes of practice, incorporating the principles of the ICC and IBA codes;
> − that advertising is clearly recognizable as such, and that there is a clear separation of advertising and programme material;
> − that there is a total ban on the advertising of tobacco and tobacco products, and strict controls on alcohol advertising (EAAA, 1985f:1).

As we indicated in the previous chapter, the advertising business has a somewhat divided opinion on the need for such a directive.

The Confederation of British Industry (CBI) and the AA, produced the following joint statement:

> We question whether there is any need for the Community to be taking action in this area. Our main reasons for this are:
> • A common market in broadcast advertising services (both television and radio) already exists in many Member States.
> • The Treaty of Rome (mainly Articles 50 and 62) guarantees the freedom to provide services − broadcasting is such a service.
> • More fundamentally still, Article 10 of the European Convention on Human Rights firmly assures freedom of expression ...
> • No real damage or harm is being done which requires legislative remedy.
> • There has been no call for legislation from any significant number of consumers.
> • Existing Community legislation already covers cross-frontier broadcasting and advertising, by means of the Directive on Misleading Advertising.
> • A range of Guidelines, Codes and Principles already exist relating to broadcast advertising − some are long-standing and have proved their effectiveness in ensuring responsible advertising:
>   + The International Chamber of Commerce's International Code of Advertising Practice (The ICC Code);
>   + Various national codes, often based on the ICC Code;
>   + The Council of Europe's Principles on Television Advertising, Recommendations No.R(84)3 adopted in February 1984;
>   + The European Broadcasting Union's Declaration of Principles regarding commercial television broadcast by DBS (July 1983);

+ The Committee of Ministers' Declaration on the Freedom of Expression and Information (April 1982) (CBI, 1985:13,14).

Others, such as the WFA, argue that it would be desirable for a directive to lay down a framework of conditions under which advertising on television will be allowed in all Member States; these conditions should include the amount of time permitted and the times when advertising may be transmitted. Such a directive would enable international advertisers to fully exploit television to promote international brands throughout the Community.

The IAA also expressed an opinion. Its Global Media Commission, "... applauding the advances in self-regulation of advertising which have honestly and consistently been sought in many countries," passed a resolution on July 2, 1985, calling for:

> ... the lifting of arbitrary, artificial and unnecessary restrictions and their replacement by responsible freedom in
> – the use of radio and television, both terrestrial and satellite, and related distribution systems,
> – the amount of advertising time permitted in all electronic media;
> – the use of all advertising in all aspects of the print media;
> for the benefit of consumers, producers of goods and services and advertisers everywhere (IAA, 1985b).

Apart from the merits or demerits of a directive on this subject, one wonders if such a directive will not be overtaken by events before the ink dries. The usual time between drafting a directive and its approval and implementation is rarely less than five years. Considering the speed of technological progress, cheap private reception from all over the world, may well be available before any regulatory action can be taken.

There is yet another point to consider. Later in this chapter we shall deal in some detail with the COE's convention of human rights and particularly the right to freedom of expression as embodied in Article 10 of this convention. The Commission refers in its green paper to this convention and its provisions on the freedom of expression, which should re respected, regardless of frontiers; if such freedom includes "commercial speech," as most people believe it does, this would not only seriously affect any future regulation of advertising at national or international levels, but it might in this particular case bring out the need for a reconsideration by the Commission of its own proposals in connection with cable and satellite. Not only restrictions in Member States, but also some of those proposed in the green paper, could well be considered to infringe upon rights covered in Article 10.

Finally, while our discussion on the subject of television advertising has centered on the Common Market and on a proposed directive for the twelve Member States, it would be perfectly possible for an advertiser within the Community to call on broadcasters outside the EC, who might not necessarily wish to adhere to EEC rules.

In discussions at the International Telecommunications Union (ITU) in 1981, for example, the East Germans said that under certain conditions they might let any advertiser use an externally directed broadcasting station based on their territory. It has been argued that European governments could in such a case forbid reception by their citizens, or forbid the sale of a decoder needed to receive such programs. One might wonder however if the human rights convention would not prevent governments from taking such restrictive action.

In summing up it would appear that the future of television as an advertising medium, may depend less on further technological progress than on advertisers wanting to use already existing television technology for their international brands in order to reach global audiences. The potential of global television advertising is enormous, but it may still take some time to overcome problems regarding international trade marks, copyrights, advertising regulations, languages, and − last but not least − the production of attractive programs, before it will have reached the level of acceptance that so many advertising people expect. However, during 1985 and 1986, already over 100 advertisers have used Sky Channel as an international medium. Among them well known multinationals, such as Coca Cola, Kodak, Rank Xerox, Timex, Kellogg, Philips, Renault, Unilever (Wood, 1986). It confirms the increasing interest of international advertisers in reaching audiences on a pan European basis.

Under these circumstances it is not surprising that the dramatic technological developments have stirred the activities of those supranational organizations that take an interest in consumer protection and advertising regulation.

Activities of other supranational organizations

Since the launch of the Commission's consumer programs, other organizations operating in the same sphere have either started or accelerated their activities. Roger Underhill wrote:

> For reasons which are not hard to understand there are few institutions more affected by the "global village" concept than communications and marketing. Of course, we have all seen it coming, but somehow it has still crept on us with a speed we were not prepared for. But global villages, like tribal ones, need head-men and the rush is on to see which of our transnational rulers is to have the most influence. The United Nations and its many agencies, the Council of Europe and its Committees, OECD, not to mention the European Commission, are just some of the bodies which daily put more and more pressure on national governments and thus on national legislation and attitudes. And more and more are they concerning themselves with legislation and attitudes affecting marketing and communication − at a time when both technology and social opinion are themselves introducing changes like we have never seen before (Underhill, 1981a:16).

There are a great number of international organizations involved in consumer affairs but the actual number of people that represent regulatory bodies and trade associations in the field of consumer affairs is rather small. This is perfectly understandable since the circle of knowledgeable people on such a specialized subject is limited. The consumerist merry-go-round therefore often carries the same people, who only change hats in accordance with the occasion. Some argue that this is a good thing because it keeps undesirable elements away from the conference table; others worry that an insufficient number of new and fresh ideas are put forward, or that introvert and inbred thinking could develop. Also, there is the concern that some civil servants seem to have a personal interest in prolonging discussions indefinitely.

Let us now take a closer look at some of these organizations, their influence on consumer affairs and on the regulation of advertising throughout the Community.

There are two categories of supranational organizations that we must consider: (1) the *intergovernmental bodies*, which have official status and authority to make recommendations for legislation to Member States. Apart from the EC which is unique in that it can produce legislation, this category includes the COE, the OECD and UN's agencies, such as ECOSOC and UNESCO. (2) *Non-governmental organizations*, which do not have any authority to introduce or propose legislation but who often are consulted by governments or intergovernmental bodies and who sometimes develop their own codes or other voluntary controls on advertising, to be adhered to by their members; this category includes a great number of organizations, representing either the business community in general or specific industries. From this category we already discussed the ICC, the BEUC and those NGOs who are a member of the EAT, but we should also pay attention to UNICE, IOCU and COFACE who equally have an interest in matters concerning advertising.

We will now look at the COE, the OECD and two UN agencies, belonging to the first group, and at UNICE, IOCU and COFACE, belonging to the second category.

The Council of Europe

Founded in 1949, with now 21 European nations,* and joined by Finland and the Holy See as observers, it represents some 380 million people and concerns itself with subjects such as the environment, human rights, social and economic affairs, education, culture, public health and consumer protection. It is a forum for cooperation

---

* Austria, Belgium, Cyprus, Denmark, Federal Republic of Germany, France, Greece, Iceland, Ireland, Italy, Liechtenstein, Luxembourg, Malta, the Netherlands, Norway, Portugal, Spain, Sweden, Switzerland, Turkey and the United Kingdom.

between the member countries, with the objective of promoting greater unity among them. It cannot take binding decisions, but its deliberations have a profound effect on decision makers at both national and international levels.

Its Parliamentary Assembly, not to be confused with the EP, offers a useful platform for national parliamentarians to air their views, to exchange information and to influence public opinion, European governments, and legislators at national and international levels. Some people question the real importance of the assembly describing it as a debating society with no real power. Others have a much higher opinion of the activities and achievements of this Parliamentary Assembly and the COE as a whole.

It should not be forgotten that it was the COE which as far back as 1968 formed a working party on the subject of misleading advertising, producing a report in March, 1972 that would lead to the Consumer Protection Charter being approved by the Council's Consultative Assembly in 1973. This Charter contained the five basic rights which would later form the basis of the EEC's First Consumer Program; it was the COE that in Salzburg in September, 1968 ran its first Symposium on the subject of "Human Rights and Mass Communications;" it was this Council that in February, 1984 — before the EEC published its green paper on cable and satellite — adopted a recommendation on the principles of television advertising. There can be no question that in the field of advertising the COE plays an important role. From 1976 to 1981 it operated mainly through its Mass Media Committee, the "Comité Directeur sur les Moyens de communications de Masse" (CDMM). In 1981 the work of this Committee was transferred to the human rights sector of the COE. It was then made into the Council's steering committee and became the official organ of the Council on all media.

> The philosophy behind the allocation of mass media activities to the human rights sector is that these activities are closely linked with the basic values which constitute the foundation of the Council of Europe. The proper functioning of free and autonomous media and the availability of a plurality of information sources and of communication links are essential for democracy and for international understanding. Freedom of information is not only a fundamental right per se, but also facilitates the exercise of other fundamental rights (Council of Europe, 1984a:1).

The steering committee, on which all 21 Member States are represented, is supported by two sub-committees: (1) the Committee of Experts on Media Policy and (2) the Committee of Legal Experts in the Media Field. The steering committee's main focus is on:

(1) mass media and human rights;

(2) cable television, satellite broadcasting and other new media; and

(3) intellectual property rights (Council of Europe, 1983).

The Human Rights Convention

The Convention for the Protection of Human Rights and Fundamental Freedoms, better known as the European Convention on Human Rights (ECHR), was signed in 1950 and came into force in 1953. It "... covers the most important of the civil and policital rights enshrined in the United Nations Universal Declaration of Human Rights of 1948" (Council of Europe, 1979:17). Whenever the need arises the catalogue of guaranteed rights is extended by additional protocols.

It is important to note that this Universal Declaration has been transformed into legal obligations by Member States

> ... by creating an effective international judicial system for guaranteeing human rights ... The rights defined in the Convention are safeguarded by two independent bodies, namely a Commission and a Court, as well as by the Committee of Ministers of the Council of Europe.All the Council of Europe member states, except Liechtenstein, which became a member of the Council only recently, have ratified the Convention and are thus bound by its provisions (Council of Europe, 1979:17).

> The Commission comprises one independent expert for each contracting party, the Court is composed of one independent judge from each of the twenty-one Council of Europe member states (Council of Europe, 1979:18 – 19).

Article 10 of the ECHR is extremely important and directly relevant to advertising. The rights to freedom of expression and information are anchored in this article:

1. Everyone has the right to freedom of expression. This right shall include freedom to hold opinions and to receive and impart information and ideas without interference by public authority and regardless of frontiers. This Article shall not prevent States from requiring the licensing of broadcasting television or cinema enterprises.
2. The exercise of these freedoms, since it carries with it duties and responsibilities, may be subject to such formalities, conditions, restrictions or penalties as are prescribed by law and are necessary in a democratic society, in the interests of national security, territorial integrity or public safety, for the prevention of disorder or crime, for the protection of health and morals, for the protection of the reputation of rights of others, for preventing the disclosure of information received in confidence, or for maintaining the authority and impartiality of the judiciary.

It would lead us too far afield to describe in detail the various steps and actions taken with regard to the Convention, but an important further decision to strengthen the Convention was taken by the Committee of Ministers of the European Council on April 29, 1982, when a Declaration on the Freedom of Expression and Information was adopted. Because of its importance it is included here in full:

DECLARATION
ON THE FREEDOM OF EXPRESSION AND INFORMATION
(Adopted by the Committee of Ministers on 29 April 1982 at its 70th Session)

The member states of the Council of Europe,

1.   Considering that the principles of genuine democracy, the rule of law and respect for human rights form the basis of their co-operation, and that the freedom of expression and information is a fundamental element of those principles;

2.   Considering that this freedom has been proclaimed in national constitutions and international instruments, and in particular in Article 19 of the Universal Declaration of Human Rights and Article 10 of the European Convention on Human rights;

3.   Recalling that through that convention they have taken steps for the collective enforcement of the freedom of expression and information by entrusting the supervision of its application to the organs provided for by the convention;

4.   Considering that the freedom of expression and information is necessary for the social, economic, cultural and political development of every human being, and constitutes a condition for the harmonious progress of social and cultural groups, nations and the international community;

5.   Convinced that the continued development of information and communication technology should serve to further the right, regardless of frontiers, to express, to seek, to receive and to impart information and ideas, whatever their source;

6.   Convinced that states have the duty to guard against infringements of the freedom of expression and information and should adopt policies designed to foster as much as possible a variety of media and a plurality of information sources, thereby allowing a plurality of ideas and opinions;

7.   Noting that, in addition to the statutory measures referred to in paragraph 2 of Article 10 of the European Convention on Human Rights, codes of ethics have been voluntarily established and are applied by professional organisations in the field of the mass media;

8.   Aware that a free flow and wide circulation of information of all kinds across frontiers is an important factor for international understanding, for bringing peoples together and for the mutual enrichment of cultures,

I.   Reiterate their firm attachment to the principles of freedom of expression and information as a basic element of democratic and pluralist society;

II.   Declare that in the field of information and mass media they seek to achieve the following objectives:

a. protection of the right of everyone, regardless of frontiers, to express himself, to seek and receive information and ideas, whatever their source, as well as to impart them under the conditions set out in Article 10 of the European Convention on Human Rights;

b. absence of censorship or any arbitrary controls or constraints on participants in the information process, on media content or on the transmission and dissemination of information;

c. the pursuit of an open information policy in the public sector, including access to information, in order to enhance the individual's understanding of, and his ability to discuss freely political, social, economic and cultural matters;

d. the existence of a wide variety of independent and autonomous media, permitting the reflection of diversity of ideas and opinions;

e. the availability and access on reasonable terms to adequate facilities for the domestic and international transmission and dissemination of information and ideas;

f. the promotion of international co-operation and assistance, through public and private channels, with a view to fostering the free flow of information and improving communication infrastructures and expertise;

III. Resolve to intensify their co-operation in order:

    a. to defend the right of everyone to the exercise of the freedom of expression and information;

    b. to promote, through teaching and education, the effective exercise of the freedom of expression and information;

    c. to promote the free flow of information, thus contributing to international understanding, a better knowledge of convictions and traditions, respect for the diversity of opinions and the mutual enrichment of cultures;

    d. to share their experience and knowledge in the media field;

    e. to ensure that new information and communication techniques and services, where available, are effectively used to broaden the scope of freedom of expression and information.

This Declaration was seen by many as a reinforcement of the Convention and as the COE's answer to UNESCO's New World Information and Communication Order (NWICO) that seriously infringed on the right to freedom of expression which the Council guards with zeal.

There is some difference of opinion as to whether or not "commercial speech" is covered by the Convention. The Human Rights Commission has confirmed that "commercial speech" merits protection under Article 10, yet there are countries where national courts have interpreted freedom of expression more narrowly.

It would be important to advertising if the European Court of Human Rights in Strasbourg would decide that "commercial speech" is covered by the Convention. Such a decision would be binding for Member States and would have far reaching consequences for the freedom to advertise throughout Europe. For example, the Netherlands excludes advertising for commercial purposes from the constitutional provisions guaranteeing freedom of expression. If the Court in Strasbourg should decide otherwise, the Dutch Constitution would have to be altered.

Similarly, a manufacturer who believes that a restriction of his advertising violates Article 10 of the ECHR, once he had exhausted all legal means in his own country, could in seventeen out of twenty-one Member States (which have also allowed legal persons to submit applications), bring the matter before the European Commission of Human Rights; this body can decide to bring the matter before the European Court, whose verdicts are binding.

While therefore it is not surprising that the advertising business attaches great importance to the interpretation of Article 10, it is strange that it took so long to "discover" this aspect of the subject. The Human Rights Convention has after all been in force since 1953, so one could have expected that Article 10 would have been brought out earlier in the discussions about restrictions in the use of advertising. The advertising business now hopes that if Article 10 covers "commercial speech" some of the restrictions on communicating with consumers, as introduced by governments or proposed by the Commission, will be undone. The advent of satellite broad-casting and the advertising it will carry, has in any case accentuated the need for a decision in this respect.

The ICC considered the issue to be of sufficient importance to organize a Symposium in Paris on January 18, 1985 on the subject of "The Freedom of Commercial Communications and the Impact of the European Convention on Human Rights."

In its invitation, the ICC pointed out that "The Symposium will thus provide a unique forum for studying an issue which is not only central to the future of cross-frontier broadcasting, but of increasing importance to the much broader question of communications freedom, both within the European Community and in a wider context" (ICC, 1985a).

In preparation for this Symposium, the ICC requested two British lawyers to prepare a paper on the subject, and asked Sir James Fawcett, D.S.C., who was a member of the ECHR from 1962 to 1984 and its president for three successive terms from 1972 to 1981, to write an introduction to these papers. This Introduction, which includes Sir James' definition of "commercial speech," stated:

> Freedom of expression includes the right to receive and impart information and ideas, and this study asks how it covers 'commercial speech,' those statements and communications published through the media that invite commercial transactions – the advertisement of products and services ... The study stands out in its realism over the combination of social policy and law, it recognises the ambiguity of status and function of many State agencies, which it well calls 'private government,' and it demonstrates beyond doubt that freedom of expression includes 'commercial speech,' and that this may be regulated or restricted only if this is necessary, under a pressing social need, to meet one or more of the prescribed purposes in Article 10(2). The deep analysis of what is necessary in this sense, with indications of a number of existing restrictions which are not, makes the study a decisive authority on 'commercial speech' (Lester and Pannick, 1984:5).

From the study itself we quote the Summary of Conclusions:

> For the reasons set out below, it is our opinion that:
> (a) The right to freedom of expression covers 'commercial speech', that is a statement, such as an advertisement, which proposes a commercial transaction. One important reason for this is that in western democracies with market economies the free flow of such information is vital to the ability of consumers to make informed decisions about the various products and services available to them. Article 10 covers all types of speech, irrespective of content or medium. Article 10 does not give commercial advertisers any special rights: it similarly applies, for example, to a consumer organisation which is prohibited from buying media time or space to express its views on the safety or quality of products or services. (The German Federal High Court of Justice has ruled that satirical anti-cigarette advertising by non-profit making health organisations is permissible).
> (b) Freedom of speech is not absolute. But the only circumstances in which a Member State may validly interfere with freedom of expression (whatever the medium through which the opinions, information or ideas are expressed) is if the conditions stated in Article 10(2) are satisfied. Unless those conditions are satisfied, an interference with freedom of expression will be in breach of the Convention.

(c) To justify an interference with freedom of expression under Article 10(2) the Member State must show – and the burden is on it to do so – that there is 'a pressing social need' for the restriction on free speech for one of a number of purposes (such as the protection of health or morals, or the protection of the rights of others) set out in Article 10(2).

(d) Each interference with freedom of expression has to be justified by the State under these criteria. The fact that the State acts in good faith, or has had the restriction complained of for a long time, does not make the interference valid under Article 10.

(e) Many existing restrictions on freedom of expression in a commercial context appear to breach Article 10. Important examples are restrictions on the content of advertising, in many Member States, for example under the United Kingdom Independent Broadcasting Authority's Code of Advertising; the effective prohibition of advertising, for example on cable television and pay-TV in Belgium, Norway, Sweden and Denmark; quantitative restrictions on television advertising in many countries. In all cases, the State is required (if challenged) to explain why there is a 'pressing social need'' for restricting free expression to advance one of the purposes listed in Article 10(2).

(f) Member States have a duty to ensure that State practice is compatible with Article 10. Where Member States are in breach of this duty, a victim may (as explained in paragraph 2 above) take legal proceedings or any other effective steps to draw this to the attention of the State and thereby to require the State to change the offending practice (Lester and Pannick, 1984:9 – 10).

The authors conclude:

... Member States have, in many respects, failed to recognize their obligation to assess whether there really is a pressing need for the restrictions they impose on the freedom of commercial speech. In many cases, restrictions continue to be imposed simply because they always have been. Article 10 requires Member States to prove, if challenged, that such restrictions are necessary in a democratic society for an authorised purpose. Furthermore, Article 1 of the Convention requires Member States to secure to everyone within their jurisdiction the rights guaranteed by Article 10. We have no doubt that in important respects State practice is incompatible with the obligations imposed on Member States by Article 10 (Lester and Pannick, 1984:38).

The study mentions some additional practical consequences if "commercial speech" is covered by the ECHR; the authors of the study question the legality under Article 10(2) of restrictions on television advertising in France, for tourism, the press, records, textiles, computers and margarine. They note that comparative advertising is prohibited or restricted in a number of Member States. But as long as the comparative information is neither false nor misleading, restrictions on it are a breach of Article 10. Neither could a state justify the prohibitions on television advertising such as those imposed in Belgium, Denmark, Norway and Sweden. Nor do the authors believe that it is the task of the State to regulate the content and quantity of broadcast advertising, unless there is a pressing social need for one of the purposes listed in Article 10(2).

At the ICC Symposium, Dr. Frits Hondius, Secretary to the Committee of Ministers of the COE, added a creative dimension to the argument. He said:

There is one form of expression which I personally regard as being tremendously important in connection with advertising – and fortunately I have not seen any litigation on it –, i.e. artistic expression. Here in Paris I call to mind the famous pre-war posters of 'Dubo-Dubon-Dubonnet' or the 'Etoile du Nor' which have made a highly original contribution to modern advertising art. Reference to advertising as 'a highly visible and audible form of artistic *and other expression*' appears in the Explanatory Memorandum to the Council of Europe's Recommendation (84)3 on Television Advertising, which is further proof of the fact that European Governments regard advertising as a form of expression (Hondius, 1985a).

Before leaving this important subject, a note of warning: If it were one day established that "commercial speech" is covered by Article 10 of the ECHR, this cannot be regarded as a blanket decision; Lester and Pannick point out: "No one case will resolve all the issues of freedom of commercial speech under Article 10. The Commission and the Court will decide only those principles relevant to the facts of the specific cases before them" (Lester and Pannick, 1984:37). It must also be remembered that if Article 10 covers commercial speech, self-regulatory measures could also be subject to its provisions, so each and every voluntary agreement may then need to undergo careful scrutiny. Thus, the advertising business may have to accept uncertainty for some time. But the debate that was accelerated by the ICC meeting in Paris, will continue. In fact, a case about the restrictions on advertising pharmaceuticals in France, will soon be brought before the Court in Strasbourg.

It is clear that the issue of freedom of expression, coupled with an ICC plea after its Symposium in Paris, calling for "a minimum of state interference in broadcasting of all types" (ICC, 1985b), are of vital importance to the future of the advertising business in Europe. This is particularly true with regard to the subject of controversial issues which we raised in the previous chapter. Our point of view and our recommended policy on these issues, as indeed on all issues where advertising restrictions are concerned, are based upon and fully in accordance with Article 10 of the ECHR and Lester and Pannick's interpretation of it.

We therefore hope that the COE, as the Custodians of the ECHR, will soon be in a position to definitely pronounce that "Commercial speech" is indeed covered by the convention.

Organisation for Economic Cooperation and Development

The OECD was established in 1948 and called the "Organisation for European Economic Cooperation;" it was part of the Marshall Plan for European recovery. It was renamed in 1960 when Canada and the United States joined; Japan became a full member in 1964, Finland in 1969, Australia in 1971 and New Zealand in 1973.

The OECD now has 24 members representing a total population of approximately 800 million.*

The objectives of the OECD are to promote economic growth of the member countries, to help the less developed countries both within and outside its own membership and to expand trade throughout the world.

The OECD probably is best known for its annual forecasts and recommendations with regard to key global economic issues. Other aspects of the work of the OECD include fostering cooperation between member countries on economic issues, energy problems, trading systems, financial and social affairs (including consumer protection), education, environmental problems, science, technology, industry, agriculture and fisheries.

The OECD has a "Committee on Consumer Policy," comprised of a representative from each Member State. Its "Terms of Reference" were renewed on October 1, 1982 and are expected to remain in force until December 31, 1987. They include as matters of priority, the following areas and policy objectives: (1) product safety, (2) consumer policy and international trade, (3) transparency of the market, (4) consumer policy issues in the service sector, (5) consumer redress, and (6) consumer representation (OECD, 1982a). The committee is active in many areas of importance to consumers, and has published a number of reports on specific issues, such as package tours, bargain price offers, mail order trading, premium offers, consumer credit, energy conservation, and endorsements in advertising. Its report on "Advertising Directed at Children" received wide publicity and a great deal of attention in many different quarters (OECD, 1982b).

The OECD's Committee on Consumer Policy examines and comments upon questions regarding consumer policy in the various countries. It contributes to increased cooperation between its member states in the field of consumer affairs in close cooperation with other bodies and institutions involved in these matters. The committee gives high priority to developments in international trade and their consequences for consumers in the countries concerned. In a Symposium on "Consumer Policy and International Trade," in Paris, November 27 – 29, 1984 and organized by the OECD's Committee on Consumer Policy, the relationship between consumer interests, economic policy and international trade were discussed:

> Consumers collectively have a wide and direct interest in economic policy and international trade. Their specific interests include the enjoyment of rising living standards, efficient use of economic resources and stability in the general level of prices. Enhanced competition, improved information

* In alphabetical order, the full members of the OECD are: Australia, Austria, Belgium, Canada, Denmark, Finland, France, Germany, Greece, Iceland, Ireland, Italy, Japan, Luxembourg, the Netherlands, New Zealand, Norway, Portugal, Spain, Sweden, Switzerland, Turkey, United Kingdom and the United States. Yugoslavia enjoys special status and participates in certain aspects of the work of this organization.

to consumers, and better quality and safety of products and services are among the basic aims of consumer policies and, at the same time, are relevant for international trading relations. On the other hand, the development of national consumer policies, in particular the introduction of product-related safety, packaging and other requirements, while not designed to restrict imports, may have an impact on international trade (OECD, 1984:3).

The regulation of advertising was not specifically mentioned on the printed program but one of the three plenary sessions was devoted to "The Impact of Consumer Protection on International Trade." The discussion demonstrated clearly how important the OECD believes it is for governments to limit as much as possible the introduction of restrictive measures on international trade. This was confirmed by the adoption of an "Indicative Checklist for the Assessment of Trade Policy Measures," consisting of thirteen questions, enabling member governments to undertake a systematic and comprehensive evaluation of proposed trade measures, and thereby contributing to the liberalization of trade, a clear consumer objective (OECD, 1985:14 – 15).

The Committee's formal outside contacts include as advisory bodies a Business and Industry Advisory Committee (BIAC) and a Trade Union Advisory Committee (TUAC). Since the OECD embraces 24 countries, it finds it difficult to maintain regular contacts with NGOs operating only within the Common Market. However, on an informal basis the views of international consumer organizations are obtained.

The OECD does not have executive authority, but the advertising business should not underrate the influence which its Committee on Consumer Policy can exert on governments and their consumer policies. The OECD may not take initiatives in the field of consumer affairs or advertising regulation, but it certainly influences those who do.

The United Nations

The UN is the largest international organization in the world that is involved in consumer affairs and advertising. The activities of UN agencies concerned with consumer affairs and advertising have grown at an astonishing rate in recent years. Murray Weidenbaum of Washington University lamented in an address in New York in December, 1983: "It is ironic that while its peacekeeping activities are experiencing such poor results, the United Nations is in a growth phase in its attempts to control private enterprise" (Weidenbaum, 1983:1).

Before illustrating the relevance of this point to advertising, it is useful to recall the structure of this vast organization. Primoff and Primoff, Counselors at Law, in Washington D.C. wrote in 1979:

> The organs of the United Nations proper are the General Assembly; under the General Assembly, the Economic and Social Council and Trusteeship Council; the Security Council, the International

Court of Justice; and a Secretariat headed by the Secretary General. The General Assembly is the deliberative body of general competence, and has precedence over and control of the Economic and Social Council and the Trusteeship Council. The General Assembly may discuss, consider, recommend and initiate studies; but none of its actions, nor those of those two Councils, are binding (Primoff, 1979:3).

The United Nations has a number of units interested in matters that are important to advertising, business and consumers. The Commission on Transnational Corporations, established in 1974, has prepared a Code of Conduct for Multi-Nationals. The WHO designed the International Code for Breast Milk Substitutes. It combined forces with another UN agency, the Food and Agriculture Organization (FAO) to form the "Codex Alimentarius Commission" to deal with content, manufacturing, distribution, labelling and presentation (including advertising) of foodstuffs. In addition, GATT and the UN Conference on Trade and Development (UNCTAD), have started to look into the movement of services as well as the traditional work they have done on goods. Advertising has been singled out as one of the main services to be addressed. Finally, the World Intellectual Property Organization (WIPO) not only considers advertising in terms of copyrights, but is now concerning itself with prior consent for broadcasting via satellite, a matter already regulated by the ITU which set up the agreements of the World Administrative Radio Conference (WARC) on satellite footprints.

While decisions of these UN bodies are not binding on the Member States of the Community, there can be no question that their work sometimes has had an effect on the Commission in Brussels. For example, the proposed directive on Claims in Food Advertising is a result of FAO/WHO initiatives.

There are two UN organizations that are of especially great significance to advertising:

(1) The Economic and Social Council (ECOSOC) and its work in the field of consumer protection;

(2) The United Nations Education, Scientific and Cultural Organization (UNESCO) and its MacBride Report on a New World Information and Communication Order.

ECOSOC and consumer protection guidelines

The United Nations' Economic and Social Council examines and makes recommendations on international economic, social, cultural, educational and health issues. The Council comprises 54 members, 18 of whom are selected each year to 3-year terms by the General Assembly. It is aided by separate regional commissions for Europe, Asia and the Far East, Latin America and Africa (Reader's Digest, 1982:423).

In September, 1982, the UN Secretariat circulated draft guidelines for consumer protection to governments for their comments. In May, 1983 a revised draft of the

Guidelines was prepared for submission to the UN ECOSOC meeting in Geneva in July, 1983. The Guidelines contained six objectives, with particular reference to "The needs of developing countries:"

(a) to assist countries in achieving adequate protection for their propulation as consumers;
(b) to facilitate production patterns geared to meeting the most important needs of consumers;
(c) to encourage standards of ethical conduct for those engaged in production and distribution of goods and services to consumers;
(d) to curb business practices at the national and international levels which adversely affect consumers (including abuses of a dominant position of market power by private and public enterprises);
(e) to stimulate the development of independent consumer groups; and
(f) to further international co-operation in the field of consumer protection (ICC Note, 1983).

The above objectives in the UN document were translated into the following guidelines, which show a remarkable resemblance to those included in the EEC's First Preliminary Consumer Protection Program. These guidelines are intended to secure the following legitimate needs of consumers:

(a) the physical safety of consumers and their protection from potential dangers;
(b) the protection of consumers' economic interests;
(c) access of consumers to the necessary information to make informed choices according to individual wishes and needs;
(d) consumer education;
(e) availability of effective consumer redress
(f) freedom to form consumer groups or organizations and the opportunity of such organizations to be consulted and to have their views represented (ICC Note, 1983).

Murray Weidenbaum, in rejecting the UN guidelines both on principle and in particular, criticized the "sweeping consumer protection code that would create new obstacles to international trade via controls on product advertising, safety, quality and pricing" (Weidenbaum, 1983:5).

Another outspoken critic of these UN activities is Jeane Kirkpatrick, until recently the United States Permanent Representative to the United Nations. She wrote: "The range, the sheer proliferation of United Nations activities at regulation of international business is really awesome" (Kirkpatrick, 1983).

She also strongly criticized the UN guidelines for consumer protection:

Although ECOSOC's involvement with this issue began from an ostensible concern that developing countries did not have adequate domestic policies and capabilities in the field of consumer protection, the proposed guidelines are intended to apply to *all* nations. The guidelines go far beyond the kind of noncontroversial standards that would readily be met by nations with advanced consumer protection legislation. As we stated at the July 1983 session of ECOSOC, the US view is that 'as currently worded, the guidelines are a Pandora's box for ill-conceived meddling in the affairs of member states; that they offer a rationale for all sorts of wrong-headed interference in domestic economies; and that they can be construed in such a way as to permit massive interference in international trade, affecting the exports of both developing and developed countries' (Kirkpatrick, 1983).

The ICC also commented on these guidelines; it made a number of important general points, such as its concern about over-regulation, the need to pay more attention to the cost/benefit aspects of consumer protection measures, and the advantages of self-regulatory mechanisms, which "are often more effective, less costly and less cumbersome than government regulation in meeting consumer protection requirements" (ICC Note, 1983:4).

The ECOSOC meeting in Geneva in July, 1983 was attended by an ICC delegation led by the chairman of its Commission on Marketing, Mr. Kenneth Fraser, who presented an oral statement in which he made the following key points:

- the draft Guidelines seemed to be inspired by notions of central economic control, paying insufficient regard to the nature of a free-market economy and the fact that in such economies companies insensitive to consumer interests eventually went out of business;
- there is substantial overlap of interests between business and consumers. For example, two major consumer objectives are freedom of choice and the right to information. Business could not make its optimal contribution to society unless the freedom of the consumer to choose, and the freedom of business to make choice available and to communicate with consumers, were both recognised and respected;
- consumer policy, be it national or international, should be a joint effort between the business community and other interested parties as appropriate;
- the purpose of any international Guidelines should be to provide a broad framework of universal validity, applying equally to domestic and foreign-owned, private, state-owned, cooperative and mixed-owned enterprises. It should not attempt to cover specific situations of one single group of countries, or one type of branch of industry (the existing draft has sections on pharmaceuticals and food), nor to cover issues that go beyond consumer protection;
- the current draft made insufficient allowance for the consumer protection measures – self-regulatory, legislative, or through voluntary agreement – that have already been taken in many countries. There is a basic assumption throughout the draft Guidelines that policies need to be developed or strengthened, where in fact this may not be required;
- the ICC was willing to put its extensive experience on this question at the disposal of the UN and member governments (ICC Annual Report, 1983:15).

The UN guidelines were finally approved by consensus but *ad referendum*, by the General Assembly during its 39th Session on December 18, 1984. On April 9, 1985, during the Second Session of the General Assembly, they were unanimously passed without further amendments.

In their final form, the guidelines represented a substantial improvement over the 1983 draft; they gave recognition to consumer protection measures that already existed in many countries and they accepted as adequate, voluntary codes and agreements to ensure consumer protection (ICC Note, 1985).

At the end of the 39th Session of the UN, mentioned above, the USA again expressed its serious misgivings about the growing UN role in the regulation of business, confirming the concern which has been expressed by other prominent American citizens earlier in this chapter.

UNESCO and the New World Information and Communication Order

UNESCO was formed in 1945 and now has a constituent membership of 160 countries. According to Article I, 1 and 2(a) of UNESCO's Constitution, its purpose is "to contribute to peace and security by promoting collaboration among the nations through education, science and culture;" it is to accomplish these aims "... through all means of mass communication ..." (Primoff, 1979:34).

In advertising circles, UNESCO became best known (or some would say notorious) for its "New World Information and Communication Order," published and known as the MacBride Report. The NWICO originated at a UNESCO conference in Nairobi in 1976 and was adopted by consensus at the UNESCO conference in Belgrade in October, 1980. The NWICO recommended severe limitations in the freedom of expression in the mass media. Although these recommendations were to be applicable to all nations, they were designed mainly to "help" third world and Eastern Bloc countries where governments felt the need for restrictions on the freedom of speech.

In a presentation to the International Advertising Association in New York on December 14, 1983 Leonard H. Marks, then Secretary-Treasurer of the World Press Freedom Committee and a former Director of the United States Information Agency, said:

> At the outset, it is important to recognize that the NWIO has never been defined — it is a concept that has emerged from long and sometimes acrimonious debate; regardless of how it is described, there is no doubt that it means a change in the status quo of the free press, and for those who are dependent on the free flow of information, whether advertisers, readers, listeners or viewers.
>
> To some, the NWIO means licensing of media, censorship by governments and a code of conduct defining the responsibility of a journalist. Others would add a demand for a greater share of the electromagnetic spectrum involving short wave broadcasting or space frequencies (Marks, 1983:1).

It is not possible for us to analyse here in detail the entire 312 page "MacBride Commission Report on Communication and Society Today and Tomorrow." We note only its recommendation that information via the mass media should be subordinate to state control and that it attacked advertising directly because of its assumed control of media and alienation of local cultures. The MacBride Report expressed outspoken bias against advertising, against multinationals and against media that are supported financially by revenues from advertising and are not state controlled.

Article 72 indicates the tenor of the MacBride Report regarding advertising:

> 72. Advertising has become an enormous world-wide activity and exists in practically every country. In the mid-1970's the total billings spent on advertising in the world was $33 billion. Its place in any communication system rests mainly on economic as well as political considerations. In some countries, it has a minor role and is in the nature of a public service. In other countries, advertising is itself a major industry and an important form of communication in its own right. Advertising is essentially a communication activity, part of the communication process and system, aiming to promote the sale of a good, commodity or service, to advance an idea or to

bring about some other effect desired by the advertiser. In today's world it is part of the cultural landscape, and increasingly influences so-called mass culture; it is thus seen by many as a threat to the cultural identity and self-realization of many developing countries; it brings to many people alien ethical values; it affects and can often deform ways of life and life-styles. On the other hand it represents a major source of revenue for mass media and thus influences to a greater or lesser extent their whole range of activity and orientation; it becomes blended into other communication contents; either in an overt or disguised way it can pervert mass media action in the political, cultural and entertainment area. In many societies, advertising contributes efficiently to the generation of consumer demand and of a mass market, but its influence on the consumer and on the mass media may also be decisive and negative. Anywhere, it can contribute to raising aspirations and can be a motivating force for an improved quality of life, but it can also contribute mightily to rising frustrations and to consumerism (MacBride Report, 1980).

The above statement is reminiscent of an earlier summary by Covington and Burling of Washington, D.C., noting the ambivalence of the MacBride Commission regarding advertising:

In general, advertising does not receive favorable or even balanced treatment. The Commission finds itself on the horns of a dilemma. On the one hand, it admits in the Interim Report that advertising often provides an essential mechanism for meeting the steadily increasing costs of transnational communication. On the other hand, the Interim Report expresses fear of advertising as a threat to cultural integrity that distorts the contents and quality of the information disseminated by the mass media and tends to cause homogenization of the public while frustrating people by creating unrealizable consumer desires (Covington and Burling, 1978:39 – 40).

The advertising business had not been sufficiently alert to these developments that had been in the making for many years. Debates about the free flow of information, and the concern of developing nations that this flow had acquired too much of a one-way character, started shortly after World War II. Gradually, more and more developing nations, many of which were not ideologically in harmony with modern capitalist societies, had joined the UN. There was growing concern that economically advanced countries would control and dominate information coming into third world countries. These fears were accelerated by the lead of the USA in satellite and computer technology. Many felt that Western influence had to be halted or at least reduced.

The advertising business' reaction to the Belgrade resolution was not immediate and forceful. Governments did not take any immediate action either. The business world apparently did not take UNESCO very seriously since its recommendations were not binding; it was uncertain who would organize and finance the many recommendations of the MacBride Commission; implementation would cost a great deal, and industry was not likely to pay for it.

However, the media were immediately concerned and did take action. At the invitation of the World Press Freedom Committee, a group of 60 print and broadcast organizations from 24 countries met in May, 1981 in Talloires, France to discuss the defense of press freedom. UNESCO's Director-General Amadou-Mahtar

M'Bow was a guest speaker. He faced an angry audience that accused UNESCO of transforming the press into an instrument of government, which M'Bow heatedly denied (*Time Magazine*, 1981). A second meeting organized by the same group, took place in September, 1983 also at Talloires. Representatives from 40 press organizations again discussed the situation and possible solutions.

Although advertising did not play an important part in the deliberations of the MacBride Commission, it was not excluded from the recommendations restricting the freedom of communication. In Belgrade at the time the NWICO was accepted, the advertising business was represented by Mr. Jean-Max Lenormand, then a Director of McCann-Erickson International in Paris and past President of the EAAA. Mr. Lenormand, with the help of his head office, had been instrumental in organizing studies and making recommendations for action by the advertising business. He commented on the meeting:

> In reality, the resolution is a compromise with the terms under which the socialist countries have accepted to suppress interior and exterior obstacles to the free circulation of information and admit that there might be 'plurality of information sources and currents.'
>
> On the other hand, the so-called Western countries accepted the adoption of 'the elemination of the negative effects from certain public or private monopolies and from excessive concentrations.'
>
> This means that Western countries have admitted that international press agencies and large multinational trusts could be the object of very special surveyance. This consensus was reached as a result of weariness all round following two years of discussion.
>
> Are the consequences serious?
>
> It is hardly likely, because this would not be the first time that a resolution from UNESCO (it wasn't voted upon) was not followed up, since it is up to each state, or each government if you prefer, to decide if and how they are to apply it. It is hard to see, not only for the immediate future, but even in the distant future, how Western governments could interfere in the 'organisation' of their mass media, because during the meetings in Belgrade they continually defended the total freedom of mass media!
>
> In conclusion, it should be noted that the text of this consensus was the object of express reserves from the British, American and Danish delegations.
>
> Finally, the principle of creating an 'international program for the development of communication,' supervised by an Intergovernment Council from 35 members and not by the UNESCO secretariat, was adopted.
>
> Just who is going to finance this program is still to be worked out, and since it won't be the Western countries, it is hard to imagine which country would accept the charge. As far as advertising is concerned, it did not seem to be the subject of a great deal of discussion, because in fact the debate was centered more upon the protection of journalists and the status of the press. But of course, the subject was not far below the surface (Lenormand, 1981).

Since 1981 not much of importance has surfaced to contradict Lenormand's expectations. The USA and the UK have meanwhile withdrawn from UNESCO because of alleged mismanagement and politicizing of non-political issues; other Western countries also have expressed dissatisfaction with the direction in which this UN agency seems to be going and have threatened to leave it. A study by 21 present and former UNESCO officials has been published in a report entitled "The Critical Analysis of the Program." "The Report charges that the United Nations Educational, Scientific and Cultural Organization's programs suffer from duplication and overlapping, unsatisfactory guidance and a failure at top management levels to coordinate activities" (*International Herald Tribune*, September 8 – 9, 1984).

The severe attacks on UNESCO may well affect the future of the NWICO, and without substantial financial aid, which is unlikely to come from Western countries, it will be difficult to put the new "Order" into effect. Yet, documents emanating from an official UN body may still have great consequences. The NWICO was accepted in Belgrade by consensus and such consensus offers at least moral support to countries in the developing world that might use such agreed upon principles as a model to introduce domestic legislation. As Leonard Marks said, when describing a UNESCO Conference in 1976: "UNESCO is not the villain: It adopted no resolutions, nor took action on the subjects, but it is the host where a virus is planted and the germ of an idea is nurtured" (Marks, 1983:9).

Notwithstanding the doubts about the future of UNESCO and the MacBride recommendations, which – most importantly – have not yet been implemented anywhere, the advertising business must remain alert. If these recommendations were to be applied one day, the consequences for advertising could be serious, especially advertising addressed at the population of third world nations. However, recent contacts between UNESCO and the IAA with regard to its education program, may contribute to a better relationship between this UN agency and the business world.

Murray Weidenbaum in the conclusion of an address in New York in 1983 adds some useful thoughts:

> For the UN to focus on the private company doing business in world markets at a time of the Iraq – Iran War, the fighting in Lebanon, and the strategic rivalry between the USSR and the US reminds me, sadly, of the ostrich with its head in the sand. Or perhaps, it is a means of diverting attention from the shortcomings of its basic activity. In any event, the role of the UN as peacekeeper deserves renewed emphasis in the dangerous world in which we live. The member nations must face the major threats to peace and try to deal with them. They should not be diverted from this fundamental responsibility by assuming the role of global 'nanny' or international business 'cop,' functions which the UN is not geared to handle and which are inconsistent with its basic and still unfulfilled mission (Weidenbaum, 1983:13).

Ambassador Jean Kirkpatrick concludes in a similar vein:

> Doubtless, international regulation is needed in a good many domains. Doubtless, consumers in remote places need protection against unscrupulous multinationals. (They need protection in ways that do not inhibit economic development and growth, I may say, as well). And doubtless, too, all of us need protection against the arrogance of the new international 'new class' (Kirkpatrick, 1983).

The comments of Weidenbaum and Kirkpatrick illustrate that consumer protection and government control of the mass media are primarily political issues and should be treated as such. The activities of ECOSOC and UNESCO underscore this conclusion. Although this observation applies to all intergovernmental organizations, it is particularly evident in the case of the UN, where the influence of third world nations and their political aspirations are strong. The so-called "Group of 77," now a group of 127 developing countries, has the support of the Eastern Bloc. This group exerts considerable influence on the policies and programs of the UN. Industry and the advertising business have therefore every reason to be particularly concerned about the activities of UN organizations.

After this discussion of three intergovernmental organizations of varying significance to consumer affairs and advertising regulation within the Community, we turn our attention to UNICE, which represents industry in Community matters, to the IOCU, a worldwide consumer organization, and to COFACE, concerned with matters regarding the family inside the Community.

Union of Industries of the European Community

UNICE, which refers to itself as the "spokesman for European industry," is an association of industrial and employers' federations. Its member federations are the central industrial and employers' federations from all EEC Member States and from all European Free Trade Area (EFTA) countries.

UNICE will respond to, and take part in, all matters of importance to European industry that come out of the Directorates-General of the EC. Its Marketing and Consumer Affairs Working Group consists of a mixture of representatives from industrial federations and corporate executives at the national level.

On October 8, 1981, the executive committee of UNICE asked this group "to prepare, in consultation with the federations, guidelines for the benefit of companies in the Community and the associated countries" (UNICE, 1983:2). These guidelines were published on March 2, 1983. They contained the following description of their purpose:

> The purpose of the present guidelines is to contribute to the fostering of the economic health of our society and to the preservation of the freedom of choice of the consumer; to clarify concepts; to define the responsibilities of the participants in the market economy, each of whom has a role to play; to promote the education and information of the consumer; to provide Federations and their members with guiding principles; and to encourage cooperation with the authorities – all endeavours which cannot fail to have a beneficial influence on the economic operation of our society and to build an unbiased image of industry and commerce in the eyes of the public (UNICE, 1983:3).

The document contains the UNICE position on the rights and duties of companies, as well as the rights and duties of consumers. With regard to the latter group it stated laconically: "This aspect has been largely overlooked so far" (UNICE, 1983:5).

The UNICE document also dealt extensively with the five basic consumer rights included in the EEC's Consumer Programs. It also considered the relationships between industry and consumer organizations:

> Throughout this paper, the need to maintain contacts with and to inform the consumer, consumer associations and similar bodies, has been stressed. A climate of confidence and cooperation must exist between the economic partners. When codes of practice are being prepared, industry is advised to consult consumers before taking decisions. It is difficult to assess the extent to which consumer associations reflect the true opinions of consumers. Nevertheless, their observations, criticisms and suggestions, which are often constructive, should be carefully listened to. When the wishes expressed by associations are of a political nature, tend to reduce the freedom of choice of the consumer, or do not coincide with his genuine interests (especially through the failure to grasp the basic inter-dependence of industry and the consumer), the company will of course recognise that the final arbiter is the individual consumer (UNICE, 1983:11).

With regard to advertising regulation the UNICE document said:

> By and large, except as regards health and safety, industry prefers not to have legal regulations, but to introduce systems based on self-discipline. These systems can be improved in the light of experience (without the time-consuming and inflexible procedures associated with legislation), and where desirable, in consultation with consumer associations. Trade associations contribute to the development of legal rules where these are agreed to be necessary. They do not favour an excessive proliferation of regulations, which might create legal uncertainty, paralyse industry, and entail costs out of proportion to the benefits expected to accrue to the economic partners (UNICE, 1983:11 – 12).

In consumer affairs UNICE has also been involved in the discussions on the recently approved directives on product liability and on misleading advertising, the directive on information about dangerous products, the directive for unit pricing of non-foodstuffs, the proposed directive on consumer credit, the communication on unfair contract clauses, and others. UNICE takes a special interest in health and safety aspects of consumer products. In general, it considers that achieving the internal market is the best way of ensuring that consumers' interests in the European Community are protected.

UNICE is also interested in consumer education. With regard to this last subject, the group sponsored a Colloquium on "Education in Economics and the World of Business," in Brussels on December 5, 1984. It is of interest to note that some of the conclusions of this Colloquium paralleled those of the COE's seminar on problems of consumer education, held in Germany in November, 1984. Representatives from the teaching profession that attended the UNICE Colloquium, drew attention "to the growing need ... to make people more aware of the advantages of a market economy," and that "certain economic faculties and a few specialised or general schools of education (at all levels of teaching) were ill-informed of the advantages of the market economy and of the role played by business organisations. It was evident that those who suffered from this state of affairs were schoolchildren and the business community" (UNICE, 1984a:3).

In the field of consumer affairs, UNICE follows EEC initiatives and recommendations, but is unlikely to take the initiative to propose new regulations regarding advertising. Rather, it studies Commission proposals and responds with an industry point of view. It recognizes EAT and WFA as the two spokesmen, as far as industry is concerned, at EEC level. Advertising is relatively unimportant compared to other matters on which UNICE represents industry. Nevertheless the advertising business has established a good working relationship with UNICE, which is an ally in the defense of consumers' freedom of choice and in favor of self-regulatory systems of advertising control.

International Organization of Consumers' Unions

Another international organization that deserves attention is the IOCU founded in 1960 by consumer groups in Australia, Belgium, Netherlands, UK and USA. In 1985 its members include 135 consumer organizations from 52 countries.

The IOCU central office is located in The Hague, Netherlands, with a regional office for Asia and the Pacific in Malaysia. Mr. Lars Oftedal Broch of Norway heads the IOCU's central office in The Hague. He stresses the international character of the IOCU, especially activities in third world nations, which are "more dramatic" than IOCU activities in Europe (Lars Broch, 1984). Mr. Peter Goldman, former President of the IOCU, adds that in 1974 the IOCU decided "to gear itself more to the needs of consumers in the Third World" (IOCU Brochure:30).

Although European consumer organizations that are members of both the BEUC and the IOCU might find some duplication, Mr. Broch points out that BEUC's main purpose is to represent consumers in Europe, whereas the IOCU represents consumers worldwide. However, the IOCU is important because it assisted in drawing up the original UN Guidelines for Consumer Protection.

Advertising is not one of the IOCU's main preoccupations, although many of its activities have a direct bearing on it. The organization's main concerns are the health and safety aspects of certain products, particularly if they fall into the hands of an unsophisticated public. The marketing practices of babyfoods, pharmaceuticals and pesticides are typical examples.

The most visible of IOCU's activities is undoubtedly its Consumer Interpol, set up in 1981; it "... scrutinizes consumer goods and services – sounding the alarm if damaged, faulty or otherwise hazardous goods are off-loaded onto unsuspecting markets. The ensuing publicity makes it hard for the manufacturer to dump the standard goods elsewhere" (IOCU Brochure:28).

Consumer Interpol, with support from the United Nations, (since the IOCU has consultative status with the UN's ECOSOC) had by 1984 compiled a list of over a thousand products and chemical substances and the names of their manufacturers, to provide an early warning system for problems that might arise.

It is to be regretted that few contacts exist between the IOCU and the advertising business. Some even describe IOCU as the organization the least friendly inclined toward marketing and advertising and their role in our society. It remains remarkable that those organizations, which have, or should have, the closest relationships with consumers, are the least accessible to industry for a dialogue about the interests of those consumers. The IOCU, along with the BEUC and the CCC, do not appear to be willing to respond to overtures of cooperation from industry, as recommended by the Commission. The bias against business is still considerable.

Other important organizations and issues

Apart from the intergovernmental and non-governmental organizations we have discussed that may have an influence on advertising and its regulation throughout Europe, there are other organizations with which the advertising business will wish to maintain contact. These will include the many national and international trade associations representing specific product categories, who will often take part in discussions on an *ad hoc* basis. The same will apply to an organization like the COFACE. This confederation acts in an advisory capacity to the Commission on matters regarding the family, such as advertising and children. COFACE, with an office in Brussels, has representatives on its Assembly from each Member State. At the beginning of 1985, 50 organizations from the then 10 Member States were members of COFACE. Although advertising is not its primary concern, in its European Family Manifesto of 1984, COFACE called for adoption of Community legislation on consumer credit and misleading advertising. The latter subject has meanwhile been resolved by the 1984 Directive (Crane, 1985:23).

The activities of these many intergovernmental and non-governmental organizations are not limited to the issues discussed in this book. There are many other subjects of a general or specific nature which any of the supranational organizations or their institutions may deem worthy of study and regulatory measures, for example: sex in advertising, poster sites, the advertising of metal detectors, a code of conduct on distribution and use of pesticides, rules on quick frozen foods, the marketing of cocoa and chocolate products, the use of works of art in advertising, the increasing importance of sponsorship in advertising, and the constant threat of taxation of advertising expenditures. These are examples of issues that already are, or may be subjected to regulation. As we said earlier, this book cannot possibly deal with each of these subjects in any detail. The authors have confined themselves to a discussion of the main principles underlying regulatory efforts and have used examples by way of illustration only. Those readers who wish to inform themselves in greater detail about any of these issues concerned are advised to consult their national trade associations.

However, the above list of outstanding subjects, together with those discussed in this book clearly illustrate the need for the business world to be alert and able to act and react quickly and decisively. The advertising business will have to be adequately organized to deal with old and new issues, as they arise. This situation requires first and foremost a strong and united representation of advertising interests at national and international levels.

Key perspectives

There seems to have been a gradual improvement in the consumer image of advertising and in the relationships of the advertising business with the Commission — as well as with other supranational organizations. Contacts between the business community and consumer groups at the international level still leave much to be desired.

We have made a number of recommendations that are intended to further improve relationships between the various parties in the regulatory process and to ensure a better understanding among future generations of the role of advertising in society and in the economic process. This effort seems to be necessary in light of the increasing complexities in communicating messages to consumers throughout the Community and Europe as a whole. Technological advances such as cable and satellite transmission in broadcasting have far reaching consequences for international trade and for the advertising to support its expansion. The discussions of the Commission's green paper "Television without Frontiers" and Article 10 of the ECHR have given new meaning to the concepts of freedom of choice and freedom of expression, both of vital importance to the future of the Community and what it stands for.

The Commission's consumer programs require continuing attention. But also numerous other supranational organizations now take an active interest in consumer affairs and advertising regulation. Clearly there must be international order in the use of old and new media crossing many borders. But how far should such order go and who should be responsible for the rules? It will have been noted that while the supranational organizations we discussed do not necessarily cover the same audience in the same territories, there is considerable overlap of interest. This proliferation and duplication of efforts in the field of regulatory activity indeed concern us deeply. How long will this kind of extravagance be sustainable and allowed to continue? We shall come back upon this important point in our final chapter.

Chapter V

Preparing for the future

"It is bad enough to know the past,
it is intolerable to know the future."
Somerset Maugham, British writer

"The future is the past in preparation."
Pierre Dac, French writer

Introduction

We shall be saying No to scepticism,
No to defeatism, and No to all excuses.

This challenging statement by Jacques Delors, as new President of the Commission, in his inaugural address in January 1985 to the EP (*Europe 85*, 1985c:6) sets the tone for the last chapter of this book. We now consider some vital political and economic trends in Europe, followed by statements by the Commission regarding its future general policies and by a discussion of the contribution the advertising business can make towards a "People's Europe." We shall then deal with some aspects of international advertising in the future and the latest trends in consumerism in Europe and the USA. This will lead to a discussion of: (1) the Commission's future consumer policies embodied in its white paper "Completing the Internal Market" and (2) Commissioner Clinton Davis' document "A New Impetus For Consumer Protection." We shall then cover the activities of other supranational organizations in the field of consumer affairs and the precarious duplication of intergovernmental bodies in this area. The case for self-regulation, coupled with a minimum of governmental intervention, should be the thread running through the combined efforts of leaders of industry, educators and advertising practitioners, in speaking out on the role of advertising in today's and tomorrow's economy and society. Our final observations will include comments on the future need for a united business world to continue its policies in defense of established freedoms, to the benefit of industry and the advertising business as well as the buying public.

Trends and megatrends

In October, 1983 the Commission published a brochure entitled "The European Community and Consumers" (*European File*, 1983). It contained an overview of consumer protection developments. Its first paragraph was a condensed copy of the first paragraph from the General Considerations of the First Consumer Program. This paragraph contained a number of questionable assertions, as discussed in Chapter II. In June – July, 1985 the Commission produced a similar brochure, again entitled "The European Community and Consumers" (*European File*, 1985). This 1985 brochure repeated in only slightly modified form the first paragraph of the 1983 brochure:

> The variety and complexity of the goods and services available to consumers often cause confusion and frustration. Over the years, as prosperity has increased, marketing conditions have been transformed and the traditional relationships between supplier and consumer have been overturned. At one time the consumer shopped locally in a limited market where he often knew the supplier personally. Nowadays the consumer faces a mass market where producers and retailers are more or less faceless, have gained considerable power through the process of mergers and are better placed than the shopper to control market conditions. For this reason, consumers are becoming increasingly conscious of the quality and safety of goods. They crave objective information on which to base their purchase, according to their needs and financial means. They also want an improved right of redress if the goods or services purchased do not match up to expectations (*European File*, 1985:3).

It is rather disturbing to see how little the attitude of the Commission has changed over a period of ten years and how it retains statements that were already out of date when they were first made. The allegations of so many years ago about consumer confusion, frustration and inability to make good choices in today's markets, continue to lack supporting evidence and are not convincing. With increasing levels of education, consumer sophistication and confidence to act, the Commission today has even fewer advocates to support its position than in the mid-1970s.

It is not easy to comprehend why the Commission over all these years has not examined seriously the changing marketplace in European countries, especially prevailing trends in buying habits, consumer motivations and preferences. The Commission can represent the real interests of consumer only if it is aware of the everyday concerns of consumers to fill their shopping baskets with products to satisfy today's needs in an efficient and economic manner. The Commission must do more than repeat phrases that were of doubtful validity in the mid-1970s and have even less credibility in the mid-1980s.

However, as we shall see later, there are indications that the Commission appointed in January 1985, now seems to have set a new course with regard to its consumer policies. One can only hope that when executing these policies, the Commission will fully take into account the continuing changes in the pattern of consumer attitudes and habits.

The subject of "change" has even reached the popular literature. In *Megatrends: Ten New Directives Transforming Our Lives*, John Naisbitt highlights well-known developments which are of relevance to the regulatory efforts of the Commission and others in Europe. He writes:

I do not want to minimize the importance of Sputnik and Columbia in opening up the heavens to us. But what has not been stressed enough is the way the satellite transformed the earth into what Marshall McLuhan called a global village. Instead of turning us outward toward space, the satellite era turned the globe inward upon itself. (McLuhan saw television as the instrument that would bring about the global village; we now know it is the communication satellite.)

Today's information technology – from computers to cable television – did not bring about the new information society. It was already well under way by the late 1950s. Today's sophisticated technology only hastens our plunge into the information society that is already here (Naisbitt, 1982:12).

Michael Parsons, an advertising agency executive in the UK, comments:

If there is one theme that seems to run through all the thinking on tomorrow, it is that as the world gets smaller so it gets more complicated.

The shrinking is caused by what Naisbitt describes, with that economy of description, as the advent of the 'globalized information economy.' In other words, of fewer than four syllables, high tech is going to make one hell of an impact. Naisbitt puts it more succinctly when he writes that 'we now mass-produce information the way we used to mass-produce cars.'

Electronic innovations, computer technology and new information systems have produced a new economic structure. Industrial society is dead, information society is born (Parsons, 1984).

To those involved in the international aspects of business and advertising, the third of Naisbitt's ten megatrends, the critical restructuring from national economies to a world economy has been of great importance for many years. The point is not at all new to Europeans, but sometimes it seems to be neglected. Naisbitt notes also that "The globalization of our economies will be accompanied by a renaissance in the language and cultural assertiveness ... the Swedish more Swedish, the Chinese, more Chinese. And the French, God help us, more French" (Naisbitt, 1982:76).

Those who know Europe well, can only confirm Naisbitt's point. We need only to look at Switzerland with its four different languages, or the separatist movement in the Basque and Catalunian regions of Spain which, much to the confusion of visitors and tourists, have reintroduced their own languages, which were strictly forbidden during the Franco regime.

Naisbitt has reminded not only Americans but also forward-looking Europeans of the difficult problems that society has faced for many decades to keep pace with technological developments. "Embracing the future," is an especially complex task for Europe, which must consider the diversity of languages, cultures, conflicting political opinions and clashing economic interests. Let us therefore briefly examine the Europe of today from a political and economic point of view. A first impression, unfortunately, is that the future is not very bright.

Scott Sullivan, the European Regional Editor of *Newsweek* magazine, begins a rather depressing article entitled "The Decline of Europe" with a quote from Luigi Barzini, well known author of *The Italians*:

> We Europeans have been reduced to the role of the Greeks in the Roman Empire. The most useful function an Italian or a Frenchman can perform these days is to teach an American or a Japanese the proper temperature at which to drink his red wine (Barzini, as quoted by Sullivan).

Sullivan continues:

> ... Western Europe, the proud old continent that dominated world history for two millenniums, is stagnating economically and faltering politically. After 30 years of nearly uninterrupted growth, the postwar European economic miracle has spluttered and died out. World leadership in science, technology and commercial acumen has passed to the United States and Japan ...
>
> A growing number of younger Europeans are simply rejecting the positivist values that fueled progress in the past. Others are worrying openly about the survivability of European culture. 'Unless we can revive the idea of a united states of Europe' says the eminent French historian Fernand Braudel, 'we won't be able to rescue European culture, not to mention the European economy' (Sullivan, 1984:44).

Mentioning the "always more" syndrome – more pay, more fringe benefits, more job security, more privileges – which Sullivan finds one of the central issues of the European malaise, he turns his attention to what he calls "The Mess in the EEC." He notes that Europe's industrial, commercial and technological problems must be tackled on a multinational basis, with the "... Brussels-based European Economic Community ... overseeing such efforts." He continues: "... it has failed lamentably to live up to its early promise as a stimulator of European unity and progress. It has bogged down in bureaucratic trivia and allowed its energies to be dissipated in sterile quarrels over agricultural issues" (Sullivan, 1984:49).

Newsweek editor Sullivan was not the only person disappointed with the lack of EEC progress in stimulating European unity. The Commission's official publication, *Europe*, also had difficulty in hiding its displeasure. The failure of summit meetings in Athens (December, 1983) and in Brussels (March, 1984) led to the following statements:

> A failure of the European Council is not a failure of the European Community.
>
> Decisions must be taken that will enable the Community to honour its pledges to itself, to its citizens and to non-member countries.
>
> We must return to the Treaty procedures – the only ones whereby the higher interest of the Community can once again be made central (*Europe 83*, 1983:3).

The last of the above quotes is a thinly concealed criticism of the summit meetings. Although the Rome Treaty did not authorize or even mention summit meetings, they were the vehicle to initiate the Commission's consumer protection programs.

After the unsuccessful Brussels summit meeting, *Europe* reported an interview with Commission President Gaston Thorn, in which "... he condemned what he described as 'the general unwillingness to compromise,' but ... [defended] the right of member states to protect their vital interests" (*Europe 84*, 1984:3). Thereby he pinpointed one of the weaknesses of the EEC. It is not able to take decisions by majority vote.

All this, we regret to say, does not make pleasant reading – particularly the point which President Thorn makes about excessive nationalistic tendencies among the Member States of the Community. This situation worries those who would like to see a strong and united European continent.

However, there also have been positive signs. For example, we should recognize that the Council of Ministers have approved several programs which should bring about greater unity of purpose among Member States in fighting competition from the great industrial powers, the USA and Japan. The Community promotes technological cooperation through the "European Strategic Programme of Information Technologies" (ESPRIT), through a program called RACE ("Research and Development in Advanced Communications Technologies for Europe"), and through a program referred to as BRITE ("Basic Research in Industrial Technologies for Europe"), the latter being

> ... a research and development programme, designed to strengthen the competitiveness of a whole series of industrial sectors which are not as much in the public eye as the new information technology sector, but whose role is just as vital for the economy: motor vehicles, chemicals, shipbuilding, clothing and textiles, building, machine tools, electrical equipment, furniture and other durable goods (*Unice Informations*, 1984b:11).

In addition, President Mitterrand from France took the initiative for yet another plan for technological cooperation between governments and industrial concerns, called EUREKA ("European Research Coordination Agency"). It was well received by governments and industry and a number of specific projects have been agreed upon.

Christopher Tugendhat, a former Vice-President of the Commission, also saw signs of a new willingness among Member States to move towards true European union. Although he did not mention these European projects by name, he was clearly in favor of them:

> The way forward must be through bringing the member states together in a network of co-operative ventures that will enable them to overcome problems that would otherwise be beyond them, and to achieve together what they could not achieve alone. To some this may not seem as dramatic, or as inspiring, an approach as that which takes as its starting point a massive transfer of powers to the centre, and as its ultimate objective the creation of a United States of Europe on the American model. But in practice it is likely to prove more durable and more capable of achieving the first objective of the Treaty of Rome, namely an 'ever closer union among the peoples of Europe.' By union I mean a sense of common purpose and shared interests that transcends the individual identities of separate states (*Europe 85*, 1985b:16).

These thoughts are welcomed by many who believe united action by Europeans is the key to competing successfully with Japan, the USA and especially with the emerging industrial nations such as Korea, Taiwan and others. But it is also believed by some that re-industrialization may be less important to Europe's future than nurturing the industries that comprise the new information and service economy, which is already quite advanced in Europe, Japan and the USA. The re-emergence of entrepreneurship, especially in new industries may be even more vital to Europe than emphasis on traditional industries. Of course, basic industries will remain important to Europe, but the resurgence of private enterprise, the rise of service industries and the innovations of small, new businesses, as they have helped the USA to overcome some of its problems, may also be of paramount importance to Europe.

It is hazardous to make forecasts about probable future economic and political developments. However, apart from the above-mentioned significant economic aspects of European recovery, there are also indications of a political nature that Europe might soon be entering a new era.

First, French President Mitterrand in a speech to the EP on May 23, 1984 revived the idea of a European Union, which had been recommended as far back as 1976 by Mr. Tindemans of Belgium. Mitterrand also made a plea for the return of majority voting within the EEC. The remarkable thing about this proposal was that it was one of Mitterrand's predecessors, president De Gaulle, who had brought majority voting in the Council to an end, thereby crippling the ability of this body to make quick decisions.

Mitterrand's speech, it should be said, did not come unexpectedly. On July 9, 1981 the EP had accepted a motion by Altiero Spinelli and other enthusiasts for the European cause, to prepare a proposal for the reform of the Community. Following this mandate, the EP set up a Committee for Industrial Affairs in January, 1982, chaired by Mauro Ferri. On February 14, 1983 a proposal for constitutional reform was passed by the EP with a large majority.

It is a most ambitious plan. Before this new "European Treaty of Union" can become a reality, it must be ratified by all Member States and approved by at least two-thirds of the European Community's electorate. Even though rapid progress and agreement cannot be expected, it is of interest to see what some of the important features of this new Treaty could eventually be:

> In terms of its function it is in effect a constitution, in that it redefines the competencies and institutions which will form the new political corpus of the European Union.
>
> In terms of its form, however, it is an international treaty, in that only the member states will be competent to accept its content, subsequently ratify it, and finally implement the Union which they are invited to join.
>
> From the point of view of its content, the draft Treaty establishes a system which, while preserving the existing Community terminology for reasons of continuity, in fact establishes a new division of powers and a new system of decison-making.
>
> In effect, it will fall to the elected Parliament and the Council of Union (made up of representatives of goverments) to approve the principal rules of the Union and its laws. The intended procedure gives power of co-decision to these two institutions, both as regards organic laws (which will require

a larger majority in both bodies) and as regards ordinary laws.

The new procedure will be more effective, thanks to a system of deadlines which will prevent decisions being delayed indefinitely by either Parliament or the Council.

The proposed system maintains the central role of the Commission, which will retain its right of initiative (a right which the Parliament and the Council will also have to a certain extent) and will also take an important part in the process of drawing up legislative acts (*Europe 84*, 1984a:9).

Sandro Pertini, past President of the Italian Republic, speaking to the EP in April, 1984, one month before Mitterrand made his speech to the same audience, gave his full support to the new draft Treaty.

One month later, in June, 1984, when the Heads of State met for their Summit Meeting at Fontainebleau in France, it was decided

... to set up an ad hoc Committee consisting of personal representatitives of the heads of state and of government, on the lines of the Spaak Committee.* The Committee's function will be to make suggestions for the improvement of the operation of European cooperation in both the Community field and that of political, or any other, cooperation (*Euro Forum*, 1984:(i)).

In March, 1985 this committee, under the chairmanship of Senator Dooge from Ireland, reported to the European Council. It recommended objectives for European union, and the improvement of the decision-making mechanism and procedures to be followed to arrive at a Union. No final decisions were taken, but Commissioner Carlo Ripa de Meana expressed the progress made:

The Community has sewn up − even if the wounds have not totally healed − the disputes which have marked the present phase of integration, and has decided to welcome two new members. Everybody now agrees in stating − and the Commission has been saying it for years − that the Community of twelve member states will only be able to work out its own role if it is prepared to change. Otherwise, decision-making will be paralysed, wrangling will start all over again, and further development of the Community will be impossible for a long time to come (*Euro Forum*, 1985:ii)

Another indication of a refreshing change in the Commission's attitudes and its future plans, was the first speech by Jacques Delors in his capacity as new President of the commission. In his speech to the EP in Strasbourg on January 14, 1985, President Delors spoke on: "The Thrust of Commission Policy." He made a passionate plea to accept the challenge of getting a disunited Europe back on its feet again. He said:

So it is that a new Commission appears before you, imbued with intellectual humility and great political resolve. Personally, I am more aware of the humility. I have often wondered why the Community, with its committed and talented leadership, has never got off the ground; why it has failed to attain the objectives enshrined in the Treaty, objectives in which there was a measure of

---

* The Belgian Minister for Foreign Affairs, Paul-Henri Spaak, chaired a Committee in 1955, preparing a Report that would become the basis of the two treaties establishing the EEC and Euratom.

consensus; in short, why it has failed to bring about the economic, social and monetary integration which is vital to the advancement of our ten nations. Forgive me if I come up with a rather trite thought, born of experience. I believe that the engineers of European integration are fumbling not over 'what has to be done' but rather over 'how to go about it.' We can no longer blame the crippling weight of the crises, the absence of political will or the inertia of national officialdom. We need to look further and, here again, there is a glimmer of hope: the European Council is now as anxious as this House to improve the performance of the institutions (Delors, 1985:2).

Discussing the weaknesses and the strengths of the present European economy, Jacques Delors observed:

European industrial society used to be a model of efficiency. It is less so today – there can be no doubt about it. It is fighting for its life – that is quite clear. Reforms are needed – nobody denies it. But the principles still hold good, because they are based on the idea of a balanced relationship between society and the individual.

What we lack, apart from a certain degree of self-confidence, is the benefit of scale and the multiplier effect. This can only result from a more united and more integrated Europe. In its four years in office, the Commission proposes to take decisive steps in three directions:
– a large market and industrial cooperation;
– the strengthening of the European Monetary System;
– the convergence of economies to lead to higher growth and more jobs (Delors, 1985:11).

The new President also expressed appreciation for the initiatives to improve the functioning of the Commission and other EC institutions. But he sounded the following note of warning: "... I fear that institutional issues would lead to the adoption of diametrically apposed positions which each side could invoke as a pretext for doing nothing" (Delors, 1985:22).

Having assured the EP that the Commission will do all in its power to avoid this outcome, Delors then mentioned the three major challenges that must be met:

First, the challenge of approach: we must demonstrate that we can act as twelve, and not simply mark time or muddle through from one day to the next.

Second, the challenge of influence: we must ensure that the Community speaks with one voice and plays its part on the stage on contemporary history.

And lastly, the challenge of civilization: in a world of change, we must reaffirm our values and fuse the sometimes contradictory aims and aspirations of our contemporaries into new constructs (Delors, 1985:26).

A few months after Mr. Delors' address to the EP, the Commission published its official "Programme for the Commission for 1985." The program echoed the thoughts expressed by the President in January. It devoted only four out of the 110 pages of the document to consumer protection, but it also contained the following important points about the Commission's overall policy:

1. The four main goals are to strengthen Europe's economic structure, to transform the Community into 'an influential actor on the world stage,' to create greater involvement of European citizens in the policies of the Commission and to 'set the Community on the road to European Union' (Commission of the EC, 1985a:1).
2. 'A barrier-free economic area cannot operate without ground rules. The plan is not therefore to deregulate at any price but to simplify by replacing the profusion of national rules with common or largely harmonized ones' (Commission of the EC, 1985a:6).
3. The Commission officially confirms its policy 'to strengthen people's sense of belonging to the Community;' it will run information campaigns and make use of special events (European Music Year, International Youth Year, the European Yacht Race) 'to increase awareness of the European dimension' (Commission if the EC, 1985a:107).

A few months later Lord Cockfield, the responsible Commissioner for the Internal Market, released a white paper "Completing the Internal Market." This document opened new perspectives on the ideal of achieving a European Common Market. We shall come back to this important display of the Commission's plans and intentions when discussing the Commission's future consumer policy. At this point we express the hope that the Council of Ministers and Governments of Member States will be as enthusiastic about these new policies as the Commission is. It would be tragic if harping on procedural details were allowed to stifle the new drive for rapid progress toward European economic unity.

It is in any case encouraging to note that at a summit meeting in Luxembourg on December 2 – 3, 1985 the Heads of State agreed to make fundamental changes in the Treaty of Rome:

> The reform package provides for majority voting by the Council of Ministers in certain areas where a unanimous decision is now required, and it strengthens slightly the powers of the European Parliament. It also covers monetary cooperation, research and technology, environmental protection and social policy (*European Community News*, 1985:1).

The timing of these initiatives is particularly important because they coincide with growing confidence in the European economy. "Coming out of the slump – at last, signs that Europessimism has run it course," ran a headline in *Time Magazine* (1985:34). The positive attitude of European citizens toward unification is equally important. According to a Eurobarometer survey published by the Commission, 52% of those questioned want "the kind of political union there is between the 50 states of the USA or the 10 provinces that form Canada" (*Europe 85*, 1985a:23).

These positive signs of new initiatives and developments toward a united Europe are promising, and one can only hope that the recommended projects, together with a redivision of responsibilities and working procedures of the Commission, will be implemented soon. These actions would enhance the image of the Community and its Commission in the eyes of the world and it would also increase confidence in

Europe's political leaders to achieve greater unity of purpose among Member States. The new developments do not yet give us reason to rejoice but they certainly are steps in the right direction.

The contribution of the advertising business to a "People's Europe"

As we have seen, it is the Commission's earnest desire to create greater awareness among European citizens of its policies. Commissioner Clinton Davis talks in one of his papers of a "people's" and a "citizens'" Europe (Commission of the EC, 1985b). It is the logical consequence of a decision at the Fontainebleau summit meeting in June 1984 when

> The Heads of Government decided that the Community should strengthen and promote its identity and its image both for its citizens and for the rest of the world. They agreed on a series of measures, some of which will be implemented in the near future, such as the 'European Passport' (*Europe 84*, 1984b:10).

An *ad hoc* committee for a "people's Europe" was set up under the chairmanship of the Italian representative, Mr. Andonnino. The "People's Europe Committee" submitted reports in March and in June, 1985 which were approved by Heads of State. They formed the basis for the Commission's new policy regarding a better understanding and a closer involvement of the public in its work.

This policy of the Commission falls on fertile ground. The advertising business has long felt strongly about the lack of serious efforts to improve the image of the EEC, and has repeatedly volunteered to help. It simply is unrealistic to expect that the public at large will understand the basic concept of the Rome Treaty to bring about a united Europe, unless better explanations are given. The advantage to European citizens to open frontiers, to lift trade barriers, and to create a genuine "common market" are not self-evident. Acceptance of the body that tries to achieve these ambitious aims must also be established before results that impress, can be expected.

Several years ago the advertising business offered to help the Commission to improve its reputation and acceptance by European citizens. At the time the Commission did not show much interest in such help from professional communicators. This has now changed. The Commission appears to be ready to seek support and active participation of the advertising business to achieve its objectives. This constitutes a major step forward. It is an idea whose time has come. The IAA, under the leadership of its Vice-President Albert Brouwet, acting in close cooperation with the EAAA and other members of EAT, is working toward a closer relationship between the Commission and the advertising business. A plan has been drawn up for a number of public service activities aimed at involving European citizens in the objective of the Commission, thereby improving its image. The Commission will entrust a few carefully selected international advertising agencies with the preparation of a number of campaigns on such important issues as unemployment, a European passport, civic rights, road safety and others. (*Official Journal of the European Communities*, 1985.)

We hope that all parties concerned — governments, the advertising business, the media and of course the Commission — will cooperate fully in making these campaigns successful. The activities will require funds to achieve long-term objectives. In the past, advertising was sometimes used to try to accomplish short-term goals, such as getting voters to the polls to elect the EP. These attempts have done the image of advertising more harm than good. They were typical examples of expecting too much from advertising, especially the mistaken belief that short bursts of advertising could sell an unacceptable product. With worthwhile issues and an adequate budget covering a number of years, it may be possible for advertising to create a more positive attitude among Europeans toward the EC. By the time of the elections for a new EP in 1988, the number of voters can then perhaps be increased over that of 1980 and 1984.

Against this brief recapitulation of relevant trends in Europe and how the advertising business can contribute to achieving a greater unity of purpose, let us now briefly review some aspects of international advertising and how it fits into this scene.

The future of international advertising

This book is not about international advertising but about the regulation of such advertising. However, we cannot very well deal with the subject of regulation without highlighting some of the trends in the complex world of international brand marketing. There can be no doubt that future market conditions will be characterized by fundamental changes in consumer demand, the means to communicate with consumers and the necessary diversity of products to satisfy them.

The words "mass market" no longer properly describe future marketing opportunities. We may instead be entering a new era of fragmentation and individualism. An aging population will have great influence on the marketing picture, as will a large teenage market with high disposable income. High-tech areas centered on the service sector will offer new opportunities, as will health-care products for the elderly. Much emphasis will be on leisure markets and home-based activities. As in the USA and in other developed markets, diversification will be one of the key words applicable to the European market with its 350 million people (*Business International*, 1984a). "All purpose" products were fine until consumer sophistication forced manufacturers to change direction. Naisbitt characterizes the shift: "... a narrow either/or society with a limited range of personal choices ... exploding into a free-wheeling multiple-option society" (Naisbitt, 1982:2).

But how can diversification and market fragmentation be compatible with the growth of cable and satellite television that offer advertisers the opportunity to convey the same messages to millions of consumers, irrespective of nationality? Does the future lie with international brands? Or are we witnessing the return to the sandwich man and town crier, telling everyone on Main Street where to buy the best hot dogs? Will the future be narrowcasting instead of broadcasting? What about the rise of Direct Mail advertising? These and other important questions affect the very nature of advertising, its creative product, and the consequences of regulating it. Ronald Beatson, Director-General of the EAAA, says: "Horizontal and vertical marketing can both be right, but on different occasions" (Beatson, 1984b:41).

We would expect that there will indeed remain a number of "local excitement" brands, which will be marketed on a nation-by-nation basis and on an even narrower market segmentation basis. "These brands will answer the needs of those who would indeed prefer everything to come in thirty-one different flavors" (Naisbitt, 1982:232).

But there will also be increasing numbers of international brands, marketed in essentially similar ways to similar market segments in different countries – despite the many differences in language, culture, habits and social customs. These brands are already with us. The need to find new economies of scale, the scarcity of outstanding creative talent and the availability of international media have caused many international advertisers to give new thought to their product and promotional policies. As a result, proven advertising ideas are used in a large number of countries, with and without local adaptation. There is nothing new in this. International advertising has long existed. The only new element is the anticipated greater availability of media to carry such advertising.

Thus we can expect a certain polarization in the marketing and advertising of goods and services, with purely local brands competing with those which because of their universal advertising promise and recognizable name and package design can make full use of international media.

If this picture of the future advertising scene in Europe is to be fulfilled, barriers to efficient expansion of international trade must be reduced or removed quickly, especially restrictions on activities that relate to brand names, product formulations, patents, copyrights and, of course, advertising.

There is also another very important barrier to be removed, sometimes referred to as the "not-invented-here-syndrome." It is a strange phenomenon in this age of satellite and computers, but there still exists a core of marketing and advertising people who believe that using the good work of colleagues from other countries will diminish their own importance. They refuse to accept that adapting imported ideas to local circumstances can be as creative a job as producing the original. A bad adaptation can easily destroy an advertising idea's effectiveness. Many central managements try to overcome this resistance by expecting their national colleagues to turn down an international advertising idea for adaptation only, if research confirms that a local idea can be expected to be more effective in the marketplace.

As the ultimate success of international advertising fully depends upon consumer' acceptance of it, it is gratifying to know that consumers' opinions of advertising show a positive trend. But what about the views of those who claim to represent consumers? What are the latest trends in attitudes towards advertising among consumerists and consumer movements? "But of course" as Jeremy Bullmore says, the consumer movement "wasn't, accurately, a movement *of* consumers; it was a movement initiated by a relatively small group of concerned people *on behalf* of consumers" (Bullmore 1982). Let us then, before dealing with the Commission's new plans, listen to this "group of concerned people." Let us consider consumerism and where it stands today. Is it still a live issue? It it dormant? Preparing for a comeback?

The voice of consumerism

Consumerism certainly has not disappeared entirely, nor is it likely to. Today it no longer has the militant character of earlier years. However, its representatives are still very active. When the Directive on Misleading Advertising was approved by the Council of Ministers in June, 1984 some in the consumer movement took this opportunity to press for more action. For example on July 25, 1984 the CCC presented a memorandum to Commissioner Narjes, asking him what he intended to do about the outstanding issues. They asked: What about home accidents, cosmetics, labelling of dangerous substances, package tours, consumer education in schools, or health and safety standards for products in trade? They made the point that "... a third programme hardly has any credibility when only one-tenth of the first and second programmes is implemented," and "... with the transnational expansion of information and communications services, consumer protection in such areas as advertising, contracts, protection of privacy or freedom of information badly needs redefining and updating to technological progress on a European basis. What is being done in this area?" (CCC Bureau, 1984). The CCC continued: "... The Bureau urges above all that the implementation of the consumer programme should be given clearer sense of direction. This is the only possible response to the disastrous attempt by the Council of Ministers for the second year running to cut the consumer budget by 50%" (CCC Bureau, 1984).

This was a fair request to make. But the new Commission, as we shall see, has interpreted it in a way which may not entirely conform to the wishes of consumer groups but which in any case demonstrates a "clearer sense of direction."

It is in this respect important to remember that while the Commission makes recommendations, it is the Council of Ministers that takes the binding decisions.

Many people believe that all EC administrative units are one coherent body with the various departments guided by the same priorities. This is not so. There are, for instance, considerable differences between the priorities of the Commission and those of the Council of Ministers. The Commission is a body of professionals, "who shall be chosen on the grounds of their general competence and whose independence can be fully guaranteed," as stated in Article 157 of the Rome Treaty. In the case of consumer affairs, the Commission's task is to prepare agreed consumer programs as efficiently and effectively as possible. The Council of Ministers, on the other hand, is a political body; its members are Ministers of Governments of Member States, and their priorities are governed by political and economic considerations which are not always identical with those of the Commission.

While the laborious working methods of the Commission partly explain the slow progress which consumer organizations attacked so vigorously, it appears as if consumer groups, such as the CCC and the BEUC, are partly to blame themselves. We wonder if more and quicker progress would have been possible, if only these consumer bodies would have been more willing to enter into positive and constructive discussions with industry. Consumer organizations were rarely prepared to sit around the table with representatives from the advertising business to thrash things out. Those who held extreme points of view resisted such discussions. The result was polarization instead of cooperation.

By way of illustration, we would like to quote from the "Concluding Remarks" by Mr. Thierry Bourgoignie, then Head of the Consumer Law Research Centre in Belgium, on the occasion of the Bremen Seminar in November, 1983. Bourgoignie in summing up the results of the Bremen meeting said: "A first remark I would like to make is that there was a consensus among the participants recognizing that the need for intervention in the market in order to give the consumers better protection is not being questioned" (Bourgoignie, 1984:308).

Having thus confirmed the desire of the participants to intervene, without reference to the reasons for the necessity for such intervention, Bourgoignie concluded:

> Substantial efforts have to be made by consumer representatives and consumer lawyers in the next few years in order to resuscitate the public constituency that the consumer movement may have lost to some degree in the past few years. There is a need for a revival of the consumer movement in Europe. The relevance of such an approach has been emphasized by many consumer leaders and analysts of the consumer movement in the US who use such suggestive terms as 'grassroots democracy,' 'new populism,' or the 'backyard revolution' (Pertschuk, 1982). This implies the use of mechanisms such as grassroot citizens organizations, direct citizen participation and activism. It may also involve reflexive law or soft-law instruments. Only such action would increase the policy-makers' sensitivity to consumer demands, revive the need for social regulation, and thereby create the conditions for legitimate public involvement in consumer matters (Bourgoignie, 1984:319).

It is of interest to note that this rather aggressive attitude is not shared by the Commission. The Commission continues to advocate dialogue, which Jeremiah Sheehan described again at the Bremen Seminar:

Dialogue is likely to yield agreement only when there is strong motivation, such as the threat of imminent proposals for legislation. Even then, results will tend to ensue from dialogue only when those proposals are likely to be adopted, i.e., when there are strong indications that the political will exists on the part of member states to adopt them. In fact, we have suffered for years in the Community from the absence of such will. Another circumstance which might induce agreement would be that "framework" legislation already existed which permitted action to counter abuse of consumer rights. Thus, for example, if the EEC Directive on Misleading Advertising came into force in all member states, there could be an advantage for advertising practitioners to adhere to a code or codes in particular sectors, such as advertising to children or advertising of medicinal products, since such adherence might constitute a defense against claims that particular advertisements are misleading. Similarly, a Community Law on unfair terms in consumer contracts could result in voluntary agreements on standard form contracts for particular product categories such as automobiles or electro-domestic durable goods. However, neither of these laws yet exist at Community level, so the conditions for dialogue in the interests of negotiating voluntary codes of conduct are not yet present.

If we assume that the environment for negotiation develops progressively, over coming years, due to the circumstances just outlined, then *dialogue may become an important element of strategy for the late eighties and could be retained in a third consumer programme to be adopted at EEC level for that period* (Sheehan, 1984:294 – 295, italics supplied).

One would have difficulty in finding two more contrasting points of view; on the one hand the consumer activist who uses ideological language; on the other hand the appeasing voice of a senior representative of the Commission, who did not then know that there would not be a third consumer program but who was fully aware of the need to compromise.

While grassroots consumer bodies are not flourishing, pressures from consumerists will keep European governments, the Commission and other supranational organizations busy for a long time to come. Because consumerism is an accepted policy for politicians to champion, consumerism in Europe, in one form or another, will remain very much alive.

Against this background, we would now like to turn to the situation in the USA, which may provide some perspectives that help us to understand the situation in Europe.

Advertising and consumerism in the USA

Despite all the difficulties, the possibilities for fruitful dialogue between the European business community and consumer groups seem to be better than they are in the USA. According to Leonard Matthews, president of the American Association of Advertising Agencies: "... there is *no* formal or informal contact between the advertising industry and consumer groups." In a letter to one of the authors of this book he continues:

It's our view that consumerists do not really represent the consumer but are an elitist group who formed their organizations at their own initiative. Their general attitude is that the consumer is not well-informed and is manipulated by the advertiser and marketer. Further, their view is that how the consumer acts in the marketplace is not a reliable indicator of consumer wants and needs and that the consumer does not know what's best for the consumer. They feel that they know better what's best for the consumer (elitist) and it's their function to force marketers and consumers to conform to their views. Of course, they try to enlist government agencies in their views (Matthews, 1984).

Although there is much similarity between the situation in the USA and in Europe, fortunately there are in Europe examples of excellent relationships between producers and national consumer organizations, such as in the UK and in the Netherlands.

As in Europe, consumerism in the USA is also a relatively low key issue at the moment. But this situation is not likely to be permanent, and one must anticipate that the character of consumerism will once again become more militant.

With regard to the decline of militant consumerism in the USA, Matthews writes:

There are two reasons ... A less sympathetic government ear to consumerists is one reason. Another is a strong trend in the US toward a more traditional and conservative attitude toward business on the part of the general public ... The 60s and 70s saw the era of non-conformity, anti-establishment, liberal anti-business attitudes. College graduates all wanted non-business careers. In this atmosphere consumerism flourished because it was anti-establishment. The 1980 presidential election saw the turn in these events. Government had overstepped its place in our lives. Big government had gone beyond Big Brother to become Big Bother. People were fed up with government looking over their shoulder. College graduates became interested in business careers again and advertising agencies became popular once more as a socially acceptable place to work.

Our most active threats in the US, and around the world, are the threats against tobacco and alcoholic beverages. The hidden agenda of the anti-groups is the elimination of all advertising for these products. Such things as health warnings in ads and packages are only way-stops along the road to total abolition of advertising. They know that the prohibition of the sale of tobacco, beer, wine and liquor will not work but they hope that abolition of advertising, over time, will reduce consumption.

We can expect a continuous attack on the advertising of these products until they achieve this end ... In my contact with consumerists I find them just as zealous, just as idealogically opposed to the free market and to free advertising as ever. They are relatively dormant for the reasons I have mentioned earlier. They are remarkably unmoved by the facts. They don't want facts which run counter to their preconceived notions (Matthews, 1984).

Matthews' comments were not merely an attempt to provoke indignation. According to the AAAA *Washington Newsletter* of February/March 1985, bills have been proposed in nine American states to restrict or ban some or all advertising for alcoholic beverages, and the US Congress has asked for a study to be made regarding the advertising of these products.

On February 7, 1985, Leonard Matthews, speaking as President of the AAAA and also in the name of the American Advertising Federation (AAF) and the

Association of National Advertisers (ANA) gave testimony before the US Senate Subcommittee on Alcoholism and Drug Abuse about the attitude of the American advertising community toward alcohol abuse in the USA.

Matthews explained how the advertising business actively supported public service campaigns combatting alcoholism, alcohol abuse and drunk driving. He also explained why the AAAA, AAF and ANA so adamantly opposed proposals to ban advertising for alcoholic beverages. He said that alcohol beverage advertising does not create the problems, and banning advertising cannot solve them.

In summing up it would seem that because of the unique cooperation within the EAT, and because of the, albeit modest, contacts with consumer representatives at various levels, the European advertising business is in a better position than its US counterpart to prevent a destructive militant consumer movement from making a comeback.

Pertschuk's ghost

Europeans should be anything but complacent about this situation. One has only to read the words of former FTC Chairman Michael Pertschuk in his recent book to realize the dangers from those consumer activists who hold almost fanatic beliefs in the importance and the righteousness of their mission (Pertschuk, 1982). Pertschuk was instrumental in the shaping of regulatory policy in the USA in the 1960s and 1970s. He also refers to a book by David Vogel with the revealing title *The Inadequacy of Contemporary Opposition to Business*:

> Did we not, ... [this writer asks] bring much of our misery upon ourselves by embracing intrusive, meddlesome, inefficient, overreaching, centralized, bureaucratic regulation? And did we not thereby debase the public currency of all regulation? (Pertschuk, 1982:137).

Pertschuk answers:

> No. And yes. I have argued strenuously in these pages that the consumer movement was laid down primarily by the reaction and revolt of business – though business was able to exploit the diffuse public dissatisfaction with government and regulation to legitimize the dismantling of consumer and other regulations that have retained undiminished popular support (Pertschuk, 1982: 137 – 138).

These two quotations illustrate that regulatory activities in the USA have been different from those in Europe. The waves of advertising regulation in Europe were not high enough to lead to open public dissatisfaction. Yet, the lessons learned from the American experience, as reported by Pertschuk, are also relevant to the European situation:

But there were lessons learned, sometimes painfully, in the course of transforming the consumer impulses of the sixties into the mature consumer regulation of the seventies. There were also lessons we refuse to learn.

We *have* learned greater respect for somber, unsentimental analysis of the effects of regulation. We, and here I believe I speak for many who view themselves as consumer advocates, *have not learned to accept that the injustice and inequity arising from inequality of bargaining power must be excluded from public policy if they cannot be measured in the economists' models* (italics added).

We have learned to pay greater heed to the social value of the entrepreneur, to value market incentives as a creative force for productivity and growth. But we will not learn to *tolerate the force with which those very incentives sweep aside the moral and ethical constraints that mark civilized society* (italics added).

We have learned that we must be accountable for the costs and burdens of regulation. But *we will not concede that the economist's useful, but imperfect, tool of cost – benefit analysis dictates policy judgements on what is right and what is just* (italics added).

We have been taught respect for a fallible bureaucracy's limitations in shaping human behavior. But *we will not abandon faith in the role of government in a democratic society to redress inequity and to give appropriate expression to those non-market values people hold deeply* (italics added) (Perschuk, 1982:137 – 138).

In the last four paragraphs of the above quote we have highlighted with italics the attitudes and the ideology that will continue to influence future consumerist activities. These attitudes are also prevalent among consumerists in Europe. But we should also highlight one of Pertschuk's main conclusions. He sums up the trend in the USA by observing: *"So the central lesson is, simply, regulatory humility"* (italics added) (Pertschuk, 1982:139). We suggest that European regulators should heed it also.

But Pertschuk has more to offer. He has acquired a certain realism that is appropriate for today and the future, and for Europeans as well as Americans. He grudgingly admits that regulators have learned from economists:

... [to] *think through* the reality of what we believed we were achieving with our intervention in the marketplace.

... They [economists] ask 'what do you think you are accomplishing with this rule? Who will benefit, who will pay? What else will happen as a result of this rule; who among competitors will be the winners and the losers? In curing this marketplace failure, what others may you inadvertently cause,and what healthy market signals will you distort? Is there a less intrusive, less costly way to remedy the problem? ... How secure are you that the world will be a better place for your intervention than if left alone?' (Pertschuk, 1982:139).

Pertschuk then gives consumerists, the advertising business and government officials a useful list of specific questions and issues to keep in mind when considering new regulatory requirements. He says "the prudent regulator should ask:"

1. *Is the rule consonant with market incentives to the maximum extent feasible?*

   Respect for the power of self-interest – of market incentives – is surely one of the salient substantive lessons learned by consumer advocates in the past two decades ...

2. *Will the remedy work?*

In the sixties there were certain goals we pursued because they intuitively seemed self-evidently right ... in most cases the effectiveness of a remedy will increase in direct proportion to the extent to which it seeks to utilize market incentives rather than stifle them ...

3. *Will the chosen remedy minimize the cost burdens of compliance, consistent with achieving the objective?*

Whether it took 'stagflation,' the revitalization of business political action, the regulatory reform movement, or the loss of our own primitive faith in the miraculous innovative capacity of American business to convince us, let there be no doubt that the regulatory calculus must seek to minimize not only paperwork burdens but, more important, regulatory impediments to innovation, flexibility and productivity ...

4. *Will the benefits flowing from the rule to consumers or to competition substantially exceed the costs? ...*

One issue popular among consumer advocates – popular, in fairness, because it evokes broad grassroots support – is the effort to maintain individual price marking of supermarket items and to resist replacement of such markings by shelf markings and computer printouts. That cause has always left me insecure, because I know of no evidence to suggest that individual price marking will benefit consumers sufficiently to offset the costs (which, of course, are passed on) of the labor-intensive price-marking process ...

5. *Will the rule or remedy adversely affect competition?*

The economists can surely take deserved credit for alerting us to the anti-competitive dangers in direct regulation of rates or entry into a marketplace. To their alarms can be traced much of the progress made in recent years toward eliminating such regulatory burdens on competition ...

6. *Does the regulation preserve freedom of informed individual choice to the maximum extent consistent with consumer welfare?*

The regulator must respect the manifest preference of Americans for free and informed choice over government intrusion that constrains choice. In what regulator's bosom does there not dwell a latent 'nanny,' solicitous of the health and well-being of his or her fellow citizens, fearful of senseless risk ... This regulatory itch must be resisted ...

7. *'States' rights' may be a tarnished symbol, but the federal regulator needs to ask, 'To what extent is this problem appropriate for federal intervention and amenable to a centrally administered national standard?'*

Appropriate regulatory humility encompasses restraint in federal intervention in decentralized industries composed of small local enterprises and restraint in the expansion of the growth and reach of centralized federal bureaucracy. Where federal action *is* appropriate, such humility also counsels simple, flexible, regulatory mechanisms policed, wherever practical, through citizen self-help or with the aid of local law-enforcement authorities (Extracted from Pertschuk, 1982:141 – 150).

The above points indicate newly found respect for the market system, cost/benefit analysis, the importance of competition, free and informed consumer choice rather than government intervention, and the activities of states (applicable to

Member States in Europe) rather than centrally administered standards (applicable to the EEC in Europe).

European consumerists should face and answer the same questions. If US consumerists can learn from experiences, so can Europeans. Professor Norbert Reich is correct when he says: "... Pertschuk's book should be read by every European consumer advocate and regulator" (Reich, 1983:240). We would add that readers should focus not only on Pertschuk's litany of regulatory successes and failures, and on his support for "resurgent consumer entrepreneurial politics" (Pertschuk, 1982:119ff) as a prescription for future consumerist activism; readers should also consider the lessons he presents in the final chapter of his book (Pertschuk, 1982:137 – 156).

Mr. Pertschuk's opinions are particularly important to Europeans because of his prominence as a former Chairman of the FTC in the USA, and especially because of the respectability of his views in the consumer activist community, world wide. If consumerists accept some of his views, they ought to consider also some of the qualifications he places on them, particularly the lessons he has learned in recent years about the need for regulatory humility.

Even if European consumerists have misgivings about these lessons, they form a solid base on which to begin constructive dialogues between consumerists, government officials and the advertising business.

The interesting point, and perhaps a tragedy of the relationship between the regulators and the business community, is that the argument between the two parties is not so much about the need to serve consumers, but about the manner in which some consumerists, both in Europe and in the USA, continue to expect others to accept their opinions without evidence. We suggest that the focus should be on evidence, not ideology; on cooperation not polarization; and on dialogue, not monologues.

Learning to live with consumerism

It is quite possible for the advertising business to live with a form of consumerism which does not maintain rigid preconceived ideas about what should and should not be done. Nobody is right or wrong all of the time. In this connection, it is of interest to listen to another voice from the USA. Robert J. McEwen, professor of Economics at Boston College, made a speech to an AVON International Consumer Leader Forum on June 21 – 22, 1982 in Tokyo. Professor McEwen has been closely connected with consumer developments in the USA and we believe his conclusions may apply to the situation in Europe:

> 1. I am convinced that the 'consumer consciousness' of the public has been raised to such an extent that, in one sense, it alone can justify a claim of victory for the consumer movement in the

up-grading of public awareness. This is true to such an extent that I believe it is not possible for business ever to go back to the old days. This, I think, is a very consoling conclusion, if it's true as I believe it to be, because it means that there can now be more reliance on the self-policing of the marketplace by aroused and alert consumers working with a new generation of sensitive business managers.

2. Wise businessmen have now seen that their proper stance in the 80's is to anticipate consumer problems and head them off before they develop. Therefore, enlightened businessmen have established well-staffed consumer affairs departments that maintain close connection to the consumer world — both the consumer world of action and the consumer world of ideas and education. These companies and these managements have accepted the idea that their long-run success depends on avoiding situations in which confrontation is inevitable. Instead, they are listening to consumer concerns and consumer complaints early enough to do something about them without great cost to both sides.

3. The government activity in the consumer field should never be totally eliminated but well may be reconsidered and reexamined to see which parts of it are absolutely necessary and which parts of it can be phased out without great loss. I, for one, am convinced that it's total folly to say that we can repeal all consumer laws on the books and return to the unprotected condition of consumers that existed before the consumer movement took its recent course. Anyone who asks for that ... is inviting a retrogression in public policy and inviting a return to the militant combat of confrontational challenges that existed for two decades ...

4. Consumer leaders themselves must address a twin problem facing them right now, one part of which is the fragmentation and the splintering of the consumer interest movement into so many special interests that the total consumer interest and the single consumer voice is being lost. The other problem that consumer leaders must face is that we must set a priority list of important things that need action and subordinate on that list things that do not really need to be done, especially if they impose relatively great burdens on producers or consumers. I think there have been examples where consumer demands have gone too far and have been excessive and have started a backlash, not merely among the suppliers but among the general public too. Unfortunately, it is the history of social movements to allow themselves to be carried away to extremes and to allow their demands to get unreasonable. The inevitable backlash from such a development can damage the very essential and substantial needs and gains of the social movement that have already been achieved ... (McEwen, 1983:65–67).

Against this background, let us now look at the new program and policies of the Commission which was appointed in January, 1985 for a period of four years.

The Commission's future consumer policies

"We are fighting a constant battle to hold on to what we have — it isn't easy to accept no role in promoting consumer welfare — the Common Market should not only exist for agricultural purposes, it should be a real common market for all its people" (Sheehan, 1983b). This *"cri de coeur"* from Jeremiah Sheehan, head of the Commission's Directorate for Consumer Affairs, reflected sincere concern for the future of the Commission's consumer programs. However, during the first half of 1985, the new Commission published the following documents, reflecting new optimism for what Sheehan called "a real common market:"

"The Thrust of Commission Policy," a statement by Jacques Delors, the new President of the
Commission, to the European Parliament in Strasbourg on January 14, 1985;
    "Programme of the Commission for 1985," an undated document from the Commission, pub-
lished in January, 1985;
    "Ten Years of Community Consumer Policy, A Contribution to the People's Europe," an
undated document for use within the Commission, prepared by Stanley Clinton Davis, responsible
for the Commission's Consumer Protection Policy (DG XI), published in January, 1985;
    A most important White Paper on "Completing the Internal Market" (COM(85)310 final), of
June 14, 1985, prepared by Lord Cockfield, responsible for the Commission's Internal Market
(DG III) and presented to the European Council's Meeting in Milan on June 28 – 29, 1985;
    "A New Impetus for Consumer Protection Policy" (COM(85)314 final), June 27, 1985, pre-
pared by Commissioner Clinton Davis.

We have already quoted from the first two documents, cited above, but all five make
interesting reading. The review "Ten Years of Community Consumer Policy" not only
gives an interesting overview of the work of the Commission in the field of consumer
affairs, but it clearly replaces the earlier Annual Progress Reports that were foreseen
in the EEC's first consumer program and from which we have quoted in our book.
The last two documents, however, are of considerable significance to the advertising
business and we would therefore like to deal with each of them in some detail.

The White Paper on "Completing the Internal Market"

The essence of Lord Cockfield's white paper lies in the intended removal of physical,
technical and fiscal barriers for the creation of an internal market, and by doing so
"... establish the foundations for an even closer union among the European peoples,
resolved by common action to ensure the economic and social progress of their
countries by eliminating the barriers which divide Europe ..." (*Rome Treaty*, 1957:1).

    The Commission now sees the completion of the internal market as an important
prerequisite for achieving a united Europe and has allowed for a period of eight
years, that is until 1992, to achieve this ambitious objective.

    Some of the most important points from the white paper, including those which
affect the advertising business, can be summarized as follows:

- ... the general principle should be ... that, if a product is lawfully manufactured and
  marketed in one Member State, there is no reason why it should not be sold freely throughout
  the Community. Indeed, the objectives of national legislation, such as the protection of human
  health and life and of the environment, are more often than not identical.
- If a Community citizen or a company meets the requirements for its activity in one Member
  State, there should be no valid reason why those citizens or companies should not exercise their
  economic activities also in other parts of the Community.

- A clear distinction needs to be drawn in future internal market initiatives between what is essential to harmonize, and what may be left to mutual recognition of national regulations and standards; this implies that, on the occasion of each harmonisation initiative, the Commission will determine whether national regulations are excessive in relation to the mandatory requirements pursued and, thus, constitute unjustified barriers to trade according to Articles 30 to 36 of the EEC Treaty.
- Legistlative harmonisation (Council Directives based on Article 100) will in future be restricted to laying down essential health and safety requirements which will be obligatory in all Member States. Conformity with this will entitle a product to free movement.
- The practice of incorporating detailed technical specifications in Directives has given rise to long delays because of the unanimity required in Council decision making. Henceforth, in those sectors where barriers to trade are created by justified divergent national regulations concerning the health and safety of citizens and consumer and environmental protection, legislative harmonisation will be confined to laying down the essential requirements, conformity with which will entitle a product to free movement within the Community.
- The Commission will review all pending proposals in order to withdraw such proposals as are considered to be non-essential or which are not in line with the new strategy.
- In accordance with the Treaty objective of creating a common market for services, all those who provide and relay broadcast services and who receive them should be able, if they wish, to do so on a Community-wide basis. This freedom goes hand in hand with the right of freedom of information regardless of frontiers (EAAA, 1985d).

The business world understandably welcomes the new policies of the Commission, which it has long advocated. In an EAAA Newsletter, the reaction of a large part of the advertising community was summarized as follows:

> The White Paper proposes that the Commission should forget its one-time aim of harmonizing every part of economic life. Such a policy was utopian, unworkable and unnecessry. The Commission instead should seek for mutually-acceptable standards which would leave national governments room to make their own regulations for products made in their own markets should they so wish, but would guarantee that products produced in other Member States, so long as they reached basic Community standards, should be given free access.
> Lord Cockfield's suggestions approach brilliance in their simplicity, by mostly reversing traditional national arguments about sovereignty. National sovereignty will not be threatened. Member States can make what laws they like for their own home-produced products, but of course if they do adopt more stringent rules than the accepted EEC norms they will be putting their products at a disadvantage to those imported from other Member States which impose simply the basic EEC's norms (EAAA, 1985c:8).

It is clear from the above that future policies of the Commission will differ quite markedly from those of its predecessors. The emphasis will be on coordination rather than on harmonization, "framework" directives will be developed, grouping products together for which essential safety or health requirements can be specified. The fact that the unified internal market should also include Community-wide broadcasting, throws a new light on the Commission's green paper "Television without Frontiers." If Community-wide broadcasting is to be achieved, questions regarding advertising and related matters, such as copyright, will have to be resolved before international trade will be able to fully exploit new opportunities throughout the Common Market.

It is against this background that we next discuss the document from Commissioner Clinton Davis "A New Impetus for Consumer Protection Policy." Interestingly enough the document starts off with the important question why achievements have fallen short of the intention of the consumer programs. The same question is also discussed in the Commission's "Ten Years" document.

Why have the consumer programs not been successful?

Combining the points made by the Commission in its "Ten Years" and "New Impetus" documents, the main reason given for the disappointing record are the following.

(1) The 1975 consumer program had drawn "its inspiration from the ideas of the consumer movement prevailing at the end of the sixties and the beginning of the seventies" (Commission of the EC, 1985b:58), when a consumer society with an abundance of goods and services called for Commission protection from recently developed production and marketing techniques. "The dynamism and aptitude of undertakings to cope with new requirements facilitated the evolution of legislative and administrative regulations and the growth of social transfers" (Commission of the EC, 1985b:58).

(2) Implementation of the consumer programs came up against an economic environment in disarray, the oil shock of 1973, increasing unemployment and soaring inflation; "Governments and industry were both reserved about the two programmes, pleading that the cost of regulation was an extra financial burden to them when they were already feeling the effects of recession" (Commission of the EC, 1985c:3).

(3) "... Community policy, although deriving from programmes and priority actions unanimously approved by the Council is falling foul of objections on the part of several Member States relating to the delimitation of the spheres of responsibility of national and Community bodies ... this attitude has delayed adoption by the Council of several Directives and has caused the European Parliament to examine in a highly critical spirit the proposals submitted" (Commission of the EC, 1985b:59).

(4) The unanimity required for the harmonization of laws under Articles 100 and 235 of the Treaty is largely responsible for the long delays in the adoption of measures by the Council of Ministers. "A good example is the Commission proposal for the control of doorstep selling: a Community agreement has been blocked by one Member State for over a year" (Commission of the EC, 1985c:5).

In studying these four points, it is of interest to observe that they fail to answer the most critical question: *Was an international consumer protection policy really necessary?*

At no time has the Commission produced compelling concrete evidence on the need for a consumer protection policy, or the need to regulate advertising at the international level. It is accepted that it is the proper function of the EC to bring into line existing laws and regulations in Member States which could adversely affect the creation of a Common Market as part of a united Europe. However, such harmonization need not have resulted in a program that went far beyond minimum requirements. The Commission has not been able to make a convincing case that its far reaching plans for the protection of the consumer against perceived abuses in the marketplace, justified the mammoth efforts mounted to curb such abuse. Certainly the advertising business should be diligent to avoid any serious abuses in the marketplace. But more importantly it should be remembered that consumers, on whose behalf the Commission is supposed to act, have never expressed any great concern about an occasional breach of the rules of honesty and decency as they inevitably occur from time to time in any business or professional activity. The entire subject had become a political issue when in 1972 Heads of State, more by way of an afterthought than as an act of deliberate policy, agreed that consumer protection should become a Community responsibility.

The Commission now mentions a number of reasons why its programs have failed, but it omits the most important one, namely that these programs did not appeal strongly to the average European citizen. They were the brainchild of politicians, encouraged by the leaders of a few consumer organizations who were not always seen to be acting for purely non-selfish reasons. The fact that the European Economic Community did not mean much to the European population did not help either.

However, once the political decision to draw up a consumer protection program was taken, and the wheels in Brussels started turning, it became clear that there were a number of additional factors that caused the unsatisfactory results. These factors are:

(a) The ambitious nature of the first consumer program (mentioned earlier in Chapter II). The following 20 product categories and general issues were marked as "priorities," to be dealt with within four years, by any standards an impossible task: (1) foodstuffs, (2) cosmetics and detergents, (3) utensils and consumer durables, (4) cars, (5) textiles, (6) toys, (7) dangerous substances, (8) materials coming into contact with foodstuffs, (9) medicines, (10) fertilizers, pesticides and herbicides, (11) veterinary products and animal feedingstuffs, (12) conditions of consumer credit, (13) misleading advertising, (14) unfair commercial practices, (15) product liability, (16) quality of services, (17) information concerning goods and services, (18) comparative tests, (19) study of consumer behavior, and (20) information on prices (see Appendix I).

(b) Too few people on the staff of the Commission had sufficient knowledge of how advertising works; thus they drafted regulations on a subject they knew too little about.

(c) The Commission made insufficient use of the knowledge and experience of international marketing and advertising operators who were prepared to help solve problems with which they were familiar and that were of immediate interest to them.

(d) Not enough civil servants were sympathetic to the argument that advertising should be permitted to support legitimate products and services with legitimate means of communication.

The Commission appointed in January, 1985 shows every intention of wanting to avoid the mistakes of the past. It is clearly set on a course to achieve economic unity in Europe within the next few years. The business world welcomes these plans and will undoubtedly support the Commission in carrying out its new policy as effectively and efficiently as possible.

A new start seems to have been made. Let us therefore now review the plans of the Commission with regard to advertising in greater detail.

A new impetus for consumer protection policy

One month after the statement by President Delors to the EP in Strasbourg, the new Commissioner for Consumer Affairs Mr. Stanley Clinton Davis, gave his views on future consumer policy to the Internal Market and Consumer Council, held in Brussels on February 11, 1985. His statement was called "A New Impetus for Consumer Protection Policy" and preceded the publication of an official document under the same title on June 27, 1985. He said:

> One of the main concerns of the European Community is to develop a Europe of tangible benefit to all of its citizens, with policies that have a relevance to everyday life. The Commission therefore intends this year to give a new impetus to our programme of consumer protection, at a time when the Community is making strenuous efforts to open up its internal market and to remove obstacles which obstruct the flow of goods and services between Member States.
>
> As we work to remove existing barriers to trade, we must ensure that the consumer, benefitting from wider choice, is not put at risk from defective or dangerous products and services. In short, we must ensure that the consumer gets a fair deal in his transactions with the producers of goods and services. We therefore intend to concentrate our efforts in three main fields:
> − consumer health;
> − consumer safety;
> − economic interests of consumers (Clinton Davis, 1985).

Although not repeated in the official document, these paragraphs nevertheless form the basis of future consumer policy, which the Commissioner later defined as follows:

> − Products traded in the Community should conform to acceptable safety and health standards;
> − Consumers must be able to benefit from the Common Market.
> − Consumer interests should be taken into account in other Community Policies (Commission of the EC, 1985c:9 − 10).

In implementing the first of these objectives, the Commission has adopted a new approach to what it calls "technical harmonization:"

> ... This will allow products for which essential safety or other mandatory requirements can be specified in common to be grouped together in Council Directives. Detailed specifications of product characteristics will be left to the European standardisation bodies CEN and CENELEC, which will be mandated by the Commission to prepare common standards to satisfy the mandatory requirements. Pending the completion of common European standards, existing national standards which satisfied the mandatory requirements will be accorded Community-wide recognition so that the products to which they relate can circulate freely in the Community (Commission of the EC, 1985c:6)

Like UNICE, which has always taken a special interest in the safety aspects of consumer protection, the BEUC has followed up the Commission's intentions to give high priority to safety and health standards by publishing a "Manifesto for Consumer Safety in Europe." The manifesto was the subject of a special number of *BEUC News* and started with the following statement:

> The consumer organizations in Europe are faced with a dramatic situation: the number of domestic accidents continues to increase from year to year. At least 30,000 dead and 40 million injured every year in the ten Member States of the European Community (official figures by the EEC Commission). According to the latest estimates from the Commission, the number of dead could, in fact, be nearer 100 deaths per day and 70 million home accidents per year (*BEUC News*, 1985:3).

The Manifesto continues to analyse the types of products contributing to this alarming situation; it says:

> Nothing is being done in Europe to remedy this situation and it is estimated that there are more than 200 million dangerous products which could, and ought to have been recalled (*BEUC News*, 1985:3).

However, with regard to the "technical harmonization," as now envisaged by the Commission, BEUC observes in its manifesto that this "is a step in the right direction to encourage the drawing up of new standards" (*BEUC News*, 1985:10).

Pending these developments, BEUC and its member organizations will intensify their own efforts on product testing. They would also like to strengthen the European Consumer Interpol and improve its links with the rest of the world.

The second main objective of the Commission concerned consumers' benefits from the Common Market. The Commission stated:

> If the common market is to be fully effective, it must be made easier for consumers to buy goods in other countries, to use them at home, to get them repaired like domestically purchased products, and to see complaints handled effectively. Consumers generally are unaware of their existing rights or the advantages to be obtained by exploiting differences in prices prevailing between Member States and on the operation of customs control for Community citizens at Member States' frontiers within the common market. Better information for consumers is prerequisite for the improved operation of competition ... (Commission of the EC, 1985c:16).

Finally, as far as the third objective of the Commission is concerned, the Commission intends to extend the role of the CCC in advising the Commission on matters concerning consumer affairs in the widest sense of the word.

Directives completed, pending and planned

As of the end of 1985, the following three directives in the field of advertising had been formally approved by the Council of Ministers:

> Directive 79/112/EEC of 18 December 1978 relating to the Labelling, presentation and advertising of foodstuffs for the ultimate consumer (OJ No L 33, 8.2.79).
>   Directive 79/581/EEC of 19 June 1979 on consumer protection in the indication of the prices of foodstuffs (OJ No L 158, 26.6.79). (Author's Note: this directive is in the process of being revised).
>   Council Directive 84/450/EEC relating to the approximation of the Laws, regulations and administrative provisions of the Member States concerning misleading advertising (OJ No L 250, 19.9.84) (Commission of the EC, 1985b:Annex III).

With regard to new proposals, Commissioner Clinton Davis stated in his "New Impetus" document: "As a first step in its plan to give new impetus to consumer policy, the Commission is transmitting to the Council a number of proposals" (Commission of the EC, 1985c:23); they include a proposal:

> (1) for the amendment of existing legislation on the labelling of foodstuffs;
> (2) for the regulation of package tour contracts, to be adopted by the council by 1987;
> (3) for the introduction of consumer education in primary and secondary schools.

In the same document, the Commissioner announced a number of other proposals under consideration:

> 1. A proposed directive on the advertising of proprietary medicinal products of November 28, 1980 had been withdrawn because according to *Campaign* of August 19, 1983, Commissioner Narjes, then responsible for consumer affairs did not see any chance that it would win acceptance; however '. . . there will be a reassessment of the situation with a view possibly to presenting new proposals' (Commission of the EC, 1985c:13).
> 2. As already indicated in the Preamble to the Directive on Misleading Advertising, the Commissioner will consider proposals on the subject of 'unfair' and 'comparative' advertising, of which adoption by the Council of Ministers is expected by 1989.
> 3. In order for consumers to be able to buy goods in other states and complying with the Commission's intentions expressed in the second main objective for future consumer policy, the proposed Directive on Consumer Credit, adopted on February 27, 1979 (OJ No C 80, 27.3.79) is maintained 'to facilitate the creation of a common market in credit' (Commission of the EC, 1985c:17).
> 4. As a consequence of the Commission's second objective, the Commissioner will make proposals concerning protection against unfair contract terms, such proposals to be adopted by the Council of Ministers by 1989.

5. The Commission will pursue proposals in the green paper "Television without Frontiers," in-cluding restrictive measures on tobacco and alcohol advertising and on advertising to children.

In his earlier document of January, 1985 dealing with the review over the last ten years, Commissioner Clinton Davis had mentioned a number of other directives affecting advertising that were already before the Council of Ministers. As he did not state his intention to withdraw these proposed directives, one must assume they stand:

1. A proposal for a directive concerning liability for defective products, adopted on September 9, 1976 (OJ No C 241, 14.10.76). (Author's Note: this directive was approved by the Council of Ministers on July 25, 1985; see OJ No L 210, 7.8.1985).
2. A proposal for a directive to protect the consumer in respect to contracts which have been nego-tiated away from business premises, adopted on January 17, 1977 (OJ No C 22, 19.1.77).
3. A proposal for a directive relating to claims made in the labelling, presentation and advertising of foodstuffs for sale to the ultimate consumer, adopted on April 13, 1981 (OJ No C 198, 6.8.1981).
4. A proposal for a directive on toy safety, their physical and mechanical properties and their flammability, adopted on June 23, 1983 (OJ No C 203, 26.7.1983).
5. A proposal for a directive on consumer protection in the indication of prices for non-food pro-ducts, adopted on December 15, 1983 (OJ No C 8, 13.1.1984) (Commission of the EC, 1985b:Annex IV).

Although the above proposals comprise the official plans of the Commission in the field of consumer protection, the indicated priorities may change and new topics for regulation may be considered. The Commission is after all subject to pressures from many different sources. Political expedience may from time to time overrule careful planning. For example, as we shall discuss later, the BEUC has made strong demands for virtually forbidding all advertising for pharmaceutical products. Advertising of alcoholic beverages might also become the subject of renewed regula-tory activity. If such lobbies succeed, the advertising business will face another onslaught on the right to advertise legitimate products.

Negative harmonization

Apart from the Commission's future plans with regard to consumer protection and advertising regulation, international advertisers are at least as concerned about existing legislation in Member States with regard to the formulation, packaging and advertising of products and services. Such legislation should be reconsidered in the light of the Commission's new policy.

Commissioner Clinton Davis refers in his "New Impetus" document to:

... consumer protection ... being the basis for deciding whether a national law should be permit-ted to stand even if it was causing a barrier to trade. Where a national law would fail to meet this criterion, its elimination constitutes a 'negative' harmonisation at Community level in contrast to the 'positive' kind brought about by Community legislation (Commission of the EC, 1985c:6 – 7).

This idea was not new. Jeremiah Sheehan, the Commission's Director of Consumer Affairs, referred to the possibility of negative harmonization at the Bremen Meeting in November, 1983.

The example of the Kellogg commercial, which we discussed in the previous chapter illustrates the significance of negative harmonization, or deregulation, to international advertisers. It should receive high priority by the Commission, national governments and the business community. Negative harmonization may be at least as quick and effective as "positive" harmonization to break down barriers which retard the expansion of international trade.

With regard to a proper dialogue between consumer representatives "... and those of other economic agents in the market, notably manufacturers, distributors and the advertising profession," the new Commission's position mentions self-regulation in a positive way:

> ... [the] expressed ... hope that this dialogue might lead to voluntary agreements in the form of European codes of conduct ... has not yet been translated into reality. Indeed it has become clear that such codes could be largely deprived of effect if they were not associated with appropriate Community legislation. Backed up by Community law, however, codes of business practice have an analogous position to product safety standards. The Commission will consider what scope there may be for pursuing this approach and will make appropriate proposals (Commission of the EC, 1985c:21).

Interestingly, the Commission does not attribute the failure of the dialogue to the unwillingness of any of the parties to participate in such dialogue, but to the lack of sufficient legal backing. However, with the notable exception of the UK, most European governments have not viewed such legal backing (or minimum standards of enforcement) as a base for self-regulation. If they would do so, perhaps the Commission's "hope" may be more likely to be achieved.

The advertising business has in any case a clear indication of the future intentions of the new Commission. Although the attitude toward advertising and the chances of greater recognition of the advantages of self-regulation have improved, the business world should not become complacent. The program of the new Commission will still demand much time and energy from the advertising business, especially through the EAT. Moreover, it is regrettable that so much time and energy must be devoted to rationalizing the activities of the many other organizations discussed in the previous chapter. This raises again the question of overlap and duplication.

The duplication of intergovernmental activities

We touched on this point at the end of the previous chapter. We now illustrate our concern by considering a typical housewife somewhere in the Community, about to do the grocery shopping for her family. With the shopping list in her basket she will visit the supermarket in her neighborhood, walk along the shelves, select the products of her choice, pay and go back home to prepare the meal for the family. Her choice in the supermarket will have been based upon her own experience with the products concerned or perhaps on the recommendation of a friend; she may also have checked comparative prices in newspaper advertising or seen a commercial on television and decided to give certain brands a try. It is an almost daily event of little significance and consequence; she has done it a thousand times and has rarely had reason to be dissatisfied or to complain. And yet, there are at least half a dozen governmental and intergovernmental bodies that to some extent are concerned about her buying decisions and her ultimate well-being. She is no doubt blissfully ignorant of the "guardian angel" activities of (a) her own government, (b) the Commission of the EEC, (c) the European Parliament, (d) the Consumers' Consultative Committee, (e) the Council of Europe, (f) the Organization for Economic Cooperation and Development, and (9) the United Nations. All of these bodies will either take decisions or make recommendations, based upon essentially the same set of consumers' rights and consumer protection guidelines. Their programs, even allowing for partially different areas of operation, show remarkable similarity. Yet, they all have their own executives, secretariats, offices, etc.; the costs are difficult to estimate but no doubt the amount of taxpayers' money involved is very great indeed.

When discussing this matter with Mr. Frits Hondius, Secretary Committee of Ministers of the COE, he said:

> ... there is of course a certain overlap between international organizations working on the same subject ... one must compare it with a number of circles fitting into another but forming one unity ... the EEC is the smallest circle, dealing with ten countries and about 270 million people ... it fits into a larger circle which is the Council of Europe with twenty-one members and about 380 million inhabitants ... the two circles fit into the OECD which has twenty-four members representing however something like 780 million people ... finally, the three circles are surrounded by the fourth one, the United Nations, covering the entire world ... the four circles cover different territories ... the one is more sophisticated than the other ... the larger the circle, the more general its objectives and recommendations will have to be ... the United Nations could not very well think in terms of directives ... the important point to remember is that the four circles must in the end represent one ultimate purpose, such as consumer protection ... there must therefore be close cooperation between all of them ... (Hondius, 1984b).

Mr. Lars Broch, Director-General of IOCU, confirmed this point of view and added that the UN Consumer Guidelines had to a large extent been based upon the work done by the Commission in Brussels (Lars Broch, 1984).

While we respect these opinions on the overlap between international organizations, we note also that one must consider not only the cost/benefit aspects of consumer protection by governmental and intergovernmental bodies, but also the amount of time and money that private industry must devote to maintain contact with these many different organizations.

Consider the situation with regard to consumer protection by the EEC and the COE. The EEC now has twelve members, the COE has the same twelve plus nine. There is considerable duplication of effort. Since this duplication often is unproductive it is not surprising that at the European Council Meeting in Milan in June, 1985 better and closer cooperation between these two organizations was recommended. This cooperation should lead the COE in the future to concentrate on specific areas where it has traditional strengths – health, culture, education, human rights and legal protection. Other issues, especially consumer protection, would be handled on the basis of a "watching brief."

While the logic of cooperation and specialization cannot be denied, some doubt that a strict division of responsibilities will indeed be achieved. There have always been understandable but regrettable jealousies between the EEC and the COE. One must wait and see if the latter organization will be prepared to forego continuation of its early initiatives to regulate television advertising. It might well endeavor to compete with the Commission in a field as important as this one, and in which it took the first steps.

Thus, the chances that governments will seriously reconsider, let alone reduce, their commitments in the field of consumer affairs at the international level, are very small. Also, since consumer protection is a political issue, financial/cost considerations are not likely to be paramount in leading to specialization. Finally, even if the Commission and the COE came to a better division of responsibilities, governments would no doubt argue that the OECD and the UN, which also deal with less sophisticated nations outside Europe that expect guidance on consumer policies, should receive continued support.

However, if the business world succeeds in maintaining high standards for self-imposed controls, continuously updating and perfecting the various systems of advertising self-regulation, it is probable that the interest of governmental and inter-governmental bodies in the regulation of advertising, which in any event is only a small part of their total consumer programs, will gradually wane. Such a trend is already apparent in the latest documents from the Commission. One can safely assume that the Commission now recognizes the positive contribution that advertising can make to "completing the internal market." This changed attitude can no doubt be attributed on the one hand to increased appreciation of the function of advertising by consumers and governments alike, and on the other hand to a gain in the prestige or acceptability of self-regulation. Some will even argue that the new policy on consumer protection would not have been possible if it had not been for the growing realisation that voluntary controls can and will do a satisfactory job in most Common Market countries.

The case for self-regulation

I   We believe that the primary function of advertising is to inform the public of the attributes of goods and services and to induce their purchase. We deplore the use of advertising primarily as an instrument to disparage a competitive product or service or to attack the truthfulness of competitive claims. Such abuse of advertising tends to destroy believability in all advertising claims and to cause grave damage to the system of private competitive enterprise.

II We believe that the sponsor of the advertising message has an especial responsibility for the content of the message. We deplore claims of facts that cannot be verified by objective tests. Anyone using the advertising message to mislead, confuse or deceive the public is acting irresponsibly and to the detriment not only of his own advertising but of all advertising.

III We believe that advertising is a social form of the public good and we support advertising that contributes to the general welfare of the public. We deplore advertising that does not adhere to generally accepted standards of good taste and morality.

IV We believe that all those engaged in advertising should work together in the public interest and their own interest to advance these advertising principles. We shall therefore lend our best efforts to further every movement designed to preserve, elevate and implement these standards (de Win, 1983:Annex 1).

The above statement stems from a publication as far back as November, 1911 by *Printers Ink*, then a well known American advertising trade magazine. The statement was one of the earliest expressions indicating the genuine desire for high standards to be applied to advertising. While discussion of these principles has taken place in the USA and in Europe for a very long time, little progress was made until the 1960s (see Chapter I). But since the 1930s the ICC has encouraged the advertising business in many countries to develop self-regulatory systems, and ICC codes have indeed influenced such systems greatly.

For a variety of reasons, mostly relating to the inability of self-regulatory systems to achieve early acceptance by advertisers, advertising agencies and advertising media, it was not until the 1960s, when consumer pressures were at their peak, that self-regulation received serious attention from the advertising business. Since then, however, considerable progress has been made and while voluntary advertising controls have not yet been able to achieve their full potential, countries like the UK, France and the Netherlands have shown the way by developing self-regulatory controls that appear to work to the satisfaction of many parties.

This point is of special significance in the light of the Commission's willingness, expressed in its second consumer program, to favorably consider "the establishment of specific agreements between the various interests" (Appendix VI, p.320). In fact, shortly before the Commission sent its proposed second consumer program for approval to the Council of Ministers, Commissioner Richard Burke made an important statement. Meeting with the EAAA in Brussels on March 22, 1979, he

... paid tribute to the effectiveness of voluntary codes of conduct in the commercial field and particularly with regard to advertising. He implied strongly that the Commission was now prepared to make more use of these in its work towards the protection of the consumer and possibly to rely less upon Directives based on legal processes. Mr. Burke suggested that while such a course might not be appropriate across the whole field of advertising, he was nevertheless prepared to test its efficacy in certain specific areas and in particular that of advertising directed to children, which is, of course, a high priority in Brussels (AA, 1979).

As we shall discuss later, agreement on the specific issue of advertising directed at children, has not yet been reached but this need not affect the general principles underlying the drawing up of voluntary codes, as included in the second consumer program.

It would seem that apart from the control of advertising in electronic media (which may require a framework directive to ensure similar basic conditions throughout the Community), voluntary regulation, backed by national legislation in each country to provide a foundation, has the potential to control advertising more effectively than any other method or system. It should therefore be a matter of high priority to industry and the advertising business not only to support existing systems of voluntary controls, but to introduce such systems and enforcement agreements where they do not yet exist. It should also be in the best interests of consumer organizations and government officials not only to support the advertising business in these endeavors, but to participate constructively in them. Experience of the advertising business in the UK suggests numerous ways of fostering effective cooperation between business, consumer associations and government, so as to enhance the important contribution that voluntary controls can make to prevent advertising abuses in the marketplace, thus benefitting both consumers and advertisers alike.

The ICC Code of Advertising Practice has been the basis for most existing codes of advertising introduced by national or international trade associations. We restrict our discussion of these codes to a few product categories, selected because of their somewhat controversial nature. A typical example is "The European Code of Standards for the Advertising of Medicines," adopted by the European Proprietary Medicines Manufacturers' Association. The latest version of this code dates back to March, 1977. It not only provides "guidance [for] all concerned with the advertising of medicines to the public," but it lists in a separate section a great number of diseases to which, neither directly nor indirectly, any reference shall be made in advertisements. In its Introduction, the AESGP says the following:

> This Code has been introduced to assist companies in producing advertising which is truthful and honest and which takes into consideration the interests of public health. It is designed to establish identical standards for such advertising throughout Europe. As such it is not intended to replace the existing legislation which varies from country to country. However, members of the AESGP believe that the prime responsibility for a high standard in advertising must always rest with the member of the association concerned (AESGP, 1977).

Another example is the "Code of Pharmaceutical Marketing Practices" of 1981, with its Supplementary Statement of March, 1982 that lays down procedures "to deal with alleged breaches in the observance of the Code" (IFPMA, 1985:21). The Code contains strict rules about information in the advertising of pharmaceutical products. (1) Statements in promotional communications should be based upon scientific evidence; (2) Information as to the safety of pharmaceutical products should be subject to the legal, regulatory and medical practices of each country; and (3) Clearance by the responsible pharmacist should be obtained before advertising is released.

The Code was developed by the International Federation of Pharmaceutical Manufacturers Association (IFPMA) in Geneva, and has been recommended to its 43 member organizations throughout the world. The Code is intended to be a model for its members and does not replace similar codes already in force in many countries. One of these national codes has been developed by the Association of the British Pharmaceutical Industry (ABPI, 1984) and goes in much greater detail than the "master code" with regard to statements in, and procedures for clearance and control of advertising of pharmaceutical products in the UK.

Apparently these actions are not considered adequate by consumer organizations. The BEUC produced a new report on the market of pharmaceuticals in the EC and said in a press release, on September 19, 1985:

> Any regulation of advertising for pharmaceutical products must serve above all to protect public health and aim at objective information for doctors and consumers. In the long run, responsibility for this information should be guaranteed by competent organizations independent from the pharmaceutical industry. For the transitional period, it is desirable to move towards a gradual limitation of pharmaceutical advertising by a minimal directive, the first form of advertising to be forbidden being advertising in cinema and on radio and television (EAAA, 1985e:5).

As this example shows, forces to curb legitimate advertising are still at work, even for products which have passed safety and health tests.

Unfortunately, an industry's desire to draw up a code in cooperation with a consumer organization can meet with difficulties because of the lack of sanctions that industry can impose. After long negotiations, EAT reached agreement with COFACE on May 4, 1982 on "Rules for Conduct on Advertising for Toys." The agreement contains seven non-controversial and explicit articles, which members of organizations belonging to the EAT, will have no difficulty to adhere to. Yet, the agreement has not yet been signed by COFACE, partly because there have been problems over the translation of the agreement in several languages, a serious problem indeed, but mainly because the EAT is not in a position to impose sanctions, it can only make recommendations to its members.

This point about lack of sanctions, so often raised by the Commission and by consumer groups, is in our opinion grossly overrated. Since 1979, when the Commission openly encouraged industry to draw up voluntary codes of conduct, the acceptance and reputation of self-regulation as an effective control mechanism have in the opinion of many people increased considerably. This is also in part due to the fact that the media in countries such as the UK, France and Holland, can and do refuse advertising that contravenes self-regulatory codes. More importantly, to advertisers it is vital that consumers should have confidence in their advertising. Therefore most advertisers want to be associated with voluntary agreements drawn up by their own trade associations, and few major businesses refuse to cooperate. It is also of interest to note that the Commission in principle now accepts a combination of legal and voluntary controls. In its Directive on Misleading Advertising of September, 1984 it states:

> ... persons or organizations regarded under national law as having a legitimate interest in prohibiting misleading advertising may:
> (a) take legal action against such advertising: and/or
> (b) bring such advertising before an administrative authority competent either to decide on complaints or to initiate appropriate legal proceedings (Chapter III, Table III, Art.4.1).

Clearly, codes and other voluntary agreements depend for their success on the honesty, integrity and ethical standards which each individual must accept for himself. He who wants to be a thief, can easily become one. Earl Warren, the US Supreme Court Justice once said:

> In civilized life, law floats in a sea of ethics. Each is indispensable to civilization. Without law we would be at the mercy of the least scrupulous; without ethics, law would not exist.

Earl Warren's statement is confirmed by the practical experience in the marketplace: the combination of voluntary advertising controls, backed up by legislation, can indeed work well. There seems in any case to be little reason to refuse to enter into a voluntary agreement because of lack of official sanctions.

To underline the importance to advertisers to adhere to agreed rules, the ISBA in the UK has produced an excellent guide in which it warns advertisers what may happen to them if they do not check carefully every advertisement before approving it. In its brochure the ISBA says the following:

WHAT YOU DON'T KNOW ABOUT SELF-REGULATION COULD HURT YOU

An offending advertisement will not be accepted by publishers.

A persistently offending advertiser will find himself a marked man and reputable media won't want to trade with him.

Transgressions can become public news, reported in the press and on television to the discomfort – or worse – of the products and advertisers concerned.

Your signature approving something that does not comply with the Codes can bring you, as well as your product, into disrepute.

Every abuse increases the risk of statutory controls being introduced – less flexible, less pratical, less sensible than the Codes we have now (ISBA, undated).

We would like to refer readers with a special interest in the details of self-regulation to the several excellent publications on this subject, such as those published by the IAA. They and others are included in the References at the end of this book.

Achievements to date

There can be no doubt that the concerted actions of a united industry during the hectic years of the 1960s and the early 1970s have been fruitful, especially by contributing to a somewhat more constrained course by regulators. There were of course other important factors which brought about such change, including the questioning attitude of many governments to some of the Commission's proposals. Recession and stagnant economic conditions were also important. However, it cannot be denied that the advertising business played a significant part in defending some of the basic values of the market system during this period. This success was due not only to the united way in which the business community responded to perceived threats, but also to the backing it received from its silent partner, the consumer and his/her acceptance of the role of advertising in daily life.

If it had not been for the quality of advertising and the application of self-imposed rules in the production and placing of it, industry would not now enjoy the confidence of the consuming public. Without positive consumer attitudes toward advertising, the industry could not have acted with the self-confidence it demonstrated during those crucial years. Advertising also re-established itself in the eyes of governments and intergovernmental bodies as an important factor in the economic process.

Future strategy

While much has been achieved in the past, much still remains to be done. Now that the Commission seems to have changed some of its attitudes toward advertising regulation, it must now practice what it preaches. The political influence of consumer groups in Western Europe and of other intergovernmental bodies is still strong. Active consumerists are found in many circles and although they are a minority, they still have an attentive audience for their grievances and protestations. Many civil servants will try to hold on to what they have achieved, finding it difficult to concede defeat and to run the risk of losing their jobs. Also at the national level much remains to be done. Not all politicians in high government positions have accepted a policy of deregulation. Many influential people remain to be convinced about the positive role of advertising in today's economy and society.

Alan Wolfe sums it up as follows:

> If those working in business believe that what they do is legitimate, and that the wealth created by the production and marketing of profitable goods and services is beneficial to society – then they must take note that there are many people who think otherwise.
>
> These opponents can be found in many places, and for a variety of reasons not all equally obvious. They have collectively built-up a pressure for increasing the number of legal and moral constraints on business activity in general and the multi-national companies in particular.
>
> Experience shows that provided a source of pressure is detected early, it and its arguments can be successfully countered. This is done by a combination of monitoring, lobbying, government and public relations, and corporate advertising. Such activity must be backed of course, by "good behaviour" policed by visible self-regulation.
>
> Trade and professional bodies should form the spear-heads of the business lobby, but all companies and those responsible for their policy have a duty to give their full support. (Wolfe, 1985:12).

The AA in the UK has in this context identified nine influential groups which it describes in its new action plan as follows: "(1) Consumerists; (2) Educationalists; (3) Employees/Workforces; (4) Government; (5) Media; (6) New Advertisers; (7) New Moralists; (8) Shareholders; and (9) Top Businessmen" (AA, 1985:2).

Whether used at the national or international level, the arguments do not differ basically from those which the advertising business laid down in the 1970s, which we discussed in Chapter III:

> Industry's stance was going to be in defense of consumer's freedom of choice and the business community's freedom of speech, as indivisible components of a market economy, coupled with effective and efficient controls of advertising, based upon codes and other voluntary agreements. The positive role and contribution of advertising in society and as part of private enterprise were to be updated and presented to relevant audiences at national and international levels.

We see no reason to suggest any basic changes. These objectives should continue to be the same for many years to come. But, the advertising business will have to adapt the specific arguments and presentation of them to changing circumstances at national and international levels.

While we have confined ourselves mainly to a discussion of steps taken at the international level, we would like to underline that success or failure in the defense of the interests of the advertising business depends largely on close contacts with, and full cooperation from trade associations at the national level. Very often a development of importance to the advertising business will start in one country. It can spread easily to others, unless an "early warning" system, such as immediately informing the EAT Secretariat in Brussels, is used to alert the total advertising business in Europe. "The ideal situation is when we can orchestrate [twelve] national lobbies to coincide with the central thrust being made by EAT in Brussels. It does not happen that often, but we are getting better at it" (Underhill, 1985:65). Thus, the discussion in the following pages on structure and organization at the international level will be based upon the common objectives of the total European advertising business. A combination of activities at the national and the international levels is necessary to ensure optimal success for all concerned.

Structure and organization

The formation of the EAT as the representative body for the entire advertising business was instrumental to defend the interests of business efficiently and effectively at the international level. The formation of this group and the authority it acquired were only possible through the unlimited support of its founders: advertisers, advertising agencies and media.

It is also essential in the future for the advertising business to continue to give its undaunted support to the national and international trade associations, to which much of the day-to-day responsibilities are delegated and which are doing such an excellent job. However, ultimately the entire subject of consumer protection and its effects on business, is the responsibility of senior management. A successful response to those who threaten the freedom to sell and advertise will therefore only be possible if boards and senior managements of businesses involved in international trade and communication with consumers across borders, accept this responsibility as one of their high priorities.

The subject is not of equal imporance to all advertisers. The significance of advertising varies considerably from company to company and from industry to industry. Consequently, the level of management that will be made responsible within a corporation, as well as the amount and type of support for the necessary activities, will also vary.

In the past, the advertising business has been most fortunate in this respect. Many of its senior executives were available on call to support, or to participate actively in meetings, together with the relevant trade associations, and to help decide on actions to be taken on behalf of the entire business community. There is no reason to believe that the business world will not continue this commitment. In this connection, we would make two observations:

(1) Experience has shown that well-intended action by individual companies or their executives, is less effective in most cases than bringing one's influence to bear in a joint effort in the name of the entire industry. While some corporations are not sympathetic toward discussing issues, even of a general nature, with their competitors, collective action through the trade associations concerned, has proven to be more effective.

(2) There often is an attitude among the leaders of businesses to expect others to do the job, particularly if the problems do not seem to demand immediate attention. Yet, when the situation becomes urgent they will be among the first to complain that nothing was done.

The two points made above stem from experience in the mid-1970s when the international trade associations in the field of advertising were rightly expected to negotiate with the Commission and others on behalf of the entire advertising business. This could only be done efficiently and effectively by falling back on the help of many executives who were prepared to make themselves available for the common cause.

It is with these thoughts in mind that we suggest:

Recommendation V

Following what is already being done by many corporations whose advertising within the Community is affected by regulation, it is recommended that these international corporations make such internal arrangements as will be necessary to keep abreast of relevant developments in the field of consumer protection, at both national and international levels.

Such arrangements often will include the appointment of an executive to act as the first point of contact with national and international trade associations, so that they can represent effectively the interests of the total industry at all levels.

There is one more step that will assist the advertising business to cope with the many regulatory issues it faces. It concerns a successful scheme that was introduced several years ago in the USA by the AAAA. At the time the US advertising business was inundated with an avalanche of regulatory activities from many different government agencies. The AAAA set up arrangements whereby member advertising agencies make promising young executives available "on loan" to the AAAA office in Washington. These executives work on specific assignments with regulatory bodies on issues of importance to the advertising business. The loaning advertising agency continues to pay the salaries of these executives during the loan period. The AAAA pays their out-of-pocket expenses during their stay in Washington. After one year they return to their agencies, much wiser for the experience.

Making allowances for the many differences that exist between the regulatory situation in the US and Europe, perhaps it would be worthwhile to consider a similar scheme for the advertising business in Europe. Earlier in this chapter, when describing the activities of the many supranational organizations in the field of consumer affairs, we pointed to the large number of contacts required by those who represent the interests of the advertising business. This prompts us to suggest:

Recommendation VI

It is recommended that the European advertising business consider the possibility of setting up a "Loaned Executive Assignment Program" (LEAP) along the lines of the US scheme.

Advertisers, advertising agencies and media would make young executives available on a temporary basis, to join the secretariats of international trade associations and accept specific assignments in the field of advertising regulation.

Such an arrangement would: (a) reduce the burden on the secretariats concerned, (b) contribute to a better relationship between the partners in the field of regulatory activity, and (c) contribute to a better understanding of the main issues by those who will later carry responsibility for their solutions.

One final point to be made on this subject concerns the need for the advertising agency business to be organized on a worldwide basis. We are reminded of Boddewyn's comment: "No country is a regulatory island anymore. Therefore, advertisers and their counsel must pay constant attention to what is happening abroad ..." (Boddewyn, 1983c:3).

While advertising agency associations in the world's most important trade centers have an excellent relationship and can rapidly exchange information and experience on any subject of mutual concern, they are not organized on a worldwide basis as their main counterparts – the advertisers and the media – have done. In today's world "without frontiers" it could strengthen the weight of their arguments if the advertising agency organizations were also seen to represent the interests of their members on a global basis.

This point came up during an Annual Meeting of the AAAA in Phoenix, Arizona, in 1978, when the question of a closer relationship between the AAAA, the EAAA, the Institute of Canadian Advertising and the Advertising Federation of Australia, was discussed and warmly applauded. It would seem that the case for a future more formal relationship, which need not entail the setting up of new structures or secretariats, would be a strong one.

Speaking out

> ... But, my friends, when you ask the American public to name some consumerists, nobody mentions the *real* consumerists, the men and women, the structure and system, which have created and are creating what is clearly and often enviously seen around the world as an economic demi-paradise ... (Seaman, 1973:19).

This paragraph is from a 1973 presentation in the USA entitled "Will the *real* consumerists please stand up?" At the time criticism of advertising in the USA was at a peak. In his presentation, Seaman severely attacked the excessive influence of American legislators on industry and the manner in which it tried to communicate with consumers; he made a passionate plea for the *real* consumerists to please stand up. His plea is as important today in Europe as it was then in the USA.

For many years to come, industry will have to dispel erroneous views of advertising. It should be permitted the freedom of expression it needs to fulfil its function properly – to inform consumers and to help produce sales. Regulation should not force advertising to become dull and boring, which can so easily happen if fantasy and sparkle are curbed. Regulators should give Jeremy Bullmore's "virtues of competitive persuasion" the fair chance they deserve (Bullmore, 1978).

Advertising must continue to speak out strongly. Despite the comment of some who feel that the concept of "freedom" is heavily overworked, those in favor of freedom of choice and freedom of expression should stand up and be counted.

The voice of captains of industry

Advertising people should not be the only advocates of the case for advertising. They should use their considerable gifts of persuasion to get more captains of industry to present their views publicly. Through their authority and prestige business leaders are in a unique position to influence governments and other key personalities at national and international levels regarding advertising regulation. In speech and in writing they should advance the principles of a market economy and its advantages to the public. Nobody is in a better position than these acknowledged leaders of industry to explain why it is easier to harm an economy than to repair it. They should explain how entrepreneurial spirit will be encouraged if regulations are limited. They should stress how restrictions stifle those who dare to innovate and express the optimism the world needs so badly. They can explain why industries that do not take into account the habits, preferences and tastes of consumers, will soon be out of business.

Governments and others will listen to those who run the businesses that helped to create today's society, attacked by some, cherished by most.

The voice of the academic world

There are also educators in universities who understand the benefits of the market system and advertising's role in it. They should be encouraged to speak out, not only in the classroom, but also in their published articles and books. Their research should be supported so that the results can be made available to consumerists and government officials who often more readily heed the writing of educators than the voice of advertising executives. The ideas of intellectuals sometimes become the policies of tomorrow's politicians and leaders in society. Also, nobody is in a better position to influence future leaders while they are in a formative stage.

Concluding remarks

The saga of international regulation of advertising in the European Economic Community will continue. Commissioners will come and go. One consumer program will replace another. Directives will be proposed, amended, withdrawn or approved. Those who favor or oppose private enterprise and a market economy, deregulation and preservation of some of the basic freedoms we have discussed, will continue their debate.

Amidst these endless arguments most consumers no doubt will remain largely undisturbed, as in the past. The shopping basket will have to be filled, a choice of products or services will have to be made. Little will consumers care about the activities of those who claim to act on their behalf and in their interests. They will in large measure trust the quality of products and services they acquire and the advertising that is done for them.

This puts great responsibility upon the shoulders of industry and the advertising business, that will have to act as the custodians of the freedoms that enable manufacturers to sell and advertise and consumers to select and choose. However, if the leaders of industry and the advertising business jointly continue their efforts to accelerate the positive and economic trends that appear to be developing, enhance the growing understanding and acceptance of advertising, but also support, develop, and constantly improve self-regulatory advertising controls, they will act to the benefit of consumers and society as a whole.

While the spirit of deregulation is gradually growing in Europe, there still is regulatory pettiness that can kill the hard-to-come-by entrepreneurial initiatives of imaginative business leaders. If a few European governments were to be replaced by ones that would reverse the deregulatory trend, the advertising business would be among the first to feel the effects.

For these reasons, the job which the business community has done is by no means finished. It will have to be continued with undaunted vigor, strengthened by the knowledge that there now is increasing acceptance of advertising's role toward creating to-morrow's Europe. But Pertschuk and his European counterparts are still with us. There is no room for complacency.

During the last fifteen years the advertising business has gone through one of the most hectic periods of its long history. However, it has not only survived but emerged stronger than before. This transition has required strength and singleness of mind by those involved in preserving the freedoms they inherited from others. But it has also required willingness to accept change and renewal as prerequisites for a successful future. Change and renewal are not always popular, but without them little can be accomplished. In his book *Self-Renewal*, John Gardner says: "The renewal of societies and organizations can only go forward if someone cares" (Gardner, 1963:XV). This book has been written for those who care enough to take part in the never ending task of renewal. We hope that many will accept the challenge.

List of abbreviations

AA	The Advertising Association
AAAA	American Association of Advertising Agencies
AACP	Association des Agences Conseils en Publicité (Association of Advertising Advisory Agencies)
AAF	American Advertising Federation
ABPI	Association of the British Pharmaceutical Industry
AEF	Advertising Educational Foundation
AESGP	European Proprietary Medicines Manufacturers' Association
AIG	Advertising Information Group
ANA	Association of National Advertisers
ASA	Advertising Standards Authority
BCAP	British Code of Advertising Practice
BEUC	Bureau Européen des Unions de Consommateurs (European Office of Consumer Organizations)
BIAC	Business and Industry Advisory Committee
BRD	Bundesrepublik Deutschland (Federal Republic of Germany)
CAEJ	Communauté des Associations d'Editeurs de Journaux de la CEE (Association of Newspaper Editors in the EEC)
CAP Committee	Code of Advertising Practice Committee
CARU	Children's Advertising Review Unit
CBI	Confederation of British Industry
CCC	Consumers' Consultative Committee
CDMM	Comité Directeur sur les Moyens de Communications de Masse (Steering Committee on the Mass Media)

CEBUCO	Centraal Bureau Couranten Publiciteit (Dutch Central Office Newspaper Publicity)
CEN	European Committee for Standardization
CENELEC	European Committee for Electrotechnical Standardization
CES	Confederation of European Trade Unions
CIAA	Commission des Industries Agricoles et Alimentaires (Commission of Agricultural and Nutritional Industries)
CNP	Conseil National de la Publicité (National Advertising Council)
COE	Council of Europe
COFACE	Committee of Family Organizations in the EEC
COREPER	Committee of Permanent Representatives
DBS	Direct Broadcast Satellite
DG	Director-General or Directorate-General
DWR	Deutscher Werberat (German Advertising Council)
EAAA	European Association of Advertising Agencies
EAEC	European Atomic Energy Commission
EAT	European Advertising Tripartite
EBU	European Broadcasting Union
EC	European Community
ECHR	European Convention on Human Rights
ECLG	European Consumer Law Group
ECOSOC	Economic and Social Council (UN)
ECS	European Communications Satellite
ECSC	European Coal and Steel Community
EDMA	European Direct Marketing Association
EEC	European Economic Communtiy
EFTA	European Free Trade Area
EGTA	European Group of Television Advertising
EP	European Parliament
ESC	Economic and Social Committee
ESOMAR	European Society for Opinion and Marketing Research

ETUC	European Trade Union Confederation
EURATOM	European Atomic Energy Commission (also known as EAEC)
EUROCOOP	European Organization of Consumer Cooperatives
EUTELSAT	Committee of Telecommunication Authorities
FAEP	Fédération des Associations d'Editeurs de Périodiques de la CEE (Federation of the Periodical Press of the EC)
FAO	Food and Agriculture Organization
FCC	Federal Communications Commission
FEPE	Fédération Européenne de la Publicité Extérieure (Outdoor Advertising Association)
FIEJ	Fédération Internationale des Editeurs de Journaux (International Federation of Newspaper Publishers)
FIPP	Fédération Internationale de la Presse Périodique (International Federation of the Periodical Press)
FIVS	Fédération Internationale des Vins et Spiritueux (International Federation of Wine, Spirit, Eaux-de Vie and Liqueurs Trade and Industry)
FSS	Fixed Service Satellite
FTC	Federal Trade Commission
GATT	General Agreement on Tariffs and Trade
GNP	Gross National Product
GWA	Gesellschaft Werbeagenturen (Association of Advertising Agencies)
IAA	International Advertising Association
IBA	Independent Broadcasting Authority
ICC	International Chamber of Commerce
IFPMA	International Federation of Pharmaceutical Manufacturers Association
INFOTAB	International Tobacco Information Centre
INTELSAT	International Telecommunications Satellite Organization
IOCU	International Organization of Consumers' Unions
IPA	Institute of Practitioners in Advertising
IPRA	International Public Relations Association
IS	Information Seeker

ISBA	Incorporated Society of British Advertisers
ITCA	Independent Television Companies Association
ITU	International Telecommunications Union
IUAA	International Union of Advertisers' Associations (now WFA)
MEP	Member European Parliament
MMDS	Multichannel Multipoint Distribution System
NAB	National Association of Broadcasters
NAD/NARB	National Advertising Division/National Advertising Review Board
NCC	National Consumer Council
NGO	Non-Governmental Organization
NWICO	New World Information and Communication Order
OECD	Organization for Economic Cooperation and Development
OE-CMT	European Organization of the World Federation of Workers
OJ	Official Journal (of the EC)
PAGB	Proprietary Association of Great Britain
RTL	Radio Television Luxembourg
SMATV	Satellite Master Antenna Television
TDFI	French Satellite Project
TELE-X	Swedish Satellite project
TEL-SAT	Swiss Satellite Project
TUAC	Trade Union Advisory Committee
TV-SAT	German Satellite Project
UK	United Kingdom
UN	United Nations
UNCTAD	UN Conference on Trade and Development
UNCTC	UN Centre on Transnational Corporations
UNESCO	UN Education, Scientific and Cultural Organization
UNICE	Union of the Industries of the European Community
USA	United States of America
UWG	Gesetz gegen den unlauteren Wettbewerb (Law against misleading advertising)
VCR	Videocassette Recorder

WARC	World Administrative Radio Conference
WATC	World Administrative Telecommunication Conference
WFA	World Federation of Advertisers (formerly IUAA)
WFPMM	World Federation of Proprietary Medicine Manufacturers
WHO	World Health Organization
WIPO	World Intellectual Property Organization
ZAW	Zentral Ausschuss der Werbewirtschaft (Central Committee for Advertising)

APPENDICES

I. *Council Resolution of 14 April 1975 on a preliminary programme of the European Economic Community for a consumer protection and information policy*, Brussels: Official Journal of the European Communities, Volume 18 No C 92/1 – 12, April 25, 1975.

II. *Memorandum on approximation of the laws of Member States on fair competition: Misleading and Unfair advertising*, Directorate-General for Internal Market of the Commission of the European Communities, Working Document No.2, XI/C/93/75 – E, Brussels: November, 1975.

III. *Joint reply and Memorandum from the International Union of Advertisers Associations and the European Association of Advertising Agencies, signed by the Presidents of these associations, Messrs. George Cordier and Rein Rijkens, to the Directorate-General for Internal Market of the Commission of the European Communities, Mr. Fernand Braun, regarding the first preliminary draft directive concerning the approximation of the laws of Member States on fair competition: Misleading and Unfair Advertising*, Brussels: April 14, 1976.

IV. *Explanatory Memorandum on a Proposal for a Council Directive relating to the approximation of the laws, regulations and administrative provisions of the Member States concerning Misleading and Unfair Advertising*, Commission of the European Communities, Doc. COM(77)724 final, Brussels: March 1, 1978.

V. *Explanatory Memorandum on an Amendment to the Proposal for a Council Directive relating to the approximation of laws, regulations and administrative provisions of the Member States concerning Misleading and Unfair Advertising*, Commission of the European Communities, Doc. COM(79)353 final, Brussels: July 10, 1979.

VI. *Council Resolution of 19 May 1981 on a second programme of the European Economic Community for a consumer protection and information policy*, Brussels: Official Journal of the European Communities, Volume 24 No C 133/1 – 12, June 3, 1981.

Appendix I

Preliminary consumer protection and information program of the EEC

THE COUNCIL OF THE EUROPEAN COMMUNITIES,

Having regard to the Treaty establishing the European Economic Community;

Having regard to the communication from the Commission on the preliminary programme of the European Economic Community for consumer information and protection;

Having regard to the Opinion of the European Parliament([1]);

Having regard to the Opinion of the Economic and Social Committee ([2]);

Whereas, pursuant to Article 2 of the Treaty, the task of the European Economic Community is to promote throughout the Community a harmonious development of economic activities, a continuous and balanced expansion and an accelerated raising of the standard of living;

Whereas the improvement of the quality of life is one of the tasks of the Community and as such implies protecting the health, safety and economic interests of the consumer;

Whereas fulfilment of this task requires a consumer protection and information policy to be implemented at Community level;

Whereas the Heads of State or of Government, meeting in Paris on 19 and 20 October 1972 confirmed this requirement by calling upon the institutions of the Communities to strengthen and coordinate measures for consumer protection and to submit a programme by January 1974;

([1]) OJ No C 62, 30.5.1974, p.8.
([2]) OJ No C 97, 16.8.1974, p.47.

APPROVES the principle of a consumer protection and information policy and the principles, objectives and general description of action to be taken at Community level as set out in the preliminary programme annexed hereto;

NOTES that the Commission will at a later date submit suitable proposals for the implementation of this programme, using the ways and means mentioned therein;

UNDERTAKES to act on the abovementioned proposals, if possible within nine months of the date on which they are forwarded by the Commission.

ANNEX

PRELIMINARY PROGRAMME OF THE EUROPEAN ECONOMIC COMMUNITY FOR A CONSUMER PROTECTION AND INFORMATION POLICY

INTRODUCTION

1. The strengthening and coordination of action for consumer protection within the European Economic Community, aims which were emphasized by the Heads of State or of Government at the Paris summit conference in October 1972, constitute a manifest and widely felt need. The debate in the European Parliament on 20 September 1972, which stressed the need for a coherent and effective consumer protection policy, various subsequent statements made both in the Parliament and in the Economic and Social Committee, work already done in this field by the Community and the Member States and by several international organizations, particularly the Council of Europe and the OECD, bear witness to such a need.

   The time has now come to implement a Community policy for consumer protection which, by marshalling, strengthening and supplementing the Community's work in this field, affirms its involvement in improving the quality of life of its peoples.

2. The wide range of experience in the countries of the enlarged Community favours the development of new ideas in the consumer field which, together with the many developments which have taken place in all Member States, point the way to a new deal for the consumer and ways to find a better balance in the protection of his interests.

3. The consumer is no longer seen merely as a purchaser and user of goods and services for personal, family or group purposes but also as a person concerned with the various facets of society which may affect him either directly or

indirectly as a consumer. Consumer interests may be summed up by a statement of five basic rights:

(a)   the right to protection of health and safety,

(b)   the right to protection of economic interests,

(c)   the right of redress,

(d)   the right to information and education,

(e)   the right to representation (the right to be heard).

4.   All these rights should be given greater substance by action under specific Community policies such as the economic, common agricultural, social, environment, transport and energy policies as well as by the approximation of laws, all of which affect the consumer's position.

Such action falls within the context of a policy for improving the conditions of life in the Community.

5.   This paper sets out the objectives and general principles of a consumer policy. It also sets out a number of priority measures to be taken during the coming years. In such a large and developing field it seemed preferable to limit the amount of work in the initial phase, on the understanding that new guidelines could be evolved on proposals from the Commission as the programme progressed.

I. GENERAL CONSIDERATIONS

A. THE CONSUMER AND THE ECONOMY

6.   While consumer protection has long been an established fact in the Member States of the Community, the concept of a consumer policy is relatively recent. It has developed in response to the abuses and frustrations arising at times from the increased abundance and complexity of goods and services afforded the consumer by an ever-widening market. Although such a market offers certain advantages, the consumer, in availing himself of the market, is no longer able properly to fulfil the role of a balancing factor. As market conditions have changed, the balance between suppliers and customers has tended to become weighted in favour of the supplier. The discovery of new materials, the introduction of new methods of manufacture, the development of means of communication, the expansion of markets, new methods of retailing – all these factors have had the effect of increasing the production, supply and demand of an immense variety of goods and services. This means that the consumer, in the

past usually an individual purchaser in a small local market, has become merely a unit in mass market, the target of advertising campaigns and of pressure by strongly organized production and distribution groups. Producers and distributors often have a greater opportunity to determine market conditions than the consumer. Mergers, cartels and certain self-imposed restrictions on competition have also created imbalance to the detriment of consumers.

7. Trade practices, contractual terms, consumer credit and the very concept of competition itself have all developed.

   Such changes have merely accentuated the abovementioned imbalances and made consumers and governments more aware of the need to keep the former better informed of their rights and protected against abuses which might arise from such practices.

   Thus practices which were once regarded in many countries as unfair solely in terms of competition between producers (misleading advertising, for example), are now also considered from the point of view of relations between producers and consumers.

8. Attempts have been made to correct the imbalance of power between producers and consumers mentioned in paragraphs 6 and 7. Increasingly detailed information is therefore needed to enable consumers, as far as possible, to make better use of their resources, to have a freer choice between the various products or services offered and to influence prices and product and market trends. Thus studies, surveys and comparative tests have been carried out on the quality and usefulness of products and services on price policy, market conditions, consumer behaviour and the rationalization of work in the home, etc.

9. Well aware that as individuals they have very little power, consumers are understandably trying to form organizations to protect their interests, and calls for greater consumer participation in decision-making have likewise become more numerous.

B. THE EUROPEAN ECONOMIC COMMUNITY AND CONSUMERS

10. The preamble to the Treaty establishing the European Economic Community cites as one of the basic aims of the Community 'the constant improvement of the living and working conditions' of the peoples constituting the Community. This idea is elaborated in Article 2 of the Treaty which includes among the tasks of the Community the promotion of 'harmonious development of economic activities, a continuous and balanced expansion, an increase in stability, an accelerated raising of the standard of living'.

To achieve this aim, a number of steps have already been taken in accordance with the form and means provided by the Treaty.

11. Article 39 of the Treaty contains a direct reference to consumers. It states that the objectives of the common agricultural policy include the guaranteed availability of supplies and the stabilization of markets, and then mentions also the aim 'to ensure that supplies reach consumers at reasonable prices'.

12. In dealing with rules on competition, Article 85(3) of the Treaty makes authorization for certain agreements between undertakings subject to the consumer receiving 'a fair share' of the resulting benefit, while Article 86 gives as an example of unfair practices 'limiting production, markets or technical development to the prejudice of consumers'.

13. Annex 1 contains a note of action of interest to consumers taken by the Community so far.*

Annex 2 contains a selection of Council Directives of interest to consumers.*

Although the general Community policy is the outcome of a compromise between the conflicting economic interest and diverse policies of the Member States, it is apparent that progress has been made in consumer protection and information; however, further progress must still be made.

II. OBJECTIVES OF COMMUNITY POLICY TOWARDS CONSUMERS

14. Given the tasks assigned to the Community, it follows that all action taken has repercussions on the consumer. One of the Community's prime objectives, in general terms, is therefore to take full account of consumer interests in the various sectors of Community activity, and to satisfy their collective and individual needs. Thus there would seem to be a need to formulate a specific Community consumer information and protection policy. In relation to the other common policies, such a policy would take the form of a general guideline aimed at improving the position of consumers whatever the production, distribution or service sector in question. The aims of such a policy are to secure:

A.   effective protection against hazards to consumer health and safety,

B.   effective protection against damage to consumers' economic interests,

C.   adequate facilities for advice, help and redress,

D.   consumer information and education,

E.   consultation with and representation of consumers in the framing of decisions affecting their interests.

* Not included in this publication.

A. PROTECTION OF CONSUMER HEALTH AND SAFETY

15. Measures for achieving this objective should be based on the following principles:

    (a) *PRINCIPLES*

        (i)   Goods and services offered to consumers must be such that, under normal or foreseeable conditions of use, they present no risk to the health or safety of consumers. There should be quick and simple procedures for withdrawing them from the market in the event of their presenting such risks.

            In general, consumers should be informed in an appropriate manner of any risk liable to result from a foreseeable use of goods and services, taking account of the nature of the goods and services and of the persons for whom they are intended.

        (ii) The consumer must be protected against the consequences of physical injury caused by defective products and services supplied by manufacturers of goods and providers of services.

        (iii) Substances or preparations which may form part of or be added to foodstuffs should be defined and their use regulated, for example by endeavouring to draw up in Community rules, clear and precise positive lists. Any processing which foodstuffs may undergo should also be defined and their use regulated where this is required to protect the consumer.

            Foodstuffs should not be adulterated or contaminated by packaging or other materials with which they come into contact, by their environment, by the conditions in which they are transported or stored or by persons coming into contact with them, in such a way that they affect the health or safety of consumers or otherwise become unfit for consumption.

        (iv) Machines, appliances and electrical and electronic equipment and any other category of goods which may prejudicially affect the health and safety of consumers either in themselves or by their use, should be covered by special rules and be subject to a procedure recognized or approved by the public authorities (such as type approval or declaration of conformity with harmonized standards or rules) to ensure that they are safe for use.

        (v) Certain categories of new products which may prejudicially affect the health or safety of consumers should be made subject to special authorization procedures harmonized throughout the Community.

    (b) *PRIORITIES*

16. In order to promote the free movement of goods, the Community is already actively pursuing a policy of approximation of laws in the agricultural, food-stuffs and industrial sectors. The Council has adopted several programmes[1] relating to specific fields, with a view to harmonizing the provisions laid down by law, regulation or administrative action in the Member States. These pro-grammes establish priority objectives for the approximation of legislation and a timetable for achieving them. The fields which are of special importance for the protection of the consumer's health and safety are the following:

  - foodstuffs,

  - cosmetics and detergents,

  - utensils and consumer durables,

  - cars,

  - textiles,

  - toys,

  - dangerous substances,

  - materials coming into contact with foodstuffs,

  - medicines,

  - fertilizers, pesticides and herbicides,

  - veterinary products and animal feedingstuffs[2].

17. In this field the Community will:

  - implement the programmes referred to in paragraph 16, particularly as regards consumer priorities;

  - continue to study the results of current research into substances which may affect the health or safety of consumers, as mentioned particularly in paragraph 16 and, if necessary, take steps to coordinate and encourage such research;

  - determine those products or categories of products which, because of the hazards they present to health or safety, should be subject to harmonized authorization procedures throughout the Community.

[1] – General programme for the elimination of technical barriers to trade in industrial products and foodstuffs resulting from disparities between the provisions laid down by law, regulation or administrative provisions in the Member States, laid down by the Council resolution of 28 May 1969 (OJ No C 76, 17.6.1969, p.1) and supplemented by the Council resolution of 21 May 1973 (OJ No C 38, 5.6.1973, p.1).
  – Action programme of 17 December 1973 on industrial and technological policy (Council reso-lution of 17 December 1973, OJ No C 117, 31.12.1973, p.1).
[2] Council resolution of 22 July 1974 (OJ No C 92, 6.8.1974, p.2).

B. PROTECTION OF THE ECONOMIC INTERESTS OF THE CONSUMERS

18. This kind of protection should be ensured by laws and regulations which are either harmonized at Community level or adopted directly at that level and are based on the principles set out below(*).

(a)   *PRINCIPLES*

19. (i)   Purchasers of goods or services should be protected against the abuse of power by the seller, in particular against one-sided standard contracts(*), the unfair exclusion of essential rights in contracts, harsh conditions of credit, demands for payment for unsolicited goods and against high-pressure selling methods.

(ii)   The consumer should be protected against damage to his economic interests caused by defective products or unsatisfactory services.

(iii) The presentation and promotion of goods and services, including financial services, should not be designed to mislead, either directly or indirectly, the person to whom they are offered or by whom they have been requested.

(iv)   No form of advertising − visial or aural − should mislead the potential buyer of the product or service. An advertiser in any medium should be able to justify, by appropriate means, the validity of any claims he makes.

(v)   All information provided on labels at the point of sale or in advertisements must be accurate.

(vi)   The consumer is entitled to reliable after-sales service for consumer durables including the provision of spare parts required to carry out repairs.

(vii) The range of goods available to consumers should be such that as far as possible consumers are offered an adequate choice.

(b)   *PRIORITIES*

20. (i)   *To harmonize the general conditions of consumer credit, including those relating to hire-purchase*

Studies carried out following the recent development of credit facilities show that the consumer needs help in this field.

21.   On the basis of studies already carried out by its own departments and by national authorities, the Commission will submit proposals on the general conditions of consumer credit.

(*) See paragraph 48.

22. (ii)   *To protect the consumer by appropriate measures against false or mis-leading advertising:*

   –   by establishing principles for assessing the extent to which an advertisement is false, misleading or generally unfair;

   –   by taking steps to prevent the consumer's economic interests from being harmed by false, misleading or unfair advertising;

   –   by studying methods of putting a rapid end to deceptive or misleading advertising campaigns and ensuring that advertisers' claims are valid;

   –   by studying the possibility of counteracting the effects of false or misleading advertising, for example by publishing corrective advertisements;

   –   by studying the problems arising in connection with reversal of the burden of proof.

23.   *To this end, the Commission will:*

   –   build upon the work already done(*), supplementing it where necessary by specific studies;

   –   proceed with the work being done in connection with the harmonization of laws;

   –   submit appropriate proposals to the Council.

24. (iii)   *To protect consumers from unfair commercial practices*, for example in the following areas:

   –   terms of contracts(*),

   –   conditions in guarantees, particularly for consumer durables,

   –   door-to-door sales(*),

   –   premium offers,

   –   unsolicited goods and services,

   –   information given on labels and packaging, etc.

25.   To this end, the Commission will:

   –   collate the measures already taken by the Member states and the studies already made or being made by international organizations;

   –   submit all appropriate proposals to the Council.

(*) See paragraph 48.

26. (iv) *To harmonize the law on product liability so as to provide better protection for the consumer*

27.   To this end, the Commission will submit appropriate proposals to the Council on the basis of studies already carried out or in progress(*).

28. (v)   *To improve the range and quality of services provided for consumers*

29.   In this complex and, for the most part, little-researched field, there is great scope for discussion and action on the part of the Community. The Commission will carry out a study in this area. It will report its conclusions before 31 December 1975, and, if appropriate, submit proposals.

30. (vi) *To promote the more general economic interests of consumers*

          In order better to satisfy the individual and collective needs of consumers, solutions should be sought to certain general problems such as:

          — how the individual can obtain better value for money for the goods and services supplied;

          — how waste can be prevented, particularly as regards:

              – packaging,

              – the life of goods,

              – the recycling of materials;

          — how protection can be provided against forms of advertising which encroach on the individual freedom of consumers.

31. Given that the concern for such matters is relatively recent, the Commission will endeavour to establish through research a basis for future action.

C. ADVICE, HELP AND REDRESS

(a) *PRINCIPLES*

32. Consumers should receive advice and help in respect of complaints and of injury or damage resulting from purchase or use of defective goods or unsatisfactory services.

    Consumers are also entitled to proper redress for such injury or damage by means of swift, effective and inexpensive procedures.

(*) See paragraph 48.

(b) *ACTION*

33. To this end, the Commission will:

    (i)   study:

            —   systems of assistance and advice in the Member States

            —   systems of redress, arbitration and the amicable settlement of disputes existing in the Member States,

            —   the laws of the Member States relating to consumer protection in the courts, particularly the various means of recourse and procedures, including actions brought by consumer associations or other bodies,

            —   systems and laws of the kind referred to above in certain third countries;

    (ii)   publish papers synthesizing and comparing the advantages and disadvantages of the different systems, procedures and documentation relating to consumer assistance, advice and to redress and legal remedies;

    (iii)   submit, where necessary, appropriate proposals for improving the existing systems and putting them to better use;

    (iv)   study the feasibility of a procedure for exchanging information on the outcome of action for redress and legal recourse relating to products mass-marketed in all or several Member States.

D. CONSUMER INFORMATION AND EDUCATION

Consumer information

(a) *PRINCIPLES*

34. Sufficient information should be made available to the purchaser of goods or services to enable him to:

    —   assess the basic features of the goods and services offered such as the nature, quality, quantity and price;

    —   make a rational choice between competing products and services;

    —   use these products and services safely and to his satisfaction;

    —   claim redress for any injury or damage resulting from the product supplied or service received.

(b)   *PRIORITIES*

35. (i)   *Information concerning goods and services*

      —   to formulate general principles which should apply in the preparation of all specific directives and other rules relating to consumer protection;

      —   to lay down rules for the labelling of products for which specifications are harmonized at Community level. These rules should provide that all labelling must be clear, legible and unambiguous;

      —   for foodstuffs, to draw up rules stating clearly the particulars that should be given to the consumer (e.g., the nature, composition, weight or volume, the food value, the date of manufacture or any other useful date marking, etc.);

      —   for products other than foodstuffs, and for services, to draw up rules stating clearly the particulars which are of interest to the consumer and which should be given to him;

      —   to draw up common principles for stating the price and possibly the price per unit of weight or volume;

      —   to encourage the use and harmonization of systems of voluntary informative labelling.

36. (ii)   *Comparative tests*

Comparative tests are another source of information. Such tests may be carried out by state-financed bodies, private bodies or a combination of the two. These bodies would have much to gain from a coordinated exchange of information(*).

The Commission will take the necessary steps to ensure that the bodies carrying out comparative tests in the Member States cooperate as closely as possible, particularly by conducting tests jointly and even by laying down similar standards for such tests.

37. (iii)   *Study of consumer behaviour*

In order to establish an integrated policy on consumer information and education, more needs to be known about consumer behaviour and attitudes. The Commission already conducts regular consumer surveys on certain aspects of the Community's economic situation. It will continue these surveys and extend them to other subjects, in cooperation with Member States, consumer organizations and other bodies, so as to learn more about the needs and behaviour of consumers within the Community.

(*) See paragraph 48.

38. (iv)   To inform consumers in simple terms of measures taken at national and Community level which may directly or indirectly affect their interests.

39.   For the Commission, such action will comprise in particular:

    —   setting out the categories of consumer information aobut goods and services which are most needed for consumers in the Community and preparing documentation on that basis;

    —   providing an increasing amount and range of clear information on consumer matters being dealt with by the Community, in close co-operation with Member States and consumer and other organizations;

    —   encouraging the production of television and radio programmes and films and the publication of press articles, etc., on consumer topics;

    —   publishing an annual report on steps taken by the Community and the Member States in the consumer interest by legislation and its implementation, information, consultation and coordination.

40. (v)   *Information on prices*

           Consumers should be informed of the factors determining prices within the Community.

           Such information will be supplied by the Commission, particularly in the annual report mentioned in paragraph 39.

41.   The Commission should continue to carry out surveys of retail prices and endeavour to inform the public as soon as possible of price differences within the Community.

Consumer education

(a)   *PRINCIPLE*

42. Facilities should be made available to children as well as to young people and adults to educate them to act as discriminating consumers, capable of making an informed choice of goods and services and conscious of their rights and responsibilities. To this end, consumers should, in particular, benefit from basic information on the principles of modern economics.

(b) *ACTION*

43. (i) *Promotion of consumer education*

In order to further the advance of consumer education by providing advice and opinions at Community level, the Commission should undertake further studies in cooperation with Member States and consumer organizations.

The object of such studies, carried out in conjunction with experts from the Member States, should be to determine methods and suggest materials for the encouragement of consumer education in the curricula of schools, universities and other educational establishments.

44. (ii) *Training the instructors*

Training those who are to instruct others is a necessary task on which a number of ideas have been advanced. For instance, centres could be set up in the Member States to provide such training, based on the results of economic and sociological research. Exchanges of ideas, of staff and of students between such centres have also been considered. The Commission will encourage work in this field.

45. (iii) *Dissemination of a wide range of information*

As part of its general information policy, the Commission will encourage the exchange and dissemination of information on topics of interest to consumers, in cooperation with national authorities and bodies concerned with consumer affairs. Publication of the annual report referred to in paragraph 39 will also provide a means of increasing consumer awareness.

E. CONSUMER CONSULTATION AND REPRESENTATION

(a) *PRINCIPLES*

46. When decisions which concern them are prepared, consumers should be consulted and allowed to express their views, in particular through organizations concerned with consumer protection and information.

(b) *ACTION*

47. In this field, the Commission will:

    (i)   carry out on the basis of existing studies(*) a comparative study of the different procedures for consumer consultation, representation and participation currently employed in the Member States and in particular the rules and criteria relating to how representative consumer organizations are and whether they are to be recognized by the authorities;

    (ii) encourage organizations representing consumers to study certain matters of particular importance for consumers, to make known their views and coordinate their efforts;

    (iii) promote exchanges of information between Member States on the most appropriate way of providing consumers with channels through which to be consulted or to express their views.

III. IMPLEMENTATION

48. In implementing its programme, the Commission will take full account of studies and other work already carried out by the Member States, international bodies(¹) and consumer organizations, and will collaborate with them so as to enable the Community to take advantages of work already in progress.

    In this context, cooperation with the Council of Europe and OECD is of particular importance in view of the work (indicated by an asterisk in this programme) undertaken by these organizations on subjects relating to consumer protection and information.

    The importance of such collaboration cannot be over-emphasized and everything possible will be done to maintain and develop the close links and harmonious relations already established or in the making in the field of consumer affairs.

49. This text should be regarded as the first stage of a more comprehensive programme which might need to be developed at a later date. The aim is to complete this first stage within four years.

(*) See paragraph 48.
(¹) The bodies with which collaboration will be maintained include:
   − United Nations; United Nations Educational, Scientific and Cultural Organization; World Health Organization; Food and Agriculture Organization and Codex Alimentarius; Organization for Economic Cooperation and Development; Council of Europe; Nordic Committee on Consumer Matters;
   − International Standards Organization and International Electrotechnical Commission; European Committee for Standardization and European Committee for Electrotechnical Standardization.

Appendix II

Memorandum on first draft Directive on Misleading and Unfair advertising

Table of contents

I. The present situation

1. *Introduction*

   Advertising has played an important part in the development of the modern industrial economy in its role as intermediary between producers and consumers. By directing consumers' attention to the relative merits of the various products the market has to offer it has promoted efficiency of distribution and consumer choice and enabled local or regional production to develop on a national scale.

   However, with the development of mass markets, modern advertising techniques, and the competitive drive within a society, there is a temptation for a producer of goods to base his advertising less on the inherent qualities, price, usefulness or differences of his product but on false or misleading information.

   This has important repercussions on the competitive character of the market. The consumer who is subjected to misleading advertising is prevented from making the right consumer choice and the producer who employs such methods acquires an unfair advantage over his competitors.

   The essential needs of a society are not well served by such distortion of the truth or of competition and it is therefore essential to regulate such abuses.

2. *Misleading advertising*

   The laws in the Member States on misleading advertising show considerable differences in treatment.

   (a) The *traditional* remedy was that of unfair competition which protected the producer (and indirectly the consumer) against the unfair competitive practices of his competitors. Liability was established by proof that the advertiser

   (1) had misled the public

   (2) by means of false statements

   (3) and had thereby taken clients or customers away from competitors.

   As can be seen from (1) and (3) this approach required proof that the individual competitor had been injured and the public had actually been misled. In all the Member States other than France, the United Kingdom and Ireland, it is now sufficient if false statements were made and there was a risk the public would have been misled thereby. Proof of actually misleading the public and thereby actually diverting clients is no longer required. Injury is inferred from the risk that the public would be misled.

In France it is still necessary to prove injury or damage though this may be very small. In the case of actions by trade associations a simple 'corporate injury' is considered sufficient.

In Holland and Italy there must be proof however of some injury even though it may only occur in the future, that is if there is only a potential injury or risk thereof.

In the United Kingdom and Ireland there is no comprehensive legislation on misleading advertising in general though certain aspects are covered by criminal legislation and contract and tort law.

As the law has developed in the Member States the same rights of action have gradually been granted to groups or associations of producers as to the individual producer. This means that, with the exception of the above-mentioned States, they can take action on the basis of their general right to protect their interests though there has been no definite or specific injury to the interests of one of their members.

There has been a similar development in regard to consumers. While the individual consumer, unlike the individual producer generally has to prove damage, some remedies, and in particular the remedy of injunction, have been extended to consumer associations on the basis of their general right to protect their collective interests.

(b) There is a difference in interpretation of the concept of risk whether certain advertising should be considered to have misled the public. The most liberal position is that adopted by the Italian Courts. Mis-statements are tolerated, in particular when expressed in general terms. But some cases of mis-statement have also been allowed in regard to precise and concrete facts. It is felt the risk of misleading the public is small given its awareness of advertising techniques.

In Germany on the other hand, mis-statements are not allowed unless they are very obviously exaggerations. Belgium and Luxembourg have, in recent years, tended to follow the German example while France and Holland though also adopting a strict view, allow some further exceptions e.g. general publicity bearing on the quality of goods.

3. *Comparative advertising*

In all the Member States other than Ireland, the United Kingdom and the Netherlands there is general agreement that in principle comparative advertising should not be allowed except in self-defence or where there is an objective comparative assessment of technical systems or where the comparison is requested by a customer.

In the Netherlands there is authority to the effect that some forms of true comparative advertising should be allowed. However there are no decisions of final authority on this point.

In the United Kingdom and Ireland there is no specific regulation of comparative advertising.

4. *Denigration*

In all the Member States other than Ireland, the United Kingdom, discrediting the reputation of a rival, whether by discrediting his products, his business methods or even his family or personal reputation in a way that injures him in his business is considered unfair competition. This is so even where the allegations are true. It is considered unfair that an individual should base his reputation on the destruction of that of his rival.

In Ireland and the United Kingdom denigration which is untrue and which destroys the reputation of a competitor would be covered by the law of defamation. This is a more restricted concept however than that of denigration.

This principle includes comparative advertising which is not based on facts which are fairly selected and unlikely to mislead, that is, the sort of comparative advertising which is prohibited in most Member States. Such prohibited comparative advertising denigrates another's goods, and indirectly his reputation, by means of misleading and unjustified comparisons.

The legal concept of denigration is used in some Member States to control comparative advertising or set out its limits. But it goes further than this as it also covers the situation where no comparison is involved and where advertising is directly defamatory of a rival's reputation.

II. The effects of the Common Market of this legal situation and the need to approximate the laws governing misleading advertising

The different legal provisions in the Member States concerning the form of protection to be given and its interpretation directly affect the establishment and functioning of the Common Market in several respects.

1. *Protection and information of the consumer*

    (a) One of the chief objectives of the Communities is the promotion of the harmonious development of economic activities by the establishment of a Common Market. This means that all aspects of economic activity must be taken into account including that of the consumer, whose role in the development of the modern economy must be protected in any balanced and harmonious development of economic activity.

The consumer cannot properly fulfill his function of final arbiter in the market economy unless he is protected against misleading advertising. A Directive on misleading advertising must therefore include as wide a protection as possible against the effect of widespread abuse of the advertising media.

Furthermore this protection can be adequately assured only if similar remedies are granted to consumers throughout the Common Market. Any measure of harmonisation must therefore include similar remedies which shall be made available to all consumers in the EEC.

(b)   In addition to the need to prohibit advertising which misleads, it is also important to harmonize the existing rules and differences between them which also create distortions of competition and impede the free flow of goods. The full range of goods or services that might otherwise be available to the consumer is impeded by differences in the national rules. This is discussed more fully in the following paragraphs.

2.   *The free movement of goods and services*

Advertising has kept pace with the enormous development in inter-state trade resulting from the creation of the Common Market, in the sense that advertising campaigns are now increasingly planned outside a national context. If a firm plans to sell its products in four Member States, there are likely to be substantial economies in the adoption of a single advertising campaign, rather than four wholly separate campaigns. The way in which this can be achieved is by enabling national advertisers to plan a common advertising concept susceptible to relatively minor changes in cases where national marketing needs, as distinct from national advertising laws, differ.

Common rules on advertising standards will facilitate the planning of a common advertising campaign for a particular product and will therefore facilitate the development of interstate trade and the development of a Common Market.

3.   *The distortion of competitive conditions*

(a)   The adoption of common rules on advertising will reduce distortions of competition which the differences in national rules at present bring about.

These distortions arise because an advertiser in country A will be able to use his campaign in another state B with similar rules. But an advertiser in country C will not if the rules in country C are substantially different from those in B. The advertiser in country A will have an advantage over the advertiser in C who will have to invest in more than one advertising campaign if he is to advertise successfully abroad.

It is true that conditions (cultural, linguistic, etc.) in B may dictate a different kind of advertising campaign from the kind which would be appropriate in A; but here again our premise has been that in fact there is a great deal of scope for common advertising campaigns. This is borne out by the actual increase in such campaigns and the general increase in interstate trading.

(b)   In any event, advertising campaigns which may have been planned primarily for national markets do in practice cross national frontiers; this is particularly true of radio and television (especially cable television) and of certain categories of journal. Campaigns may in fact have a national objective but an international impact. Consequently, the advertiser who does not wish to run the risk of advertising in a way which offends another Member State's laws must tone down his campaign in the national market with a possible loss of competitive advantage there. This is clearly unsatisfactory.

(c)   Different advertising laws also tend to distort competition in border regions, as Professor Ulmer of the Max-Planck-Institut in Munich has pointed out in his study of the laws on unfair competition in the Member States. This occurs because the consuming public in proximity to a border also carries out a substantial percentage of its purchases on the other side of the border. The result is that if advertising rules on one side of a border are more favourable, the consumer will be more tempted to purchase on that side than on the other; the traders on one side of the border are thereby placed in a more favourable position than those on the other. The amount of trade in question cannot be considered negligeable given the number of people living in border regions or in towns and cities in close proximity thereto within the Common Market.

(d)   The points already considered concern the effect on free movement of goods of the different national treatment of misleading advertising. Distortions of competition also arise however from the failure to regulate misleading advertising at all the present inadequacies in such regulations. Deception of the consumer will in all probability lead him to make the wrong choice in his purchase of a particular product; and the producer who employs deception acquires an unfair advantage over his competitors who may be producing better quality goods. The distributive function of advertising is distorted and the proper functioning of the market is upset.

This is true of those Member States where there is no regulation of advertising or where such regulation can be considered inadequate; this distortion is compounded by differences in regulation as between Member States which accentuate the difficulty for the consumer to make the right choice.

III. Work undertaken in regard to regulation of misleading advertising and approximation of the laws thereon

1. *Private organisations*

   The Commission recognises the valuable work carried out by various voluntary associations, in establishing systems of self-regulation, in devising codes of advertising conduct and, not least, in helping the Community in its preliminary enquiries into the legal problems of misleading advertising. Broadly speaking, the voluntary associations fall into three categories: those representing advertisers, those representing advertising agencies and those representing the media.

   At Community level, the advertisers are represented by the EEC group of International Union of Advertisers Associations, and the advertising agencies by the EEC group of the European Association of Advertising Agencies. Both these bodies have submitted memoranda to the Commission on misleading advertising and, through their chief executives or committee members, have made available their knowledge and experience in frequent discussions with members of the Commission's staff.

   There have also been discussions with the representatives of the media, such as the International Federation of the Periodical Press; and with some of the leading figures in national advertising bodies, such as the Union Belge des Annonceurs, the Zentralausschuss für Werbewirtschaft (ZAW) in Germany and the Advertisers Association in the United Kingdom (the two latter bodies also submitted memoranda).

   Most, if not all, of the voluntary bodies so far mentioned participate in the deliberations of the International Chamber of Commerce and in particular of the ICC's Marketing Committee; and throughout the Commission preliminary enquiries it has been of incalculable value to be able to refer to one of the principal documents emanating from the Marketing Committee, namely, the ICC Code of Advertising Practice. Indeed, the Commission's proposals are largely based on the ICC Code, most of the departures from the Code being dictated only by the need to give legal form to general principles.

   Some advertising associations have submitted their views on the need for harmonisation of laws on misleading advertising to the Commission. Their attitude has been that Community legislation could enhance the authority of their self-regulatory organisations provided the importance of their role was in some way recognised in the legislation.

   The Commission's services view is that this is an entirely reasonable suggestion. Voluntary organisations have a valuable and useful part to play in establishing standards for the proper and balanced development of advertising and reconciling the various interests of advertisers and consumers.

In furtherance of this objective procedures for settling conflicts which could otherwise be settled only in Court are of some importance. They have two advantages — they are less expensive than litigation and a certain flexibility is retained by arbitration bodies which are not bound by precedent. Advertising guidelines can be developed more quickly and efficiently by such means.

However, the settlement procedures of such voluntary organisations can be effective only if they are backed by legislative authority such as this Directive is designed to provide. Article 8 of the Directive is included to encourage individuals to have recourse to the settlement procedures of voluntary organisations but it in no way derogates from the right of recourse established by the Directive.

2. *The Council of Europe*

The Council of Europe has been active in the field of consumer affairs for a long time and its most recent efforts have been crowned by the adoption of Resolution 521 (1972) on Consumer Protection Policy and Recommendation 624 (1971) on the legal protection of consumers. Further work has been devoted to the development of a consumer protection Charter.

In regard to the specific question of misleading advertising the Council of Europe adopted Resolution (72)8 on Consumer Protection against misleading advertising on 18 Feburary 1972. This resolution makes a very strong statement in favour of harmonising the laws on misleading information and spells out the various means whereby this should be achieved. In so far as possible the Draft Directive attached to this Memorandum (W.Doc. No.3) gives effect to the provisions of the Resolution.

3. *The Commission of the European Communities*

The Commission's work in relation to misleading advertising has been part of its general efforts in the field of unfair competition. For several years the Commission has studied the problems of ensuring observance of the rules on unfair competition within the Common Market and has taken several initiatives in this respect:

(a)   The Commission asked the Max-Planck-Institut für ausländisches und internationales Patent-, Urheber- und Wettbewerbsrecht in Munich to undertake a study of the relevant comparative law to ascertain the differences between national rules on fair competition liable to affect the development of the Common Market. This study was ably undertaken by Professor Eugen Ulmer of the Institute and an international team of outstanding scholars in the field: The study comprises five volumes and is being published in several languages. The study is currently being enlarged to take account of the laws of the new Member States and this new part of it is due in the course of 1976.

(b) In July 1968, the Commission sent to the governments of the original Member States a Report on the harmonisation of legislation concerning unfair competition (Doc.XIV/5593/68 of 24 April 1968) based on the study published by the Max-Planck-Institut and pointing out the priorities and the need for action in this sector.

(c) At the same time, the Commission informed the Member States that it was sending a questionnaire to a selection of European associations representing commercial and industrial interests to find out precisely what disadvantages resulted from divergences in legislation. The replies received were summarized (Doc.2715/XIV/70 of 5th February 1970) and were favourable to some action being taken by the Commission, in particular in the field of misleading advertising.

(d) On the basis of these replies Working Document No.1 (Doc.XIV/156/72 of 28th February 1972) was prepared and submitted to Member States (including the three new Member States) and the first meeting of government experts was held in November 1972. The Working Group agreed that misleading advertising was one of the topics in the list of topics discussed that should be given priority in any further action undertaken by the Commission in the field of Fair Trading Practices.

(e) In December 1973, the Commission submitted a Preliminary Community Programme for Consumer Information and Protection to the Council (amended version of 21 May, 1974, Doc.SEC(74)1939 final).

This Programme includes protection of the consumer against false or misleading advertising in its list of priorities particularly 'by establishing principles for assessing the extent to which an advertisement is false, misleading or generally unfair' and 'by taking steps to prevent the consumer's economic interests from being harmed by false, misleading or unfair advertising', (SEC.22(ii) of the Programme). Many other features of the Programme establish the general principle of consumer protection against misleading information and the need to supply the consumer with information which is sufficient for him to protect himself.

IV. Basic principles underlying the substantive rules

A. Scope of the rules

1. *Misleading advertising*

Substantial differences exist in the interpretation of 'misleading advertising' by the Courts in the Member States. The aim of the Direcitve is to define the constitutive elements of deception in advertising as accurately and widely as possible and by pinpointing the most common abuses to reduce as far as possible the different interpretations given by judge-made law in the various Member States.

Bearing this in mind the draft Directive contains a short article (art. 1) requiring Member States to prohibit misleading advertising. This is followed by a general clause (art. 3) which sets out the criterion by which advertising may be judged to be misleading, and this is completed by three sub-sections which set out the circumstances in which advertising is most commonly misleading e.g. on matters of quality, conditions of sale etc.

The Directive contains an additional article (art. 4) setting out some of the commonest forms that deception takes e.g. providing inadequate information or making unsubstantiated claims, and other common abuses which it was considered important to regulate.

The Directive is flexible however and only sets out a system of miminum rules. There is room for adoption by national Courts to new situations or circumstances requiring a different approach. This is guaranteed by the existence in article 2 of a general clause. But the discretion of national Courts in regard to the most obvious and common abuses is limited by the other provisions of the Directive.

It is thereby hoped to establish a new balance between judicial flexibility and the need to reduce differences in interpretation of the rules on misleading advertising within the Common Market. The Directive will also establish higher standards in advertising which will be of benefit to both consumer and producer.

Professor Ulmer has pointed out in his comprehensive study of Unfair Trade Practices in the Community that such a balance would be an essential part of any successful attempt to regulate misleading advertising on a Community basis. A general clause is necessary because a comprehensive definition of misleading advertising would be too restrictive of the scope of a proposed Directive; but ground rules for interpretation would have to be included or there would be no uniformity in the rules established by the Common Market. A Directive would add nothing to the existing situation in those circumstances.

(a)   The general definition of misleading advertising sets out the criterion of liability, namely the risk that the public or the reasonable man would be misled. In all the Member States, except Ireland and the United Kingdom (where this matter is not regulated comprehensively), the burden of proof (leaving aside intention or 'faute' of the advertiser) traditionally required the plaintiff to show that

(i)   he actually suffered an injury whether as a producer in the same sector by losing customers or as a consumer by purchasing an unwanted article, and

(ii)   this was due to advertising which misled the public as well as the plaintiff.

Now the position is different on both counts. The individual competitor or consumer and groups of competitors or consumers may take action for an injunction without proving injury to themselves. Nor is it required that they show the public has actually been misled. It is sufficient if they show that the advertising created a risk that the public would be misled, and that a reasonable member of the public would have been misled.

This development arose out of the difficulty for a producer or a group of producers or consumers to demonstrate the general injury they have suffered which is nonetheless perfectly real. They do not have to prove specific damage. The law in most Member States only requires that they show a risk that the public would be misled and the court may infer therefrom that injury has resulted to the general interest.

The requirement that a plaintiff need only show that there was a risk that the public would be misled is also simple and more effective. Traditionally the plaintiff had to adduce in court the testimony of a representative group of people who claimed that they had actually been misled. It is far better to have the court decide that a reasonable man would be misled by the advertising in question.

In cases of actual injury the Directive confirms the rights granted in all Member States to such individuals or groups of individuals as actually suffer specific damage (art. 7(a) and (b)).

The Directive requires that criminal remedies be available to individuals or groups of consumers or competitors in addition to the remedy of injunction or damages (art. 7(a) and (b)).

The criterion of deception is independent of whether statements are false, true or partially true etc. as deceptiveness is the determining factor.

(b)   In several Member States misleading advertising is prohibited by means
        of a general clause supported by a list of the circumstances or facts con-
        cerning which advertising is frequently misleading. This list sets out the
        important points concerning which the consumer must not be misled such
        as the nature, quality, price of the goods etc. In a comprehensive regula-
        tion of misleading advertising this is an important element, and the list
        established in the Directive sets out a comprehensive and non-exhaustive
        list of the most obvious conditions surrounding the sale of goods which
        should not be distorted so as to mislead the public. This is in line with the
        general policy mentioned in para. 1 of specifically including as many com-
        mon abuses as possible in the definition to narrow possible divergences in
        interpretation by the national courts.

(c)   The actual techniques of presenting deceptive information to the con-
        sumer are also constitutive elements of misleading advertising. Examples
        are the partial presentation of the truth in a way that is misleading or
        claims that are not substantiated put forward as positive truths. It was felt
        that this was an important element in the fight against misleading adver-
        tising and has also been included in the Directive.

(d)   The definition of advertising has been made as wide as possible and such
        matters as political advertising and appeals by recognized charities, pro-
        vided they have a commercial or professional side to them, are also
        included. Personal promotion by salesmen is included but in this case just
        as in the cases mentioned above national Courts have the task of setting
        out the limits of application of the Directive. There are obviously some
        exceptions that will need to be made but it was considered best to leave
        this to the national Courts. The clearest example of this is the case of
        political advertising which raises constitutional issues. (It is not intended
        to include purely editorial matters in the scope of the Directive but again
        the issue is left to the national Courts which may decide to include it in
        certain limited circumstances.)

(e)   Both goods and services are included and both are widely defined. There
        does not seem to be any topical reason why misleading advertising should
        be confined to one specific set of goods or services. Advertising can be
        misleading no matter what is advertised.

2. *Unfair advertising*

(a)   Article 5 contains a list of common abuses which have not been regulated
        before in the Member States, except by the various self-regulatory bodies
        including the International Chamber of Commerce. Examples of such
        abuses are the exploitation of young children, or of the superstition or

fear of the public at large. They do not for the most part constitute deceptive advertising and they have therefore been placed under a different heading namely 'unfair advertising'. Both denigration and comparative advertising have been placed under the heading 'unfair advertising', but without prejudice to the application of the rules on misleading advertising.

(b)   *Comparative advertising*

As we have seen (see p. 274-5) in most Member States, comparative advertising is generally prohibited but certain exceptions are allowed in the case of self-defence or where there is an objective comparative assessment of goods or services where such assessment is necessary to demonstrate the advantages of one set of goods or services over the others. An exception is also allowed in the case where a customer requests such a comparison.

The Directive makes a wider allowance for comparative advertising. It only prohibits it when it consists of misleading advertising or when it is based on an unfair selection of facts. To put it another way, comparative advertising is allowed

(i)   if it is not misleading;

(ii)   if it is based on a fairly selected set of facts;

(iii)   if it is a direct comparison which is not based on any set of stated facts or analytical comparison – for example a statement that 'Beer is best' implies that beer is better than other drinks, but it is not considered to be an especially harmful sort of advertising and it does not come within the scope of the Directive.

Comparative advertising made in self-defence must comply with the ordinary rules laid down in the Directive for comparative advertising as otherwise it would compound any existing or alleged abuse or offence. Further action may be taken by someone who feels aggrieved under art. 7(d) which provides for a system of correction and apology.

An exception for the case where a customer requests a comparison is not made as it is difficult to visualize a customer asking to be misled or misinformed. It is in the interest of both advertiser (he wants to avoid suit) and customer, that misunderstanding should be avoided. This can best be achieved by not allowing this exception.

(c)   *Denigration*

Denigration of a competitor in a way which affects his business by attacks on his products or business methods or even his personal qualities or attributes is prohibited in most Member States whether the allegations made are true or false. This is so because it is felt to be unfair that an individual should base his own reputation on the destruction of the reputation of his competitors

The definition of this abuse includes comparative advertising, and also covers the situation where no comparison is involved or where there is a direct slander. Art. 5 is designed to cover the latter as comparative advertising is covered by art. 6.

The Directive prohibits denigration of a competitor by means of advertising where such attacks are of a personal nature. This prohibition is absolute as it is difficult to conceive of such personal attacks being either fair or relevant.

Other attacks on the goods or firm of a competitor must be judged according to their degree of fairness. The fairness of such attacks must be judged along lines similar to the criteria used in evaluating comparative advertising which also generally consists of an indirect attack on a competitor's commercial reputation. Obviously false or deceptive attacks would not be considered fair. The area of discretion here basically concerns those allegations about a competitor's commercial reputation which are true and can be substantiated.

B. The person against whom the claim would be brought

1. *Misleading advertising*
   (a) The actual bodies or individuals who should be responsible for misleading advertising include the advertiser himself, his advertising agent and persons or bodies in control of the advertising media. The person whose goods or services are being advertised bears the principal responsibility. But the responsibility of the advertising agent is also quite clear as he is the actual creator of the advertisement. Those in control of the media have a general responsibility to society for the programmes they convey and their responsibility extends to the advertising they include in their programmes. The draft Directive embodies these views. Those responsible should consist of those ultimately responsible for action taken. It is not intended to make subordinate employees liable.
   (b) As to the question of fault or intention on the part of the person against whom the claim is brought, the laws in the Member States show a certain variation.

In Germany and Italy for example an injunction may be requested without proof of fault or intention on the part of the defendant. In France and Belgium it is sufficient to prove that the defendant was negligent. In the United Kingdom and Ireland there is no precedent to go by as there is no specific law on misleading advertising, but in theory an injunction could be granted without proof of intention or negligence, that is on the basis of strict liability. However in all Member States intention or fault has been required where damages are sought or in criminal actions in relation to misleading advertising. Again, in the United Kingdom and Ireland there is no specific precedent in relation to misleading advertising but the general rule is that intention or fault are required in criminal actions or negligence in civil suits for damages. The draft Directive dispenses with a specific requirement of fault or intention in regard to injunction only in view of the importance of a simplified remedy of injunction for the overall success of the Directive. The other procedural aspects are left up to the Member States.

2. *Unfair advertising*

The same principles set out above in relation to the person or persons against whom a claim may be brought in regard to misleading advertising shall apply in regard to both comparative advertising and denigration. No difference in treatment is required.

C. Remedies

The following paragraphs apply to misleading and unfair advertising.

1. *Injunctions*

As we have seen the general trend in some Member States has been to develop the remedy of injunction without the need to prove fault or intention on the part of the defendant or that damages were caused to the plaintiff.

This is the most important and useful remedy available in the context of misleading advertising because the damage which can be caused by advertising can be caused in a very short space of time and it is important to be able to act fast to remedy the situation. In addition to this it is often difficult to prove damage to an individual or collective interest; this is not because the damage hasn't occurred or is not real but because actual proof is difficult. The absence of a requirement that fault or intention be proved in some Member States is also in accordance with the need to act with speed in these cases.

Another advantage of allowing injunctions without proof of damage is that class actions become possible, the damage to the general interest of a group does not have to be specifically proved but may be inferred by the court from the circumstances or deceptiveness of the advertising. Class actions are important because more often than not it is representative organisations of consumers or producers who have the necessary expertise and financial backing to ensure effective control of advertising and protection for the interests these organisations represent.

Including the right to injunction without proof of damages in a Directive poses certain problems for Member States such as the United Kingdom or Ireland which do not allow injunctions unless specific damage is proved. But what is proposed in the draft Directive is a limited extension of the right to injunction without damages which will be confined to the sector of misleading advertising where it is both suitable and necessary. This does not amount to a general reform or harmonisation of the remedy of injunction but to a limited adaptation of the remedy to the needs of the situation.

The Directive also contains the idea in article 7 that fault or intention need not be proved in the case of injunction. This is to facilitate recourse to this procedure and ensure the necessary speed to provide an effective remedy.

2. *Criminal remedies and actions for damages*

The draft Directive also requires that if criminal remedies are made available in the Member States for breaches of the law on misleading advertising groups of consumers or producers will be able to initiate criminal proceedings. It also extends this right of consumer or producer groups to the normal action in damages which is only available in some countries to the individual and not to groups.

Appendix III

Joint reply and Memorandum from the IUAA and EAAA to first draft Directive on Misleading and Unfair advertising

First preliminary draft Directive concerning the approximation of the laws of Member States on fair competition: Misleading and Unfair advertising

The International Union of Advertisers' Associations (IUAA) and the European Association of Advertising Agencies (EAAA) greatly appreciate the opportunity given to them to present their preliminary comments on the first preliminary draft Directive concerning the approximation of the laws of Member States on misleading and unfair advertising.

Our Associations wholeheartedly agree with the intention of the Commission to improve, where necessary, the standards of advertising, to eradicate abuse, where it occurs, in the form of misleading or unfair advertising, and to strengthen its power to deliver its essential social and economic contribution to consumers as well as industry.

There is, however, an opinion amongst various bodies representing advertising that the measures suggested to achieve this goal are too elaborate and far-reaching, that they represent a considerable sharpening of the present legislation in the Community seen as a whole, and that the aim of Articles 3 and 100 of the Rome Treaty regarding the safeguarding of a proper functioning of the Common Market could be achieved, as far as advertising is involved, by a less degree of detailed legal harmonisation than proposed in the draft Directive.

We have expressed in the enclosed Memorandum our comments on various parts of the draft Directive and the Memorandum covering it, which we hope may be helpful to you. Our views, which we have tried to make constructive and positive, can be summarised as follows:

If it is decided that there are factors which call for some harmonised law on misleading advertising, then any Directive to this end should:

(a)   be brief and basic, and leave to the national Courts and self-disciplinary bodies the necessary flexibility in interpreting what is misleading or unfair advertising, having regard to each country's public attitudes, traditions and cultural requirements on this matter;

(b)   limit itself therefore to a simple and brief definition of advertising which may mislead a reasonable person in a material degree; of advertising which may be harmful to the public in some other way; and of unfair advertising. There should be no reference to misleading 'by omission', or any of the very controversial clauses in Article 4;

(c)   define advertising as 'paid communication of a commercial or professional character, whether by public or private enterprises or charitable institutions';

(d)   include a specific reference to comparative advertising, which should be allowed in all countries of the Community, provided that it is not misleading or unfair, denigratory or taking advantage of the goodwill of a competitor;

(e)   encourage and acknowledge self-disciplinary controls as a means of the implementation of the Directive (the important role of self-disciplinary bodies is fully recognised in Section III:1 of the Memorandum covering the draft Directive);

(f)   provide for the speediest possible process by court order or some alternative method as Member States consider appropriate, against the publication or further publication of misleading or unfair advertisements, unless suitably amended, as a result of decisions by Courts or self-disciplinary bodies;

(g)   reserve the sole right to initiate criminal proceedings to a public prosecutor or equivalent public authority;

(h)   as far as other remedies are concerned, leave Member States to choose the measures of enforcement which are appropriate within their own legal system; EEC Directives have, as far as we know, not in the past covered legal procedures for enforcement, and we would question the suitability of abandoning this practice in the field of advertising, where many factors contribute to great differences in the systems now in operation in the various Member States.

We would appreciate the possibility to present further comments during the progress of the draft Directive towards a proposed Directive. We are, of course, at your full disposal at any time, if there are any special questions where we could be of assistance.

MEMORANDUM
FROM
THE INTERNATIONAL UNION OF ADVERTISERS' ASSOCIATIONS (IUAA) AND
THE EUROPEAN ASSOCIATION OF ADVERTISING AGENCIES (EAAA)
ON THE
PRELIMINARY DRAFT DIRECTIVE ON MISLEADING AND UNFAIR ADVETISING

I. INTRODUCTION

In its introduction, the Memorandum covering the proposed Directive on Misleading Advertising, pays a just tribute to the importance of advertising in a modern industrial economy. Indeed the effect on industry and commerce of a major interference with the capacity of the producer to communicate with the consumer about his products could be very damaging to a free enterprise economy and to modern society. The effect of a major curtailment of advertising on the financial viability of the press, broadcasting, and all communications would be most serious.

It is, therefore, somewhat alarming to find that, in the next paragraphs of the Introduction, the character of the Directive takes its shape from criticisms of advertising which, while doubtless valid about occasional advertisements, are described, without any evidence or proof, as if they were a widespread and general cause of 'distortion of the essential needs of society', and that this had important repercussions on the competitive character of the market. The Memorandum might imply in the second paragraph of point II:1, also without any evidence or proof, that there is 'widespread abuse of the advertising media'. This is, definitely not a true description of the actual situation in the Member States.

It is alarming because, in framing a proposed law to deal with occasional abuses of the freedom of communications, the precise terms of the Directive are such as would make it difficult for the advertiser to communicate with his market.

It must surely be the intention of the Commission, and one with which the IUAA and the EAAA would wholeheartedly agree, to improve the standards of advertising, to eradicate the fringe of abuses, and to strengthen its power to deliver its essential economic contribution and serve the very real needs of the consumer. But the effect of the detail provisions of the Directive, if it became law in each country, would almost certainly be to raise doubts about almost any advertising. Judgements based on the letter of a law such as the Directive suggests, would (under criminal and civil penalties) create such uncertainty in the minds of advertisers and media that they might well be reluctant to risk publishing anything that might be normally regarded as effective advertising. It must be remembered that advertising can only exist if it promotes the knowledge, the acceptance, reputation and demand for a product or service, and so produces a sales revenue that pays for the cost of advertising. It is in the inevitable nature of advertising that it is *promotional*; that is, it puts the product or its performance in a favourable light. What is needed is to ensure that such promotion is truthful in substance and honest in implication, and that the impression given by words, pictures or nuances is not such as to mislead reasonable people (who themselves are well aware of the partisan nature of advertising) into unwise purchases; but at the same time to ensure that the consumer has access to knowledge of what is on offer.

Unfortunately the exact terms of the Directive go much further than this objective. It is said in the Memorandum covering the Directive that it was designed to propose 'minimum rules'. In fact, the proposed rules represent a considerable sharpening of the legislation about advertising as it now exists in the Community as a whole. It is for these reasons that our Associations feel bound to ask for some fairly major revisions of the text of the Directive, as detailed in the following pages.

There is only one further general comment we would wish to make. Every country in the Community already has laws (or is in the process of passing laws) against misleading advertising. These provisions appear to be to the satisfaction of the national governments, and they have the advantage, in what is essentially a subjective area of criteria, of meeting the differing needs and cultural requirements of the different nations. We wonder whether any good purpose will be served by trying to 'harmonise' this legislation *in detail*. There is very little substance in the argument for harmonisation outlined in Section 2 of the covering Memorandum, referring to the free movement of goods and services. The occasions when any advertising campaign can be planned to cover all the Community countries are few and far between. Differences in the marketing situation, in language, in cultural reactions to words and pictures, are too great. It is common practice in the business to re-examine every proposed campaign when considering its suitability for some other country, and there has been no problem in taking into this re-examination the question whether the laws of that other country require some special amendment in addition to those necessitated by other factors. In practice they very seldom do, because the criteria of what is misleading or unfair are much the same everywhere in the Community and the ICC Code is used internationally as a guide. While we accept that 'harmonisation' is an integral part of the Community's policy, we believe that the harmonisation of a simple basic law, with maximum national flexibility in operation, would secure the purposes of this particular case and of the Treaty of Rome better than one which prescribes as much detail as the present Directive.

II. STUDY OF CLAUSES IN THE DIRECTIVE

In this Memorandum we are confining ourselves to the broad issues raised by certain Articles and Clauses. We have made no attempt yet to deal with the details of wording which may need further amendment and clarification.

Article 1 – No broad comment.

Article 2

Paragraph 1 – We believe that it is necessary to have a strict division between editorial content and advertising. Therefore, we would suggest that the word 'paid' be inserted before 'communication' which corresponds with the common business practice all over the world.

In our opinion it would be of value to indicate that the Directive shall be applicable to both public and private enterprises and also charitable institutions. As the Directive now is drafted it seems to embrace only misleading and unfair advertising by private individuals in the course of occasional commercial transactions. We would doubt that this is desirable.

Article 3 – The inclusion of the words 'by omission' in a law – and this relates also to Article 4(b) referring to the 'insufficient information' – create a new dimension to the concept of 'misleading' and one which would contribute seriously to the risk we mentioned in our Introduction of creating great difficulties for all advertising. It is all very well to argue that the question of what has been omitted that ought to have been included will be decided by common sense in the courts. The fact is that the letter of this law opens the door to penalties and injunctions for virtually every advertisement ever published, and there is no assurance that in a multiplicity of jurisdictions there will not be many judgements which, based on the letter and not on a common sense interpretation, will create great difficulty in framing advertisements, or at best an endless series of expensive legal appeals.

There is no product, however good and serviceable, which has no negative to it in terms of performance, formula, price or some other factor, or for some people at some time, or on some other ground. Your Memorandum quotes 'Beer is best' as an acceptable advertisement; we feel certain that some courts in some countries would say that a poster saying 'beer is best' is omitting essential cautions. Advertisements, to be effective, have to be simple and preferably short; on television the limitations of time are obvious.

We take the view therefore that either these words 'by omission' should be omitted or else that they should be qualified by definitions of the matter which should not be omitted (where relevant) such as poison, fire or health hazards, attached to the product.

We understand from the Memorandum covering the draft Directive that the test of whether an advertisement is misleading or not should be made with reference to the likelihood of a *reasonable man* being misled by it. This is not, however, what the Directive specifies. There is an important difference between what words may be reasonably understood as saying, which depends on logic and syntax, and what a reasonable man understands them as saying, which depends additionally upon the extent of information he already has and his experience. Target groups for the advertising message vary widely and so does their understanding. We would also urge the inclusion (as in the UK Trade Descriptions Act) of the qualifying words 'in a material degree' applied to the word 'misleading'. There is at present a dangerous vagueness about the whole definition.

Article 4 – We have strong objections against this article.

All experience in the EEC countries shows that there has been no need, to-date, to specify detailed rules as has been done in Article 4. It is quite evident that provisions corresponding to what has been laid down in Article 3 have been sufficient guidance for courts and self-disciplinary bodies to issue judgements in cases of misleading and unfair advertising.

Incidentally, the phrasing of Article 4 is evidently largely derived from scientific literature about the legal usage in the United States, and it carries with it the dangers inherent in any transfer of legal vernacular from one legal system to essentially different ones, and from scientific literature to statute law.

The problem with this Article is that the wording of its clauses is too broad and too rigid. If a case were to be judged on the literal wording of the suggested clauses (b) to (g), it would be virtually impossible for an advertiser to frame a useful advertisement. Moreover, the subjective element, as opposed to objective fact, entering into this judgement would be considerable.

Where provisions like this are interpreted by a Code of Practice Committee, or by an experienced court such as the German Courts, they are treated with common sense and flexibility so that the good intentions are realised, but within the boundaries of normal commercial practice and national traditions and attitudes. But such clauses interpreted by less experienced courts throughout the Community, which treated the letter of the law as rigidly binding, (and who should blame them?) would produce a very different result, which might well create a situation where manufacturers under threat of crinimal and civil penalties, preferred not to risk advertising at all.

In our view Article 4 should be omitted.

Article 5 – We would suggest that it would make a tidier structure to the Directive, if this Article were married with Article 3 thus defining 'Misleading' and 'Unfair' in a single conspectus.

Article 6 – There seems to be a widespread confusion, even within the advertising profession about the term 'comparative advertising'. We would propose that the Directive should be applicable only to cases where there is a comparison in which the other person is either named or otherwise made clearly unambiguously identifiable. Comparative advertising should only be allowed provided that it is not misleading or unfair, denigrating or taking advantage of the goodwill of a competitor. We would, however, like to underline that such comparative advertising, in order to comply with the above rules, can only be done in very rare cases. All experience from the Member States confirms this observation.

Articles 7 and 8 – We cannot accept the present wordings of these two Articles, which represent very substantial sharpening of the legislation now in force in the Member States.

This Directive is, we believe, the first Community document to prescribe legal procedures. We wonder whether it is a wise move and a good precedent, especially in the field of advertising where so many factors contribute to great differences in the systems now in operation in the various Member States, to try to supersede the traditional laws and procedures in such cases, which are working satisfactorily to meet the national needs of each country.

We propose that Articles 7 and 8 should be amalgamated into one article and that the wording of this new article be based on the following observations:

a. The important role of self-disciplinary controls has been fully recognised in Section III:1 of the Memorandum. The Directive should, therefore, go much further than the present wording, to encourage and acknowledge self-disciplinary controls as a means of implementation of the Directive.

b. We fully agree that the Directive should provide for the speediest possible process, by court order or some alternative method as Member States consider appropriate, against the publication or further publication of misleading or unfair advertisements, unless suitably amended, as a result of decisions by Courts or self-disciplinary bodies.

c. The right to initiate criminal proceedings should be reserved to a public prosecutor or equivalent public authority.

d. Finally the paragraph 7(d) is a dubious compromise in its wording between those who favour 'corrective' advertising and those who do not, and must lead to some rather ridiculous decisions. You will be aware of course that our Associations are totally opposed to the principle of admitting 'corrective advertising' as a penalty as explained in earlier memorandums.

e.   The Directive should leave to Member States, as far as other remedies are concerned, to choose the measures of enforcement which are appropriate within their own legal system.

Article 9 – We believe that it would be appropriate to leave more time than 12 months for bringing into force the measures necessary to comply with the Directive.

Articles 10 and 11 – No comment.

Conclusion – We appreciate that the effect of our comments above may appear to be somewhat negative and unconstructive. We have, therefore, framed a series of eight considerations on which, in our view, a harmonised law would be effective and helpful and would ensure the benefits of honest advertising for manufacturers and for consumers. These proposals have been set out in a letter which we are sending to Mr. F. Braun, covering this Memorandum.

Appendix IV

Explanatory Memorandum Proposal for a Directive on Misleading and Unfair advertising

I. INTRODUCTION

1. Advertising is an integral part of the system of mass production and distribution serving the general public. Manufacturers of goods and providers of services need the opportunity to inform and remind the public of what they have to offer. Such a system of information is useful to the economics of production. Consumers need information on goods and services so that they can make their choice between the many alternatives.

    Advertising has the additional effect of stabilizing employment by ensuring the steady disposal of production; it provides the basis for competition in the marketplace, and encourages product development and innovation and the provision of low-cost goods and services previously regarded as too expensive for the mass market. In addition, advertising makes a vital contribution towards the cost of the media.

2. However, the process can give full value to the public only if advertising is honest and truthful. Should advertisers give false or misleading information, consumers might be led to buy something which they would not otherwise have bought. Furthermore, those who advertise in this way secure an advantage over competitors because consumers may leave out of consideration what the latter have to offer precisely because of this advertising's influence on them.

3. Unfair advertising makes use of inadmissible means to influence consumer behaviour in the marketplace, especially by giving improper information about competitors or by exploiting the trust or credulity of consumers.

    Misleading advertising and unfair advertising are improper ways of influencing the market process; consumers and also competitors and the public in general must be protected against them.

II. THE LEGAL SITUATION IN THE MEMBER STATES

4. Misleading and unfair advertising is generally considered illegal in the Member States. A feature of the present legal situation is that legislation on advertising, and in particular misleading and deceptive advertising, is not set out in a special law but embodied in many laws with a general or specific objective, e.g. laws on fair competition, food, cosmetics, pharmaceuticals, chemicals, etc. For this reason, only a few of the major laws of Member States can be cited below.

5. In *France* the 'Loi d'orientation du commerce et de l'artisanat' of 1973 forbids advertisement containing false or misleading statements. Infringements are prosecuted under criminal law. Injunctions may be issued against those who advertise using misleading statements. When a court takes a decision on an infringement of the ban on misleading or false advertising it may require the publication of corrective statements. Consumer associations have a right of action in the general interest of consumers. A draft law now under discussion provides for a considerable reinforcement of criminal sanctions; in future, fines could be as much as 50% of the outlay on the advertising.

6. In *Belgium* the 'Loi sur les pratiques commerciales' of 1971 forbids the misleading advertising of movable property. Infringements are prosecuted under criminal law. Associations also have a right of action. In Belgium and in *Luxembourg* there are also many specific laws for special sets of circumstances. The competition legislation of both countries includes general clauses for the protection of competitors and consumers.

7. In *Italy*, the general clauses against unfair competition of Article 2598 No.3 and the more specific provision of Article 2598 No.2 of the Codice Civile cover individual cases of misleading advertising. The provisions seek to protect competitors rather than consumers, but there are specific provisions in economic administrative law to protect consumers.

8. In the *Netherlands* there is no general legislation on misleading advertising. Under Article 1404 of the Burgerlijk Wetboek misleading advertising may constitute an illicit act whereby the person responsible is liable to pay compensation. Article 328 bis of the Wetboek of Strafrecht forbids misleading the public for the purpose of gaining a competitive advantage.

   A draft law, 'Regelen omtrent de privaatrechtelijke bescherming tegen misleidende reclame', has been under discussion since 1975. It makes provision for the addition to the Burgerlijk Wetboek of provisions making misleading advertising illegal, requiring those responsible to pay compensation and enabling the courts to require a corrective statement to be published. Trade and consumer associations are also to have a right of action.

9. In the *United Kingdom*, apart from the common law, which also applies to advertising, over sixty Acts of Parliament and many regulations deal with advertising in general or with individual aspects of advertising. The main general Acts are:

   (i)   the Misrepresentation Act, 1967 which grants a person led to make a contract as a result of misrepresentation concerning a product the right to apply for rescission or claim damages or both, as the case may be;

   (ii) the Trade Descriptions Act, 1968 which bans false descriptions of goods, false or misleading information about products or false statements about certain services, a ban enforced through criminal sanctions;

   (iii) the Fair Trading Act, 1973 which gives the Director-General of Fair Trading extensive powers of investigation in the field of advertising, powers which may lead to the banning of certain practices.

10. In *Ireland* penalties are imposed for false information about products under certain conditions under the Merchandise Marks Acts, 1887, 1931 and 1970, and there is a Bill which makes provision for banning false or misleading advertising of goods or services and for penalties for infringements.

11. In *Germany* the 'Gesetz gegen den unlauteren Wettbewerb' lays down provisions on the problems in question; Article 3 aims at the discontinuation of misleading advertising used as an instrument of competition in business. Article 13 gives trade associations and consumer organizations a right of action against advertisements under specific conditions.

12. In *Denmark* the 'Lov om markedsføring' has been in force since 1975. It provides for the prohibition of business acts contrary to good marketing practice. Improper, incomplete or misleading information likely to influence supply or demand is forbidden, and there are penalties for infringements. A Consumer Ombudsman monitors observance of the law.

III. OBSERVATIONS ON THE DIRECTIVE

1.   *General*

13. This Directive is based on Article 100 of the EEC Treaty. The laws of the Member States on misleading and unfair advertising directly affect the functioning of the common market.

   One of the tasks of the Community is to promote throughout the Community a harmonious development of economic activities and an accelerated raising of the standard of living. Differing degrees of legal protection from country to country for consumers and competitors, whose behaviour is determined by the various rules on fair competition, hinder or prevent the achievement of these goals. Moreover, in view of the development of media techniques, advertising increasingly reaches beyond the frontiers of individual Member States and directly addresses consumers in other Member States. This is particularly true with the products of large firms. Laws which differ from country to country therefore jeopardize the effective protection of those involved in the economic process.

14. The different laws also affect the free movement of goods and services. Differences in the laws make it impossible to plan and conduct advertising campaigns beyond the frontiers of a Member State. If certain advertisements are allowed in one Member State but banned in another it is difficult, particularly in border areas between two or more Member States, to operate a uniform marketing system for goods or services. The greater expense of planning and conducting several advertising campaigns simultaneously also affects the advertiser's competitive position. Furthermore, a skilful salesman may be able to secure competitive advantages over his competitors by exploiting differences in the laws. Equality of competitive opportunities, however, is one of the prerequisites for the common market.

15. On 14 April 1975, the Council of Ministers of the European Communities adopted a 'Preliminary programme of the EEC for a consumer protection and information policy'([1]). In it the Council laid down the following principles, among others: no form of advertising should mislead the consumer; any advertiser should be able to justify, by appropriate means, the validity of any claims he makes; all information provided in advertisements must be accurate.

The Council instructed the Commission to continue its work on the approximation of laws and to submit to the Council appropriate proposals to protect the consumer against false or misleading advertising (Items 19(iv) and (v), 22 and 23 of the programme). The proposal for a Directive is a measure to implement this part of the programme.

16. As implemented the Directive would involve amending legislation in several Member States, the European Parliament and the Economic and Social Committee must be consulted (second paragraph of Article 100 of the EEC Treaty).

([1]) OJ C 92, 25.4.1975, p.1.

2. *Commentary on the individual Articles*

Article 1

This article defines the objective of the Directive, which is the protection of the consumer, persons carrying on a trade, business or profession as well as the interests of the public in general, against unfair and misleading advertising. The choice of remedy and the decision whether these measures are to be under civil law, criminal law or administrative law are left to the discretion of Member States.

Article 2

This article contains definitions of the most important concepts used in the Directive.

The definition of *advertising* is broad in order to cover the diversity of advertisers and media. No reference is made to the number of persons addressed by an announcement to be regarded as advertising.

Since such announcements must be made 'in the course of carrying on a trade, business or profession for the purpose of promoting the supply of goods and services' neither political advertising nor advertising by private individuals falls within the scope of the Directive. The same applies to reports on comparative tests by independent organizations, since they do not have the task of promoting the sale of goods or services.

Editorial matter in newspapers, on the radio or on television will not usually be covered by the Directive either, not being designed to promote the sale of goods or services. The opposite is true where material is ordered and paid for by an advertiser. Individual cases in which an announcement presented in the form of editorial matter nevertheless has to be regarded as advertising because of its entended purpose — a purpose recognizable from the contents — are not to be singled out by means of a definition, rather will a decision on the matter be left to the discretion of the courts or other competent authorities, on the basis of an assessment of all the facts of the case.

The concept of *'misleading advertising'* is based on the misleading nature of the advertising, having regard to its total effect. Thus a false announcement, say, in an advertisement is not nullified by a supplementary or corrective statement elsewhere, in an out-of-the-way place.

Whether an advertisement is misleading or likely to mislead depends on who is addressed or reached by it. Provision is made for only one exception to this rule, i.e., where it could not reasonably be foreseen that certain persons would be reached by an advertisement. Advertising exclusively for a specialist audience may be presented in ways which are not readily comprehensible to the layman, and may mislead him in some circumstances. If it cannot be foreseen that such an advertisement will reach a non-specialist audience it is not to be considered misleading if nevertheless it comes to the notice of a layman.

The form of words 'unless . . .' has been chosen deliberately in order to stress the exceptional nature of this provision.

Article 3 and Article 4 should also be considered in determining whether an advertisement is misleading.

'Unfair advertising' is considered illegal in all the Member States, although the concept has different meanings. Often, an advertisement is unfair because personal attacks are made on competitors or improper references are made to their commercial activities. However, unfair advertising also prejudices the interests of consumers. Playing on the anxieties of a consumer, or exploiting his consumer's lack of experience, for example, gives the advertiser an unjustified competitive advantage over competitors, while prejudicing the interests of consumers whose decisions are influenced by subjective factors.

The languague of subparagraph (e) is general to cover cases which are not expressly mentioned in the above definition but which, at the discretion of a court or of another competent authority, must also be regarded as unfair advertising.

The definition of 'goods' includes both movable and immovable property. Advertising which publicizes rights and obligations includes in particular advertising which publicizes specific trade marks or names.

Article 3

This Article contains a non-exhaustive list of aspects which are to be taken into consideration in determining whether advertising is misleading or unfair. Those called upon to assess advertising are therefore obliged to examine in each case the features of advertising mentioned in this Article.

Paragraph 2 mentions a particularly important case of misleading advertising. Indeed a false impression can equally well be produced by the omission of material information. For this reason, such omission is also to be regarded as misleading. The advertiser is at fault in this case because he could have prevented the misunderstanding by providing full information for the persons addressed or reached. An advertisement is also misleading if, because information is omitted, expectations are aroused which the advertiser cannot satisfy. This would apply, for example, to an advertisement publicising the sale of a product at a special price when the advertiser has in stock only a few of the articles concerned, but does not make this fact known and thus arouses in consumers the expectation that he has a reasonable supply.

Article 4

The Article indicates that comparative advertising *per se* is neither misleading nor unfair. Indeed, comparative advertising may give the consumer useful and valuable information about goods and services and help him decide what to buy. Moreover, comparative advertising may also be in the interest of competitors, by giving them an opportunity to bring out more clearly the features of their products. It therefore seems appropriate for comparative advertising to be declared admissible under certain conditions.

The first condition of admissibility is that it compares material points. It is not enough to compare some insignificant aspect of two products, since such a comparison does not really give the consumer or the public in general more information. As the second condition is a comparison of 'verifiable' details the advertising statement 'Product X is better than product Y' would not be admissible either. Moreover, comparative advertising must also respect the general principles regarding misleading and unfair advertising.

Comparative tests carried out by consumer organisations or the editorial staff of newspapers are not 'advertising' within the meaning of the Directive and so do not fall within the scope of Article 4.

Article 5

This Article relates to measures against misleading or unfair advertising. The choice of remedies is left to each Member State, insofar as these are adequate and effective measures.

The second paragraph gives those affected by misleading and unfair advertising a right of action. The same right is to be given to associations with a legitimate interest in the matter, i.e. consumer organisations and trade associations in particular. Experience shows that individual consumers are rarely prepared to take a matter of misleading and unfair advertising to court, since they do not as a rule suffer financial loss from individual advertisements.

The right of action of associations seems a suitable means of ensuring that action is taken against misleading and unfair advertising in general, thereby providing effective protection for consumers and competitors.

The third paragraph lists three of the measures which the Member States are to adopt, as a minimum requirement, in order to take effective action against misleading and unfair advertising.

Subparagraph 1 concerns decisions on the discontinuation of misleading and unfair advertising. Such decisions cannot be made dependent on whether the advertiser (culpably) acted deliberately or negligently, since − where the protection of consumers and competitors is concerned − all that matters is the effect of the advertising and not the reasons for the use of misleading or unfair advertising material. To make it possible to stop advertising campaigns quickly, if necessary, and therefore to prevent damage from arising or being aggravated, provision is made for decisions on the discontinuation of advertisements to be taken by an expedited procedure.

Subparagraph 2 enables courts to require the publication of their decisions or of corrective statements. In certain cases, corrective statements may offset the effect of a misleading or unfair advertisement, and therefore to a large extent restore the competitive situation to its state before the misleading or unfair advertisement was made. Moreover, the bad publicity attaching to a corrective statement would discourage advertisers from using misleading or unfair information. The question of when it is appropriate for courts to decide on the publication of corrective statements in specific cases must be left to their discretion.

Subparagraph 3 seeks to ensure that the civil law, administrative law or criminal law sanctions are sufficient to deter advertisers from any sort of misleading or unfair advertising. Consequently, the scale of the advertising, the extent of the prejudice and the advertiser's economic benefit are also to be taken into consideration when sanctions are imposed.

Article 6

As a general rule, the burden of proof of the misleading and unfair nature of an advertisement lies with the plaintiff. Article 6 makes an exception to this rule, by providing for a reversal of the burden of proof in one particular case. Any advertiser who makes a factual claim must bear the consequences if the validity of his claim cannot be proved. This reversal of the burden of proof is not unreasonable, since the advertiser has it in his power to avert such consequences by exercising discrimination in his choice of advertising material. Consumers or competitors, on the other hand, are in no position to prove that a factual claim is wide of the mark. An advertiser claiming, for example, that his product has no side effects or has been scientifically tested is in a better position to prove the accuracy of these claims, say by supplying research findings. If he is not in a position to do so it is therefore to be expected that he will not make such factual claims in his advertisements.

Use of the expression 'burden of proof' indicates that the burden of proof is reversed only in case of dispute, i.e. in proceedings before courts, an Ombudsman, or an authority hearing complaints, etc. Of course, this provision does not in any way oblige the advertiser to provide information to a competitor or a consumer. It must not be used for discovering information or manufacturing processes or other business secrets.

Article 7

This Article specifically mentions bodies set up by business circles for the self-policing of advertising, thereby recognizing these bodies and their usefulness. Neither their existence nor their scope will be affected by the provisions adopted to implement the Directive. They will be able to go about their business exactly as before. Article 7 simply specifies that those affected by misleading and unfair advertising shall in any case have the right to refer the matter to independent courts.

Article 8

This Article allows the Member States, exceptionally, to adopt or maintain more exacting provisions to protect the consumer against misleading or unfair advertising. More exacting provisions may be justified as regards the advertising of certain products, e.g. narcotics, weapons, medicines, tobacco products, and food, or as regards advertising through certain media, e.g. on television or by telephone.

Appendix V

Explanatory Memorandum Amendment Proposal for a Directive on Misleading and Unfair advertising

Amendment to the proposal for a Council Directive relating to the approximation of laws, regulations and administrative provisions of the Member States concerning Misleading and Unfair Advertising (submitted by the Commission to the Council pursuant to Article 149(2) of the EEC Treaty)

SUMMARY

The text submitted for approval by the Commission and transmitted to the Council contains amendments to the proposed Directive concerning Misleading and Unfair Advertising (OJ No C 70, 21.3.1978, p.4). The amendments follow in large part the requests made by Parliament and the Economic and Social Committee. Many cover points of detail. However, the amendment to Article 5 of the Directive introduces a substantial change because it admits an alternative to litigation as a means of controlling misleading and unfair advertising in the form of an administrative authority. This is the existing and preferred form of control in some Member States and its omission from the original text of the Directive created a good deal of controversy. Its inclusion under the proposed amendment to Article 5 would not rule out recourse to a court of law if the administrative authority failed to act properly, effectively or at all.

EXPLANATORY MEMORANDUM

I. INTRODUCTION

The amendments in the text which follows reflect certain requests resulting from the Opinion of the Economic and Social Committee([1]) and the Resolution of the European Parliament([2]).

II. COMMENTS ON THE ARTICLES

Article 1

Parliament has requested that the expression 'objective of the Directive' should be replaced by 'the *purpose* of this Directive' in the English text only of the Directive. It is considered unnecessary for the Commission to introduce the amendment under the Article 149(2) procedure. Although this drafting is more elegant, it does not change the meaning of the original text. In this case, as with other suggested drafting improvements of the same nature, it could be implemented in the Council when revised texts are prepared.

Article 2

'Advertising'

In order to clarify the point that advertising may be oral or in writing, or represented pictorially, it is proposed to amplify the text to indicate that for the purposes of the Directive advertising means the making of a representation in any form.

Parliament has also requested an amendment to indicate that advertising is directed at the general public or a part thereof. However, this is inconsistent with Article 1, which also refers to other interests, and would thus lead to difficulties of interpretation. It is, therefore, proposed not to incorporate this amendment.

'Misleading advertising'

In the view of the Economic and Social Committee, this definition should not be subject to a limitation excluding persons who would not foreseeably be reached by the advertising in question. However, it would seem better to retain the definition in its present form. In the case of trade or specialised advertising, advertisers are reasonably entitled to assume a certain degree of knowledge on the part of the persons addressed and should not have to frame their advertisements on the assumption that they might be seen by a member of the general public.

([1]) Dated 5 April 1979.
([2]) Dated 8 May 1979.

'Unfair advertising'

(a) Parliament requests the deletion of 'improper' from the original text, so that any reference to nationality etc., which casts discredit on another person, falls within the definition of unfair advertising. This amendment clarifies the text and it is proposed that it should be adopted.

(c) Both the Economic and Social Committee and Parliament have made the point that appeals to sentiments of fear may be justifiable to indicate to the public the need to take certain protective measures, for example, to acquire accident or life insurance. Only where such sentiments are abused is advertising unfair. It is proposed that the text be amended in this sense.

(d) Parliament has requested that this part of the definition, which was omitted in error from the original text in the French version, should specifically relate to discrimination on the grounds of sex, and should also incorporate forms of discrimination included in paragraph (c) of the original text. It is proposed to accept this precise re-formulation, which also complies more closely with existing laws in some Member States and in this respect responds to the view expressed by the Economic and Social Committee.

(e) In the original text, this paragraph referred to exploiting the trust, credulity or lack of experience of a consumer. However, the term 'exploits' is neutral and both Parliament and the Economic and Social Committee request that the text should indicate that advertising is unfair where it abuses the trust, credulity or lack of experience of consumers. It is proposed to adopt this amendment.

Parliament has also requested that the second part of paragraph (e) should be deleted altogether. The effect of the paragraph is to introduce a general definition of unfair advertising, which on one view is too broad and vague. On the other hand, others take the view that the definition of unfair advertising *should be* expressed in general terms so as to permit the law some scope for development. Since this is a point of principle for some Member States, it is proposed that it should be left for discussion in the Council.

'Goods'

The Economic and Social Committee has also called for the inclusion in the Directive of a definition of services. However, since the word 'services' is used in the Directive in its natural and ordinary meaning, it is not proposed to adopt this request.

Article 3(1)

The English text only should be amended to be consistent with the revised definition of 'advertising' in Article 2.

Article 3(2)

Both Parliament and the Economic and Social Committee have requested that an advertisement shall be regarded as misleading when it is not readily recognisable as an advertisement. It is proposed to adopt this amendment.

The original text indicates that an advertisement is to be regarded as misleading when by omission it arouses expectations which the advertiser cannot satisfy. As such expectations may be entirely subjective, it is proposed to amend the original text to refer to *reasonable* expectations which the advertised goods or services cannot satisfy.

Article 4

This Article concerns comparative advertising, which the Economic and Social Committee requests should be authorised for a trial period. It is not proposed to adopt this request. Comparative advertising is already legal in a number of Member States. The question of authorisation, therefore, does not arise for those countries and a limited authorisation only for Member States which do not recognise comparative advertising as legal would be inappropriate in a Directive for the approximation of laws.

Article 5

The original text of the Directive proposed that persons or associations concerned by misleading advertising should be able to seek recourse in a court of law. However, some countries prefer to exercise control through an administrative authority. This is already the case, for example in Denmark where the Consumer Ombudsman has this task, and in the United Kingdom, where the Independent Broadcasting Authority has a statutory duty to control broadcast advertising. Parliament has proposed that this system should continue to be possible under the Directive as an alternative to litigation at first instance, provided that certain conditions are fulfilled. They are detailed in the proposed Parliamentary amendments to Article 5, and make it clear that if the administrative authority fails to fulfil or abuses its function, the courts shall have the last word.

It is proposed to adopt the Parliamentary amendment with two reservations. The first concerns the proposal that an administrative authority may be the chosen means of control only in those countries where it already exists. However, if control by an administrative authority is viable, it should be open to any Member State to choose it. Secondly, it would be desirable to clarify the text by indicating that an administrative authority must apply reasonable standards. In its present form, the Parliamentary amendment refers to the improper exercise of powers and this could be understood as limited to procedural abuses only.

The original text was intended to exclude the need to prove that a misleading advertisement had been published intentionally or negligently. However, in referring to the absence of fault it has been misunderstood and it is proposed to clarify the text accordingly.

Article 6

Parliament has proposed that this Article should be renumbered 7, and that the original Article 7 should be renumbered Article 6. Nothing in the Directive is intended to damage the self-regulatory system of control operated by the advertising industry in several Member States, and Article 7 is to this effect. To clarify the point, Parliament has proposed that the original Article 7 should stand next to Article 5 in the revised text. It is proposed to follow this request.

Article 7

The original Article 6 now becomes Article 7. Because of the implications of the reversal of the onus of proof proposed in this Article, Parliament requests that its provisions be limited to civil and administrative cases. This amendment should be accepted. In some Member States it is a fundamental principle of criminal law that the prosecution must prove the guilt of the accused and that the accused should not be obliged to prove his innocence. However, even in its amended version, the Directive does not oblige Member States to refrain from reversing the burden of proof in criminal cases.

Article 9

The Economic and Social Committee recommends that the Directive should allow Member States 24 months to comply with its provisions. It is, therefore, proposed to amend the text in this sense. It is also proposed to accept the Parliamentary amendment which would require Member States to communicate to the Commission the texts of all provisions of national law which they adopt in the field covered by the Directive.

Appendix V

COMMISSION

Amendment to the Proposal for a Council Directive relating to the approximation of the laws, regulations and administrative provisions of the Member States concerning misleading and unfair advertising(¹)

Original text	Amended text
ARTICLE 2	ARTICLE 2
For the purpose of this Directive:	For the purpose of this Directive:
— 'Advertising' means the making of any pronouncement in the course of a trade, business or profession for the purpose of promoting the supply of goods or services;	— 'Advertising' means the making of a *representation in any form* in the course of a trade, business or profession for the purpose of promoting the supply of goods or services;
— 'Misleading advertising' means any advertising which is entirely or partially false or which, having regard to its total effect, including its presentation, misleads or is likely to mislead persons addressed or reached thereby, unless it could not reasonably be foreseen that these persons would be reached thereby;	Unchanged.
— 'Unfair advertising' means any advertising which:	— 'Unfair advertising' means any advertising which:
(a) casts discredit on another person by improper reference to his nationality, origin, private life or good name; or	(a) casts discredit on another person by (*1 word deleted*) reference to his nationality, origin, private life or good name; or
(b) injures or is likely to injure the commercial reputation of another person by false statements or defamatory comments concerning his firm, goods or services; or	(b) Unchanged.
(c) appeals to sentiments of fear, or promotes social or religious discrimination; or	(c) *abuses or unjustifiably arouses sentiments of fear*; or
(d) clearly infringes the principles of the social, economic and cultural equality of the sexes; or	(d) *promotes discrimination on grounds of sex, race or religion*; or
(e) exploits the trust, credulity or lack of experience of a consumer, or influences or is likely to influence a consumer or the public in general in any other improper manner;	(e) *abuses* the trust, credulity or lack of experience of a consumer, or influences or is likely to influence a consumer or the public in general in any other improper manner;
— 'Goods' means property of any kind, whether movable or immovable, and any rights or obligations relating to property.	— Unchanged.

(¹) OJ No C 70, 21 March 1978, p.4.

Original text	Amended text

ARTICLE 3 — ARTICLE 3

ARTICLE 3	**ARTICLE 3**
1. In the determining whether advertising is misleading or unfair, pronouncements shall be taken into consideration concerning in particular:	1. In determining whether advertising is misleading or unfair, *representations* shall be taken into consideration concerning in particular: (English text only)
(a) The characteristics of the goods or services, such as nature, performance, composition, method and date of manufacture of provision, fitness for purpose, usability, quantity, quality, geographical or commercial origin, properties and the results to be expected from use;	Unchanged.
(b) the conditions of supply of the goods or services, such as value and price, conditions of contract and of guarantee;	Unchanged.
(c) the nature, attributes and rights of the advertiser, such as his identity, solvency, abilities, ownership of intellectual property rights or awards and distinctions.	Unchanged.
2. Advertising shall in particular be regarded as misleading when it omits material information, and, by reason of that omission, gives a false impression or arouses expectations which the advertiser cannot satisfy.	2. Advertising shall in particular be regarded as misleading when *it is not readily recognisable as an advertisement or* when it omits material information, and, by reason of that omission, gives a false impression or arouses *reasonable* expectations which the *advertised goods or services* cannot satisfy.

ARTICLE 5 — ARTICLE 5

ARTICLE 5	**ARTICLE 5**
Member States shall adopt adequate and effective laws against misleading and unfair advertising.	Member States shall adopt adequate and effective laws against misleading and unfair advertising.
Such laws shall provide persons affected by misleading or unfair advertising, as well as associations with a legitimate interest in the matter, with quick, effective and inexpensive facilities for initiating appropriate legal proceedings against misleading and unfair advertising.	Such laws shall provide persons affected by misleading or unfair advertising as well as associations with a legitimate interest in the matter, with quick, effective and inexpensive facilities for either *(a)* initiating appropriate legal proceedings against misleading or unfair advertising; or *(b) bringing the matter before an administrative authority with adequate powers.*

Original text	Amended text

Member States shall in particular ensure that:
- the courts are enabled, even without proof of fault or of actual prejudice:

(a) to order the prohibition or cessation of misleading or unfair advertising; and
(b) to take such a decision under an accelerated procedure, with an interim or final effect;
- the courts are enabled:

(a) to require publication of a corrective statement; and
(b) to require publication of their decision either in full or in part and in such form as they may judge adequate;
- the sanctions for infringing these laws are a sufficient deterrent, and, where appropriate, take into account the financial outlay on the advertising, the extent of the damage and any profit resulting from the advertising.

- the courts *or the administrative authority, as appropriate*, are enabled, even without proof of *intention or negligence* of actual prejudice:

(a) to order the prohibition or cessation of misleading or unfair advertising; and
(b) to take such a decision under an accelerated procedure, with an interim or final effect;
- the courts *or the administrative authority, as appropriate*, are enabled:

(a) to require publication of a corrective statement; and
(b) to require publication of their decision either in full or in part and in such form as they may judge adequate;

Member States shall ensure that the consequences of infringing laws and decisions in the field of misleading and unfair advertising take into account the extent of the harm.

Where the abovementioned powers are entrusted to an administrative authority, the authority shall not be controlled by advertising interests, shall be obliged to give reasons for its decisions, and shall be under a duty to exercise its powers so as effectively to control misleading and unfair advertising; and procedures shall exist whereby improper exercise by the authority of its power or improper failure by the authority to exercise its powers or to apply reasonable standards can be reviewed by the courts at the request of the parties.

ARTICLE 6

Originally Article 7 – Unchanged.

ARTICLE 6

ARTICLE 7
(Originally Article 6)

Where the advertiser makes a factual claim, the burden of proof that his claim is correct shall lie with him.

Where the advertiser makes a factual claim, the burden of proof that his claim is correct shall *in civil and administrative proceedings* lie with him.

Original text	Amended text
ARTICLE 9	ARTICLE 9
Member States shall bring into force the measures necessary to comply with this Directive within eighteen months of its notification and shall forthwith inform the Commission thereof.	Member States shall bring into force the measures necessary to comply with this Directive within twenty-four months of its notification and shall forthwith inform the Commission thereof.
Member States shall communicate to the Commission the text of the main provisions of national law which they adopt in the field covered by this Directive.	Member States shall communicate to the Commission the text *of all provisions* of national law which they adopt in the field covered by this Directive.

Appendix VI

Second consumer protection and information program of the EEC

THE COUNCIL OF THE EUROPEAN COMMUNITIES,

Having regard to the Treaty establishing the European Economic Community,

Having regard to the proposal from the Commission([1]),

Having regard to the opinion of the European Parliament([2]),

Having regard to the opinion of the Economic and Social Committee([3]),

Whereas, pursuant to Article 2 of the Treaty, the task of the European Economic Community is to promote throughout the Community a harmonious development of economic activities, a continuous and balanced expansion and an accelerated raising of the standard of living;

Whereas the improvement of the quality of life is one of the tasks of the Community and as such implies protecting the health, safety and economic interests of the consumer;

Whereas fulfilment of this task requires a consumer protection and information policy to be implemented at Community level;

Whereas the Heads of State or of Government, meeting in Paris on 19 and 20 October 1972, confirmed this requirement by calling upon the institutions of the Communities to strengthen and coordinate measures for consumer protection;

([1]) OJ No C 218, 30.8.1979, p.3.
([2]) OJ No C 291, 10.11.1980, p.35.
([3]) OJ No C 83, 2.4.1980, p.24.

Whereas the Council Resolution of 14 April 1975 provides for the implementation of a preliminary programme of the European Economic Community for a consumer protection and information policy(¹);

Whereas the aims and principles of this policy have already been approved by the Council;

Whereas the preliminary programme of 14 April 1975 should be brought up to date to ensure the continuity of the measures already undertaken and enable new tasks to be undertaken in the years 1981 to 1986;

APPROVES the guidelines set out in the annexed action programme;

NOTES that the Commission will submit suitable proposals for the effective implementation of the programme;

UNDERTAKES to act on these proposals, if possible within nine months of the date on which they are forwarded by the Commission or, if the case arises, of the date on which the opinions of the European Parliament and the Economic and Social Committee are forwarded.

ANNEX

SECOND PROGRAMME OF THE EUROPEAN ECONOMIC COMMUNITY FOR A CONSUMER PROTECTION AND INFORMATION POLICY

I. INTRODUCTION

1. The adoption by the Council on 14 April 1975 of a preliminary four-year programme of the Economic and Social Committee for a consumer protection and information policy was the first stage in the Community's measures on behalf of customers.

    Measures taken or scheduled in accordance with the preliminary programme contribute towards improving the consumer's situation by protecting his health, his safety and his economic interest, by providing him with appropriate information and education, and by giving him a voice in decisions which involve him.

(¹) OJ No C 92, 25.4.1975, p.1.

Very often these measures have also resulted in either eliminating non-tariff barriers to trade or harmonizing the rules of competition by which manufacturers and retailers must abide.

2. The purpose of this programme is to enable the Community to continue and intensify its measures in this field and to help establish conditions for improved consultation between consumers on the one hand and manufacturers and retailers on the other.

   This programme, for which it is appropriate to envisage a duration of five years if it is to be fully implemented, retains in its entirety the inspiration, objectives and underlying principles of the first. Like its predecessor, it is primarily concerned with the need to enable the consumer to act with full knowledge of the facts, and to hold the balance between market forces. To do this, he must be able to exercise the five basic rights which the preliminary programme conferred on him. They are:

   — the right to protection of health and safety;

   — the right to protection of economic interests;

   — the right of redress;

   — the right to information and education; and

   — the right of representation (the right to be heard).

3. Nevertheless in the current difficult economic situation, a situation characterized by a slowdown in incomes growth, continuing unemployment, and the various economic consequences of the energy dependence which affects most Member States, consumers are obliged to pay more attention to the way in which they use their income, particularly as regards the quality of goods and services bought, so as to derive the maximum benefit from it. Very special importance therefore attaches in this context to action relating to consumer protection with regard to the quality of goods and services, the conditions affecting their supply, and the provision of information about them. It follows, moreover, that, where appropriate, more attention than previously must be given to two questions which have assumed considerable importance for the consumer in the current economic climate, namely:

   — the price of goods and services, regarding which the Community already exerts some influence, notably in the common agricultural policy but also in the competition policy;

   — the quality of services — both public and private — which account for an ever-growing share of household expenditure.

4. Moreover, without in any way ceasing to ensure that the rights listed above are complied with, the consumer policy, which has hitherto been mainly defensive, should become more positive and more open to a dialogue in order to establish the conditions in which the consumer can become a participant in the preparation and implementation of important economic decisions which concern him first and foremost as a buyer or a user, and which very largely determine his individual or collective living conditions. This approach corresponds to the spirit and the letter of the definition of the consumer given in the preliminary programme(¹). There are, however, several prerequisites to such a policy, notably:

    (1) that while continuing to voice its proper concerns, the consumer movement will progressively take into account the economic and social implications of the decisions on which it might wish to be consulted;

    (2) political and economic decision-makers should be willing to take consumers' views into account through the appropriate channels when preparing and implementing decisions which are likely to affect consumers' interests in the short or long term.

5. The Community's efforts should be directed towards fulfilling these prerequisites. Steps have already been taken along these lines. At Community level, consumer opinion has been taken more and more into consideration by Community bodies and institutions. For their part, consumer organizations are being progressively drawn into considering consumer policy in a wider context. Nevertheless, there is still some way to go. In particular the Community should try to encourage a dialogue and consultation between representatives from consumers and representatives from producers, distributors and suppliers of public or private services with a view, in certain cases, to arriving at solutions satisfactory to all the parties in question.

6. Although legislation both at national and Community level will still be needed in many cases in order to ensure that the consumer may exercise the fundamental rights listed above and that the market operates properly, the application of certain principles might also be sought by other means, such as the establishment of specific agreements between the various interests held, which would have the advantage of giving consumers additional assurances of good trading practice.

    The Commission will endeavour to facilitate the elaboration and conclusion of such agreements, on an experimental basis, for example, in certain fields of after-sales service and in areas involving aspects of professional ethics.

(¹) 'The consumer is no longer seen merely as a purchaser and user of goods and services for personal, family or group purposes but also as a person concerned with the various facets of society which may affect him either directly or indirectly as a consumer.'

7. Obviously, the use of this voluntary formula should in no case prejudice the application of existing laws and regulations, nor exclude the adoption of statutory and administrative provisions at either national or Community level.

8. To sum up, the new programme is meant to:

   (1)   continue measures to protect and inform consumers, begun under the preliminary programme, the reasons for which and whose objectives and principles can only be confirmed. As a general rule, the Commission endeavours to take account of consumers' interests when framing any policy having a bearing on consumers, notably in regard to agriculture, competition and industrial policy. In such measures, besides questions of safety and quality, the problems posed by prices and their disparities and by the quality and prices of services cannot be ignored. With regard to prices, the Commission should give increasing attention to consumer interests in the definition and in the application of Community policies (agricultural, competition, industrial, etc.) which can influence those interests. It will also be appropriate to ensure that scientific enquiries into price disparities are pursued and made use of to a greater extent than in the past.

   (2)   seek to create the conditions for a better dialogue and closer consultation between representatives of consumers, producers and distributors.

II. IMPLEMENTATION OF THE PROGRAMME

9. The measures proposed in this programme are set out in the order of the objectives aimed at (already stated and approved in the preliminary programme), namely:

   A.   protection of consumers against health and safety hazards;

   B.   protection of consumers' economic interests;

   C.   improvement of the consumer's legal position (help, advice, the right to seek legal remedy);

   D.   improvement of consumer education and information;

   E.   appropriate consultation with and representation of consumers in the framing of decisions affecting their interests.

10. The programme will be carried out, as was the preliminary one, by using the appropriate means laid down in the Treaty. Bearing in mind the number of interests involved, Commission will undertake very wide consultations, notably through its Consultative Committees, before forwarding proposals for implementing measures.

11. In addition, the Commission will not fail to continue its close cooperation with international bodies such as the Council of Europe and the OECD which are concerned with consumer problems and to make use of their contributions in this field.

A. PROTECTION OF CONSUMER AGAINST HEALTH AND SAFETY HAZARDS

12. **Principles**

The preliminary programme laid down the following principles, which remain applicable:

(1) goods and services offered to consumers must be such that, under normal or foreseeable conditions of use, they present no risk to the health or safety of consumers. There should be quick and simple procedures for withdrawing them from the market in the event of their presenting such risks;

in general consumers should be informed in an appropriate manner of any risk liable to result from a foreseeable use of goods and services, taking account of the nature of the goods and services and of the persons for whom they are intended;

(2) the consumer must be protected against physical injury caused by defective products and services supplied by manufacturers of goods and providers of services;

(3) substances or preparations which may be contained in or be added to foodstuffs should be defined and their use regulated, for example by endeavouring to draw up in Community rules, clear and precise positive lists. Any processing which foodstuffs may undergo should also be defined and their use regulated where this is required to protect the consumer;

foodstuffs should not be adulterated or contaminated by packaging or other materials with which they come into contact, by their environment, by the conditions in which they are transported or stored or by persons coming into contact with them, in such a way that they affect the health or safety of consumers or otherwise become unfit for consumption;

(4) machines, appliances and electrical and electronic equipment and any other category of goods which may prejudicially affect the health and safety of consumers either in themselves or by their use, should be covered by special rules and be subject to a procedure recognized or approved by the public authorities (such as type approval or declaration of conformity with harmonized standards or rules) to ensure that they are safe for use;

(5)   certain categories of new products which may prejudicially affect the
       health or safety of consumers should be made subject to special authoriza-
       tion procedures harmonized throughout the Community.

13. **Priority measures**

On the basis of the principles set out above, the Commission will continue to
expand its activities in accordance with the guidelines set out below, its prime
objective being to make consumer goods and services safer to use and to promote consumer health protection. In addition, for goods or services which
appear on the market or are developed in such a way as to jeopardize the safety
or health of consumers, the Commission reserves the right to propose, if need
be, suitable measures to supplement, pursuant to these principles, the priority
measures already planned.

14. 1. **Harmonization of laws on certain products**

The Community will develop and pursue its work on harmonizing the laws on
certain products in order both to encourage the free movement of such goods
and to regulate the marketing and use of substances or products likely to affect
the health or safety of consumers. Harmonizing measures will cover, as required,
the properties of products, notification or approval procedures, methods of
analysis and testing, labelling and safety standards. Moreover, an important
part of these permanent activities is related to the application of Directives
already in force or to be adopted as the programme is implemented, particularly
in the framework of the committees on adaptation to technical progress.

All this work will be carried out with the help of the most reliable and advanced
scientific and technical expertise available. The Commission will thus continue
to consult the Scientific Committees for Animal Nutrition, Food, Pesticides,
Cosmetology, Toxicology and Ecotoxicology.

Harmonization will be directed chiefly towards the following types of product.

15. 1. (a) **Foodstuffs**

The Community has developed two types of action with regard to foodstuffs,
namely horizontal (general measures on additives, materials and objects coming
into contact with foodstuffs, special foods) and vertical (measures on specific
products).

The Commission will continue its work in this field by:

—   monitoring the application of Council Directive 79/112/EEC of 18
     December 1978 on the approximation of the laws of the Member States
     relating to the labelling, presentation and advertising of foodstuffs for
     sale to the ultimate consumer(¹), particularly as regards misleading claims,

(¹) OJ No L 33, 8.2.1979, p.1.

the ingredients of alcoholic beverages, derogations regarding ingredients and the date of minimum durability of products;

— monitoring the adaptation of the Directives adopted to scientific and technical progress;

— introducing other measures on, for example, flavouring, surface sprays used on fruit, vegetables and cheeses, baby foods, deep-frozen foods and pesticide residues;

— putting forward suitable proposals when consumer health problems arise unexpectedly (as has already occurred with erucic acid, vinyl chloride monomer residues and saccharine);

— examining certain nutrition problems (effects of certain foodstuffs on health, food labelling, etc.), in particular as regards consumer education and information; if necessary, it will submit appropriate proposals;

— participating in standardization activities in the Codex alimentarius, with particular reference to the implementation or preparation of guidelines.

16. 1. (b) Cosmetics

Council Directive 76/768/EEC of 27 July 1976 on the approximation of the laws of the Member States relating to cosmetic products([1]) enumerates a number of tasks of a scientific and technical nature which will be performed; these include:

— permitting or prohibiting the substances listed in Annex IV to the Directive which are at present provisionally allowed;

— drawing up, on the basis of scientific and technical research, proposals for lists of authorized substances which could include antioxidants, hair dyes, preservatives and ultraviolet filters, taking into account in particular the problem of sensitization;

— adapting the Directive to technical progress, particularly by introducing the methods of analysis necessary for checking the composition of cosmetic products, by determining criteria of microbiological and chemical purity and methods for checking compliance with these criteria and, finally, possibly by amending Annex II to the Directive, which lists substances which cosmetic products must not contain.

([1]) OJ No L 262, 27.9.1976, p.169.

17. 1. (c) **Textiles**

With regard to the safety of textiles, the Commission will continue to study problems of textile inflammability, with particular reference to health risks liable to result from the use of fire-proofing substances.

The Commission will likewise examine risks arising from the use of raw materials or other substances such as colouring agents.

18. 1. (d) **Toys**

The work already in hand as part of the proposal for a Directive on the approximation of the laws of the Member States concerning toy safety([1]) will be continued and proposals for directives will be prepared on the physical and mechanical safety, inflammability, toxicity and electrical safety of toys.

19. 1. (e) **Pharmaceutical products**

Several Directives have been adopted on pharmaceutical products for human use, particularly on conditions of marketing, provisions on standards and protocols and the colouring agents used. In addition, two proposals for directives are now being discussed on pharmaceutical products for veterinary use which may have indirect influence on consumer health. The Commission will continue its work in this area and in particular submit to the Council a proposal for a Directive on the advertising of pharmaceutical products.

20. 1. (f) **Dangerous substances**

The Commission will continue its work on dangerous substances for which there are already Directives on classification, labelling, packaging and use, and will concentrate on dangerous preparations. In particular, the Commission will study the safety problems associated with household use of products in which such preparations are employed (cleaning materials, for example) and, if necessary, submit appropriate proposals.

21. 1. (g) **Tobacco and alcohol**

After carrying out comparative studies on measures taken or planned by Member States with regard to tobacco and alcohol, the Commission will:

– assess to what extent divergences in measures taken by Member States in regard to these products affect the Community market and, where necessary, make appropriate proposals;

– take such other initiatives, in support of actions undertaken in Member States, as may be appropriate in the more general context of problems associated with the use or abuse of such products by consumers.

([1]) OJ No C 228, 8.9.1980, p.10.

22. 1. (h) **Manufactured products**

The Commission will continue its work on motor vehicle components and other manufactured products likely to affect consumer safety and health.

In particular, the problem of the inflammability of materials used in manufacturing furniture or for fitting out buildings (furnishing materials in general and various internal and external covering materials) will be examined.

23. 2. **Monitoring product safety**

Implementation of measures adopted in various fields concerning the protection of consumer health and safety in respect of which action to harmonize laws has already been taken (food additives, cosmetics and pesticides) requires the national authorities supervising their application constantly to improve the methods used, in line with industrial developments and the advance of scientific knowledge; there are largely similar problems in making such improvements in all the Member States, particularly when it comes to working out ways and means.

The Community should therefore draw up a list of control systems in Member States in order to remedy any difficulties or shortcomings, for example, by developing more effective control methods or by the exchange of experts or information between laboratories.

To this end, the Commission will organize meetings between representatives of specialized laboratories existing in the Member States and, if necessary, submit appropriate proposals to the Council.

24. 3. **Research**

The Commission will continue to examine the results of studies in the various fields likely to further the cause of product safety and, where appropriate, will take steps to coordinate and encourage such studies.

25. 4. **Information on products**

To comply with the principles set out above, the fullest and most objective information possible must be available on the various aspects of product safety. This information should suggest the direction the work should take by facilitating the selection of priorities.

26. (a)   With this in view, the Commission has already sent the Council a proposal for a Decision introducing a Community system of information on accidents in which products are involved, outside the spheres of occupational activities and road traffic[1]; the purpose of this system would be to enable detailed statistics to be compiled.

[1] OJ No C 252, 24.10.1978, p.2.

(b)   In addition, with a view to promoting objective and detailed documentation on the properties of products likely to affect consumer health and safety, the Commission will, by taking appropriate steps, endeavour to survey existing data bank systems, further their development and facilitate access to them.

27. As the information system referred to in point 26 is not designed for adopting emergency measures, the Commission has proposed that a system be set up at Community level for the rapid exchange of information on dangers arising from the use of consumer goods. Such a system would enable the responsible authorities to take necessary measures promptly to ensure public safety.

B. PROTECTION OF THE ECONOMIC INTERESTS OF CONSUMERS

28. Principles

The preliminary programme set out a number of principles which are still relevant:

(1)   purchasers of goods or services should be protected against certain unfair sales practices and in particular against the vendor's standard contracts, the exclusion of essential rights in contracts, harsh conditions of credit, demands for payment for unsolicited goods and high-pressure selling methods;

(2)   the consumer should be protected against damage to his economic interests caused by defective products or unsatisfactory services;

(3)   the presentation and promotion of goods and services, including financial services, should not be designed to mislead, either directly or indirectly, the person to whom they are offered or by whom they have been requested;

(4)   no form of advertising should mislead the potential buyer of the product or service. An advertiser in any medium must be able to justify, by appropriate means, the validity of any claims he makes:[1]

(5)   all information provided on labels at the point of sale or in advertisements must be accurate;

(6)   the consumer is entitled to reliable after-sales service for consumer durables, including the provision of spare parts required to carry out repairs;

(7)   the range of goods available to consumers should be such that as far as possible consumers are offered an adequate choice.

---

[1] This principle will apply in observance of existing criminal law provisions in the Member States.

29. On the basis of these principles and pursuant to the preliminary programme, the Commission has submitted proposals for Directives which are still under discussion by the Council bodies.

    The following are the texts concerned:

    – a proposal for a Directive to protect the consumer in respect of contracts which have been negotiated away from business premises([1]);

    – a proposal for a Directive relating to the approximation of the laws, regulations and administrative provisions of the Member States concerning misleading and unfair advertising([2]);

    – a proposal for a Directive relating to the approximation of the laws, regulations and administrative provisions of Member States concerning liability for defective products([3]);

    – a proposal for a Directive relating to the approximation of the laws, regulations and administrative provisions of the Member States concerning consumer credit([4]).

30. **Continuation of action provided for under the preliminary programme**

    The Commission will pursue the action already begun under the 1975 programme which it has not been able to bring to a conclusion, particularly as regards certain unfair commercial practices.

    The Commission has already started work on unfair terms in contracts, with the help of government experts, as a basis for a Community measure. Meanwhile, legislation has been adopted in several Member States, and the Commission will submit, as a first step, a discussion paper in which it will set out all the problems which this subject involves and the various options open with a view to harmonizing those aspects of competition which may be affected by disparities in this area. After wide-ranging consultations on this discussion paper, the Commission will put forward suitable proposals, where necessary.

31. Within the framework of the general activities already undertaken, the Commission will also study the promotion of the interests of specific groups of underprivileged consumers in order to cater better for their particular needs.

    Action taken by the Commission on competition, pursuant to Articles 85 and 86 of the Treaty, contributes to this end in being opposed to certain business practices likely to have a detrimental effect on consumer prices or in being intended to prevent such practices.

([1]) OJ No C 22, 29.1.1977, p.6.
([2]) OJ No C 70, 21.3.1978, p.4.
([3]) OJ No C 241, 14.10.1976, p.9.
([4]) OJ No C 80, 27.3.1979, p.4.

32. Under the common agricultural policy, the Commission has taken into consideration the effects of the common farm prices and the level of supplies on the Community market on the interests of consumers, as envisaged among the objectives of Article 39 of the Treaty. The Commission has also consulted consumers when drawing up the price proposals submitted to the Council.

    The Commission will continue to take consumer interests into account in the implementation of this policy.

33. In general, it is important to take into consideration the economic repercussions which certain factors such as the scarcity of resources, shorter working hours and the use of new data-processing and telecommunications technology may have on consumption patterns and producer-distributor-consumer relations. The Commission will carry out further studies and will submit suitable proposals, where necessary.

34. **Expansion of Community action on services**

    Because of the growth in the number and importance of services, the part they take up in household expenditure and the opening of the frontiers of Member States to an increasing number of them, there should be a strengthening of consumer protection in this sector, notably in the matter of quality of services and their price transparency([1]).

    Services account for a growing proportion of economic activity in the Member States of the Community, where they employ on average about half the working population and are a field in which manpower often represents a high proportion of added value. The term 'services' in fact covers a very wide range of activities, in which changes in productivity vary considerably from one to another. However, it is possible to identify three broadly common features:

    —   expenditure on services is increasing rapidly in absolute terms and as a proportion of the household budget;

    —   whereas the quality and performance of industrial products can be defined with a relatively high degree of objectivity, any assessment of the quality of a service rendered is often more subjective and thus the comparison becomes less reliable;

    —   a large – sometimes the largest – proportion of services activities consists of collective services where the public sector or the quasi-public sector has a near monopoly on supply and where market forces operate only partially, as regards both the fixing of prices and determination of the quality of the services offered.

([1]) In view of the increasing importance of this sector, the Commission organized a colloquium of consumer organizations on the theme 'The consumer as user of services' in October 1979.

The Commission will study the following three areas and, if appropriate, put forward suitable proposals. With due regard for the significance of such measures for consumer protection and the effects of differences in Member States' legislation on the proper functioning of the common market.

35. (a) **Commercial services connected with products**

The terms of after-sales services for consumer durables are of particular importance, especially in view of the increased useful life of certain goods. With this in mind, the Commission will examine ways of improving the quality of the after-sales service provided by producers and suppliers and by undertakings which carry out maintenance and repairs, in particular as regards the guarantee period, wider use of firm estimates, the drawing up of detailed invoices, product transport and out-of-service costs, and the availability of replacement parts.

The Commission will study the means necessary for this purpose and will take the appropriate steps with a view to improving conditions of warranty on the part of the producer and/or supplier and after-sales service either by legislation or, where appropriate, by agreements between the parties concerned for *inter alia* the improvement of contract terms. Priority will be given to warranties and services associated with motor vehicles and electrical household appliances.

36. (b) **Commercial services not connected with products**

This heading covers a wide variety of activities of increasing importance in meeting the needs of consumers, both as individuals and collectively, particularly tourism, consumer credit and insurance. The Commission will carry out studies on the development of these services and how they are provided. If necessary, the Commission will put suitable proposals to the Council and/or encourage the adoption of voluntary agreements for improving the general conditions under which these services are provided.

37. (c) **Public and quasi-public services**

A number of services essential to consumers are provided by public and quasi-public services, notably electricity, gas and water supplies and transport. In these areas consultation should be encouraged between the main public services and administrative authorities of a commercial character and the representatives of consumers. To this end, the Commission will prepare a report on consumer representation, concentrating on those services which are international in character, with a view to putting forward suitable proposals, where necessary.

C. ADVICE, HELP AND REDRESS

38. **Principles**

The preliminary programme states that 'consumers should receive advice and help in respect of complaints and of injury or damage resulting from purchase or use of defective goods or unsatisfactory services' and that 'consumers are also entitled to proper redress for such injury or damage by means of swift, effective and inexpensive procedures'.

In 1975 the Commission held a symposium on legal and extra-legal means of consumer protection which in particular made it possible to analyse:

- systems of assistance and advice in the Member States;
- systems of redress, arbitration and the amicable settlement of disputes in the Member States;
- the laws of the Member States relating to consumer protection in the courts, particularly the various means of, and procedures for, obtaining legal remedy, including actions brought by consumer associations or other bodies;
- systems and laws of the kind referred to above in certain third countries.

Suggestions put forward at the symposium can be classified under five heads:

1. the need to improve consumer information and education;
2. the need to set up conciliation bodies either to take preventive action to put an end to certain reprehensible practices by amicable arrangement, or to settle by mutual agreement disputes between consumers and tradesmen or suppliers of services;
3. the setting up of arbitration bodies;
4. the simplification of legal procedures for settling disputes over small sums of money;
5. assigning responsibility for consumer protection to consumer groups, public authorities or institutions like the ombudsman.

This matter has already been the subject of a most constructive debate in the European Parliament and the Economic and Social Committee.

Although limited, the Community's action in this area will seek to make a useful contribution to the implementation of suggestions made in the analysis referred to above. The work done by the Council of Europe on legal aid will also be drawn upon, as well as the studies undertaken by the European University Institute in Florence.

39. **Priority measures**

The Commission will continue to study the procedures and channels for obtaining legal remedy which exist in the Member States, particularly with regard to the right of consumer associations to institute legal proceedings, the simplification of court procedures and the processing of individual petitions, the development of amicable settlement procedures and the admissibility of proceedings by consumers against public undertakings administered according to commercial criteria. It will publish a discussion paper on all these matters, taking into account the different experience gained and the procedures applied in the Member States.

The Commission will also continue, where necessary, to encourage national or local schemes facilitating consumers' access to the courts and the settlement of the more common or minor disputes, and will publish the results.

D. CONSUMER INFORMATION AND EDUCATION

40. **Consumer information**

Principles

Sufficient information should be available to the purchaser of goods or services, and to the general public, to enable him to:

— assess the basic features of the goods and services offered, such as the nature, quality, quantity, energy consumption and price;

— make a rational choice between competing products and services;

— use these products and services safely and to his satisfaction;

— claim redress for any injury or damage resulting from the product supplied or service received.

Following a study of the feasibility and value of drawing up general rules on labelling for all mass-consumption non-food products, it would appear to be more useful to work out rules for each specific category of products so that they are more directly related to the properties of each product.

41. **Priority measures**

Under this programme, the Commission will take the following measures:

— include in any proposals on given products or services which it puts to the council special provisions to take account of their specific properties, with the aim of guaranteeing that the consumer receives proper information on the properties and the quality of the goods and services supplied;

- organize consultation meetings between the representatives of consumers, producers, distributors and suppliers of services as a means of promoting the introduction and development of a voluntary labelling system or of any other voluntary means (such as instructions for use or packaging) of informing consumers about the capabilities of certain kinds of products or services;

- encourage cooperation between carrying out comparative testing, particularly in the case of tests on products and services which are available in several Member States at the same time;

- conduct a more general information campaign on national and Community activities which are directly or indirectly relevant to the interests of consumers by:(¹)

  - regularly publishing releases and by holding briefing sessions for radio and television reporters and for the specialized press of consumer associations;

  - organizing meetings of consumer organizations to enable them to discuss the development of the consumer movement in Europe and of consumer protection in the Community;

  - publishing a periodical report on the state of consumer protection in the Community which will cover the work done in this field and the development of the consumer movement at Community and national level.

42. In implementing this programme, particular attention will be paid to information on prices. This is essential for the proper functioning of competition, which can also be expected to have a positive effect in attenuating inflationary forces, and for ensuring a better choice for consumers.

It is important that as far as possible the market itself should be so structured as to facilitate the adjustment of demand to price changes, primarily through increased transparency. This implies in appropriate cases action in three directions:

- the consumer should be informed about the value for money of products and services (particularly as regards conditions of warranty and after-sales services) on offer by means of fuller information on products, wider

---

(¹) As part of its general information policy, the Commission will endeavour to take specific steps to inform the general public of the present Community programme, the activities undertaken and the results obtained.

publication of the results of comparative tests and the provision of information to consumers on identical products which they cannot recognize as such;

– the consumer should be informed about prices themselves by improvement of the regulation on price marking, including prices per unit of measurement, although no encouragement must be given to price-fixing practices that may adversely affect competition;

– the consumer should be informed about price differences, particularly in the localities accessible to him, by the encouragement of local or regional schemes for this purpose.

43. To this end the Commission will take supplementary measures which must in no case be price-control or price-fixing measures but must supply appropriate information to several different sections of the public. The Commission will endeavour to promote private initiatives aimed at improving consumer information on prices and comparative prices at local or regional level.

As regards price formation, the Commission will also continue to exercise its powers with regard to rules of competition under Articles 85 and 86 of the Treaty.

CONSUMER EDUCATION

44. Principle

In this area of policy, the preliminary programme states:

'Facilities should be made available to children as well as to young people and adults to educate them to act as discriminating consumers, capable of making an informed choice of goods and services and conscious of their rights and responsibilities. To this end, consumers should, in particular, benefit from basic information on the principle of modern economics.'

45. Priority measures

1. Given the powers of the Member States with regard to education and the work the Commission has already undertaken, Community action will consist in continuing the wide-ranging exchange of views on national experience and joint consideration of the aims and methods of consumer education in schools.

With this is mind, the Commission will submit to the Council a communication on consumer training.

2. It will look into possibilities in adult education, and in particular into possibilities for televised courses and study leave for officials and members of consumer associations.

3. It will give consideration to the problems which arise for underprivileged consumers.

E. PROMOTION OF CONSUMER INTERESTS

46. The preliminary programme gave priority to measures to protect consumer interests. In the course of its implementation, the idea gradually developed that the consumer should be increasingly seen as having a part to play in the preparation of economic and social decisions concerning him.

47. This development is based on a number of considerations.

The first is the value of a dialogue between consumers and producers/distributors and between consumers and the public authorities. This becomes clear once we recognize that in our society changes in economic and social policy must as far as possible be the result of consultation between all the parties concerned, including consumers, and that consumption should no longer be regarded merely as a balancing variable of economic development.

The second consideration is the development of closer cooperation between associations which could defend and promote consumers' interests and play an active part in trying to achieve the necessary balance between consumers and producers/distributors. It must be recognized that action by the individual consumer is not likely to have much effect on the mass market where he exercises his choice, while excessive growth in regulatory powers can only serve to over-institutionalize the relationships between the parties concerned.

48. Promotion of the consumer's interests could be based on the following:
   - development of procedures for consultation by the public authorities, to the appropriate extent, of representatives of consumer interests;
   - development of a regular dialogue between representatives of consumer interests and producers' and distributors' organizations;
   - more aid to organizations which represent consumers.

49. **Priority measures**

   Under this programme, the Commission will:
   - send the Council a communication on consumer association representation, criteria for representation and the approval procedures operating in

Member States. At the same time it will give details of the extent of consumer representation within the Community;

– continue to ensure that there is balanced representation of consumers on
the specialized advisory committees set up by the Commission;

– continue, and where possible increase, its aid to European consumer associations to enable them to make their viewpoint better heard, and it will
also make every effort to organize seminars for training officials from
these associations, particularly on the subject of common policies;

– foster consultation between European consumer associations and the
various business interests concerned on specific matters of common
interest;

– endeavour to promote adequate representation of consumers in standards
organizations.

References

AA (1970), *A Positive Approach to Advertising*, Report on Seminar of The Advertising Association, UK, with contributions from John Hobson (Ted Bates Advertising Agency), Tony Fisher (Unilever Ltd.), Brian F. McCabe (Foot, Cone & Belding Advertising Agency) and John Braun (Advertising Standards Authority), London: October.

AA (1978), *Opinion of The Advertising Association of the United Kingdom on the Proposal for a Directive on Misleading and Unfair Advertising*, (COM(77)724 Final), London: March.

AA (1979), a letter of April 11, 1979 addressed to the members of the Advertising Information Group, on "Advertising directed to Children."

AA (1980), *Advertising to Children*, Background Briefing No.1, London: July.

AA (1985), *Public Action Plan for the Mid-1980's (Draft)*, London: The Advertising Association, July 4.

AAAA (1973), "The Case for Advertising," *Bulletin Number 3054-0*, New York, American Association of Advertising Agencies, February 15.

AAAA (1982), *The Process of Self-Regulation in Advertising*, a presentation given by the American Association of Advertising Agencies to the Federal Trade Commission, Washington: April 21.

AAAA (1983), *The American Association of Advertising Agencies' Response to the Federal Trade Commission's Inquiry on the Advertising Substantiation Program*, New York and Washington: Board of Directors of the AAAA, July 13.

ABPI (1984), *Code of Practice for the Pharmaceutical Industry*, and the *Constitution and Procedure for the Code of Practice Committee*, 6th ed. London: Association of the British Pharmaceutical Industry, January.

Adams, Charles F. (1984), "One Parting Thought After Four Years in Washington," *AAAA Washington Newsletter*, October.

Adler, Richard P.; Lesser, Gerald S.; Meringoff, Laurene Krasny; Robertson, Thomas S.; Rossiter, John R.; and Ward, Scott, eds. (1980), *The Effect of Television Advertising on Children*, Lexington: Lexington Books.

The Advertising Association and the European Advertising Tripartite (1985), *The European Advertising & Media Forecast*, Henley-on-Thames: NTC Publications Ltd., June and October.

Advertising Age (1978), "Federal Trade Commission Staff Report on TV Advertising to Children," Summary and Recommendations, February 27.

The Advertising Educational Foundation, an undated brochure, New York.

AESGP (1977), *The European Code of Standards for the Advertising of Medicines*, Paris:March.

Anderson, Ronald D.; Engledow, Jack L.; and Becker, Helmut (1978), "Advertising Attitudes in West Germany and the US: An Analysis Over Age and Time," *Journal of International Business Studies* (Winter) 27 – 38.

Andreasen, A.R. (1977), "Consumer Dissatisfaction as a Measure of Market performance," *Journal of Consumer Policy*, 311 – 324.

ASA (1982), *Annual Report of the Advertising Standards Authority*, London.

ASA (1984a), *Annual Report of the Advertising Standards Authority*, London.

ASA (1984b), *ASA Case Report 107*, London: March 14.

ASA (1984c), *ASA Case Report 108*, London: April 11.

ASA (1984d), *ASA Case Report 109*, London: May 16.

ASA (1984e), *ASA Case Report 110*, London: June 13.

ASA (1985), *ASA Case Report 121*, London: May.

Australian Advertising Industry Council (1983), *Advertising, The People Have Their Say*, Report No.2 of the Australian Advertising Industry Council, June.

Austria Tabak Werke AG, *Werbekodex 1981*, an advertising code for cigarettes, published by the Austrian Tobacco Works, ref.no.T 82/2/1/5/i, December 1.

Backman, Jules (1967), *Advertising and Competition*, New York: New York University Press.

Barnes, Michael (1982), "Public Attitudes to Advertising," *The Journal of Advertising*, (1)119 – 128.

Barounos, E. et al. (1975), *EEC Anti-Trust Law: Principles and Practice*, London: Butterworths.

The Battle for Eyeballs (1980), a video-tape recording on new communications technology, its impact on the consumer and implications for advertising, London: SSC&B:LINTAS Worldwide, December.

Baudet, Henri and van der Meulen, Henk, eds., (1982), *Consumer Behaviour and Economic Growth in the Modern Economy*, London: Croom Helm.

Beatson, Ronald (1983a), Presentation to Council Meeting of the European Association of Advertising Agencies, Helsinki: June.

Beatson, Ronald (1983b), "Media, Public Authorities and Advertising Agencies: The New Tripartite," speech at Second International Conference on Public Service Advertising, the International Advertising Association, Brussels: September 21 – 23.

Beatson, Ronald (1984a), "The Image of Advertising in Europe," a presentation to the Annual Meeting of the American Association of Advertising Agencies, Palm Springs, California: March 19.

Beatson, Ronald (1984b), "Building Euro-Brands," Advertising Age's *Focus*, March.

Bernard, André (1985), "The Media Revolution: Heat or Light, Myth or Reality," presentation to congress International Advertising Association, Istanbul: September 10.

Bernitz, U. (1981), "Brand Differentiation between Identical Products − An Analysis from a Consumer Law Viewpoint," *Journal of Consumer Policy*, (5)21 – 38.

Bernitz, Ulf and Draper, John (1981), *Consumer Protection in Sweden*, Stockholm: the Institute of Intellectual Property and Market Law, Stockholm University.

Best, Arthur (1981), *When Consumers Complain*, New York: Columbia University Press.

BEUC (1974), *A Study of Advertising in the United Kingdom and the Federal Republic of Germany*, Brussels: European Office of Consumer Organizations.

BEUC (1980), Replies to BEUC to a Questionnaire from the Committee on the Environment, Public Health and Consumer Protection of the European Parliament, for a Public Hearing on Consumer Protection Policy, Brussels: January 17.

BEUC (1982), *The European Community Directive on Food Labelling*, Brussels: July 20.

BEUC/EAT (1982/1983), joint letters from the BEUC and the EAT of June 30, 1982 and February 15, 1983, to the President of the Council of Ministers of the EEC, on the proposed Directive on Misleading and Unfair Advertising.

BEUC (1983), *The Impact of Satellite and Cable Television on Advertising*, a Report prepared by the BEUC for the Commission of the EC, Brussels: August.

BEUC (1984), *1984 Annual Report*, Brussels: Bureau Européen des Unions de Consommateurs (European Office of Consumer Unions).

BEUC News (1984), "Europe-wide Television," a Dossier, Number 37, Brussels: July/August.

BEUC News (1985), "The Safety of Consumers in Europe," a Special Number, No.47, Brussels: September.

Beville, Hugh M. (1985), "The Audience Potentials of the new Technologies: 1985 – 1990," *Journal of Advertising Research*, (25)(J) No.12, April – May RC-3 to RC-10.

Biervert, Bernd; Monse, Kurt; and Rock, Reinhard (1984), "Alternatives for Consumer Policy: A Study of Consumer Organizations in the FRG," *Journal of Consumer Policy*, (7)343 – 358.

Bishop, F.P. (1949), *The Ethics of Advertising*, London: Robert Hale Ltd.

Bloom, Paul N., ed. (1982), *Consumerism and Beyond: Research Perspectives on the Future Social Environment*, Cambridge, MA: Marketing Science Institute.

Boddewyn, Jean J. (1978a), *Premiums, Gifts and Competitions: An International Survey*, New York: International Advertising Association, September.

Boddewyn, Jean J. (1978b), *Comparison Advertising: A Worldwide Study*, New York: Hastings House.

Boddewyn, Jean J.; and Marton, Katherin (1978c), "Comparison Advertising: A Worldwide Study," *Proceedings of the Annual Conference of the American Academy of Advertising*, Steven E. Permut, ed., 150 – 54.

Boddewyn, Jean J. (1979a), *Government Pre-Clearance of Advertisements: An International Survey*, New York: International Advertising Association, January.

Boddewyn, Jean J. (1979b), *Advertising to Children: An International Survey*, New York: International Advertising Association, September.

Boddewyn, Jean J. (1979c), *Outdoor/Billboard Advertising Regulation: An International Survey*, New York: International Advertising Association, April.

Boddewyn, Jean J. (1979d), *Decency and Sexism in Advertising: An International Survey of their Regulation and Self-Regulation*, New York: International Advertising Association, December.

Boddewyn, Jean J. (1980), *New Regulatory Developments: Reversal of the Burden of Proof, Corrective Advertising and Suing Advertisers, A 40-Country Survey*, New York: International Advertising Association.

Boddewyn, Jean J. (1981a), *Direct Mail/Direct Response*, New York: International Advertising Association, May.

Boddewyn, Jean J. (1981b), "The Global Spread of Advertising Regulation," *MSU Business Topics*, (Spring)5 – 13.

Boddewyn, Jean J. (1981c), *Endorsements/Testimonials: A 36-Country Survey*, New York: International Advertising Association, August.

Boddewyn, Jean J. (1982a), *Consumer Credit and Investment Advertising*, New York: International Advertising Association.

Boddewyn, Jean J. (1982b), *Food Advertising Regulation and Self-Regulation*, New York: International Advertising Association, March.

Boddewyn, Jean J. (1982c), "Advertising Regulation in the 1980s: The Underlying Global Forces," *Journal of Marketing*, 46(Winter)27 – 35.

Boddewyn, Jean J. (1978 – 1982), *Forbidden or Severely Restricted Advertising Practices*, New York: a series published by the International Advertising Association between 1978 and 1982.

Boddewyn, Jean J. (1983a), "Belgian Advertising Self-Regulation and Consumer Organizations: Interaction and Conflict in the Context of the Jury d'Ethique Publicitaire (JEP)," *Journal of Consumer Policy*, (6)303 – 323.

Boddewyn, Jean J. (1983b), "Outside Participation in Advertising Self-Regulation: The Case of the Advertising Standards Authority (UK)," *Journal of Consumer Policy*, (6)77 – 93.

Boddewyn, Jean J. (1983c), "The Growth of Ad-Regulation and Self-Regulation Around the World," *Advertising Compliance Service*, New York: September 19 and October 3.

Boddewyn, Jean J. (1983d), ed. *Tobacco Advertising Bans and Consumption in 16 Countries*, New York: International Advertising Association.

Boddewyn, Jean J. (1983e), *Comparison Advertising: Regulation and Self-Regulation in 55 Countries*, New York: International Advertising Association, January.

Boddewyn, Jean J. (1984a), "Outside participation in Advertising Self-Regulation: The Case of the French Bureau de Vérification de la Publicité (BVP)," *Journal of Consumer Policy*, (7)45 – 64.

Boddewyn, Jean J. (1984b), *Advertising to Children: Regulation and Self-Regulation in 40 Countries*, New York: International Advertising Association.

Boddewyn, Jean J. (1984c), "U.S. Advertising Self-Regulation: The Government as Outside Partner NAD/NARB," October (unpublished draft).

Boddewyn, Jean J. (1985a), *Medicine Advertising Regulation and Self-Regulation in 54 Countries*, New York: International Advertising Association, April.

Boddewyn, Jean J. (1985b), *Foreign Languages, Materials, Trade and Investment in Advertising: Regulation and Self-Regulation in 46 Countries*, New York: International Advertising Association, October.

Boddewyn, Jean J. (forthcoming), "Outside Participation in Canadian Advertising Self-Regulation," *Canadian Journal of Administrative Sciences*.

Borrie, Gordon; and Aubrey, Diamond (1973), *The Consumer, Society and the Law*, 3rd ed., Harmondsworth, Middlesex, England: Penguin Books, Ltd.

Borrie, Gordon (1984), *The Development of Consumer Law and Policy*, London: Stephens.

Boettcher, Winfried (1979), *Werbung im Schulbuch*, Bonn: Zentralausschuss der Werbewirtschaft e.V.

Bottomley, David (1985), personal letter to one of the authors, York: December 20.

Bourgoignie, Thierry; Delvax, Gey; Domont-Naert, Francoise; and Panier, Christian (1981), *L'Aide Juridique au Consommateur*, Brussels: Bruylant.

Bourgoignie, Thierry (1984), "The Need to Reform Consumer Protection Policy," *Journal of Consumer Policy*, Vol.7, No.2, June, 1984, Copyright© 1984 by D. Reidel Publishing Company, Dordrecht, Holland.

Brandmair, Lothar (1977), *Die Freiwillige Selbstkontrolle der Werbung*, Cologne: Carl Heymanns Verlag KG.

Brardt, Cathrin (1982), *Irreführende Werbung unter Wettbewerbsrechtlichen und Verbraucherschutzpolitischen Aspekten*, Braunschweig: Universität Göttingen.

Braun, John (1965), *Advertisements in Court*, London: David Fanning Ltd.

Braun, John (1981), "The First EEC Consumer Programme," *Viewpoint*, London: Independent Television Companies Association, Ltd., Summer.

Braun, John (1983a), Extract from submission by EEC Commission to Council of Ministers, on December 5, 1973, ref. Com(73)2108, as stated in a letter from John Braun to the authors, December 6.

Braun, John (1983b), personal discussion, London: November 17.

Braun, John (1984), "Principles of Conduct for the Direct Selling Business in Europe," *Journal of Consumer Policy*, (7)300 – 305.

Braun, John (1985), personal letter to one of the authors, London: February 8.

Breyer, S. (1982), *Regulation and its Reform*, Cambridge, MA: Harvard University Press.

Bruce, Robert R.; Keller, Bruce P.; and Cunard, J.P. (1985), *Worldwide Restrictions on Advertising: An Outline of Principles, Problems and Solutions*, New York: International Advertising Association, March 14, 1986.

Bruhn, Manfred (1982), *Konsumentenzufriedenheit und Beschwerden*, Frankfurt am Main: Verlag Peter Lang.

Brussels Meeting (1977a), Meeting with Commissioner Richard Burke and Ludwig Krämer, official of the Commission, also attended by Messrs. Nils Färnert (Director-General EAAA), Albert Brouwet (J. Walter Thompson), Julian Critchley (Conservative MP, UK), Albert Wolvesperges (SSC&B:LINTAS) and Rein Rijkens (President EAAA), Brussels: April 18.

Brussels Meeting (1977b), Meeting with Mr. Roy Jenkins, President of the Commission, accompanied by Messrs. Ludwig Krämer, Alan Dukes, Aneurin Hughes as officials of the Commission and Ms Grenfell (P.A. to President Jenkins); also attended by Messrs. André Bernard (SSC&B:LINTAS), Wolfgang Voltmer (McCann, Frankfurt), Jean-Max Lenormand (McCann, Paris), Julian Critchley (Conservative MP, UK), Nils Färnert (Director-General EAAA), Albert Brouwet (J. Walter Thompson) and Rein Rijkens (President EAAA), Brussels: June 13.

Brussels Meeting (1978), Meeting with Commissioner Richard Burke, Alan Dukes, Michel Carpentier and Ludwig Krämer, officials of the Commission, also attended by Messrs. Carl Christiansen (Unilever Germany and President Elect of the WFA), Peter Gilow (President Elect EAAA), Laurent Templier (AACP, France), David Wheeler (IPA, UK), Jules van Neerven (CEBUCO, Holland) and Rein Rijkens (President EAAA), Brussels: February 24.

Buell, Victor P. (1977), *The British Approach to Improving Advertising Standards and Practice*, Amherst: Business Publication Services, School of Business Administration, University of Massachusetts.

Bullmore, J.J.D. (1978), *Advertising and the Virtues of Competitive Persuasion*, London: Annual Review J. Walter Thompson Co. Ltd.

Bullmore, J.J.D. (1982), *The Decline of Them and the Rise of Us*, London: Annual Review J. Walter Thompson Co. Ltd.

Bullmore, J.J.D. (1983), personal discussion, London, November 16.

Bullmore, J.J.D.; and Waterson, M.J. (1983), eds., *The Advertising Association Handbook*, London: Holt, Rinehart and Winston Ltd.

Burgenmeier, Beat (1985), "Consumer Protection in Switzerland: Strengthening Countervailing Power of Competition?," *Journal of Consumer Policy*, (8)45 – 52.

Burke, Richard (1977a), "The Role of Government and Public Policy in the Advertising and Marketing Process," presentation at Second EurAm Conference, London: November 28 – December 1.

Burke, Richard (1977b), "The Consumer Voice in Europe – let us tip the balance," presentation to the European League for Economic Cooperation, London: December 8.

Burke, Richard (1978a), "Opening Address to the Third EurAm Conference," Paris: November 27 – 30.

Burke, Richard (1978b), *The European Dimension in Health Policies*, a Peter Becket Memorial Lecture at the Annual Conference of the Federated Dublin Voluntary Hospitals and St. James's Hospital, Dublin: February 22.

Burke, Richard (1979), "Controversial Controls," an article in the SSC&B:LINTAS House Magazine, and the response from Messrs. Roger Underhill and Rein Rijkens, London: Third Quarter, No.4.

Burollaud, Hélène (1973), "Government Control and Free Enterprise – Are They Compatible?" a presentation at the 23rd World Congress of the International Advertising Association, Dublin: June 6 – 8.

Burson-Marsteller (1981), *Le Pouvoir Consommateur dans la France Socialiste*, Paris: Burson-Marsteller.

Business International (1980a), *EEC Consumer Policy*, New York: December.

Business International (1980b), *Europe's Consumer Movement: 5. Self-Regulation vs Mandatory Controls*, Geneva: December.

Business International (1984a), *Europe's Changing Markets*, Geneva: February.

Business International (1984b), *Europe's Consumer Movement: Key Issues and Corporate Responses*, New York: December.

Buzzell, Robert D. (1968), "Can You Standardize Multinational Marketing?" *Harvard Business Review*, (46)(Nov./Dec.)102 – 13.

BVP (1983), *Recueil des Recommendations*, Paris: Bureau de Vérification de la Publicité, September 1.

Campaign (1983), "ASA urges rethink on Ads,", London: December 16.

Campbell, Alan (1980), *EC Competition Law: A Practitioner's Handbook*, New York: North-Holland Publishing Company.

CAP (1979), *The British Code of Advertising Practice*, London: CAP Committee, April 1979, amended September, 1981.

CAP (1984), *The British Code of Sales Promotion Practice*, London: the CAP Committee, 4th ed., September.

Carpentier, Michel (1977), "Background to Consumer Affairs: The European Perspective," presentation at Conference on "Consumer Affairs: Threat or Opportunity," London: Royal Garden Hotel, March 3.

Carpentier, Michel (1978), "The European Consumer in a Changing Society," presentation at Colloquium in Belgium, October 23 – 24.

CARU (1983), *Self-Regulatory Guidelines for Children's Advertising*, Third Ed., New York: Council of Better Business Bureaus, Inc., Children's Advertising Review Unit.

CBI (1985), *Consumer Protection in the European Community*, a joint statement from the Confederation of British Industry and The Advertising Association, London: January.

CCC (1982), Draft Opinion of the Consumers' Consultative Committee on Consumers, Alcohol Advertising and Codes of Ethics, Doc. No.CCC/71/80 rev.4, XI 225/82 – orig. Fr., Brussels.

CCC Bureau (1984), *Memorandum* presented to Commissioner Narjes by the Consumers' Consultative Committee's Bureau, Brussels: July 25.

CGT (1981), *Besoins Sociaux, Idéologies et Institutions de la Publicité*, Paris: Centre Confédéral d'Etudes Economiques.

Chamberlain, Neil W. (1980), *Forces of Change in Western Europe*, London: McGraw-Hill Book Company (UK) Ltd.

Clinton Davis, Stanley (1985), "A New Impetus for Consumer Protection Policy," a paper to the Council of Consumer Affairs Ministers, Brussels: February 11.

Close, G.L. (1983), "The Legal Basis for the Consumer Protection Programme of the EEC and Priorities for Action," *European Law Review*, August.

CNP (1983), *Bilan et perspectives de la Concentration entre les organisations de consommateurs et la profession publicitaire*, Paris: Conseil National de la Publicité.

Cockfield (1985), a statement by Commissioner Lord Cockfield in *Euro Forum*, London: July/August.

Coen, Robert J. (1984), personal letters to one of the authors, New York: October 12 and 31.

COFACE (1982), an Agreement with EAT on "Rules of Conduct on Advertising for Toys," Paris: May 4.

Cohen, Dorothy (1974), "The Concept of Unfairness as it Relates to Advertising Legislation," *Journal of Marketing*, 38(July)8 – 13.

Cohen, Ronald I. (1971), "Comparative False Advertising Regulation: A Beginning," *The Adelaide Law Review*, 4(August)69 – 112.

Commandeur, Claus; and Forster, Wolfgang (1982), eds, *Verbraucherinformation mit neuen Medien*, Frankfurt: Campus.

Commission of the EC (1979), "Second Community Programme for Consumers," *Bulletin of the European Communites*, Supplement 4/79, Luxembourg: Office for Official Publications of the European Communities.

Commission of the EC (1981a), "Consumer Education in Schools," a Working Document of the Commission to the Council of Ministers, XI/488/81-EN-rev.1, Brussels.

Commission of the EC (1981b), *Steps to European Unity*, 2nd ed., Luxembourg: Office for Official Publications of the European Communities.

Commission of the EC (1982a), *Consumer Representation in the European Communities*, Luxembourg: Office for Official Publications of the European Communities, 1983.

Commission of the EC (1982b), *The Consumer and New Information Technology*, Louvain-La-Neuve: Cabay.

Commission of the EC (1984), *Television Without Frontiers*, a green paper on the establishment of the common market on broadcasting, especially by satellite and cable, COM(84)300/5, Brussels: May 23.

Commission of the EC (1985a), *Programme of the Commission for 1985*, Brussels: March.

Commission of the EC (1985b), *Ten Years of Community Consumer Policy, A Contribution to a People's Europe*, Luxembourg: Office for Official Publications of the European Communities.

Commission of the EC (1985c), *A New Impetus for Consumer Protection Policy*, a paper from EC Commissioner Clinton Davis, Doc. COM(85)314 final, Brussels: June 27.

Commission of the EC (1985d), *Completing the Internal Market*, a paper from EC Commissioner Lord Cockfield, Doc. COM(85)310 final, Brussels: June 28 – 29.

Commission of the EC (1985e), "Consumer Redress," *Bulletin of the European Communities*, Supplement 2/85, Luxembourg: Office for Official Publications of the European Communities.

Conseil Economique et Social (1980), *Avis sur la place et le rôle de la publicité*, Paris.

Consumerism: A Growing Force in the Market Place (1973), 4th ed., New York: Burson-Marsteller Public Relations, August.

Consumerism in the Eighties (1983), a National Survey of Consumer Attitudes, New York: Louis Harris & Associates, Inc., February.

Cote, Kevin (1985), "United At Last," *Focus*, London: October, pp.10 – 20.

Council of Europe (1972), *Consumer Protection*, Report of the Working Party on Misleading Advertising, Strasbourg: March.

Council of Europe (1973), *Recommendation 705(1973) on Consumer Protection*, Twenty-Fifth Ordinary Session of the Consultative Assembly of the Council of Europe, Strasbourg: May 17.

Council of Europe (1979), *The Council of Europe, Aims – Operation – Activities*, Kehl, West Germany: Morstadt.

Council of Europe (1981), *Convention for the Protection of Human Rights and Fundamental Freedoms*, European Treaty Series 5,9,44 and 46, edition February.

Council of Europe (1982), *Consumer Protection – Training of Consumer Advisers, Professional or Voluntary*, Strasbourg.

Council of Europe (1984a), *Council of Europe Activities in the Mass Media Field*, doc. DH-MM(84)4, Strasbourg: Directorate of Human Rights of the Council of Europe, August 31.

Council of Europe (1984b), *European Standards for Television Advertising*, Recommendation No.R(84)3, Strasbourg: Committee of Ministers of the Council of Europe, February 23.

Council of Europe (1984c), *The Use of Satellite Capacity for Television and Sound Radio*, Recommendation No.R(84)22, Strasbourg: Committee of Ministers of the Council of Europe, December 7.

Council of Europe (1984d), *Freedom of Expression and Information in European Law*, DH-MM(84)3, an Information Document of the Directorate of Human Rights, Strasbourg, July 2.

Council Resolution of 14 April 1975 on a preliminary programme of the European Economic Community for a consumer protection and information policy, Brussels: Official Journal of the European Communities, Volume 18 No C 92/1 – 12, April 25, 1975 (See Appendix I).

Council Resolution of 19 May 1981 on a second programme of the European Economic Community for a consumer protection and information policy, Brussels: Official Journal of the European Communities, Volume 24 No C 133/1 – 12, June 3, 1981 (See Appendix VI).

Covington and Burling (1978), *Advertising Under Attack, a Report on Current UNESCO and International Communications Policy Developments, etc.*, Washington, DC: The Interpublic Group of Companies, December 15.

Craig, Gordon A. (1984), "The Rush to a Summit Carries Some Risks," *International Herald Tribune*, June 29.

Crane, Peggy (1985), "How COFACE Gets Involved in Family Matters," *Europe 85* (Jan./Febr.).

Crosby, Scott; and Tempest, Alastair (1983), "Satellite Lore," *International Journal of Advertising*, 2:2(April – June).

Dauner-Lieb, Barbara (1983), *Verbraucherschutz durch Ausbildung eines Sonderprivatrechts für Verbraucher*, Berlin: Duncker & Humblot.

Dawson, Charles (1985a), "TV Revolution: Why admen cannot afford to be silent," London: *Campaign*, November 22.

Dawson, Charles (1985b), "Open Skies Across Europe," London: *Media International* (12)No.131, October, 20 – 23.

Day, Barry (1967), ed., "I'm the only one who knows what the hell is going on," a discussion with Marshall McLuhan, London: SSC&B:LINTAS International, September.

Debauve (1980), Belgian Court Decision, March 18, 1980, Case 52/79, Procureur du Roi versus Marc J.V.C. Debauve and Others.

Dedler, Konrad; Gottschalk, Ingrid; Grunert, Klaus G.; Heidrich, Margot; Hoffman, Annemarie L.; and Scherhorn, Gerhard (1984), *Das Informationsdefizit der Verbraucher*, Frankfurt: Campus.

Delors, Jacques (1985), "The Thrust of Commission Policy," a statement from the President of the Commission of the EC, Strasbourg: January 14.

Drettmann, Fritz (1984), *Wirtschaftswerbung und Meinungsfreiheit*, Frankfurt: Lang.

Dunn, Samuel Watson (1974), "The Changing Legal Climate for Marketing and Advertising in Europe," *Columbia Journal of World Business*, 9(2)(Summer)91 – 98.

Dunn, Samuel Watson (1982), "United Nations as Regulator of International Advertising," *Proceedings of the 1982 Conference of the American Academy of Advertising*, Alan D. Fletcher, ed., Knoxville: University of Tennessee, 29 – 32.

EAAA (1973a), *Public Attitudes Toward Advertising*, Brussels: March 3.

EAAA (1973b), Memorandum on *Misleading Advertising: Harmonisation or Legislation*, presented to the Directorate-General Internal Market of the Commission of the EC, Brussels: June.

EAAA (1976), *Advertising and the Vatican*, a Report from the European Association of Advertising Agencies on a visit to the Vatican, Brussels: April.

EAAA (1977a), *Aide Mémoire*, a document prepared by the European Association of Advertising Agencies for a meeting with Commission President Roy Jenkins, Brussels: June 13.

EAAA (1977b), *Ten Points of Public Concern about Advertising*, Brussels: February.

EAAA (1983), *New Communications Developments*, Brussels: November.

EAAA (1984), *EAAA Newsletter*, (7), Brussels: November.

EAAA (1985a), *Next Steps*, Brussels: January 23.

EAAA (1985b), *EAAA Newsletter*, (8), Brussels: March.

EAAA (1985c), *EAAA Newsletter*, (9), Brussels: July.

EAAA (1985d), Extract from the Commission's White Paper of June 14, *Completing the Internal Market*, Brussels: July 9.

EAAA (1985e), *Next Steps*, Brussels: September 26.

EAAA (1985f), *Next Steps*, Brussels: October 31.

EAT(1982), *Advertising and the Consumers' Consultative Committee: Four Questions Discussed*, Brussels: November 16.

EAT (1983), *Self-Regulation and Codes of Practice: A Discussion Paper*, Brussels: April.

EAT (1984a), *Consumer Education Within a Market Economy*, Brussels: June 27.

EAT (1984b), *Commentary by the European Advertising Tripartite on the Commission's Green Paper, Television Without Frontiers*, Brussels: October.

EAT (1984c), *EAT Statement on the Green Paper Hearings of 12 – 13 December 1984*, Brussels: December 18.

EBU (1983), "Declaration of Principles Regarding Commercial TV Advertising Broadcast by DBS," a statement from the European Broadcasting Union, *EBU Review, Programmes, Administration, Law*, (XXXIV) No.5, 7 – 8, Geneva: September 5.

EC General Report (1984), *Eighteenth General Report EC on the Activities of the European Communities in 1984*, Luxembourg: Office for Official Publications of the European Communities, 1985.

ECLG (1983a), "Non-Legislative Means of Consumer Protection," *Journal of Consumer Policy*, (6)209 – 224.

ECLG (1983b), "Group Actions in the Consumer Interest," *Journal of Consumer Policy*, (6)325 – 350.

Engledow, Jack L.; Thorelli, Hans B.; and Becker, Helmut (1975), "The Information Seekers – a Cross-Cultural Elite," *Advances in Consumer Research*, (2)141 – 155.

Esserman, June F. (1981), ed., *Television Advertising and Children*, New York: Child Research Service.

Euro Forum (1983), "Euro-television: a Genuine Alternative," an interview with Lorenzo Natali, then Vice-President of the EC, London: September.

Euro Forum (1984), London: November.

Euro Forum (1985), Commissioner Carlo Ripa de Meana commenting on the Dooge Report from the Committee for Institutional Questions, London: June.

Europe 83 (1983), London: December.

Europe 84 (1984a), London: April.

Europe 84 (1984b), London: July/August.

Europe 85 (1985a), London: March.

Europe 85 (1985b), London: April.

Europe 85 (1985c), London, January/February.

European Community Information Service (1985), *European Community News*, No.41/1985, Washington: December 16.

European File (1983), "The European Community and Consumers," 15/83, Brussels: October.

European File (1984a), "The European Community in the World," 14/84, Brussels: August – September.

European File (1984b), "The Institutions of the European Community," 17/84, Brussels: November.

European File (1984c), "Towards a European Television Policy," 19/84, Brussels: December.

European File (1985a), "The European Community and Consumers," 12/85, Brussels: June – July.

European File (1985b), "A Community of Twelve: welcome to Spain and Portugal," 17 – 18/85, Brussels: November.

European File (1986a), "Towards a People's Europe," 3/86, Brussels: February.

European File (1986b), "An Industrial Strategy for Europe," 4/86, Brussels: February.

European File (1986c), "The European Internal Market," 8/85, Brussels: April.

The European Institute for the Media (1985), *Broadcasting Policies in the E.E.C.*, Proceedings of the Colloquia, Vol.I, Manchester: January 24 – 25.

European Parliament (1980), *Draft Motion for a Resolution on the Second Consumer Action Programme*, with an *Addendum*, of the Committee on the Environment, Public Health and Consumer Protection of the EC, Brussels: June 10/12.

European Parliament (1983), *Bibliography* (General, Powers, Members, Procedures and Rules, Activities, Direct Elections, Seat, Political Groups and Parties, Relations with other Institutions), Brussels: Directorate-General for Research and Documentation.

European Parliament (1984), *Research and Documentation Papers*, Resolutions of the European Parliament in the field of Environment, Public Health and Consumer Protection (1979 – 1984), Brussels: August.

European Society for Opinion and Marketing Research (ESOMAR), *E.S.O.M.A.R. What It Is ... And What It Stands For*, a Brochure, Amsterdam: undated.

Europese Commissie Voorlichtingsbureau Den Haag (EC Information Office The Hague) (1985), *European Almanak*, 13th ed.

Evans, Murray (1973), "Government Control and Free Enterprise – Are They Compatible?," a presentation at the 23rd World Congress of the International Advertising Association, held in Dublin, June 6 – 8.

Explanatory Memorandum on Proposal for a Council Directive relating to the approximation of the laws, regulations and administrative provisions of the Member States concerning Misleading and Unfair Advertising, Commission of the European Communities, Doc. COM(77)724 final, Brussels: March 1, 1978 (See Appendix IV).

Explanatory Memorandum on an Amendment to the Proposal for a Council Directive relating to the approximation of laws, regulations and administrative provisions of the Member States concerning Misleading and Unfair Advertising, Commission of the European Communities, Doc. COM(79)353 final, Brussels: July 10, 1979 (See Appendix V).

Fallon, M. (1982), "Some Thoughts on Non-Community Law Initiatives as Methods for European Integration in Consumer Matters," *European Consumer Law*, Thierry Bourgoignie, ed., Louvain-la-Neuve: Cabay, 271 – 303.

First Report Commission (1977), *Consumer Protection and Information Policy*, Luxembourg: Office for Official Publications of the European Communities.

Fisher, Bart S.; and Turner, Jeff (1983), eds, *Regulating the Multi-National Enterprise*, New York: Praeger.

FIVS (1980), *Code of Conduct of General Advertising Practices*, adopted by the Fédération Internationale des Vins et Spiritueux (International Federation of Wine, Spirit, Eaux-de-Vie and Liqueurs Trade and Industry), Helsinki: June 18 – 19.

Fleischmann, Gerd. (1981), ed., *Der Kritische Verbraucher*, Frankfurt: Campus.

Fulop, Christina (1973), "Restrictive Marketing Practices in the EEC," *European Journal of Marketing*, (Winter)(7) 3.

Fulop, Christina (1977), *The Consumer Movement and the Consumer*, London: The Advertising Association.

Fulop, Christina (1981), *Advertising, Competition, and Consumer Behaviour*, London: Holt, Rinehart & Winston.

Gardner, John W. (1963), *Self-Renewal*, New York: Harper and Row.

Geier, Phil (1978), an Analysis, London: *Campaign Europe*, April 24.

Gilow, Peter (1980), a presentation at the Public hearing on Second EEC Consumer Program, Dublin: February 26 – 27.

"Global Media: A Media Revolution in the Making," (1984), *Advertising Age*, December 3, 1984, 45 – 61.

Government Regulatory Issues and Advertising, Comments by the participants in the Loaned Executive Assignment Program of the American Association of Advertising Agencies, New York: Vol.I November 1979, Vol. II December 1980, Vol.III July 1982.

Green, S.R. (1976), "Advertising for Today and Tomorrow," *Open Column*, London: December.

Greer, Thomas V.; and Thompson, Paul R. (1985), "Development of Standardized and Harmonized Advertising Regulation in the European Economic Community," reprinted with permission from *Journal of Advertising*, (14)2, 1985.

Greyser, S.A.; and Diamond, S.L. (1974), "Business is Adapting Consumerism," *Harvard Business Review*, (September – October)38 – 58.

Greyser, S.A.; and Diamond, S.L. (1983), "U.S. Consumers View the Marketplace," *Journal of Consumer Policy*, (6)3 – 18.

Greyson, Leslie E. (1980), *Consumer Protection Activities in the European Economic Community*, Boston: Harvard Intercollegiate Case Clearinghouse.

Griffin, Paul (1973), "Government Control and Free Enterprise – Are They Compatible?," a presentation at the 23rd World Congress of the International Advertising Association, held in Dublin: June 6 – 8.

Grunert, Klaus G. (1982), *Informationsverarbeitungsprozesse bei der Kaufentscheidung: Ein gedächtnispsychologischer Ansatz*, Frankfurt: Lang.

Grunert, Klaus G. (1984), "The Consumer Information Deficit: Assessment and Policy Implications," *Journal of Consumer Policy*, (7)359 – 388.

Haas, C.R. (1983a), *Advertising Self-Regulation in France*, a Mimeograph, Paris: Bureau de Vérification de la Publicité.

Haas, C.R. (1983b), personal discussion, Paris: October 18.

Hahn, Rüdiger (1984), *Behinderungsmissbräuche marktbeherrschender Unternehmen*, Frankfurt: Lang.

Hall, Edward T.; and Hall, Mildred R. (1983), *Hidden Differences*, Hamburg: Stern Magazin.

Hardinghaus, Herbert; and Mildner, R. (1983), *Verbraucherbeteiligung – Konsumfreiheit und Konsumentenmacht*, Hamburg: Rohrberg.

Harris, Louis; and Associates (1983), *Consumerism in the Eighties*, Los Angeles: Atlantic Richfield Company, February.

Harris, Ralph; and Seldon A. (1959), *Advertising in a Free Society*, London: Institute of Economic Affairs.

Heslop, Alan (1976), ed., *Business – Government Relations*, New York: New York University.

von Hippel, Eike (1982), *Der Schutz des Schwächeren*, Tübingen: Mohr.

Hobson, John (1964), *The Influence and Techniques of Modern Advertising*, three cantor lectures delivered to the Royal Society of Arts, London: March 2, 9 and 16.

Hobson, John (1978), "Advertising in To-Day's Society: An Up-To-Date Assessment," *Journal of the Royal Society of Arts*, London: February.

Hoffmann, Annemarie L. (1982), *Verbraucherinteresse als Informationsproblem*, Frankfurt: Lang.

Holler, Manfred J. (1983), ed., *Homo Oeconomicus I.*, München: Leudemann.

Holliger, Eugénie (1984), "Reflections on the Swiss Approach to Consumer Protection," *Journal of Consumer Policy*, (7)266 – 268.

Hondius, Ewoud H. (1984), "Non-Legislative Means of Consumer Protection: The Dutch Perspective," *Journal of Consumer Policy*, (7)137 – 156.

Hondius, Frits W. (1984a), "Freedom of Expression and Information in European Law," address to the Canadian Institute for Advanced Legal Studies, Strasbourg: July 2.

Hondius, Frits W. (1984b), personal discussion, The Hague: October 12.

Hondius, Frits W. (1985a), a statement to the ICC Symposium on the Human Rights Convention of the Council of Europe, Paris: January 18.

Hondius, Frits W. (1985b), "Freedom of Commercial Speech in Europe," Washington, DC, *Transnational Data Report*, (VIII) No.6, 321 – 327.

House of Lords (1978), *Draft Directive Concerning Unfair and Misleading Advertising*, 38th Report by the Select Committee of the House of Lords, Session 1977 – 78, London: HMS Office, July.

Hoyos, Carl Graf; Kroeber-Riel, Werner; von Rosenstiel, Lutz; and Strumpel, Burkhard (1980), eds., *Grundbegriffe der Wirtschaftspsychologie*, München: Kösel.

IAA (1973), *The global Challenge to Advertising*, New York: undated.

IAA World Congress (1973), "Government Control and Free Enterprise — Are They Compatible?," a panel discussion at the 23rd World Congress of the International Advertising Association, held in Dublin: June 6 – 8.

IAA Resolution (1983a), *Resolution Calling for More Freedom for Use of Terrestrial and Satellite TV and Amount of Time Permitted on TV*, New York: March 8.

IAA (1983b), *Tobacco and Advertising, Five Arguments Against Censorship*, a brochure prepared by the international tobacco industry, New York: June.

IAA (1983c), *Tobacco Advertising Restrictions Around The World*, New York.

IAA (1985a), *Resolution on Self-Regulation*, adopted by the Executive Committee of the International Advertising Association, New York: May.

IAA (1985b), *Global Media Commission Resolution*, the International Advertising Association, New York: July 2.

IAA Global Media Commission (1986), *The Role of Advertising in Worldwide Media Development*, New York: January 6.

IBA (1985), *The IBA Code of Advertising Standards and Practice*, London: April.

ICC (1981a), *Cost-Benefit Analysis of Consumer Protection*, doc.376, Paris.

ICC (1981b), *Consumer Legislation*, doc.383, Paris.

ICC Note (1983), "Statement and Comments from the Marketing Commission of the International Chamber of Commerce on the UN Draft Guidelines for Consumer Protection," doc.240/150Bis, Paris: June 23.

ICC (1983), list of publications from the International Chamber of Commerce, taken from *Publicaties 1983*, published by the ICC Netherlands:

    1937 *International Code of Advertising Practice*, revised at regular intervals, most recently the fifth edition in 1973. In 1983 Guidelines for Advertising addressed to Children were included (ICC No.275/405).

    1971 *International Code of Marketing Research Practice* (275).

    1973 *International Code of Sales Promotion Practice* (275).

    1973 *International Council on Marketing Practice*, constituted in November of that year and charged with the application of the previously mentioned Codes (275).

    1974 *Advertising and Sales Promotion Expenditure* (276).

    1976 *Advertising Agencies: their Services and Relationship with Advertisers and Media* (368).

    1977 *ICC/ESOMAR International Code of Marketing and Social Research Practice* (312).

    1978 *International Code of Direct Sales Practice* (318).

    1978 *Marketing: La Discipline de la Liberté* (331).

    1979 *Reaching Agreement on a Marketing Research Project* (346).

    1979 *Media Information for Advertising Planning* (347).

ICC Annual Report (1983), *The UN Consumer Protection Guidelines*, Paris: Marketing Commission of the International Chamber of Commerce, Paris.

ICC (1984), *Law and Self-Regulation*, doc. No.240/166, Paris: April 4.

ICC Note (1985), Report to National Committees and Members of the Commission on Marketing-Advertising and Distribution of the International Chamber of Commerce, on the UN Consumer Protection Guidelines, doc.240/178Bis, Paris: January 14.

ICC (1985a), Invitation ICC Symposium on *The Freedom of Commercial Communications and the Impact of the European Convention on Human Rights (Article 10)*, Paris: October 23, 1984.

ICC (1985b), Press Release 664/552, *ICC Urges a Genuine Common Market for Advertising*, Paris.

IFPMA (1985), Code of Pharmaceutical Marketing Practices, Sixth Printing, Geneva: January.

Imkamp, Heiner (1983), book review of Werner Kroebel-Riel and Gundolf Meyer-Hentschel, "Werbung — Steuerung des Konsumentenverhaltens", Würzburg: Physika, 1982, *Journal of Consumer Policy*, (6)101 – 103.

International Herald Tribune (1984), September 8 – 9.

IOCU Brochure, *Giving a Voice to the World's Consumers*, undated.

IPA (1974), *The Structure of the EEC and the Council of Europe*, London: October (revised November 1974).

IPA (1980), *Advertising Controls Checklist*, London.

IPA (1983), *Is it Legal*, a guide to Labelling and Packaging, A.A. Painter, ed., London: June.

ISBA, *Self-Regulation and the Advertiser*, London: undated.

Janssen, Werner (1974), "Some Foreign Law Aspects of Comparative Advertising," *The Trademark Reporter*, 64(Nov. – Dec.)451 – 497.

Jenkins (1977), Address by the Rt. Hon. Roy Jenkins, President of the Commission of the EC, to the European Parliament, Luxembourg: January 11.

Joerges, Christian (1984), "The Administration of Art.84(3) EEC Treaty: The Need for Consultation and Information in the legal Assessment of Selective Distribution Systems," *Journal of Consumer Policy* , (7)269 – 292.

Joint Reply and Memorandum from the International Union of Advertisers Associations and the European Association of Advertising Agencies, signed by the Presidents of these associations, Messrs. George Cordier and Rein Rijkens, to the Directorate-General for Internal Market of the Commission of the European Communities, Mr. Fernand Braun, regarding the first preliminary draft directive concerning the approximation of the laws of Member States on fair competition: Misleading and Unfair Advertising, Brussels: April 14, 1976 (See Appendix III).

Katona, George; Strumpel, P.; and Zahn, E. (1971), *Aspirations and Affluence*, New York: McGraw-Hill Book Company.

Kirkpatrick, Jeane (1983), "Global Paternalism: the United States and the New International Regulatory Order," New York: *Outlook*, Booz Allen & Hamilton Inc.

Kirkwood, R. (1983), "Tobacco Advertising," *The Advertising Association Handbook*, London: Holt, Rinehart & Winston Ltd.

Kolstadt, Eva (1973), "Government Control and Free Enterprise – Are They Compatible?," a presentation to the 23rd World Congress of the International Advertising Association, Dublin: June 6 – 8.

Korah, V. (1975), *The Competition Law of the European Economic Community and the United Kingdom*, Hackensack, New York: Rotham.

Kroeber-Riel, W. (1980), *Konsumentenverhalten*, 2nd ed., Munich: Vahlen.

Kroeber-Riel, W.; and Meyer-Hetschel, G. (1982), *Werbung – Steuerung des Konsumentenverhaltens*, Würzburg: Physika.

Kronholz, June (1979), "Consumerism European Style," *Wall Street Journal*, November 20.

LaBarbera, P. (1980), "Analyzing and Advancing the State of Art of Advertising Self-Regulation," *Journal of Advertising*, 9(4)27 – 38.

Labour Party, *Report of a Commission of Enquiry into Advertising*, London: Labour Party (known as the Keith Report), undated.

Lars Broch (1984), personal discussion, The Hague, August 28.

Lawson, R.G. (1978), *Advertising Law*, Estover, Plymouth, England: Macdonald and Evans, Ltd.

Lawson, R.G. (1981), "Consumer Protection: World Perspective," *Consumer Legislation*, Paris: International Chamber of Commerce.

Lawson, R.G. (1982), *Advertising and Labelling Laws in the Common Market*, Bristol: Jordan & Sons Ltd.

Lenormand, Jean-Max (1981), Report of January 9, 1981 to the European Association of Advertising Agencies in Brussels, concerning a UNESCO Meeting at Belgrade on October 25, 1980.

Lenzen, Richard (1981), *Verbraucherpolitik in der EG unter Berücksichtigung der Verbrauchererziehung*, Frankfurt: Peter Lang GmbH.

Lester, Antony; and Pannick, D. (1984), *Advertising and Freedom of Expression in Europe, The Scope and Effect on the European Convention of Human Rights*, Paris: Marketing Commission of the International Chamber of Commerce.

Levin, H.J. (1967), "The Limits of Self-Regulation," *Columbia Law Review*, 67(March)603 – 642.

Levitt, Theodore (1983), "The Globalization of Markets," *Harvard Business Review*, (May/June) 92 – 103.

London Meeting (1975), Meeting between Messrs. Alan Wood, President of the International Union of Advertisers Associations and Rein Rijkens, President of the European Association of Advertising Agencies, London: August 5.

Luns, Joseph (1983), personal discussion, The Hague, August 27.

MacBride Report (1980), report from an International Commission for the Study of Communications Problems, established by UNESCO's Executive Board, Paris: October/November, 1977.

Mackaay, Ejan (1982), *Economics of Information and Law*, Boston: Kluwer.

Mähling, Friedrich (1983), *Werbung, Wettbewerb und Verbraucherpolitik*, Munich: Florentz.

de Malherbe, Armand (1979), "Can Self-Regulated Advertising Be the Best Protection of the Consumer?," a presentation to the European Association of Advertising Agencies, Brussels: March 22.

Mann, Patricia (1980), *Product Liability*, a presentation to the Council Meeting of the European Association of Advertising Agencies, Paris: April 16 – 17.

Marks, Leonard (1983), "Can a Free Press Survive in the New World Information Order?," a presentation to the International Advertising Association, New York: December 14.

Martineau, Pierre (1957), *Motivation in Advertising*, New York: McGraw-Hill Book Company, Inc.

Matthews, Leonard S. (1984), personal letter to one of the authors, New York: May 22.

Matthews, Leonard S. (1984), "Government Regulation and Self-Regulation in Advertising," a presentation to ADASIA Advertising Congress, Korea, Seoul: June 17 – 23.

McDonnell, Dennis (1978), "How Creativity Can Learn to Live with Strict Controls," London: *Campaign*, July 7.

McEwen, Robert (1982), "The Progress of the US Consumer Movement in Modern Times," a presentation given to the AVON International Consumer Leader Forum, Tokyo, June 21 and 22, 1982 and published by AVON Products Co. Ltd., January 1983.

Lord McGregor (1984), "Press Freedom – The Role of UNESCO," *International Journal of Advertising*, (2)95 – 111.

McKerracher, Keith (1984), a presentation on "How Advertising is Seen in Canada," Annual Meeting of the American Association of Advertising Agencies, Palm Springs, California: March 8.

McLachlan, D.L.; and Swann, S. (1963), *Competition Policy in the European Market*, London: Oxford University Press.

McLachlan, D.L.; and Swann, S. (1967), *Competition Policy in the European Community*, London: Oxford University Press.

McLaren, Bob (1979), a presentation on "How Are Advertising Controls Affecting the Creative Product?," at a conference of the International Advertising Association, Amsterdam: May 7 – 10.

Media International, (1979), Vol.5 No.42, December.

Memorandum on approximation of the laws of Member States on fair competition: Misleading and Unfair advertising, Directorate-General for Internal Market of the Commission of the European Communities, Working Document No.2 XI/C/93/75-E, Brussels: November, 1975 (See Appendix II).

Meyer, Heinrich (1983), *Europäische Verbrauchererziehung – Bestandaufnahme und curriculare Konzeption*, Frankfurt: Lang.

Micklitz, Hans-W. (1984), "Three Instances of Negotiation Procedures in the Federal Republic of Germany," *Journal of Consumer Policy*, (7)211 – 229.

Miller, James C. (1981), "Statement by F.T.C. Chairman James Miller at Annual Meeting National Advertising Review Board," *Better Business News & Views*, (7)4.

Miracle, Gordon E. (1974), "A Two-Nation Comparison of Advertising Law and Regulation: Norway and the United States," *Proceedings of the 1974 National Conference of the American Academy of Advertising*, Sherilyn K. Zeigler, ed., Knoxville: University of Tennessee, 323 – 333.

Miracle, Gordon E.; Ashmen, Roy; Hassenjaeger, John; Hunt, Keith; Katz, Benjamin; Preston, Ivan; and Schultz, Don (1979), *Advertising and Government Regulation*, Cambridge, Massachusetts: The Marketing Science Institute, Report No.106.

Miracle, Gordon E. (1984), "An Assessment of Progress in Research on International Advertising," *Current Issues and Research in Advertising 1984*, 135 – 166.

Miracle, Gordon E. (1985a), "A Brief History of US Advertising Self-Regulation to 1970," *Proceedings of the 1985 Conference of the American Academy of Advertising*, Nancy Stephens, ed., Tempe: Arizona State University, R2 – R7.

Miracle, Gordon E. (1985b), "New Perspectives on the Objectives, Decisions and Performance of the NAD/NARB," unpublished working paper, October.

Miracle, Gordon E. (1985c), "Advertising Regulation in Japan and the USA: An Introductory Comparison," *Waseda Business and Economic Studies*, No.21:35 – 69.

Miracle, Gordon E. (1986), "An Update on the Objectives, Activities and Performance of the NAD/NARB," forthcoming.

Miracle, Gordon E.; and Nevett, T.R. (1986), *Voluntary Self-Regulation of Advertising in the UK and the USA*, Lexington, MA: Lexington Books, forthcoming.

Mitra, G. (1983), "Advertising of Medicines to the Public," *The Advertising Association Handbook*, London: Holt, Rinehart & Winston.

Monk, Keith (1983), personal letter to one of the authors, Vevey: November 4.

Monk, Keith (1984), "International Profile of the Communication Policy in International Companies," a presentation to the International Advertising Association (Holland Chapter), Eindhoven: February 15 – 17.

de Mooij, Marieke K., "Maatschappelijke Aspekten van Reklame," (Social Aspects of Advertising), reprints of three Chapters from the *Marketing Handbook for Commercial Policy Problems*, Deventer, Holland: Kluwer.

Moskin, J. Robert (1973), ed., *The Case for Advertising*, highlights of the industry presentation to the Federal Trade Commission in the US, New York: American Association of Advertising Agencies.

Murray, James (1984), "Codes of Practice in Ireland: A Practitioner's View," *Journal of Consumer Policy*, (7)208 – 210.

Mussey, Dagmar (1984), "Wooing Ms Germany," London: *Focus*, March, 1984:31.

NAD, *Dear xxx, Your advertising has recently come to the attention of the National Advertising Division*, Guide for Advertisers and Advertising Agencies, New York: National Advertising Division, Council of Better Business Bureaus, Inc., undated.

Naisbitt, John (1982), *Megatrends*, New York: Warner Books, Inc.

NARB (1978), *A Review and Perspective on Advertising Industry Self-Regulation*, New York: National Advertising Review Board, May.

NARB, *If You Have A Complaint About Advertising*, Public Service Bulletin, New York: National Advertising Review Board, undated.

Neelankavil, James P.; and Stridsberg, Albert B. (1980), *Advertising Self-Regulation: a Global Perspective*, New York: Hastings House Publishers.

Neelankavil, James P. (1985), *Restrictions on Advertising by Media and Selected Products in 16 Countries of Europe*, New York: International Advertising Association, April.

Nevett, Terry (1982), *Advertising in Britain – A History*, London: William Heinemann Ltd.

Newell, R.P.; and Kennedy, H.M., *TV Advertising Directed at Children*, a submission by SSC&B: LINTAS through the Advertising Federation of Australia to the Public Inquiry into Self-Regulation by Australian Broadcasters, Sydney: undated.

Noël, Emile (1981), *Working Together*, Luxembourg: Office of Official Publications of the European Communities, 1982.

O'Connor, James (1981), "Evergrowing EEC Legislation – Advertisers Beware," *Viewpoint*, London: Summer.

O'Connor, James (1983a), "Impact of Regulation and Standards on New Media (in Europe)," a presentation to the International Advertising Association, New York: June 7.

O'Connor, James (1983b), personal discussion, London: August 4.

O'Connor (1984), "Success – 12 years on! The EEC Directive on Misleading Advertising is Finally Adopted," *Viewpoints News*, London: July 8.

OECD (1982a), *Resolution of the Council Concerning the Renewal of the Terms of Reference of the Committee on Consumer Policy*, Paris: October 6.

OECD (1982b), *Advertising Directed at Children*, a Report from the Committee on Consumer Policy of the Organization for Economic Cooperation and Development, Paris.

OECD (1982c), *Endorsements in Advertising*, a Report from the Commission on Consumer Policy of the Organization for Economic Cooperation and Development, Paris.

OECD (1984), *Consumer Policy and International Trade*, program of a symposium organized by the Organization for Economic Cooperation and Development, Paris: November 27 – 29.

OECD (1985), *Consumer Policy and International Trade*, Results of the 1984 symposium and program of action of the Organization for Economic Cooperation and Development, Paris: June.

Official Journal of the European Communities, (1985), a Supplement, Vol.28, concerning preparation of international publicity campaigns, Brussels: February 21.

van Os, Leo (1984), *The International Bandwagon, Fables and Facts*, a presentation to the International Advertising Association (Holland Chapter), Eindhoven: February 15 – 17.

OYEZ (1981), *Advertising and Marketing to Children: Responsibility and Effectiveness*, a one-day workshop arranged by Oyez International Business Communications Ltd., London: March 31.

Packard, Vance (1957), *The Hidden Persuaders*, New York: van Rees Press.

PAGB (1979), *Code of Standards of Advertising Practice*, rev. ed., London: Proprietary Association of Great Britain.

Painter, A.A. (1981), "The British Experience: Consumer Protection and its Impact on Business," *Consumer Legislation*, Paris: International Chamber of Commerce.

Parsons, Mike (1984), "Why Admen must act now to safeguard their Future," London: *Campaign*, May 11.

Peebles, Dean M.; and Ryans Jr., J.K. (1971), "Advertising as a Positive Force," *Journal of Advertising*, 7(2)48 – 52, 47.

Peebles, Dean M.; and Vernon, I.R. (1977), "A New Perspective on Advertising Standardization," *European Journal of Marketing*, 11(8)569 – 576.

Pertschuk, Michael (1982), *Revolt Against Regulation, The Rise and Pause of the Consumer Movement*, Berkeley: University of California Press.

Pitcher, A.E. (1985), "The Future of International Advertising," Stockton Lectures at the London Business School, London: February 14.

Poniatowski, Michel (1985), "Notre Dernière Chance Pour N'être Pas Colonisés," *Figaro Magazine*, Paris: October 12, 21 – 31.

Poole, Robert W. (1982), ed., *Instead of Regulation*, Lexington, MA: Lexington Books.

The Positive Case for Marketing Children's Products to Children (1978), comments by the Association of National Advertisers, the American Association of Advertising Agencies and the American Advertising Federation, New York: November 24.

Preston, Ivan (1983), "A Review of the Literature on Advertising Regulation," *Current Issues and Research in Advertising 1983*, 1 – 37.

Pridgen, D. (1985), "Satellite Television Advertising and the Regulatory Conflict in Western Europe," *Journal of Advertising*, 14(1)23 – 29.

Primoff (1979), *The Sources and Status of U.N. Efforts To Regulate Advertising And Other Multi-National Enterprises*, prepared for the Interpublic Group of Companies, Inc. New York: Primoff & Primoff, March 7.

Ptak, Horst; Schulz, Uwe; Puknat, Rainer; Prochazka, Michael; Brandenstein, Horst; and Nölke, Rolf (1983), *Das Informationsinteresse der Verbraucher*, Kassel: Arbeitsgruppe für Verbraucherwirtschaft an der Gesamthochschule Kassel.

Public Hearing (1980), organized by the Committee on the Environment, Public Health and Consumer Protection of the European Parliament, Dublin: February 26 – 27.

Quotations at beginning of Chapters: Huxley, Buckley, Nicolson, Somerset Maugham and Dac, from: "A Dictionary of Contemporary Quotations," compiled by Jonathan Green, published by David & Charles (Publishers) Ltd., 1982, pp.113, 25, 24; St. Francis of Assisi from: "Familiar Quotations," compiled by John Bartlett, published by MacMillan & Co. Ltd., London, Fourteenth Edition; Bevan, Samuel Johnson and King George VI from: "Advertising in a free Society," by Harris & Seldon, published by the Institute of Economic Affairs, London, 1959, p.X; Thorn from: *Europe 1981*, issue January/February.

Rask Jensen, Hans (1983), *Consumer Education in Schools*, a Report to the Commission of the EC on results of pilot project in consumer education in schools, XI/824/83-DA, Brussels.

Reader's Digest 1982 Almanac and Yearbook, Pleasantville, New York: The Reader's Digest Association, Inc.

Reich, Norbert; and Micklitz, H.W. (1980), *Consumer Legislation in EC Countries, A Comparative Analysis*, London: Van Nostrand Reinhold Co. Ltd.

Reich, Norbert; and Micklitz, Hans W. (1981), *Consumer Legislation in the Federal Republic of Germany*, New York: Van Nostrand Reinhold Co. Inc.

Reich, Norbert (1983), Book Review of Michael Pertschuk (1982), *Journal of Consumer Policy*, (6)239 – 40.

Reich, Norbert; and Smith, Lesley Jane (1983), "The Implementation of the International Code of Marketing of Breast Milk Substitutes by the EEC," *Journal of Consumer Policy*, (6)335 – 364.

Review of the UK Self-Regulatory System of Advertising Control, (1978), A Report by the Director-General of Fair Trading, London: Office of Fair Trading, November.

Rijkens, Rein (1976), a presentation at the First EurAm Conference, Amsterdam: November 8 – 11.

Rijkens, Rein (1978a), personal letter to Commissioner Richard Burke, July 17.

Rijkens, Rein (1978b), "Ad Forces Rally to Repel Their EEC Critics," *Advertising Age*, New York: August 14.

Rijkens, Rein (1978c), "Marketers and Admen Challenge EEC Directive," *Advertising Age*, New York: September 11.

Rijkens, Rein (1978d), "Tough Global Challenge Confronts Ad Industry," *Advertising Age*, New York: October 9.

Rijkens, Rein (1979), "Europe Admen Must Defend Their Industry," *Advertising Age*, New York: February 12.

Rome Treaty (1957), *Treaty establishing The European Economic Community*, Rome, March 25, 1957, London: Her Majesty's Stationery Office, 1962.

Rules for Marketing of Tobacco Products, a Voluntary Agreement, Ref.No.075, Denmark: March 13, 1980.

Ryans, John K.Jr.; and Donnelly, James H.Jr. (1969), "Standardized Global Advertising, a Call as Yet Unanswered," *Journal of Marketing*, 33(2)(April)57 – 60.

Ryans, John; and Bell, Henry (1979), "International Advertising Regulation," *Proceedings of the Midwest Marketing Association Conference*, April.

Ryans, John; and Wills, J. (1979), *Consumer's Impact on Advertising: A Worldwide Study*, New York: International Advertising Association, May.

Samiee, Saeed; and Ryans, John K.Jr. (1982), "Advertising and the Consumer Movement in Europe: The Case of West Germany and Switzerland," *Journal of International Business Studies*, 8(Spring/Summer)109 – 114.

Samsonite, (1983), Verdict of the "Cour d'Appel de Paris (13e Ch.)," April 12, 1983, *Gazette du Palais*, June 22 – 23, 1983 and the verdict of the "Cour de Cassation, Chambre Criminelle," No.83.92.070.B, May 21, 1984.

Schricker, Gerhard (1969), *Fair Trade and the Consumer in the EEC*, paper for a conference organized by the British Institute of International and Comparative Law, Cambride: March.

Schricker, Gerhard (1977), "Unfair Competition and Consumer Protection – New Developments," *International Review of Industrial Propery and Copyright Law*, 8(3)185 – 227.

Schuster, Alex (1984), "Government Monitored Codes of Practice in Ireland," *Journal of Consumer Policy*, (7)185 – 196.

Scrivener, C.; Albach, D.; and Monier, Y. (1979), *Rôle, Responsibilité et Avenir de la Publicité*, Paris: La Documentation Française.

Seaman, Alfred J. (1971), *The Power of Words*, a statement to the Federal Trade Commission, Washington: October 22.

Seaman, Alfred J. (1973), "Will the Real Consumerists Please Stand Up?," a presentation to the Tea Association of the United States of America, Inc., Arizona: October 9.

Second Report Commission (1978), *Consumer Protection and Information Policy*, Luxembourg: Office for Official Publications of the European Communities, 1979.

The Self-Regulatory System of Advertising Control – Report of the Working Party (1980), London: Department of Trade.

Shaw, Gary; and Grayson, Leslie E. (1980), *Consumer Protection Activities in the European Economic Community*, Boston: Intercollegiate Case Clearing House, 8-581-609.

Sheehan, Jeremiah P. (1983a), "Consumer Education Programs and Trends in the European Community," a presentation at a conference organized by the US Office of Consumer Affairs and AVON Products Inc., on *The Market Pacemaker ... Consumer Education*, conference proceedings, Washington, DC: US Department of State, April 25.

Sheehan, Jeremiah P. (1983b), personal discussion, Brussels: October 27.

Sheehan, Jeremiah P. (1984), "EEC Initiatives in the Consumer – Producer Dialogue," *Journal of Consumer Policy*, Vol.7, No.2, June, 1984, Copyright © 1984 by D. Reidel Publishing Company, Dordrecht, Holland.

Shepherd, Harry (1981), "Conclusion," *Consumer Legislation*, Paris: International Chamber of Commerce, Doc.383.

Sheth, Jagdish N. (1978), "Strategies of Advertising Transferability in Multinational Marketing," *Current Issues & Research in Advertising*, 131 – 141.

Skinner, Peter G. (1969), "Trade Regulation in the Common Market – The Development of a European Approach," *Columbia Journal of Transnational Law*, 8(2)(1969)246 – 278.

Smith, G. (1983), "Advertising and Children," *The Advertising Association Handbook*, London: Holt, Rinehart & Winston Ltd.

Soldner, Helmut (1978), "Vergleichende Werbung im Internationalen Vergleich," *Deutsche Betriebswirtschaft*, 38(1978)4:547 – 555.

Statistical Office of the EC (1984), *Statistical Panorama of Europe*, Luxembourg: Eurostat.

Stauder, Bernd; Feldges, Joachim; and Mulbert, Peter (1984), "Consumer Protection in Switzerland by Means of 'Soft Law' – Practices and Perspectives," *Journal of Consumer Policy*, (7)231 – 252.

Steffens, Heiko (1980), *Verbrauchererziehung*, Tübingen: Deutsches Institut für Fernstudien.

Stichting Sigarettenindustrie (1984), an *Advertising Code for Cigarettes and for Roll-Your-Own-Tobacco*, published by the Dutch Foundation for the Cigaret Industry, The Hague: May 15.

Stone, Elhanan C. (1985), *Advertising and Children*, New York: Global Products/Services Marketing Commission of the International Advertising Association, December.

Strauss, Lawrence (1983), *Electronic Marketing*, London: Knowledge Industry.

Straver, Will (1977), "The International Consumer Movement: Theory and Practical Implications for Marketing Strategy," *European Journal of Marketing*, 11(2)93 – 117.

Straver, Will (1978), "International Consumerist Movement, Theory and Practical Implications for Marketing Strategy," *European Journal of Marketing*, 316.

Stridsberg, Albert B. (1974), *Effective Advertising Self-Regulation*, New York: International Advertising Association.

Stridsberg, Albert B. (1977), *Controversy Advertising*, a Worldwide Study, sponsored by the International Advertising Association, New York: Hastings House, Publishers.

Stuyck, J. (1978), "Der Vorschlag einer EG-Richtlinie zur Harmonisierung des Werberechts," *Journal of Consumer Policy*, (2)326 – 337.

Stuyck, J. (1983a), "Tobacco Advertising Regulation in Belgium," *Journal of Consumer Policy*, (6)225 – 230.

Stuyck, J. (1983b), *Product Differentiation – The Legal Situation*, Deventer: Kluwer.

Stuyck, J. (1984), "Consumer Soft Law in Belgium," *Journal of Consumer Policy*, (7)125 – 135.

Sullivan, Scott (1984), "The Decline of Europe," *Newsweek*, April 9.

Teel, Sandra J.; Teel, Jesse E.; and Bearden, William O. (1979), "Lessons learned from the Broadcast Cigarette Advertising Ban," *Journal of Marketing*, 43(January)45 – 50.

De Telegraaf (1982), Amsterdam: April 22.

Tempest, Alastair C. (1982), "The Witches' Brew: Advertising, Satellites and the European Institutions," *Journal of Advertising*, (1)143 – 145.

Tempest, Alastair C. (1984a), "Do the European Institutions Love Marketers," a presentation at a conference on Euro-Marketing, London: January 19 – 20.

Tempest, Alastair C. (1984b), "Why We Need Advertising," *Intermedia*, (12) March.

Tempest, Alastair C. (1984c), "The European Institutions: How They Affect the Industry," *Marketing Week*, February 10, 38 – 42.

Tempest, Alastair C. (1985), "Is Commercial Speech Free Speech? A European Perspective," Washington, DC: *International Information Economy Handbook*, p.73.

Theobalds, Harry (1983), "The Rules Governing Advertising on Television and Independent Local Radio," *The Advertising Association Handbook*, London: Holt, Rinehart & Winston Ltd.

Third Report Commission (1980), *Consumer Protection and Information Policy*, Luxembourg: Office for Official Publications of the European Communities, 1981.

Thomas, Lutz (1983), *Der Einfluss von Kindern auf Produktpräferenzen ihrer Mütter*, Berlin: Duncker & Humblot.

Thomas, Richard (1984), "Codes of Practice in the United Kingdom and the Consumer Interest," *Journal of Consumer Policy*, (7)198 – 202.

Thompson, Mayo (1975), "Government Regulation of Advertising: Killing the Consumer in Order to 'Save' Him," a presentation at the Annual General Meeting of the Association of National Advertisers, Palm Beach: November 30 – December 3.

Thomson (1981), Lord Thomson of Monifieth, "Harmonisation of EEC Law," an article in *The Three Banks Review*, London: June.

Thomson (1984), Lord Thomson of Monifieth, "Cable, Satellite and the Future of Commercial Broadcasting – The British View," a presentation at the Anglo-German Chamber of Commerce, Munich: April 13.

Thomson, Peter (1979a), "The Future for Self-Regulation," a presentation at the Cavendish Conference Centre, London: September 25.

Thomson, Peter (1979b), "Advertising Control: Advertisements in Media other than Television and Radio," *The Advertising Association Handbook*, London: Holt, Rinehart & Winston Ltd.

Thorelli, Hans B.; and Thorelli, Sarah V. (1974), *Consumer Information Handbook: Europe and North America*, New York: Praeger Publishers.

Thorelli, Hans B.; Becker, H.; and Engledow, J. (1975), *The Information Seekers*, Cambridge, Mass.: Ballinger Publishing Co.

Thorelli, Hans B.; and Thorelli, Sarah V. (1977), *Consumer Systems and Consumer Policy*, Cambridge, Mass.: Ballinger Publishing Co.

Thorelli, Hans B.; and Sentell, Gerald D. (1982), *Consumer Emancipation and Economic Development: The Case of Thailand*, Greenwich, CO: JAI-Press.

Time Magazine (1981), "Confrontation at Talloires," a report on a meeting of the World Press Freedom Committee, June 1.

Time Magazine (1985), May 20.

Time Magazine (1985), November 18.

Tobacco Advisory Council (1981), *Advertising Controls and Their Effects on Total Cigarette Consumption*, London: February.

Tobacco Advisory Council and the Imported Tobacco Products Advisory Council (1983), *Tobacco Products: Advertising and Promotion and Health Warnings*, a voluntary agreement with UK Health Ministers, January.

Tofler, Alvin (1970), *Future Shock*, London: The Bodley Head Ltd.

Tölle, Klaus (1983), *Das Informationsverhalten der Konsumenten*, Frankfurt: Campus.

Trubek, D.; Bourgoignie, T.; and Trubek, L. (1981), "Thinking Federal: An Approach to Reconciling the EEC's Commitments to Consumer Protection and Economic Integration," paper presented at the European University Institute Conference, December 14 – 19, Florence, doc.IUE 227/81 Col.64.

Tugendhat, Christopher (1985), "Most people in most countries do not want to be run from Brussels ...," *Europe 85*, April.

Underhill, Roger (1981a), "The Commercial Interest Lobby," *Viewpoint*, Special Feature, Summer.

Underhill, Roger (1981b), "Talks Which May Curb the Threats of Consumerism," London: *Campaign*, November 6.

Underhill, Roger (1984), "Why We Should Welcome the New Directive," London: *Europe 84*, September.

Underhill, Roger (1985), "Advertising's Defender in the European Corridors of Power," London: *Campaign*, November 22.

Understanding Economics (1983), an educational project of the Department of Education, University of Manchester, Manchester.

UNICE (1983), *Guidelines for Consumer Affairs*, Brussels: March 2.

UNICE (1984a), *Education in Economics and the World of Business*, Report on a colloquium organized by the Union of Industries of the European Community, Brussels: December 5.

UNICE Informations, (1984b), a monthly periodical, Brussels: November 10.

Unilever Magazine, (1983), "Regulations Galore," No.48, London: First Quarter.

U.S. Council for International Business (1982), *International Information Flows*, Number 1, December.

Uustialo, Liisa (1983), "Societal Change and Challenges for Consumer Policy," *Journal of Consumer Policy*, (6)149 – 160.

Venables, Tony (1984), "European Codes: A Red Herring," *Journal of Consumer Policy*, Vol.7, No.2, June 1984, copyright © 1984 by D. Reidel Publishing Company, Dordrecht, Holland.

Waterson, M.J. (1981), *Advertising and Alcohol Abuse*, London: The Advertising Association.

Waterson, M.J. (1983a), "The Advertising of Alcoholic Drink Products," *The Advertising Association Handbook*, London: Holt, Rinehart & Winston Ltd.

Waterson, M.J. (1983b), ed., *Statistical Yearbook*, London: The Advertising Association, October.

Wedell, Georg (1985), "Television Without Frontiers," London: *Government and Opposition*, Vol.20, No.1 (Winter)94 – 103.

Weidenbaum, Murray L. (1983), "The Growth of the U.N. as a Regulatory Private Enterprise," a presentation on International Regulatory Development, sponsored by the US Mission of the United Nations, New York: December 7.

Weiss, D.; and Chirouze, Y. (1984), *Le Consumerisme*, Paris: Editions Sirey.

WFPMM, *Guidelines for Voluntary Codes of Advertising Practice and Advertising to the Public (Statement of Policy) and Retail Distribution of Proprietary Medicines (Statement of Policy)*, undated.

Whincup, M.H. (1980), *Consumer Legislation in the United Kingdom and the Republic of Ireland*, London: Van Rostrand Reinhold Co.

Whitington (1985), *Whose Tune Are We Dancing To?*, an analysis, Sydney: February.

Wikström, Solveig (1983a), "Another Look at Consumer Dissatisfaction as a Measure of Market Performance," *Journal of Consumer Policy*, (6)19 – 35.

Wikström, Solveig (1983b), "Bringing Consumer Information Systems Down to Earth; Experiences from a Swedish Experiment," *Journal of Consumer Policy*, (7)13 – 26.

Williams, J.S. (1973), "Government Controls and Free Enterprise – Are They Compatible?," a presentation at the 23rd World Congress of the International Advertising Association, Dublin: June 6 – 8.

de Win, Paul P. (1983), *Self-Regulation in the Field of Advertising*, a paper, Brussels: February.

Winkler, Heinz (1980), *Täuschende Werbung in Stichworten*, Frankfurt: Deutscher Fachverlag.

Wolfe, Alan (1983), "Public Attitudes to Advertising in the UK," *The Advertising Association Handbook*, London: Holt, Rinehart & Winston Ltd.

Wolfe, Alan (1985), *Some Disturbing Factors in the Business Environment*, London: Ogilvy & Mather Ltd., April.

Wood, David (1983), "New Media Opportunities," a presentation to the Education Conference of the International Advertising Association, London: November.

Wood, David (1985), "What the Satellite Boom Will Mean for Euro-Advertisers," *Campaign*, London: August 30.

Wood, David (1986), *New Media Presentation*, London: Ogilvy & Mather Ltd.

Woodroffe, Geoffrey (1984a), "Government Monitored Codes of Practice in the United Kingdom," *Journal of Consumer Policy*, (7)171 – 184.

Woodroffe, Geoffrey (1984b), *Consumer Law in the EEC*, London: Sweet & Maxwell.

Wright, John S.; Warner, Daniel S.; and Winter Jr. Willis, L. (1971), *Advertising*, New York: McGraw-Hill Book Company.

Yearbook Winkler Prins Encyclopaedia 1972, Amsterdam/Brussels: Elsevier.

Yearbook Winkler Prins Encyclopaedia 1980, Amsterdam/Brussels: Elsevier.

Zanot, Enic J. (1984), "Public Attitudes Towards Advertising: The American Experience," *International Journal of Advertising*, (3) 3 – 15.

ZAW (1978), *Europäische Werberechtsordnung: EEC Directive on Misleading and Unfair Advertising*, Bonn.

ZAW (1979), *Der ZAW: Aufgaben, Organisation, Mitgliedsverbände*, Bonn: Zentralausschuss der Werbewirtshcaft e.V., Oktober.

ZAW (1983), *Sober Facts on Advertising for Alcoholic Beverages*, Bonn.

ZAW (1984), "Comments on the document published by the Commission of the EC on *Television Without Frontiers*," Bonn: October 22.

Zwaan, J.W. de (1983), personal letter No.5197 to one of the authors, Brussels: October 11.

Acknowledgments

Sylvan Barnet   Chairman, Advisory Council International Corporate Members of the International Advertising Association, New York

Ronald Beatson   Director-General, European Association of Advertising Agencies, Brussels

Sir Gordon Borrie   Director-General, Office of Fair Trading, London

David Bottomley   Advertising Manager Europe, Rowntree Mackintosh PLC, York

Brandolino   President, Reader's Digest, Milan
   Brandolini d'Adda

John Braun   Consultant, European and Consumer Affairs, London; from 1973 to 1977 a senior official of the Commission of the EC, Brussels

Albert Brouwet   Senior Vice-President International, J. Walter Thompson and Vice-President, International Advertising Association, Brussels

Jeremy Bullmore   Chairman, J. Walter Thompson Company Ltd., London

Philippe Charmet   Chairman, LINTAS:PARIS, Paris

Richard C. Christian Associate Dean, Medill School of Journalism, Northwestern University, Evanston, Illinois; formerly Chairman of Marsteller, Inc., Chicago

Robert J. Coen   Senior Vice-President, McCann-Erickson, Inc., New York

Nils Färnert   Consultant, Stockholm; formerly Director-General, European Association of Advertising Agencies, Brussels

Jan Fels   Former Worldwide Ethical Officer, Reader's Digest, New York

Kenneth Fraser   Chairman, Commission on Marketing of the International Chamber of Commerce, Paris

Sidney Freedman	Responsible for Promotion of Consumer Interests in the Directorate Protection and Promotion of Consumer Interests, Commission of the EC, Brussels
S.R. Green	Past Chief Executive Officer, SSC&B:LINTAS International and Consultant to the Interpublic Group of Companies, Inc., New York
Gerald de Groot	Director, Mark Research, London
Raymond Haas	Past Director, Bureau de la Vérification de la Publicité (BVP), Paris
Bryand Harris	Consultant, European Common Market Problems; from 1973 to 1983 senior official of the Commission of the EC, Brussels
Thorof Helgesen	Managing Director, Norwegian Association of Advertising Agencies and the Norwegian Institute of Marketing, Oslo
Alexandre van Hissenhoven	Counselor to the Union of the Industries of the European Community, Brussels
Hugh Holker	Chairman, Public Action Committee, International Advertising Association, London
Frits Hondius	Secretary Committee of Ministers of the Council of Europe, Strasbourg
Kees Knook	Unilever PLC, Londen
J. Koopman	Chairman, Committee on Consumer Policy, the Organization for Economic Cooperation and Development, The Hague
Ludwig Krämer	Official of the Commission of the EC, Brussels
R.G. Lawson	Consultant in Marketing Law, Isle of Wight
Joseph Luns	Past Secretary-General, North Atlantic Treaty Organization (NATO), Brussels
Patricia Mann	Vice-President, J. Walter Thompson International, London
Leonard Matthews	President, American Association of Advertising Agencies, New York
Morgan McDonough	Past Vice-President, SSC&B:LINTAS International, New York
Keith McKerracher	President, Institute of Canadian Advertising, Toronto
Bob McLaren	International Creative Director SSC&B:LINTAS International, London

Kenneth Miles	Director, The Incorporated Society of British Advertisers Ltd., London
Herbert Mittag	President, Kammer der Gewerblichen Wirtschaft für Wien, Fachgruppe Werbung Wien (Advertising Trade Association), Vienna
Keith Monk	International Advertising Adviser to Nestlé, Vevey
Marieke de Mooij	Director, Stichting voor Reclame- en Marketingonderwijs (Advertising and Marketing Foundation), Amsterdam
Terence A. Nevett	Professor of Marketing, Central Michigan University, formerly Principal Lecturer Polytechnic of the Southbank, London
Volker Nickel	Zentralausschuss der Werbewirtschaft (Central Committee for Advertising), Bonn
James O'Connor	European Adviser, Independent Television Companies Association Ltd., London
Lars Oftedal Broch	Executive Director, International Organization of Consumers' Unions, The Hague
Leo van Os	Chairman, SSC&B:LINTAS Nederland, Amsterdam
Jan Prillewitz	Past Chief Public Relations Officer to the President of the European Parliament, Brussels
Marie C. Psiménos	First Director of the International Chamber of Commerce, Paris
Tom Recter	Legal Staff Member Consumentenbond (Consumer Union), The Hague
Lorraine C. Reid	Senior Vice-President, National Advertising Review Board, Council of Better Business Bureaus, New York
Gerrit-Jan Ribbink	Secretary, Vereniging Erkende Reclame Advies Bureaux (VEA), (Dutch Advertising Agency Association), Amsterdam
Joop Rijkens	Past Advisory Director, Moussault Advertising Agency, Amsterdam
Dieter Schweickhardt	Director Gesellschaft Werbeagenturen (GWA), (Advertising Agency Association), Frankfurt
Alfred J. Seaman	Past President, SSC&B Inc., Chairman Operations Committee, SSC&B:LINTAS International and Consultant to the Interpublic Group of Companies, Inc., New York

Jeremiah Sheehan	Director, Protection and Promotion of Consumer Interests Directorate of the Commission of the EC, Brussels
Alastair Tempest	Director External Affairs, European Association of Advertising Agencies and Secretary, European Advertising Tripartite, Brussels
Harry Theobalds	Controller of Advertising, Independent Broadcast Authority, London
Lord Thomson of Monifieth	Chairman, Independent Broadcast Authority, London
Peter Thomson	Director-General, Advertising Standards Authority, London
Roger Underhill	Director-General, The Advertising Association and Chairman European Advertising Tripartite, London
Tony Venables	Director, Bureau Européen des Unions de Consommateurs (BEUC), (European Office of Consumer Organizations), Brussels
Richard Wainwright	Member Cabinet of Commissioner Stanley Clinton Davis, Commission of the EC, Brussels
Beate Weber	Chairman, Consumer Protection Committee of the European Parliament, Brussels
David Wheeler	Director, Institute of Practitioners in Advertising (IPA), London
Irene Williamson	Director, Corporate Affairs AVON Products Inc., New York
Paul de Win	Director-General, World Federation of Advertisers, Brussels
J.W. de Zwaan	Permanent Representative of the Netherlands at the European Communities, Brussels

Subject index